"Hammond doesn't make splashy drama out of her characters' dilemmas or solve them by way of a sudden, inspirational uplift. Instead, she opens a window onto the vanishing world of small-town America, and lets the cold sea air blow in." —*San Francisco Chronicle*

"Hammond offers a nuanced look at the strains of daily life in a world of diminished possibilities. . . . What lingers here is the unflinching look at dailiness." —*Booklist*

"An exceptional debut about small-time lives and limited dreams in rural America . . . Hammond's depiction of the town and its people is refreshingly unsentimental . . . moving and deftly told." —*Kirkus Reviews*

"Hammond shines an unwavering light on a group of people who struggle to make do, yet who live their lives and cope with hardship with grace and dignity. Her clean, sharp prose, idiosyncratic dialogue, and deep insight into relationships embellish this heartfelt debut." —*Publishers Weekly*

"Earthy dialogue, precise narrative, well-placed humor, and the coverage of difficult topics (e.g., AIDS and child abuse) mark Hammond's distinctive style. . . . Recommended as a testimonial to the regenerative power of female friendship, the will to survive, and the courage to seek happiness." —*Library Journal*

"The characters take over and live on these pages. . . . Hammond is going to blow the socks off the fiction world." —Bookreporter.com

"Hammond is a gifted writer. . . . *Going to Bend* paints a picture of a town in which small triumphs can make up for large sufferings. . . . This is a delightful, spirited debut." —OregonLive.com

"Deeply moving . . . *Going to Bend* is about finding the good in people." —registerguard.com

going to bend

going

to

bend

A Novel

diane hammond

Ballantine Books · New York

2005 Ballantine Books Trade Paperback Edition

Copyright © 2004 by Diane Hammond
Reading group guide copyright © 2005 by Random House, Inc.

Published in the United States by Ballantine Books, an imprint of The Random House Publishing Group, a division of Random House, Inc., New York.

Originally published in hardcover in the United States by Doubleday in 2004.

Library of Congress Cataloging-in-Publication Data
Hammond, Diane Coplin.
Going to bend : a novel / by Diane Hammond.—1st ed.
p.   cm.
1. Fishing villages—Fiction. 2. Restaurants—Fiction. 3. Friendship—Fiction.
4. Oregon—Fiction. 5. Soups—Fiction. I. Title.
PS3608.A6956G65 2004
813'.6—dc21   2003051945
ISBN 0-345-46098-7

Printed in the United States of America

Ballantine Books website address: www.ballantinebooks.com/BRC

2 4 6 8 9 7 5 3 1

Text design by Nicola Ferguson

To Kerry and Nolan

going to
to
bend

Hubbard was one of the oldest no-account towns on the coast of Oregon. Men there fished commercially or helped others deep-sea fish for sport; they worked in the woods cutting timber, or they worked in the mill over in Sawyer, making paper amidst a great noise and stink. They lived hard, bore scars, coveted danger and died either young and violently or unnecessarily old. The women worked, or not. The children belonged to them.

Hubbard was one of those places where you could still have your choice of oceanfront trailers—old rusting aqua and silver tunafish cans with moisture problems. Highway 101, the West's westernmost route from Canada to Mexico, was the town's only through street, a straight and single shot lined with gift shops and candy shops and kite shops and a Dairy Queen, shell art and postcards and forty-six flavors of saltwater taffy, homemade right here. There was everywhere a spirit of cheer, clutter and nakedly opportunistic goodwill: what Hubbard had it would happily sell you, and if you didn't see it, just ask. Everyone loved a tourist, and the fatter the cat, the better. To a point. The locals maintained their own entrances to the Dairy Queen, Anchor Grill and Wayside Tavern: unmarked doors around back by the service entrances, where there was no parking problem.

In this town, beautiful even if no-account, lived two women, old friends, Petie Coolbaugh and Rose Bundy. Rose was a big, soft woman of calm purpose and measurable serenity. Petie was small and hard and tight and flammable, like the wick of a candle. They were both thirty-one, and ever since grade school had been celebrating good times, hunkering down in lean ones, hiding truths from each other's families, sitting up with each other's babies. In the last six weeks they had also become business partners. They made soup for a living now.

Two months ago a cafe and coffeehouse had come to Hubbard by way of a brother and sister, fraternal twins from Southern California who'd had the idea of coming north to slow down. They had bought the old barbershop at one end of town and moved in tables and church pews and giant green ferns. They bought crockery dishes, an espresso machine, quilted tablecloths and posters for the walls. They sanded the old fir floors and built a mahogany counter of great beauty and grace. They installed a tiny kitchen, named the place Souperior's, and then, instead of hiring a cook, they held auditions.

> *Bring your best soup* (they invited all of Hubbard, on index cards
> in city hall, the post office and the Quik Stop) *to Souperior's next
> Saturday afternoon. Winners get on our menu. Grand winner gets a
> job offer.*

Although Hubbard loved its tourists, resident newcomers were a source of suspicion. For a week or so the little index cards—tacked up fresh and bright among the curling notices about firewood and crab pot repairs and handmade dog figurines—excited a lot of comment, most of it skeptical. On the other hand, an invitation to compete against your neighbors didn't come along often except for the county fair, and in the end, sixty-four soups were entered in the contest and were judged during an open house and soup-feed by the cafe's owners, Nadine and Gordon Latimer. Petie and Rose won with a jointly submitted bottomfish stew born of desperation the year Eddie Coolbaugh broke his foot and couldn't work for three months. A fisherman Rose had been dating then had fed them all from the junkfish left behind on a sportfishing charter boat. Two more of Rose's soups also made it onto the menu. When she was offered the job of soup cook, she asked if she and Petie could share it. The deal was that they would supply the cafe with two fresh soups each day, Tuesday through Sunday, and they could work from home. Breads came from the Riseria in Sawyer; Nadine handled the salads herself. Every day the soups would be different until the menu was exhausted and they could start again. New soups would always be under consideration.

Rose had been working at the time as a waitress for the Anchor Grill, 3 A.M. to noon shift—a job from which she'd come and gone for years. Bad hours, good tips. Petie had been cleaning motel rooms at the Sea View Motel: bad wages, good people, good location. In either case, cooking sounded better and the money was only slightly worse. Plus as long as they could stand a steady diet of soup, they could feed their families for free.

The Coolbaughs lived in a shabby little rental on the north side of town, on a dead-end road called Heyter Place. The house was old and had been no good to start with, but Petie knew how to put a good front on things. Small, exquisite watercolors hung on the walls: still lifes of balloons and baby toys; wildflowers and action figures; cooking utensils, bouquets of keys. She'd painted the kitchen walls and ceiling brilliant white with lemon yellow trim, and even the sickly sun of winter seemed to try a little harder there. Now, in robust late September, the cheap white curtains were so saturated with light they seemed incandescent.

While Petie diced fifty carrots, Rose read aloud from the weekly newspaper about old Billy Wall, who had just been indicted on sodomy charges.

"You know what I think? Hand me that peeler." Petie weighed it thoughtfully in her hand, then pointed it at Rose. "I think if he did what those kids say he did, the guy deserves to have a bad thing happen to him. I mean worse than shame and a jail term. I mean something *bad*. They should take him just like you'd take a carrot, and peel him down real slow, you know, real *careful*, layer by layer until you've got him peeled naked as an egg, and then you bring him to Hubbard Elementary and you lock him in the gym with twenty mothers with baseball bats. You put some Gatorade in there, and some high-nutrition snacks, and maybe have an alternate or two who can substitute when one of the women gets tired." She traded Rose the peeler for a paring knife. "The son of a bitch."

For several minutes Petie's knife made sharp regular reports like gunshots on the cutting board. She had thick, strong, shiny black hair—Indian hair, although she was no part Indian—that she'd tied back from her face with an old rolled-up bandanna. Stuffed under it were some straggly ends, old bangs. She was always trying to grow out old bangs or some other hair fiasco. Once, Rose remembered, she had bleached out a central stripe in her hair. She'd looked strange as a skunk with the jet black running up against the peroxide yellow with no warning and no apology. That was back in high school, in their freshman year. Petie's mother had died four years before, and she and her father were living up at the top of Chollum Road in a twelve-foot camp trailer. Old Man Tyler had always been mean, but after Petie's mother died and he had to declare bankruptcy, he'd been even worse. But as far as Rose could tell, even before Petie's mother died, the only time Old Man Tyler had really paid attention to her was when he was yelling at her; otherwise, he took no notice. Petie swore she didn't own a dress until she was twelve, and by then it was too late to get a feel for them. She'd have gotten married in pants if she'd had her way, but Eddie Coolbaugh had balked so she was married in a homemade lace sheath Eula Coolbaugh made for her, a dress that showed how essentially boy-shaped Petie was. And how small. Everyone thought she was bigger, including Rose. In her own way, she took up a lot of space.

"What are you thinking about?" Petie said, scraping the cut carrots into a big plastic Tupperware container to use tomorrow morning.

"That time you bleached your hair out."

Petie chuckled. "I looked just like a skunk."

"That's what I was thinking. I never thought it bothered you, though. You didn't show it."

"Of course I didn't show it. I didn't tell anyone Old Man beat me over it, either."

"He did?"

"Well, he was drunk."

"Oh."

"Then again, you never really knew, with Old Man. Chances are, he would have beaten me anyway."

"What do you think will happen to those boys Billy Wall messed with? I've heard kids don't recover from something like that, ever. Do you think that's possible, that those poor kids have been ruined?"

Petie shrugged. "I don't know. They'll grow up. They'll date, they'll make stupid choices. At some point they'll realize their lives aren't nearly as good as the ones they expected. Same old same old. Everyone's ruined somewhere along the line."

Rose started to laugh. "Oh, Petie."

"Really. Sooner or later something terrible's always going to come along. It's really just a question of timing."

Rose took the carrot peeler and started scraping potatoes, a small mountain of them, into the sink. "Something terrible like what happened to those boys is not going to happen to everyone, Petie. My God."

"Of course not. It could even be something that seems like not much—moving to another town, say, or having bad acne or liking beer too much. Or it could be something quiet like hopelessness or boredom. No one ever said that ruin always comes in a big loud package."

Rose watched Petie tear apart some sprigs of parsley and toss them into one of the pots. "Well, I'm thinking I might start driving Carissa to school."

"Does she worry about the trip?" Petie stirred some heavy cream into one of the pots.

"No."

"Does she complain about having to wait after school?"

"No, but—"

"So she's a smart kid. She can take care of herself. Stir." Petie put her spoon in Rose's hand.

"You worry about the boys," Rose pointed out, stirring.

"I worry about Ryan. I *fear* for Loose. There's a difference."

Five-year-old Loose Coolbaugh (short for Lucifer, although even that wasn't his real name) was a fearless, physical kid: he would hit before he'd concede he was wrong. His playground daredeviltry had already made him, in less than a month, an object of admiration in his first-grade class. He'd been to the emergency room over in Sawyer twice in just that time period: once for a minor concussion when he swung into thin air off the monkey bars, once for stitches in his hand from an old can he'd systematically broken apart with a rock.

Ryan, on the other hand, was frail and suffered for it. At eight years old, he still had frequent asthma attacks, night fears and daytime dreads: large dogs, sneaker waves, public toilets, physical contests. He was also bookish, which no one in the family could fathom. Loose needled him mercilessly, and often got the upper hand. Eddie Coolbaugh used to push him to try harder, be bolder, cry less often, but since Loose had come along Eddie had lost interest. Petie and Rose often took turns bringing Ryan along on after-school errands, just to give him a break from the household. Petie protected him when she could, but she admitted to Rose more than once that she didn't exactly get the point of him, either.

"I think this is ready," Rose said. "It's getting late. We better go." Petie was cutting Rose's scraped potatoes and stowing them in a Tupperware container filled with water, for the morning. The finished corn chowder on the stove was one of their favorites. The other vat was lentil, a recipe of Rose's that wasn't even on the Souperior's list. The soup was supposed to have been vegetable barley, but Petie refused to fix anything submitted by Jeannie Fontineau. Jeannie Fontineau was nothing but a sad-eyed fat woman now, but she had fooled around with Eddie Coolbaugh a little bit years ago, before she got so fat but after he and Petie were married. Jeannie Fontineau wasn't the only one Eddie had ever fooled around with, but she was the first, and that made her stand out. Nadine would be mad about the soup substitution, but they'd just tell her something.

Petie stowed the Tupperware container in the refrigerator and said, "You call Nadine and tell her we're on our way. I'll load the car." The vats of soup were too hot and too heavy for either of the women to carry, so Eddie Coolbaugh had rigged up a table-high dolly for them, and a ramp down the two steps outside. From there they just slid the vats into the back of Petie's old Ford Colt. Together they jockeyed the huge pots onto the dolly and out the kitchen door. Petie disappeared down the ramp while Rose dialed. It was ten-thirty in the morning; Souperior's started serving lunch at eleven. Nadine answered on the first ring.

"You're pushing it, you guys," she said when she heard Rose's voice. She sounded unusually testy; Rose guessed it was a migraine day.

"Petie's got the engine running. Corn chowder and lentil."

"Where's the vegetable barley?"

"We got a deal on salt pork, so we switched. Does it matter? Did you publish the menu in the paper?"

"As it happens, the ad doesn't start until next week. But I'd like to have known. You should have asked me. I'm the owner. You're the employees."

"You sound like you have a headache."

"I have late soup, is what I have. Give me a break, Rose."

"We'd be there already if we weren't talking."

Nadine sighed. "You're both taking advantage of me."

"Yes," Rose said, "but we're completely supportive. Look for us in five minutes." Rose retrieved the empty dolly and closed the kitchen door behind her, smiling. She'd just been kidding about a newspaper ad.

Souperior's turned its back on the highway to moon westward from the high and rocky rim of Hubbard Bay. Petie remembered when the shambly little place had been the barbershop and all the Hubbard men had looked alike because old Walt Miller hadn't gone to barber school up in Portland yet to learn a second way to cut hair. Petie's father used to hang around the place half plowed making a pest of himself, especially after her mother died and they lost the house and had to move into the camp trailer up at the top of Chollum Road. Old Man was a contentious drunk; sometimes Walt had had to sneak out of his own shop to get away and call her to come get him. Once, while Walt wasn't looking, her father had taken his little buck knife and carved into the shop's doorjamb, *I got fucked in '74. JST*. That was the year her mother's uninsured hospital bills came to seventy-five thousand dollars and she died anyway. Walt had sanded most of the message away, but he'd left the JST as an expression of sympathy. Although the initials had been covered over with a few coats of paint by now, Petie could still feel a faint depression with her fingertips.

But Old Man had been dead for five years, Walt for two, and now Souperior's was wedged between the Kristmas Kottage and Passionetta's Fudge and Candies, its ruddy old fir floor rippling westward towards the sea. Nadine had edged the great drafty old plate-glass windows in country lace and dark-stained oak, and she hosed and squeegeed away the salt every morning from a catwalk Gordon had built for her the first week they were there. The one thing that made Nadine tolerable, in Petie's opinion, was the sense of honor with which she looked out over the foamy chop. This woman, whatever else you could say about her—and Petie hadn't found much else worth saying about her—loved the place with a deep and abiding respect. In Petie's book that nearly made up for the rest of her, which was all nerves, snip and anxiety. More than once Petie had held her up to Rose as living proof that some people shouldn't give up smoking.

Nadine met them now at the door, a thin woman with graying flyaway hair and an overbite. "This is not going to happen again," she said, holding the door as Petie staggered through with one of the pots of soup.

"There's still fifteen minutes until opening," Rose said over her shoulder. "And the soup is nice and hot. All you need is a ladle."

"That's not the point," Nadine said.

"What is the point?" Petie said, returning from the kitchen.

"The point is, I need to be able to depend on you, Patricia. The point is, my customers depend on you."

"The point is, you need to goose the guy who's sitting on your refrigerator order," said Petie, slapping Nadine lightly on the back. It always amused her to hear herself called Patricia, a name she hadn't gone by since the day she was baptized thirty-one years ago. "It's insane for us to be doing same-day cooking."

Nadine wilted. "He said there were delays at the factory. It'll be another week, maybe two."

"We could probably rent freezer space over at Pacific Seas Packing," Rose said. "It's slow right now."

"I'm not serving frozen food here," Nadine said. "Not even for one day. You know that."

Nadine didn't realize that in order to get more than one day off a week they doubled up sometimes, freezing and storing the extra batches down at the fish plant thanks to a favor owed Jim Christie, Rose's boyfriend. They thawed the soup out a couple of days ahead, reheated it that morning, and whichever of them delivered it to Souperior's put on a dirty apron saved from earlier in the week just to make it look like they'd been cooking. Rose wanted to tell Nadine the truth, but Petie thought it was nicer to just leave her in the dark, where she wouldn't worry herself.

"Look, Nadine, we're sorry," Rose said. "We didn't cut it so close on purpose. When we're cooking things we haven't made before, it's not always easy to guess the timing right. When the refrigerator gets here and we can get a day ahead of ourselves you'll be off the hook. Okay? We know how important it is. And we like this job. We're not going to let you down."

While Rose and Nadine talked, Petie walked over to the coffeepot and helped herself to a good strong cup. Whatever else, Nadine made great coffee, dark and fragrant, nothing like the weak-tea coffee they served down at the Anchor: the early morning boys took their coffee thin and watery, and hell would freeze over before they'd ever let Connie or Rose or any of the other waitresses thicken it up. Petie had worked on them every morning for two years and not one of them had given an inch. That was before Ryan was born, when she still went down every morning at six-thirty with Eddie Coolbaugh. There'd been her and Rose and pretty-faced Pogo Robinson, and Eddie, of course, plus eight or nine others in the back three booths. Petie had sat in the same chair at the same table, morning after morning, keeping a plate of eggs or pancakes going and smoking a cigarette or two, minding a cup of coffee for Rose to sneak from as she waited on them all. Petie was twenty, twenty-one then, cocky and lean, proud as hell of their new beater car and their mouse-scratchy one-bedroom apartment a block back of the highway. She could still remember all their morning go-to-work smells: the jean jackets that had aged on a barstool, the weather-beaten, sweat-permeated ball caps, the safety boots that gave off engine grease and fish, the newsprint from Dooley Burden, who had to do his crosstik. Petie and Rose and Connie had been the only women most days, and of them, Petie was the only paying customer. Petie liked it like that, liked their not talking any special way to her, liked the guff they gave, liked giving it back again. She'd even liked Eddie Coolbaugh, for that matter, with his clean pretty fingernails no matter what job he was working, his tucked-in shirt and big brass belt buckle centered like a hood ornament over his fly, the strut in his walk that almost fooled you into forgetting he was only five-seven. Eddie cared about looking good, and used hairspray on his thin blond hair long before it was fashionable, to keep it in place. In those days he still wasn't letting anyone cut it but Petie.

All those mornings at the Anchor she had slouched low and easy in the vinyl tuck-and-roll booths, thinking she had a rightful place there, and then she got pregnant with Ryan. Suddenly no one was making eye contact anymore. The boys cleaned up their jokes around her. They stopped slapping at her back pockets with newspapers or jacket sleeves when she got mouthy. Just like that, they got polite and threw her over to the women. And except for Rose, Petie had never liked women—at least women her own age—and had never known how to be around them. So she defied them and kept going down for coffee right up to the day she delivered, but once Ryan came it was over. Ryan had cried all the time and Petie's milk had backed up and clogged and she was awake twenty hours a day, sometimes more, and then Eddie Coolbaugh had started getting his hair cut by Jeannie Fontineau. No one but Rose came around for weeks, and then some of the women started to; Rose must have told them Petie was in trouble up there alone in her lousy one-bedroom with no washer-dryer. She was so crazy by then she was grateful for the company, and the world had been nothing much but women ever since. She'd gotten better at them—there were always kids to talk about, for one thing—but she never felt the same about mornings after that, or about men, either.

Petie rubbed her eyes and watched the water: medium chop, medium high tide coming in. Paul Kramer's boat *Mariah* was picking its way through the channel, loaded with rockfish. She and Rose had started cooking at five-fifteen, with a break to get everyone off to school, and Petie was tired. At least Eddie was working day shift right now at the mill over in Sawyer and would be gone until suppertime. He'd been working security there for just over a year: good job, good benefits. But when he was rotated to swing shift or graveyard it messed up their routine. He was always stirring up Loose or getting on Ryan for something, or else promising to do something with them and then not showing up.

Petie rubbed her eyes again. Something else had happened to them the year Ryan was born: Eddie Coolbaugh had gotten his first dirt bike between his legs. It was just a little gnat of a bike but he'd worked the machine until he wore it out, bumping over back trails and ripping new ones out of the woods. Broken fingers, torn-up knees, stupid stuff, but he loved it. Ever since that first bike he'd been trading and rebuilding and selling and rebuying and generally garfing up their garage and side yard. By then it hadn't mattered that much to her. Somewhere in the back draft left by Ryan and Jeannie Fontineau, the spark between her and Eddie had been sucked right out. So had the talk. Now there were just little bits of nontalk like, *Do you think that clutch is still slipping,* and *What about fixing some of that venison Luther brought by,* and *I'm going down to the Wayside to have a couple beers.* That was good-days talk. On bad days it was, *Try picking up your clothes once in a while,* and *I thought you said you were coming home for supper,* and *Why don't you be nice to Ryan for a change, he's got your blood in his veins just as much as Loose and all you do is make him feel like shit.* They mainly got along, though, as long as Eddie was working and kept his hood ornament to himself. Every once in a while Rose and her daughter Carissa came over to stay with the boys and they went and threw darts down at the Wayside like they used to, but Petie always won and that pissed Eddie off.

ROSE CAME over and sat across from Petie at the table; Nadine had disappeared into the kitchen. "We need to lighten up a little," she whispered, stirring cream into a cup of coffee. "She's pretty upset."

"Talk about needing to lighten up."

"This is her place, Petie. She can be any way she wants to. And she's got an awful lot of leftovers back there from yesterday."

" 'Each new day, new soups,' " Petie said, quoting Nadine's motto. "You know, she's going to go broke."

"God, I hope not," Rose said. "I like this job."

"It does beat getting your butt patted at four-thirty in the morning by some old boy at the Anchor," Petie said. "Or being up to your elbows in dirty sheets, like me."

"I kind of miss the boys, to tell you the truth," Rose said. "Except for the ones like old Dooley Burden, you know how he was always moving his coffee cup way over to the other side of the table and then taking a look down my shirt when I went to give him a refill." It was widely acknowledged that Rose had very pretty breasts. Just about every male customer at the Anchor had tried to sneak a peek sometime.

"I hope you didn't put up with that," Nadine said. She'd come up drying her hands on a dish towel.

"Only when I needed the tips."

"If you give in like that, you just enable the behavior," Nadine said sourly. She slid into the booth across from Rose, next to Petie.

"It's okay," Rose assured her. "They'd do it anyway."

"Hell, even I do it," Petie said. "Rose has great boobs."

Nadine sighed. "I'm never going to understand you people."

"Ditto," Petie said. "How much did that dish towel cost you?"

"Six for twelve dollars. I order them from Williams-Sonoma. It's a kitchen catalog."

"It's expensive," said Petie.

"Well, there's nothing better than good-quality cotton," Nadine said primly, folding the towel in quarters and putting it in her lap, out of sight.

"Huh," said Petie. She had just been warming up, but Rose had kicked her under the table.

"What I came over to tell you was, the soups are delicious. What gives the lentil its body?"

"You puree a little of the salt pork and add it back in," Rose said.

Petie sighed. Every day she just wanted to drop off the soup and go, and every day Nadine ended up backing them into small talk. Rose was nicer about it than Petie. *The woman's just lonely*, she would say to Petie once they'd left. *She doesn't know anyone yet and business is slow and I don't think anyone's been in love with her in a long time, so be nice. It won't kill you.* As usual, Rose was right.

"So tell us about L.A.," Petie said to Nadine, making an effort. "Give us the inside scoop."

Nadine shrugged. "There is no inside scoop. People shoot other people for no reason on the freeways. The whole place is on a seismic fault. Where most of the people can afford to live, it's ugly. Hollywood turns out to be just a state of mind." They've been over all this before.

"But what's it *like*?" Petie said. She'd never been to California, but she would like to see Hollywood, Universal Studios, Disneyland. She could do without the beaches. She'd lived around beaches for thirty-one years and they'd never done a thing for her.

"It's like anywhere else, just more expensive. People go to work too far away, they have jobs they don't like, they talk about getting out. I worked in a bookstore for seven years and I never even knew the names of the people in the shop next door. I thought a lot about rape and door locks. What do you want to hear, Patricia?"

"She wants to hear about Richard Gere," said Rose.

"Richard Gere?"

"I like Richard Gere," Petie said. "He looks like the kind of guy who isn't worrying all the time about his hair mousse."

"I never met Richard Gere," Nadine said.

Suddenly there wasn't much left to say.

Rose, who was facing the small window onto the street, suddenly leaned forward. "I think I just saw Eddie go by," she said. "Is he working a half day today?"

"No."

"Maybe he came home sick," Rose said.

"Maybe," Petie said.

"Or maybe I saw wrong."

"God, I hope so."

The street door to Souperior's jangled, and a man and a woman in expensive matching jogging suits looked inside.

"Would you have a menu?" The woman stayed in the doorway but her perfume came on in.

"We serve soup," Nadine said, getting up from the table. "Today we have corn chowder and lentil. They're both excellent."

"Oh," said the woman, backing away. "Oh, no. We wanted seafood." She turned around and left.

"All right, we'll have clam chowder," Nadine said to Rose, who'd been after her to offer it. "We'll carry it on the menu as a third soup every day. I'll pay you both an extra forty dollars a week for it."

"Forty dollars each?" said Petie.

Nadine just gave her a look.

"Oh, all right," Petie said to Nadine. She shook her purse, found her car keys and stood up to go. "Want a ride?" she asked Rose.

"I'll walk. Call me if it was Eddie."

"I will," said Petie. "If it was, pray for flu."

WHEN SHE got home Petie found Eddie Coolbaugh's old beater Ford pickup halfway up the rutted drive. Eddie was still inside, stalled behind the wheel. Petie pulled around him, parked on the hard-pack in the side yard and came back down on foot.

"Fired?"

"Quit."

"Son of a bitch." Petie walked around, let herself in the passenger side and shut the door. This was Eddie's seventh job in six years. Anybody else would have run out of places to go years ago, but everyone liked Eddie. Except for the way he looked he didn't take himself too seriously, plus he wasn't the only one around with a history of slipping: off the wagon, into adultery, out of work. He didn't even slip as often or as far as some.

"Call and tell them you didn't mean it. Say you were coming down with a migraine."

"Hell, I did mean it. The guy was getting on me about reports all the time. Report this, report that, write this down, write that down. Today he tells me he wants a shift log entry every hour, that's the latest thing. I was hired to do security, not be some fucking writer."

Eddie Coolbaugh had been a terrible student, severely dyslexic, though they hadn't known it then. By the time they'd finally figured it out, it was too late to fix it. Most people didn't know. The security job was doomed.

"Plus the little prick keeps calling me Coolpaw, thinks he's real funny," Eddie was saying. "Ha ha ha."

"You could see if they'd take you somewhere else at the mill. You could turn union, maybe."

"Sure, if they had an opening," said Eddie. "Which they don't."

"Two hundred and twenty dollars," Petie said. "We've got two hundred and twenty dollars in the bank."

"Come on, Petie, the guy's a prick."

"Yeah, well, he's a prick who was paying you a lot of money. And it was a lot of money we were *spending* every paycheck."

"I thought you'd take my side for a change."

"Honey, when you're right I'll take your side so fast your head'll spin." Petie got out of the truck and slammed the door. The truck was a piece of trash and should have been driven into a ditch and left there years ago. The door didn't even slam, it just whined and then stuck. Eddie fired up the engine and chugged along beside her, talking through the half-open door.

"Come on, Petie. I'll find something else. It's not that big a thing."

"Trust me," Petie said. "This is a big thing. Big. What's not a big thing is when you throw away a shit job. This was not a shit job, Eddie."

"You could just get it over with and hit me."

"I could," Petie said agreeably, "but I might break your nose again, and then we'd have to pay a doctor bill *we can't fucking afford*."

"Screw you, Petie, you know? You never understand," Eddie hollered. He turned the truck around in the ratty side yard and roared off. On the way by, he flipped her the bird. It had all happened before.

Petie let herself in through the kitchen and sat down at the table. The house was thick with the smell of onion and bay and salt pork and lentil. Under that was the fainter, nicer, sweeter-saltier aroma of little boys and sneakers and the morning's damp towels and laundry; and then there was the fusty odor of the house itself, with its hint of worn carpet and dry rot. And finally, faintest of all, was the scent of Petie herself, the warm soap and skin smell she had been inhaling from the crook of her arm since she was a little girl to calm herself.

While her mother was alive she used to wear some cheap sweet toilet water Petie couldn't remember the name of, and their house always smelled of that. Later, the camp trailer on Chollum Road had smelled of her father; his cigarettes, his hair oil, his diesely work clothes, all the hot pungent odors about him that were so thick she used to be afraid they'd stick to her when she left for school in the morning. Of all of them, through all the years, only Eddie Coolbaugh had no scent, none whatsoever. He never had. Even soap didn't stay on him long, even beer. Petie didn't know why that was.

The phone rang.

"Fired?" It was Rose.

"Quit. The damned guy he works for wanted him to write a lot."

"Oh, man," said Rose.

"Listen. When's Christie coming home?" Jim Christie, Rose's boyfriend, was still fishing out of Dutch Harbor, Alaska, and had been gone for two months. It was about the right time of year for him to be heading home.

"I don't know. Soon. I thought I would've heard from him by now."

"I hope whenever he does come down here, he has room for Eddie."

"I don't think you can count on it. He's not bringing a boat down with him this time. You know, I've got a little bit of money, Petie. You take it if you need to."

"Nah. We've got a little. Plus, hey, there's always the clam chowder money."

"You take that."

"We'll split it. But I wonder what she pays the Riseria for bread?"

"Not much, I bet."

"Yeah, but she was complaining the other day because she couldn't get them to do specialty breads—you know, cheese dill, honey granola, husk and stem stuff. Maybe I could make bread for her."

"You could ask. It's not much money for the work, though."

"Yeah, well, the night desk isn't open at the Sea View anymore." Once Petie had worked the graveyard shift at the Sea View Motel for an entire summer while Eddie was out of work. (Marge and Larry Hopkins wouldn't hire Eddie for the job. They told Petie very nicely that they didn't feel he could be counted on. Petie had patted Marge on the shoulder and said, "No kidding.") Ryan had been just five months old at the time, and from June through September he had slept all night under the counter in a basket, among the spare stacks of scenic drive maps and giveaway tide tables; Petie had slept nearby in a La-Z-Boy, with all the lights on and the VACANCY sign flashing. In the morning Larry would wake her up and she'd go clean rooms for a while with Ryan riding shotgun in her housekeeping cart. It was a good setup, and it lasted until Eddie got work on a construction job over in Sawyer and Petie could afford to gently break it to Marge and Larry that they no way in hell needed a night desk clerk. "Oh, we know that, honey," Marge had told Petie. "We were just waiting until Eddie found something for himself. You go on home, now." Petie had been baking her and Larry holiday treats every year since then without fail, whether or not she was working for them, and not just to celebrate the big holidays, either: Presidents' Day, the first day of spring, Groundhog Day.

"Hey," Rose's light voice came echoing down the line. "You all right? You stopped talking."

"What? Oh yeah," Petie said. "I'm fine."

Chapter 2

On its way south out of Hubbard, the coast highway dragged itself up and around a stony headland and then reeled straight down into Sawyer. It wasn't unusual, on a foggy day, to crest the cape and be blinded by sudden sunshine from a microclimate yawning on the other side.

Comparatively speaking, Sawyer was the land of riches: home of the mill, the jail, the big fish-processing plants, three supermarkets that stayed open twenty-four hours a day. En masse every morning and evening, and in a steady trickle all the hours in between, Hubbard's citizens scaled the headland and fell over the other side into Sawyer's banks, law offices, schools, pharmacies, movie theaters, car dealerships, Wal-Mart. The road could be treacherous and everyone had a story to tell about the time they'd spun out on black ice, come upon a neighbor wheels-up in a ditch, lost it going around the last curve. Last year Petie had done a three-sixty on wet pavement early one fall morning when a young buck leapt across her headlights and then disappeared into the treetops on the far side of the road. When she got home, she had found a hoofprint punched right into the middle of her grille.

Now she navigated the same curve cautiously, even though the sun was out and the road was dry. For one thing she was so tired her senses felt like they were wandering around on their own. For another thing, she didn't trust her car, a beat-to-shit Ford Colt that Eddie had picked up cheap and tinkered with everlastingly. It was an act of God when they got through a week without mechanical failure. Now she eased into Sawyer and ground to a halt in the parking lot of the Cash 'n Carry wholesale store in the center of town. Rose had wanted to come over in Petie's place but Petie convinced her that the drive and a little shopping was a joy ride compared to being stuck at home with Ryan, Loose and Eddie.

Secretly, Petie loved the Cash 'n Carry. Here was a place of plenty where you could buy toilet paper rolls in packages of three dozen and pickle slices in five-gallon drums. Disposable banquet tablecloths came in nine colors, little plastic champagne glasses were shrink-wrapped in packs of twenty-five, crepe paper was available in thousand-foot rolls. Someone was having fun.

"Hey, pretty lady. How's it going?" Approaching her from the complimentary coffee station was Bob Harle, the Cash 'n Carry's owner, a low-slung, short-legged, barrel-chested man Petie liked a lot. He always fetched her a rolling pallet personally. Now he extended a free cup of coffee.

"Same old same old. I'm getting stronger, though." Petie flexed her fingers. At the end of the first week, her hands had been so sore from kneading ten loaves of bread a day that she could hardly pick up a Kleenex. "Couple more weeks and I'll be strong enough to strangle someone if he crosses me."

"Hey, not this man," Bob said, holding up his hands. "I don't mess with you career women."

"The only thing different about this from the last twenty-two years is I'm getting paid."

"I heard you made real nice soups out there, though, you and Rose. I'll have to come by and try it one time."

"Hell, I'll just bring you a bowl of something next time I come in," Petie said. "It'll cost you less." She fingered some thirty-packs of Life Savers, like you'd buy to stock the candy shelf at the Quik Stop. She flicked the little handi-paks of Tylenol, Bufferin, Advil on a Li'l Drug Store display. You'd have to be in pain to buy this stuff. Even wholesale the little ten-packs of aspirin cost almost as much as a bottle of fifty in a regular store. Nadine probably bought things like that; her purse was probably full of little travel packs of Kleenex and pocket-sized potpourris and rose-hip essence and shit.

Bob watched her for a minute sympathetically, crossed his short arms with difficulty across his big chest.

"You don't have any job openings," she said.

"Afraid I'm full up. My boys tend to stick around, the Lord only knows why. Probably my magnetic personality. Your man still out of work?"

Petie nodded. "He's looking, though. How'd you know about that?"

"Rose told me. She worries."

"She talks."

"Nothing wrong with being out of work, Petie. It happens to a man sometimes."

"Well," said Petie. Bob didn't know Eddie Coolbaugh, didn't know about the seven jobs in six years. Rose wouldn't have said anything about that. Petie sure wasn't about to.

"These things just take time, sometimes," Bob said reassuringly.

"Well, if something does come up, though, could you call me? Or you could just call Eddie."

"I'll call you first thing," Bob said, and patted her shoulder.

Bob went off and Petie cruised the aisles slowly. She put on the Souperior's account whole wheat flour, cracked wheat flour, stone-ground flour, cornmeal, oatmeal and yeast; a brick of lard, a tub of shortening and an industrial-size bottle of parsley; a twelve-pack of peanut butter and eleven pounds of quick-frozen breaded chicken breasts for home; and a yo-yo for the boys that Bob let her have for nothing because it had gotten loose from its shrink-wrapped pack. Bob pretended he didn't notice she was buying for home and Petie believed in taking what was offered without worrying too much about the fine points. In her experience, pride only took you so far before it turned into stupidity. Old Man had turned stupid years ago and he and Petie had been hungry in that camp trailer more often than she could remember. The rest of the time they ate poverty food: boxed macaroni and cheese, canned meat, canned hash, hot dogs, all fixed on a hot plate. At school Rose brought or bought enough food for them both, and Petie took it.

After the Cash 'n Carry she decided to stop by the State Employment Division to look at the job listings. Maybe something new had come in since the last time she'd checked. She left the car under a tree to give her frozen chicken breasts every advantage.

The Employment Division was in an old cement block outbuilding of the county's mental health and family services. It was gloomy inside and smelled like work clothes and cheap perfume and Xerox copiers. Listed in the lobby on an enormous white board were all the current jobs. Grill cook, prep cook, carpenter, maid, waitress, waitress, paralegal, clerk. Delivery driver, cannery worker, bartender, nurse, bookkeeper, dishwasher, pest control . . . pest control. Petie approached a pretty girl standing behind a window at the counter like a bank teller. She had long pink Barbie doll nails and matching pink top and pink plastic earrings.

"Can you tell me anything about that pest control job?" Petie asked.

"Oh! Let's see. That's one we don't have much on." The girl paged through a ring binder efficiently with her pencil eraser. "We're listing it, but we don't have it in our files. It just says here"—the girl traced the words with one pink fingernail as she read—" 'Pest inspection/sales. Climbs under houses, in attics, crawl spaces looking for possible pest infestation, rodent nests, etc.' "

"What does it pay?"

"It looks like one thousand five hundred per month, plus commissions."

"So you find bugs and then sell people a plan to get rid of them."

"And provide relief for the guys who spray, but that's probably only during vacations and sick days and stuff. I mean, that's what I'm guessing. Like I said, we don't have much here on it. I could give you a number to call, though. Or would this be for you? I could try and set up an interview if you wanted."

"That's okay," Petie said. "Maybe I'll take the number, though."

The girl wrote it out on a little slip of paper in big round letters. "If you change your mind about an interview or you need anything else, my name is Toni and I'm here to try and help you." The girl gave Petie a nice smile.

On her way out Petie took an Employment Division registration form. Of course the girl was smiling. She had a job.

Eddie coolbaugh was in the side yard soaking car parts in an old coffee can when Petie got home. Loose was stirring them around with a stick while Eddie worked on a transmission coupling with a toothbrush. They were completely absorbed; they barely looked up when she pulled in.

"Hey," she said in their direction, struggling to drag the twenty-five-pound flour sacks out of the backseat. "Hey!"

"Go see if your mom needs help," Eddie told Loose.

"I'm doing this," Loose said.

"Well, stop doing it and help your mom."

"She doesn't need any help."

"Like hell I don't," Petie said menacingly. "Get over here and take the other end of this thing."

Loose shuffled over and lifted a corner of the flour sack between two fingers.

"Come on, Loose, will you give me a break? Try just a little bit."

"I can't. It's too heavy," he whined. He tried, and it was.

"Come on, Eddie, do you think you could put that junk aside for just five minutes and give me some help with this stuff?"

Eddie set the coupling down on a clean flannel cloth and sprang to his feet. There were still times when his bones seemed filled with air. He had been one of the most gifted hurdlers Sawyer High had ever seen. They used to joke that his legs were better than Petie's, and she had very nice legs even though she was so small.

"Think you got enough stuff there, or were you thinking of going back for a second load?" he said as they muscled two of the flour sacks out the door together.

"Funny."

"Hell, at least we're not going to go hungry," he said. "Look at all this shit. You could open a bakery."

"What do you think I'm doing in the kitchen at three o'clock every morning? Clog dancing?"

Grunting, they wrestled the load through the mudroom and into the kitchen. Petie lined up the flour sacks in the broom closet beside her ancient Hoover.

"You've got to give the old place credit," she said, panting and giving the kitchen wall a pat. "I wasn't sure the floors had it in them to stand up under this kind of weight."

Eddie smoothed back his hair, tucked in his shirt. Even in work clothes he took care with himself, fussing over missing buttons and shrunken sleeves. "Where's Ryan?" she asked. Eddie pointed at the ceiling.

"Ryan!" she called up the stairs. "You okay?"

A muffled yes came down. Hiding from Loose again.

"I stopped at the employment office while I was over there," she said.

"Yeah?" Eddie considered her with a minimum of interest and no enthusiasm.

"They're looking for someone to do pest control. It might be decent money."

Eddie looked at her.

"I brought you an application form. We could fill it out after the kids are in bed."

"You want me to get cancer?"

"Not right now, because we've only got forty-two dollars and eighty-six cents. And I just got paid the day before yesterday. C'mon, it's not going to give you cancer. You could at least look into it. It sounds like it's probably more sales than spraying and stuff, and anyway if it's hazardous it probably pays more. Plus nothing's that dangerous if you're careful. And you wouldn't have to stop looking just because you had the job."

Loose came slouching into the kitchen, dripping the oil stick all over the floor. "Aren't you coming back out? You said we were gonna rebuild the transmission."

"Out," Petie yelled. "NOW!"

Loose shuffled out, twirling the stick and dotting the walls with oil.

"You're worried about some harmless household chemicals but you let a five-year-old boy play with that shit," Petie said.

Eddie left the kitchen without a word. Petie heard Loose start crying, and when she looked out the kitchen door Eddie was ripping some part out of the boy's hand and heading for his workshop around back.

"Crap." Petie walked out into the yard and put her arm around Loose's shoulders as he stood sobbing over the coffee can of stewed parts. "Come on in, Loose. I'll fix you a nice piece of bread."

Loose drove his elbow into Petie's side and ran to the workshop.

"Damn it," Petie whispered, but her heart had gone out of it. She went back into the kitchen and dialed Rose's number. There was a God: Rose was home.

"I think there's good money in pest control. He thinks there's cancer," Petie said, describing the blowup. "Plus I charged some stuff on Nadine's account and I don't have the money to pay her back."

"You want some help?"

"Not yet. It'll probably be another three weeks or something before she gets the bill."

"Well, the good news is, she said Souperior's had a waiting line for a little while at lunch today," Rose said. "We got mentioned in the *Oregonian* travel section. Wait a sec." She put down the phone; Petie could hear rustling. "Here, listen. 'Delightful atmosphere, spectacular view, an excellent if limited fare,'" Rose read. "'Souperior's is a welcome way station for anyone passing through this tiny coastal community.' Sounds pretty good."

"Thank God. If that place goes under right now I can't swear to the safety of the dog."

Rose snorted over the receiver.

"You think I'm kidding," said Petie darkly.

"Oh, Petie, you don't even have a dog."

"Well, at the rate things are going, I might have to get one, a nice fat tender one. Where the hell is Christie, anyway? Isn't he taking a long time coming back?"

"God, it sure feels like it. I thought he'd be down by now for sure."

"Are you getting worried?"

"No, he'll be here."

"Well, I wish he'd hurry. I need someone to bail out Eddie, because I'm not getting anywhere for shit."

"So what are the boys doing?"

"Loose is sulking and Ryan's hiding. Just another fun afternoon at home."

"Is Eddie there?"

"So far."

"Then let's go for a beer, my treat. Carissa's next door, she won't be back for an hour."

"I don't know."

"I'll meet you there," Rose said, and hung up.

THE WAYSIDE was a small rickety wooden box with a front door, a delivery door, and nothing else, not a single window. At high noon it was dark as dusk inside, a place where you could have a serious drink at 9 A.M., and many did. No booths, either; people sat right out in the open at the scarred old carved-up tables (*White Lightning, Mugsy & BooBoo, 'Nam in '63, All Bikers Go to Heaven*) and took the company as it came. If you wanted to put a move on someone you went down the street to the Anchor and drank cocktails in the tuck-and-roll booths beside the tourists and the electric organ with Pinky Leonard at the keyboard.

Ron Schiffen, a regular for coffee at the Anchor and manager of the Pepsi distributorship over in Sawyer, was standing alone at the bar. He had one foot up on the rung of a barstool, and all the time he drank his beer and neatly stripped chicken wings between his teeth he absently ran the sole of his boot over and over a protruding nail. They were the slick, tooled boots of a hustler or a pool shark. At any given time he owned two pairs, his old boots and his new boots. Right now the old ones had needle-sharp toes, were scuffed to the point of colorlessness and were so perfectly broken in that each one caressed his small foot like a cheap date. The new boots, which he now wore, were oxblood with inset medallions and black-threaded swirls. They were a gift from his wife Carla and Schiff's distaste for them was absolute. It wasn't the flamboyance he minded—his favorite pair of boots ever had been an ostrich-skin pair with burnished lizard toes—but the fact that they were not a man's boot; they were the sort of foo-foo boot a woman would pick out for a man, saying, "Look, hon, aren't they *pretty*?" However, when Carla had bought them Schiff had been in the doghouse for something—he couldn't remember what, he was always in the doghouse for something—so he'd praised them to the heavens and continued to wear them every day like a hair shirt. He shuffled deeply whenever he passed through the jagged gravel of the Pepsi distributorship's parking lot.

He looked up from his beer and his ruminations about his boots when he saw Rose come in. The sight of her perked him up. He liked Rose, and missed seeing her at the Anchor, waitressing every morning. She was an easy-tempered, warm-eyed woman who knew when to pour a man a cup of coffee and how to set down a plate of eggs, a rare combination.

"Hey, Rosalie." He always called her that although her name wasn't Rosalie, just plain Rose.

"Hi, Schiff."

"You going to brighten up my afternoon?"

"Why, do you need cheering up? Is something wrong?"

"Nah. Just the four o'clock Thursday blues. I got sick of the office, I'm in trouble at home, I'm getting old."

Rose hopped up on a barstool a couple down from Schiff and his tidy pile of clean-picked chicken bones. "Why's Carla mad this time?"

"Oh, hell, it could be lots of things. I didn't get her the sofa she wanted. I came home late from work two nights in a row. I smiled at a girl on the street because she was so ugly I thought she probably needed it. God only knows."

Rose chuckled. Most of the time Schiff was a little too much of a strong flavor for her taste, all sex and big talk and buffoonery, but then he'd go and have these little lapses of honesty.

Schiff washed the grease off his fingers delicately with a paper napkin dunked in a little beer. That done, he dug his hands deep into his pants pockets and looked at her pleasantly.

"Do you know of any job openings?" she said.

Schiff raised an eyebrow and smiled the slow, infinitely suggestive smile that had gotten him into so much trouble, welcome and unwelcome, over the years. Rose snorted. "I swear I don't understand why no one's shot you yet," she said. "Not for me, for Eddie Coolbaugh."

Schiff sobered; he wasn't one to make light of another man's troubles. "They having it kind of tough?"

"They're okay but, you know. He needs to find something. Has he talked to you already?"

Schiff shook his head. "I saw him here the night he quit the mill, though. He was really toasted, he kept saying how Petie wanted him to get a job as a writer, no one could understand what the hell he was talking about. I've probably seen him a couple of times since then down at coffee but he hasn't ever said anything to me. Tell you the truth, I figured he was waiting for Christie to come home and work something out for him. Or that maybe he had something else in the bag. He was talking about buying one of my bikes. For his boy, he said."

"Oh."

Schiff sold things on the side, property, vehicles, stereo equipment, it didn't matter what, he loved the patter and the conquest. Over the years he had sold Eddie a lot of his old stuff: dirt bikes, a camp trailer, once a pickup that lay down and died three months after he bought it. Schiff set him up with a good buy now and then to keep his spirits up.

"Don't sell him anything right now, Schiff, please?"

"On my honor," he said, and then, seeing her face, "Hey. Give me a break. On *your* honor, then."

"All right."

Roy, the afternoon bartender, came out from the back and extended a remote phone in Schiff's direction. "Carla," Roy mouthed, looking skyward.

"Hi," said Schiff, already patting his pockets for his car keys. "I know. I was just leaving. Nah, it's real quiet. A couple of the guys were here, but they just left. Five minutes." He hung up the phone and gave Rose a puckish smile. "You can run, but you can't hide."

Rose nodded. "If you hear of anything, Schiff, let me or Petie know, would you? Or let Eddie know."

"You got it."

"Okay. Thanks."

Schiff shrugged on his leather jacket and watched Rose turn back to the bar. She was the sort of woman he could imagine rolling around with nice and slow in a big soft bed. He had been with a woman like her for a while after he came back from Vietnam years ago. She had been one of the nicest women he'd ever known, and he'd treated her badly; he'd seen someone else on the side the whole time, a stripper in a club, a low-challenge kind of good-time gal who hadn't gotten in the way at all until he forgot which night he was supposed to see who and the whole thing had turned to crap. He couldn't remember the nice woman's name anymore, but she had told him right up front she didn't care what he did with his own time, just as long as he came home to her at night. He'd sure fucked up with her. He sometimes wondered if Carla was some kind of payback.

R OSE ORDERED a beer for Petie just as the front door opened and Petie rushed in, brushing her hair out of her eyes with the back of her wrist. Without a word she sat down, picked up the cold beer Rose pushed towards her, and drank half.

"Eddie was bitching because he wanted to go out himself, and then Ryan got worried and wanted to come with me, which got Loose started chanting *Fraidy, Fraidy*. I told them I was going out to buy a gun."

"Oh, Petie." Rose chuckled and took a long drink. "Schiff was in here just now."

"Oh, no," Petie said. All the years she had known him, Schiff had driven her crazy. Old Man used to say, *I got no use for salesmen or fools,* and on that one point Petie totally agreed.

"He said Eddie's been talking to him about buying one of his bikes," Rose said.

"If Eddie buys one of Schiff's bikes, he'll be wearing it next time you see him."

"I talked to Schiff a little bit and he promised he wouldn't sell Eddie anything. He said he'd let one of us know if he heard about any jobs."

"Well, I picked up a copy of the paper on the way. Maybe there's something in the job listings." She slapped the paper on the bar and leafed through rapidly, pausing over a half-page advertisement for Souperior's that listed all the soups, breads and desserts for the coming week. *Soup's on at Souperior's,* it read. *Bread and dessert, too. Like you wish your mother had made.*

Petie pulled out the want ads. It was a skinny section; not much around.

"God, these are the same jobs Eddie didn't get last week. I mean, there's zip." Petie looked over the section twice to be sure, and then drained the last of her beer. Rose noticed little slack places by the corners of her mouth she'd never noticed before; her jacket collar was too big, as though she'd lost weight. Rose knew people who didn't like Petie, thought she was mean-tempered and hard as a bone. Nadine, for one, was scared to death of her. But Rose thought of Petie, with wonder, as a woman who'd crossed a landscape barren as a salt flat and come out the other side no tougher than she'd had to, and sometimes softer than she could afford.

"Hey," said Rose. "We're doing Connie's barley beef in the morning, so get some rest."

"I'm not brewing the herb stock ahead of time," Petie said. "I'm telling you that right now. She can just go and fuck the herb stock."

"No," Rose soothed. "I think we can skip that part."

. . .

EDDIE COOLBAUGH should have been home already; the boys had usually finished eating and gotten into the tub by now. Petie had finally given up five minutes ago and fed them; they were so hungry they hadn't even objected to soup again, and anyway Petie had begun to buy their cooperation with day-old Souperior's desserts, the richer the better.

Loose was telling Ryan about a rat one of his friends claimed his father had seen the night before on the bay front over in Sawyer.

"It was this long," Loose said with gusto, spreading hand and spoon twenty inches apart, dripping soup on the floor. "And that's without the tail. Creechy's dad said it was so big it didn't run, it just turned around and hissed at him. He said its eyes were red. Cool!"

Ryan shuddered faintly and stopped eating.

"Give us a break, Loose," Petie said. She was pacing from her stove to the window to her soup pot to the back door to her stove. She was worried that something had happened to Eddie. They couldn't afford for something to have happened.

"But Creechy's dad said—"

"All right," said Petie. "We heard what Creechy's dad said. Eat your dinner. And you better watch where the soup goes. In your mouth, not on the floor. Ryan, you eat a little more, too."

"Then tell him not to talk about rats anymore."

"Loosey, don't talk about rats anymore."

"Baby," Loose said to Ryan. A vicious foot scuffle broke out under the table.

Petie sprang at them and brought her fist down so hard on the tabletop that Ryan's milk sloshed out of his glass.

"Okay," she said, blowing on the side of her hand. "Now finish your dinners. It's late."

"Where's Daddy?"

"If I knew that, wouldn't I have told you the last five times you asked? Give me a break, Loose, all right? He'll be home soon."

The boys finished their meal quickly and in silence. The phone rang as Petie was clearing the table. It was Eddie.

"Hey, nice of you to call," said Petie. "Where the fuck are you?"

"Chill out, Petie. I was talking to Roy about anything he'd heard might open up."

Petie softened. That was important. "Anything?"

"No," said Eddie. "But he said he'd let me know if he hears about anything."

Petie waited silently.

"I'll be there in a little while," Eddie said.

"What do you mean, a little while?"

"Roy said he'd seen Schiff, and Schiff said he had something for me. I'm going to see if he's at the Anchor."

"Don't go talk to Schiff, Eddie. He's just going to try and sell you something. Don't let him sell you anything. *Eddie?*"

He had hung up.

Petie cleared away the dishes, washed down the table and counters, got ready for tomorrow's work and then sat at the table and put her head in her hands. She could feel her blood throbbing in her neck, as though her arteries were too tight. If Eddie didn't find a job by Friday, she would have to ask their landlord for an extra few weeks on their rent. By Friday, when their electric bill came due, they'd be totally broke. Unless, of course, they went broke sooner. If Schiff pulled a fast one, for instance. Or if Eddie did something stupid. Petie had seen the dirt bike lying dead on the lawn. She knew what was what. That bike's riding days were over for good, which meant that Eddie was probably keeping his spirits up by shopping around for another one. Cutting some stupid deal with Schiff for when he had money again.

It was suddenly too much. With fury, Petie headed for the telephone, grabbed the receiver and the phone book, and flipped to the *S*'s.

Ron schiffen had just poured a nice little Jack Daniel's for himself, lowered himself into his recliner and switched on the network news. He'd started to go by the Anchor for a quick one on his way home but found too many tourists hanging around the lounge. Sometimes it was a kick to mingle—one time he and Carla had been set up for some pretty kinky stuff after an evening of drinks and racy cross-couple flirting, until Carla figured it out—but tonight he hadn't been much in the mood. For one thing, he'd taken a fall back in the hills behind his house while he was dirt-bike riding yesterday, and now he had a gimpy leg that would never have slowed him down even five years ago.

Connie Chung came on, and Schiff kicked back and put his boots up—the old ones, welcome as house slippers after another day in Foo-Foo Boot Hell. Schiff watched for a few minutes and thought again what he always thought: Connie Chung was one fine-looking lady. Too bad about her and Maury Povitch not having any luck with kids. Connie Chung was pretty old, though. Imagine wanting kids at that age. Schiff had had himself fixed a long time ago so he'd never have to worry. He had a stepkid he hadn't seen in twelve years. And then there was Randi the Makeup Queen, sixteen and sweet as cheap syrup when she needed something, biting as turpentine when she didn't. Carla's daughter.

When the phone rang, Carla yelled at him to get it. She was always yelling at him. He got it.

"If you talk to Eddie, I'll wring your neck," a furious little voice said in his ear.

"Huh?"

"This is Petie Coolbaugh. Eddie's out there right now looking for you because Roy told him you said you had something for him. Schiff, I swear to God if you sell him your dirt bike, or if you even talk to him about the possibility of selling your dirt bike, or if you so much as *say* you've got a dirt bike to sell, I'll break your knees."

Schiff smiled a happy smile, switched off Connie with the remote and swallowed some of his drink. "Now, that's interesting. Would you actually know how to break my knees? It's not that easy, you know."

"Shut up, Schiff."

"Not that I wouldn't enjoy watching you try. You always were cute when you got mad. You get this little twitch in the corner of your mouth. I bet no one's ever told you that."

"God, Schiff. How can anyone stand you?"

"Because I'm cute. And I'm easy. Not cheap, never cheap, but definitely easy."

"Where's Carla, anyway?"

"Out of earshot."

"I could have guessed that."

Schiff chuckled silently and let Petie swing in the silence for a couple of minutes before he said, "Would you like to start this conversation over now that your hairs are back in place?"

Petie sighed deeply on the other end of the line. "Would you listen if I did?"

"Yes, I would. I'm a good listener. You should try me. So to speak."

Petie hesitated. "Just don't sell Eddie a dirt bike, Schiff, all right? Or make any deals for a future sale? I'm afraid he's going to try to work something out with you, and he can't right now. He just can't. That's all. We can't afford it, Schiff, all right?"

"You should trust me more. I already promised Rose I'd keep the bike away. I don't break my word."

"So you weren't going to try and sell him a bike?"

"No."

"Then why were you trying to find him?"

"Actually," said Schiff, beaming into the receiver, "one of my drivers quit this afternoon. I *was* going to offer him a job."

"Oh."

"G'night, Petie. And hey, thanks for calling."

He hung up the receiver gently, a happy man. Well, well, well. He'd flustered Petie Coolbaugh. God, but he'd always wanted to.

AT ONE time, after he got back from Vietnam, Schiff had worked as a carnival roustabout. It was a hard life, full of bad food, dirt, physical hardship, tents-for-two when the weather was good, a few hours' sleep grabbed in one of the mechanical trailers when it wasn't; always moving on. That was the draw, too—no threats, no roots, no carryover.

And of course, there were the girls. The carnival traveled Oregon's small-town circuit, and wherever they went there were girls cruising the midway in tight jeans, slinky skirts, oversized jackets, smoking cigarettes and talking about whether or not to punch another hole in their ears for just one more stud, half-moon or imitation diamond chip. The shy ones stayed beyond the range of Schiff's ring toss booth, watching him; the bold ones came right up with their slidey eyes, hip-shot walks, blowing smoke, lifting their hair high and slow in their hands to cool off. So many girls coming and going, orbiting around him because he looked so good: lean and hard from hoisting Ferris wheels and fun houses around, easy with a smile, always clean even if it meant bathing from the sink of a filling station restroom: no grease under his nails, always careful with his hair.

At the end of the evening some of the girls usually stayed to take him out. There'd be a few hours of hanging out in some church parking lot that stood in for a cruise strip, or at some tired A&W drive-in where they didn't serve the cars anymore but people brought their stuff out and ate in them, anyway, local habit. And by the end, when everyone else was giving up and heading for home, there was usually one girl who had fallen for him hard enough to think she understood him, or that he understood her, who'd take him at last in a backseat or on the couch of a borrowed living room at a brother's girlfriend's place. Some of them were good girls, not as tough as they wanted him to think, scared that they were actually doing what they'd only meant to think about doing. These girls he took great care with: whispered to, held hands with before and after, protected with a condom even if they said they were already on something (and this was before AIDS, so it was sheer courtesy).

And then, inevitably, there were the other girls, the hard girls who were using him to get back at a boyfriend, a husband, a mother or stepfather. As long as he kept on his toes, these girls made simple good-time lays, more like sporting events; these girls tended to be the biters, the hair-tossers, the athletic types who expected him to step lively even after fourteen hours of carnival labor and heat and dust.

Once they'd been in a small town in central Oregon, someplace Schiff couldn't remember the name of anymore. It had been June or July, just another hot day cooling into a high-desert night, except that a strange girl had come and stood on the outer fringes of his area, watching him work the girls cruising his booth. She had had a farm tan and thick, deep red hair—the red of heat, of temper—pulled back loosely with the twist tie from a bread bag. Her face was thin and cagey like a fox, and she was smiling. She looked poor and smart and a little bit dangerous.

"Hey, cowboy," she said. She crossed her arms over her chest, crossed her thin legs at the ankles.

"Hey."

"You're pretty good at that," she said.

"At what?"

She looked a passing girl up and down, and then turned back to him. For a second he panicked, wondering if she might be the kid sister of some girl he'd laid in another nearby small town, out to avenge her. But he'd have remembered anyone with family coloring like that, plus this girl looked too amused. Family members did not find him amusing. He winked.

"Move on, cowboy."

Stung, he said, "What makes you think I'd make you an offer?"

"It's almost closing time, isn't it?"

Shrewd girl.

"So what's your name?" he said. "I bet it's Joan. Or maybe Molly. Are you a nice girl, Molly? I wonder. Why have you been watching me?"

"This is a carnival, isn't it? People come for the show."

"And am I a show?"

"Best I've seen," she said.

Schiff took care of a kid and his fat girlfriend, shook down his bag of tickets, glanced at his watch. The girl was still there when he looked over. "So do people around here like you, or what?" he called to her.

The girl grinned. "Depends."

"On what?"

"Whether I like them. Now, I like you."

"Jesus. How do you act when you don't like someone?"

"Nicer."

Schiff saw the carnival boss head down the midway. You weren't supposed to just let people talk to you, you were supposed to badger them into playing a game. Schiff thrust three plastic rings at the girl. "Play," he said.

"I thought you'd never ask."

She threw the rings expertly. Poor farm kids often did; you could make ring toss games out of rope ends and a stick. The girl hooked three ringers. Schiff handed her an inflatable panda and three more rings. "You don't really like me," he said.

"Sure I do. You remind me of a dog I used to have. Always looking for something to eat, something to chase. His name was Skippy."

Three more ringers. Schiff took back the inflatable panda, handed the girl a stuffed duck. The lights flashed all over the midway: fifteen minutes until closing. He was starving. He quickly dug in his pocket and dredged up a five-dollar bill. "Hey, how about buying me a Coke and a hot dog and coming back in fifteen minutes."

"You've got class, Skip. I like that in a man." She held the folded bill up between her fingers, turned and walked off. Fifteen minutes later there was no sign of her. Half an hour later he was picking up little pieces of garbage with a nail on a stick when Little George, one of the roustabouts, showed up looking mad. "Some girl," he said, "says she's your cousin, needs to see you right away. Give me a break, hotshot."

"Freckles?" Schiff said. "Ornery-looking?"

"That's the one. No shit, she your cousin?"

"Second cousin," Schiff said. "Mean as a snake. It's okay, you can let her come on back."

"You better not let the old man see."

The girl came down the midway towards him casually, chewing. In her hands she held a final bite of hot dog, an inch of warm Coke at the bottom of a paper cup.

"Here's your Coke," she said when she reached him. She toasted him and drained it, then popped the hot dog into her mouth and licked her fingers, one by one. "My, that was tasty."

Schiff grabbed her by the arm and marched her roughly down the side of the midway, through the fairgrounds and into the street.

"Take it easy, Skippy," she said. "Or I might just take my toys and go home."

"I'm hungry," he hissed, keeping a hard grip on her arm. "And more than anything in the world I hate being hungry. Find me something to eat."

"Okay, okay. Next block," she said. "The A.M.-P.M. MiniMart. You could probably get a corn dog there, or some jo-jos or something."

Schiff didn't speak again until he'd bought himself a box of Hostess Ding Dongs, a fruit pie, a corn dog and a Coke. He was still ticked, but in the light of the store she looked younger and prettier than he'd thought, and even poorer. Her dress had been someone's housedress a long time ago, with the sleeves taken off and a plastic belt added around the waist. She fingered the merchandise while he shopped. "Did you want anything?" he said, holding the door for her when he was through.

She smiled and shook her head. She had not returned any of his change.

Schiff ate while they walked back to the high school where the fair was being held. The girl walked a little ahead. When they reached the dark school building they sat on the concrete steps. It was one-thirty in the morning and cool. The girl shivered beside him in her light ugly dress, then stopped herself by crossing her thin arms tightly over her chest.

"You go here?" he asked, nodding at the building with his head.

"Yeah."

"You like it?"

"More than anything."

"Do you ever say anything you mean?"

"Sometimes."

When he'd finished the pie, the Ding Dongs, the Coke, he felt better. Maybe he could salvage some of the evening. "So tell me about my-self," he said, belching. It was one of his standard lines and it almost al-ways worked, threw the girls off-balance.

"Why should I do that?"

"You're a smart girl. I might learn something."

"Okay, Skippy." She thought for a minute. "You like pretty women when you can get them, but if you had a choice between a pretty face and a bad body or a great body and a dog face, you'd take the body. You try to be nice, especially when it might get you somewhere, but only when you can afford it."

"What else?"

"You're going to remember me."

A pickup pulled up, a real beater, a 1954 Chevy pocked with primer and metal fatigue. It was too dark to see who was driving. The door swung out, and the girl stood up.

"Who's that?" said Schiff, standing, too.

"Time to go, Skip," said the girl.

"Who is that, someone you know? Your brother, father, what?"

She tripped lightly down the stairs.

"Hey!" he said. "What's your name?"

"Do you think you'll always wonder?"

Now, sitting in his recliner, Schiff at last figured out what it was that had always gotten him about Petie Coolbaugh. It was the dark hair that had thrown him off.

Chapter 3

JIM CHRISTIE was home.

When Rose had walked into the house last night he had been sitting at her kitchen table. He had let himself in with his key, but tentatively; he was sitting at the kitchen table with his coat still on, and when she leaned over and kissed his forehead his skin was damp with sweat, as though he'd been there awhile.

"Have you eaten yet?" she said softly.

"Not yet."

"Will you?"

"Yes," he said.

Rose moved around the kitchen, putting a beer in front of him at the table, then putting down a bowl of soup. Nothing for herself; she felt strangely light-headed and serene. Eventually Jim took off his jacket and rolled up the sleeves of what was probably his only clean shirt, a threadbare flannel one with both its cuff buttons missing. His large duffel was set in the hall; a cap was balanced carefully on top, filthy and bled of all its color by the sun and the wind.

Rose drank a beer from the bottle and watched him spoon up his soup, wipe his mouth carefully with the paper napkin she'd set at his place. He looked older and as though he'd been sick recently or maybe still was, a little. His skin seemed slacker than it had, the wrinkles deeper. His forehead was high and white without the cap; his hair, nearly as colorless as his eyes, was stiff and unkempt, as though he'd been running his fingers through it.

"Was it a bad season?" she asked.

He shrugged, one arm hooked around his soup bowl protectively on the table as though it might move away: sea habits. "We did all right. There were some big catches, but you had to be able to stay out there till you'd made quota; you needed big holds. The small boats got hurt."

"Who'd you crew for?"

"The *Betty Oh*." Rose was familiar with her; she worked out of Dutch Harbor but she was an Oregon boat, built down in Reedsport ten or fifteen years ago, a big, solid vessel that wouldn't go down easily in rough weather.

"Is Chucky Dillon still skipper?"

Jim nodded, coaxed the last drop of soup from his bowl.

"More?" Rose asked.

He shook his head, reached for a slice of almond torte Rose put in front of him—a Souperior's leftover. He ate it all without speaking, looking at his plate. Nadine was an excellent baker.

"Was it a good crew?" Rose asked when he'd finished and stacked his bowl and plate together.

"It was okay. Dillon's tough on kids, you know, he looks for drugs, throws them off if he even thinks they're holding. So people stay away. Pay's good, though, if you got nothing to hide."

The days and nights were long on the boats, and drugs were one way of getting through them, but these days the Coast Guard could board a boat anytime for inspection. If drugs were found the boat was impounded, on the spot and indefinitely, with all her gear and any catch in the holds. More than one Young Turk had come home with his head hanging, and some old ones, too. And if these men had been the ones holding they were finished; no one would forgive them for costing them the season, not the owner, not the skipper, not the crew. Men like Christie, good hands, chose their boats with care. Good skippers chose their crews the same way. Christie was one of the most sought-after hands in the business.

"Carissa will be so glad you're here," Rose said quietly, smiling. "She's next door. She and Angela are friends again."

"She still so pretty?"

"Prettier. She's growing up awful fast, though."

"What grade's she in now?"

"Eighth."

"Eighth," he said, shaking his head as though he'd been gone years, not months. He drained the last of a second beer. "She still being good to her mama?"

"Oh, yes. And you won't believe the treatment you're going to get. She's been trying out recipes for a month, waiting for you to come."

"I had some business to take care of in Dutch Harbor, took me a week or so longer than I'd expected."

"It's okay."

Christie wiped his mouth with his napkin. "Soup was sure good, Rose. Thank you."

"We're cooking for a living now, me and Petie. I'll tell you about it later, when you're not so tired."

He nodded, stood up. "I thought I'd go down to the Wayside for a little, see a few people." He shrugged his jacket on and Rose smiled mildly. It was like that between them. He'd be home again in a couple of hours, and he'd be sober. He just couldn't be with her too long at first, couldn't be in the house. He wasn't tame, that way. The first season he'd lived with them, Rose had sometimes awakened alone in bed and found him outside in his little one-man tent, the bottom of his old ratty sleeping bag just visible through the flap. It had been winter then, and rainy. And he'd always come in rested.

From the living room window, she had watched him climb into his rattletrap truck, start the engine with a rasp and ease it around her Ford. She'd stayed where she was until she could see his taillights recede and then disappear. Then she'd gone inside, cleaned up the dishes and started his laundry.

. . .

IN HIS whole life Eddie Coolbaugh had had exactly one job he'd really liked: working at Ches Stevens' NAPA Auto Parts store during high school. He'd liked all the packages of parts lined up on the pegboard displays, and the smell of the oil and metal that hung over everything like a slick. Since then, he hadn't given two damns about any job he'd had, especially not the ones that took him out on the water. He had called old Ches a couple of weeks ago to see if he needed someone, but his son had mostly taken over the operation and computerized the inventory and purchasing system and done away with all but one assistant and a freelance mechanic. Something might come open at the True Value Hardware but Eddie wasn't getting his hopes up, especially because the money was no good. He hadn't ever gotten the knack of making money. Petie was still pushing the pest control thing even though Eddie knew he'd be poisoned inside a year if he took that job, plus he hated like hell crawling into rat-turdy crawl spaces and under spidery eaves.

Petie could sure be tough on a man. She always knew her mind, for one thing. Eddie didn't always feel a certain way about a thing; he might have two or three different thoughts in the same half hour, and then again he might not care enough to have any thoughts at all. Petie was always thinking, always deciding on stuff for herself. Secretly he was proud of her, but she was a hardship sometimes. Jeannie Fontineau used to call her a tough little bit. Poor old Jeannie Fontineau, she'd gotten so fat and sloppy. If there was one thing he couldn't abide, it was a fat sloppy woman. You might not have much in this life, but pride was free.

Eddie squatted down and peered for several minutes at the carcass of his latest dirt bike, which was lying on its side in the hard-pack of the side yard. It had given up its life on a nasty little jump on Peach Tree Hill. It would cost as much to fix the bike as it would to buy another one, which was just the excuse Eddie had been looking for. Ron Schiffen had exactly the bike he wanted. Schiff was suddenly claiming the bike wasn't for sale, but Eddie had heard him talking to Dooley Burden about it at the Anchor yesterday, so he was probably just trying to jack up the price by sparking some competition, knowing how much Eddie wanted it. That was Schiff, always looking for the best angles. Eddie was going to talk to him about setting up a delayed-payment, delayed-possession deal where Schiff would keep the bike until Eddie got a job, but Eddie would have sole dibs the minute things turned around for him. It was the last week of October, and good mud-riding weather was right around the bend; Eddie couldn't stand the thought of not having a bike. Besides, he'd promised Loose he'd start teaching him some things, and he didn't want to disappoint the boy.

Eddie pulled a black plastic sheet over the twisted remains and went inside for his truck keys. The kitchen was humid with the smells of soup and bread, but everything was quiet. Petie and Rose were making their run to Souperior's with the day's haul and the boys were in school. Eddie snuck some beer money out of the peanut butter jar where Petie kept change and headed for the Wayside. He'd heard Christie had come back to town yesterday, and chances were Eddie would find him there.

When Eddie arrived Jim Christie was sitting at the bar listening to a couple of the old boys off the charters that had already come in with their loads of green tourists and bottomfish. "Guy keeps insisting he's got something big on his line, you know, big, and I keep telling the fool it's only a dang rockfish," one of the men was cackling as Eddie approached.

Eddie clapped Christie on the shoulder. "Hey, bud," he said. "Long time."

"Hey," Christie said, clasping his hand. Christie's palms were hard and rough, working hands, outdoor hands. He was in his late forties and looked older. His face had turned to hide and his eyes were small and bleary from squinting into bad weather. He wore a cap that said *F/V Betty Oh*, the boat he'd just come off. The only time Eddie had ever seen Christie without a cap was at an old mate's funeral. A wide white strip of untanned skin had stretched across his forehead like a bandage.

Eddie got a beer from Roy and he and Christie headed for a table. "So are you down for a while?" Eddie asked.

"Couple of months, three or four, maybe. Same as usual."

"Good money this season?"

Christie shrugged. Rumor had it that he was loaded, had a hundred grand, two hundred grand, a quarter of a mil stashed away in a bank up in Dutch Harbor. Rumor had it that he didn't have a penny, gave it all away every year to an old Aleut woman and her retarded son up there. When it came right down to it, no one knew a damn thing about Jim Christie, much as he was welcome in Hubbard anytime.

"Rose tell you about me yet?" Eddie asked.

"Yeah. Bad break."

"Petie wants me to do this pest control thing." Eddie shook his head.

"Good money?"

"I don't know. Maybe."

"You going to take it?"

"Nah."

Christie nodded, rubbed the condensation off the side of his beer bottle with his thumb.

"What about you?" Eddie said. "You got something lined up?"

"Not yet. I'll see who's got charter work. Something to keep me out of trouble." Christie drained the last of his glass. "You want me to put you in if something comes up?"

Eddie pulled his beer a little closer. This was what he had come for. "Yeah."

Bud Hollings and a couple of the other fishermen who'd worked out of Alaska this year, too, came in and spotted Christie at the back table. They brought their beers around and soon were talking about boats and people Eddie had never heard of, strutting and kicking the old table legs with their big heavy work boots. It was time for Eddie to leave. He was out of beer money, anyway. "Later," he said to Christie.

"Later."

Sᴜɴsᴇᴛ ᴡᴀs Nadine's favorite time at the cafe. The last rays lingered over her ferns and tablecloths, warmed the wood of her benches and floors, offered irrepressible hope, though no doubt unfounded. Dinner at Souperior's was a chancy business. Some evenings the place was full, others it was a wasteland. If the ebb and flow of customers had anything to do with the weather, Nadine couldn't see what. If it had to do with the days of the week, she hadn't figured that out, either. The only thing that seemed to make any predictable difference was advertising, so she sat on a high stool in the failing light and drafted next week's copy.

We take soup a step beyond, she wrote. *Sumptuous, scrumptious, simply delicious. In fact, souperior.* She copied down the next week's menu and ended with, *Simply souperb, seven days a week at Souperior's. In Hubbard.*

Copy complete, Nadine sniffed her pencil eraser and mulled. By her elbow was a fresh cup of coffee, which she drank way too much of and always swore she'd cut back on and then didn't. The caffeine might or might not contribute to how much she worried. Right now she worried not only about customers, menu choices and advertising strategies but also about Petie and Rose, who were working for dirt and seemed so unstable, at least Petie. Privately Nadine had decided that if business got much softer as winter arrived, she would have to let one of them go, even at their minimal wages, and pick up the slack herself. The one she'd lay off would be Petie, and she would do it badly. So she worried about that, too.

But most of all what she worried about was Gordon. His T-cell count had fallen to 130 and he had started having drenching night sweats, bad enough for him to buy a waterproof mattress pad and two extra changes of bed linens. Then there was the increasing fatigue and the more frequent bouts of what they euphemistically referred to as flu, on top of the chronically swollen glands, of course, old and familiar as cranky cell mates after two years. Was it all just more of "the process" the doctors were always referring to in L.A.? Or were they ominous portents, signs that Gordon's decaying immunological system was about to come completely unstrung and pitch him headlong into the ranks of the full-blown? If so, the whole thing was going too fast, years too fast. Hadn't Johns Hopkins released the statistic only recently that only fifty-three people out of one hundred would have broken through, a full ten years after seroconversion? Hell, look at Magic Johnson; doomed, obviously, but still playing exhibition basketball after learning of his own positive status.

Nadine couldn't tell whether Petie or Rose had figured it out yet. In a city like L.A. or San Francisco, there'd have been no hiding Gordon's HIV status, but here the plague was a distant thing happening someplace else, like famine in India. She and Gordon had agreed that they would keep his illness to themselves as long as possible, knowing that once he was widely identified as HIV positive, his involvement in the cafe would have to stop. But they had also agreed not to launch some humiliating obfuscation campaign. Both Gordon and the disease deserved greater respect than that.

Nadine took a deep breath and hopped down from her stool to put on another pot of coffee. Gordon often chided her for these kinds of fretful ruminations. Better to put the effort into solvable problems, like the fact that if the Hubbard locals would only accept Souperior's as well as the tourists did, her troubles would be over. But they seemed to be an un-crackable nut. They liked what they liked, which is to say they liked the things they'd always had. The women had contributed all the recipes, but the men didn't seem to want to come in and eat them. A few times she'd joked with Gordon that if she could figure out how to make a fried soup with brown gravy, they'd be rich.

Visibility—Souperior's needed visibility. That's what advertising did, but on Nadine's limited budget she couldn't afford more paid advertising. On the other hand, Gordon had offered an interesting idea last night. Christmas was coming, with all those people looking for gifts. They could put together a Souperior's cookbook, maybe call it *Local Flavor*. They wouldn't give away all their recipes, of course, but they'd use a lot of them, even a couple of the best ones, and attach the recipe's author's name so the local people who'd contributed them would feel famous and buy copies for gifts. Maybe they'd even do another contest for a New Recipes section. If they desktop-published the book on Gordon's computer, had it cheaply printed in Sawyer and did the spiral binding themselves, they could make a slender profit even on a small run of, say, two hundred and fifty copies. And if they didn't sell all the books by Christmas they'd just give them new covers and offer them to the summer tourist trade. Nadine could talk to the other Hubbard merchants about carrying the book in their gift shops, maybe even featuring it in their windows. She'd bring up the idea at the next meeting of the Hubbard Chamber of Commerce. It was worth a try.

The only other hurdle was editing the recipes, simplifying them and checking them for consistency. That, and getting a local name on the cover. Nadine picked up the phone and dialed. If Rose would help her for free, Nadine would make her associate editor.

In an hour, she and Rose and Gordon were seated in a back booth, hands folded around fresh cups of coffee, alone in the deserted gloom of afternoon. She did most of the talking. This was customary. Gordon rarely came forward except in a shy, apologetic way. He was diffident, balding, crumpled, brainy, afflicted with a mild stammer; graced with a certain softness, a delicacy of manners and approach. His eyes were as light and clear as swimming pool water.

Rose leaned far over the table, trying to follow them. "You mean you want Petie and me to write a cookbook?"

"Well, we want you to help edit one," said Nadine. "It would just be you, since Petie's already so busy with her bread and everything. And you don't need to write it, exactly, at least not from scratch, because of course we have all the recipes already. Just choose, say, twenty-five. And write them down the way you cooked them, make sure they have good simple directions, what order things need to be prepared in and that. From your experience."

"We haven't followed a single recipe," Rose said.

"What?"

"Well, we've stuck to the main parts, but we've adapted some things because we thought they'd taste better."

Nadine and Gordon exchanged a look.

"Won't it make people mad if they read we changed things?" Rose asked. "If you're going to use their names, I mean."

Nadine ran her hand through her hair. Sometimes she imagined she could feel the gray multiplying day by day. One morning she'd wake up and find she'd gone pure white. "We think it's very important to use their names," she tried to explain. "It would help in marketing the book locally, at any rate. Okay, let's do this. You could just edit the recipes like they were written originally, like they were submitted. Even if they won't taste quite as good."

"You mean you just want me to copy them down."

"Well," said Nadine. "Just edit them, you see."

Rose shifted uncomfortably. "I guess maybe I don't understand what you mean, edit."

Gordon nodded: he'd finally gotten it. "Where it says 'teaspoon,' you put 'tsp.,' where it says 'one-half cup,' you put '1-slash-2 cup.' Like that, you just make all the measurements and abbreviations consistent, make sure the instructions make sense, so all the cooking steps are represented. And give everything the same format—the same look."

"Oh!" said Rose, flushing. "I guess I feel stupid. That's not hard."

"No, it shouldn't be," Nadine agreed. "And then when you're done, Gordon will put it all into his computer, and out will come a book."

"Are you putting any of your salads in there?" Rose asked. "The cold salmon, dill and onion, maybe, or the crab and feta?" Three months ago Rose had never even heard of feta, but she knew what she liked.

Nadine frowned. "I hadn't thought about anything but soup. What do you think?" she asked Gordon.

"She's right. A few, though. Not enough to eclipse the soups. The soups should be the main thing."

"And a few of Petie's breads," said Rose. "Maybe five of them. And five desserts."

"All right," said Nadine, enthusiastic now. "Yes, I think so."

"Okay," said Rose.

Nadine shot Gordon another look. "There are two more things, though," she said. "The copy—the editing—needs to be finished in three weeks, if we're going to get this done in time. And we can't pay you."

"You mean do it for free?"

Now Nadine flushed. "I'm sorry, Rose. We can't afford to pay anything at all. We're doing this as a way to make more people aware of us, to try and get some more local people in here. But you'll be listed as ed-itor on the cover. Everyone in town will see that. I'm sure Carissa will be very proud."

Rose looked from one anxious face to the other. They were good people, she thought. They weren't lying; they really couldn't afford to pay. And if they didn't get more people to eat here, they couldn't afford to stay in business, either. Petie would never have done it, in Rose's place, but Rose decided to help them. It might be fun. It might even work.

"All right," she said. "Yes. All right."

"Great," said Nadine. "Oh, that's great."

"Imagine," said Rose, smiling her pretty, easy smile. "Me, writing a cookbook."

AFTER SHE left Souperior's, Rose headed out of town, up the headland and then off onto a narrow, poorly maintained spur that a long time ago had been the original coast highway. Hardly anyone took the road anymore, not even locals, and Rose loved the quiet up there after the noisy highway, and the buckled, worn-out look of the asphalt as it rose and twisted and reeled around the edges of thousand-foot drops straight to the ocean. She pulled into a gravel turnout and switched off the ignition. The day was overcast and the water far below looked sullen and metallic. At the bottom of the cliff, but across a hairpin inlet from it, a sea cave had been worn into the bottom of a sheer rock face. At low tide the cave had a gleaming black sand floor; at high tide, waves sucked and boiled around its ceiling. The place was unnamed as far as she knew and unreachable from land, and had always filled Rose with dread. Now as she stood looking she imagined someone washing in there half drowned, numb with cold and crazy with relief, only to realize that there was no way out and the tide had already turned.

Rose shuddered and crossed her arms tightly. It was a wild coast and things like that were possible. But she always had morbid thoughts the first few days Jim Christie was home, possibly to make up for all the thinking she didn't do while he was away. During his absences she wouldn't even watch the weather reports because she didn't want to know when there were storms. No one had ever told her she was being silly, either, not even Petie. Every year boats went down, men were lost.

Now, high above the ocean, she could see squalls gathering on the horizon. Let them come.

She climbed back into her old Ford, shabby and comfortable as a blown-out armchair, and, on a whim, headed for Sawyer. The road was quiet, nearly empty. Every day now there were fewer tourists, fewer RVs, fewer NO signs and more YES!es on the motels. It was everybody's favorite time of year, when the coast was left to itself.

Sawyer Middle School was a brick box around which huddled a cluster of prefabricated, freestanding classrooms. There was a plant the school always reminded her of, what was it called—hens-and-chickens. The main building had been Sawyer High when Petie and Rose were young and children didn't leave Hubbard until ninth grade. A better system. These sixth and seventh graders, so lately released from their safe little neighborhood grade schools, were too eager to be old. Rose had heard from several of Carissa's teachers that there was a startling amount of promiscuity among the girls, particularly the ones from abusive homes. Carissa's English teacher had confessed to Rose that she used to have her students keep journals for a semester, but that so many of them had confided terrible things, she didn't give the assignment anymore. Even so, she said, last year one of her students had stayed after school and whispered that her mother's boyfriend had started sneaking into her bed sometimes on the nights her mother was at work tending bar for the Elks. It hadn't been that way when Rose and Petie were growing up. The teacher had told Rose she would be leaving the school system at the end of the year to teach at a Christian school for two-thirds the pay.

Rose pulled up to the curb, switched off her car engine and had just settled down to wait when she saw Carissa bounce out of a side door, one of the first children to appear, her backpack strapped onto her small shoulders—she was delicately made instead of roomy and soft like Rose.

She was dressed to the teeth in new jeans, new shoes, a new enormous sweatshirt with an expensive brand name on the front, fancy braids—her one good back-to-school outfit. A proud, bright, healthy girl in the throes of delight. Christie was home. When she caught sight of Rose she broke into a happy smile.

"Did you bring Jim?" she said, peering eagerly in the window. She wrestled the door of the car open.

"He'll have supper with us. He's down at the docks."

Carissa tossed her backpack into the rear seat, where it landed with a heavy thud. She was a diligent student. "Did you tell him I was going to cook?"

"I told him."

"I was thinking maybe I shouldn't fry the chicken, you know, in case he's been eating a lot of fried chicken on the boat or something. I could bake it."

"Even if he's been eating fried chicken every night, sweetie, it's not going to have been home-fried chicken, and it's not going to have been you cooking it. Go ahead and fix it like you want. He'll like it either way."

"I'm so glad he's back, Mom. Aren't you?"

"Oh yes."

They drove in silence for a couple of blocks. Then Carissa said, "You know Billy Wall, who got arrested over here for doing nasty things to boys?"

Rose was startled. "How did you hear about that?"

"Oh, everyone knows. One of the boys he did that to, he's in my class."

"Well, you stay away from him."

"Why?"

"Because he's probably feeling real bad. He doesn't need kids watching him."

"I wouldn't watch him or anything."

"Well, you just keep some distance, all right? He's had some bad things done to him, and sometimes children have trouble after that."

Carissa's thoughts had turned back to home. "Mom, when Jim's away, do you think he misses us?"

"I don't know. He must, in his own way."

"I bet he can feel us missing him all the way up in Dutch Harbor. Do you think someday he might decide to just stay home?"

Rose glanced over at the small rapt face and looked away. "I don't think so, sweetie," she said gently. "No, I don't think so."

Chapter 4

Hᴜʙʙᴀʀᴅ's ᴘᴏsᴛ office was at one end of town, a flimsy old box rancid with cigarette smoke and mold. Through the service window you could see into an apartment carpeted in old apple-green shag. The post office was not part of the postal service proper, but was a concession operated by Lou and Lee Boyles, who delivered the mail in a Ford Aspen station wagon with bad shocks and one taillight out. In Gordon's opinion, whatever the Boyles were being paid by the postal service to keep zip code 97360 alive, it wasn't enough. On days like today, when he was moderately depressed, he would gladly have paid an extra penny a stamp through the next millennium just to subsidize a fresh paint job and some new Formica.

He stepped up to the free community bulletin board, pulled a pushpin from a card in his jacket pocket and tacked up his last flyer.

Watch for it! From soup to nut breads, it's Local Flavor, *featuring the best of Hubbard's souperior soups, breads and desserts. Edited by Rose Bundy, with contributions by Hubbard's finest cooks. A souperb gift choice this Christmas. A Souperior's Production.*

It was not inspired copy, but every other version Gordon had come up with relied on words like connoisseur, maestro, aficionado, tour de force, unparalleled, cuisine, extraordinaire—words that did not seem to address the general orientation or vocabulary of the average Hubbard resident. So he'd settled on this, and had spent the last two hours in Sawyer and now Hubbard posting the flyers on bulletin boards in supermarkets, the senior center, bakeries, bookstores, dental offices and the library. He and Nadine hadn't intended to do flyers at all, but business was continuing to soften, the rains were here and it would be two more weeks before Rose even completed the copy: he and Nadine were getting more nervous every day about being able to make it through the winter.

Gordon had chosen the Hubbard post office as his last stop because it gave him a chance to check the post office box he had opened here recently. He had begun receiving copies of the *Los Angeles Times*, which he read more avidly than he ever had when he lived there. He missed L.A. He found it more and more amazing that he now lived in a place where the movie theater was really called the Bijou. And although he still found the scenery magnificent, scenery didn't offer chamber music concerts or Thai cooking or cafes in which to read the Sunday paper. Of course, it also didn't hit you over the head with a bat and take your shoes and billfold on a dark night, which was more or less what had happened to him several years ago. A clean-cut, well-dressed man had run at him from a doorway, eerily silent, and beaten him viciously without ever speaking above a whisper—and then only to say, "Your wallet and shoes, please." *Please.* Gordon had thrown up his arms to protect himself; otherwise, as though in collusion, he had kept mute and done what he was told. And then, just as suddenly, he had been alone, sitting on the sidewalk bleeding and ashamed. Wasn't it somehow worse to be beaten by a polite deviant? Muggers wore grimy clothing, had dirty hair, rough speech, and you could avoid them on the street if you paid attention, which Gordon always did. But this had been impossible, without cues; it had been like being beaten by, say, a crazed accountant. His assailant had worn neat khaki pants, leather loafers; his shirt had been tucked in. *Your wallet please*, he'd whispered, after he had already broken Gordon's nose with a wood baton. What on earth could have happened? Cocaine addiction? Failure to pass the CPA exam? Or had he simply been shrewd enough to cross-dress as a different stereotype, knowing it would throw his victims off? Gordon still pondered it from time to time, though now he thought of it as an odd and somewhat humorous calamity that had happened a long time ago.

In the post office, he squared the corners of his flyer with the notices for child care, firewood and lawn mower repair, collected his papers and mail, and climbed into his car, a well-loved Peugeot whose days were nevertheless numbered for lack of service opportunities. He turned up Wilson, crossed Third, then entered Wayne Street, where Rose lived. She had promised she'd have a batch of recipes ready for him to read, her first. She had sounded nervous about it on the phone, so now he was nervous, too. He and Nadine couldn't afford any big mistakes—or even, it was possible, any little ones.

The car whined into a lower gear as he passed homes of varying degrees of squalor and disintegration, until he found the driveway Rose had described for him and pulled in behind her old car. The house turned out to be an old tan double-wide, one of the earliest models (perversely, Gordon had become something of an expert on manufactured home architecture) with none of the bay windows, novelty porches and mullions that made the newer models look so hopeful. In places the house's metal siding was dented, as though someone had butted it with a car. But there were curtains at the windows and the yard was very tidy, with several whiskey barrels holding the remains of last summer's annuals. On the lowest limb of a fir tree hung a wooden cutout of a bonneted little girl on a swing. Her skirt was made of real fabric trimmed in lace. For yard art, this was upper end. On the house next door, Gordon could see gargantuan pink wooden butterflies with three-foot wingspans nailed to the siding. Two doors down from Gordon's own apartment building in Sawyer, there was a polka-dot-painted cutout of a woman's backside bending over in the garden. Beside it was a cutout of a man's blue-jeaned backside, his hand out to steal a feel.

Rose must have been watching for him; she opened the door before he'd even knocked. She wore dressier clothes than normal: a thin, full denim skirt, matching western-style shirt, fake tooled leather belt with fake silver medallions and turquoise, western boots. Could it all have come from Wal-Mart? And yet he thought she looked very beautiful, ample in a way that you never saw in L.A.'s muscle-bound gym dolls. It disconcerted him to see her in clothes that were so different from her usual jeans, T-shirts, sweatshirts. People always led more complicated lives than he imagined or was prepared for.

He followed her into the living room, a shabby brown-paneled space furnished with mismatched furniture over which had been thrown bright crocheted afghans and scraps of lace, all of it clean and orderly. He fastened with appalled reverence on a single bookcase of pressboard and veneer occupying a place of honor along one wall. On the top two shelves were what looked like complete sets of works by Danielle Steel and Sidney Sheldon. Below them, neatly displayed, was a series of Happy Meal toys from McDonald's.

"Mine." Rose smiled when she saw where he was looking. "No one gets to touch those, not even Carissa."

"Do you collect them all?"

"Oh, no. Just the ones I really like or think might be worth something later on. Otherwise you'd need a special place to keep them all, you'd have so many. Loose and Ryan, Petie's boys, have whole shoe boxes full and we don't even take them that often."

Gordon nodded and buried his hands deep in the pockets of his corduroy trousers. It was conceivable that at that exact moment he was the only man in Hubbard wearing cuffs. He marveled that Rose would even speak to him. Sometimes when he passed by the barbershop or went into the post office, the conversation paused until he was out of earshot. It was not just his imagination, he was sure. And he minded; that was his dilemma.

Rose had walked over to a battered wood desk against one wall and was fussing with some papers, tapping them into order.

"It's not going as fast as I thought it would," she said apologetically. "I guess this probably doesn't look like much." She held out a thin sheaf of pages, handwritten on both sides of loose-leaf paper, school stuff. Gordon saw that her handwriting was firm, round and excessively legible. There were little circles instead of dots over the *i*'s, and at the end of each recipe she had drawn a happy face. With dread Gordon scanned the pages. Then he went back and began to read.

You might not feel like bothering to put the navy beans through a food mill, since no one ever uses them anymore and they take time and muscle, too, he found on one page. *Do it anyway. A food processor will leave you a jillion little pieces of navy bean skin that will stick to your teeth, your spoon and the sides of your bowl. Another thing about this soup: don't eat it the day before anything really important, as it can be cleansing.*

On another page, chosen at random, *Don't use cheap cheesecloth to wrap the herb bundle in—get the good, close-woven kind and double it. Otherwise, halfway through the cooking when there's no turning back, you'll find an empty soggy pouch and little bits of herb floating all over the place that you can never fish out and the whole thing will be ruined. We know because it happened to us.*

He read all the way through before he finally laid the pages facedown on her desk. What she'd done was delightful. In each recipe she had transcended the simple editing function he had described for her and introduced instead her simple, unpretentious, wise voice as she described shortcuts and false temptations, technical tricks and danger zones.

She watched his face and started smiling uncertainly. "Is that what you wanted me to do? Because, you know, if it isn't I could work on it some more—"

"It's wonderful! You've given it real charm. People will like this."

"Oh well," said Rose dismissively, "they all know me around here."

"I'm thinking of people who don't know you." Perhaps, if the writing bore out, there might even be a market beyond Sawyer and Hubbard, through a publisher. He'd talk to Nadine about it.

"God, I'm relieved. I've been worried all day."

"Don't worry. Write. I'll type this up and get it ready to go."

"Have you ever done this before?"

"Never. Nadine, either. But she's shrewd, so you're in good hands."

"And what about you?" Rose smiled. "What about your hands?"

Gordon shuddered faintly, but he could see that she was just feeling relieved.

Rose went into the kitchen, returning with a plate heaped with brownies and two mismatched mugs of coffee. "Carissa made the brownies last night. She's a very good baker. She says she's going to be a pastry chef when she grows up. She also says that she's going to be a pediatrician, though, so I don't know." Rose chuckled. "Jim told her once he likes brownies, so she's made him at least nine batches since he got back, and that was only a week ago. Lord only knows what she'd have done for Pogo if he'd have kept up with her."

Gordon took the plate from her and set it on a coffee table. "Pogo?" Why did so few men have normal names in Hubbard? Bob-O, Roy Boy, Jimbo, Bry.

"Carissa's father. My ex-husband."

"Oh." Gordon had never heard Rose mention a husband before. Somehow, he'd thought she'd been—what had they called them in high school?—an unwed mother. "Was he a fisherman, too?"

"Pogo? Oh, no. It's hard to say what Pogo did. He was a little like Eddie Coolbaugh that way, he drifted around. Mill work, woods work, mechanic. You know."

"Here?"

"Here first, then over in Doggett for a while. I've heard he's in Longview, Washington, now."

"You lived away from here?"

She smiled. "Umm-hmm. You thought I'd never been anywhere, didn't you? Well, it was only for a little while. Pogo had itchy feet and some buddy of his, I can't even remember who it was, got him a job at a dinky little mill over there. We were broke, though, so we went. You know where Doggett is? No? It's on the way up to Portland, maybe sixty-five miles from here."

Gordon recalled a scattering of buildings along the roadside: a shabby cafe, a combination filling station and market with dusty video posters in the window, a couple of billboards, a small shake mill. "There's not much there."

"No. A market, post office in a trailer, two taverns. You know what the kids wanted most in that town?"

Gordon shook his head. He couldn't imagine. When he'd been in school, they'd wanted world peace.

"McDonald's. While I was there the mayor even helped them get up a petition to send to the McDonald's people, saying how the city council would support a McDonald's if one came to town, but McDonald's wrote back and said there weren't enough people for them to do a good business. The kids were so disappointed."

"So what brought you back to Hubbard?"

"Oh, layoffs at the mill. Plus Pogo had started getting bored and I missed home. I was pregnant, and I didn't want to have a baby in a town where I didn't know anyone. Well, of course I knew everyone in Doggett by then, but, you know, I didn't *know* them. So we came home. Well, I did. Pogo dropped me off and said he'd let me know when he found work. I stayed with Petie and Eddie until the baby came."

"Didn't he come back?"

"At first."

"Then what?"

Rose shrugged. "You'd have to have known Pogo. I mean, you just knew you'd lose him one day, right from the get-go. Pogo didn't like people to get too close. The minute he felt cramped he'd start to rise and thin, just like smoke, until one day he wasn't there at all. I'm grateful it happened before Carissa could get to know him. He would have broken her heart."

Rose chewed the last of her brownie serenely.

"And you're not bitter?"

"Bitter? No. You know, it wasn't really personal."

"But it was hard."

Rose smiled at him, amused. "Sure."

Gordon nodded and wiped his mouth with a paper napkin. He found her story unspeakably depressing. "Do you believe there are brave people in the world?" he asked suddenly.

"Brave?"

"Brave. Courageous. People who live well in the face of terrible things."

Rose thought for a minute. "Yes, I do."

"You?"

Rose laughed. "Oh, no, not me. Nothing terrible has ever happened to me."

"Then name someone."

"Petie," Rose said without hesitation. "Petie is brave."

"Is she?"

"When God contemplates Petie, He never seems to have a break in mind. He just keeps piling it on, and it's been like that as long as I've known her, and none of it's ever been her fault. And she keeps getting up in the morning, just the same."

"Yes, but is she brave, or is she just dogged?"

Rose began to gather up their trash. "I don't know," she said. "Is there a difference?"

Maybe not, Gordon thought. Sometimes simply waking up in the morning was an act of bravery, and lasting until sunset a matter of putting your head down and following your shadow.

"Rose," Gordon said—cowardly, waiting until she went into the kitchen. "There's something you probably ought to know."

"Mmmm?" she said.

God, he hated this. "I'm HIV positive. I have AIDS. I thought you deserved to know."

She appeared in the kitchen doorway, wiping her hands on a dish towel. She looked at him with concern. "How terrible."

"It's not communicable, you understand. To you, I mean. You can't catch it by being around me."

"Yes, I know that. I'm so sorry, Gordon—I don't know much else. Is there anything I should be doing for you that I'm not?"

Gordon smiled a small, grateful smile. "No. It's enough that you didn't gasp or run."

"Is that why you and Nadine are here? Why you came to Hubbard, I mean?"

"Yes. Most everyone has died. My—my partner died this past spring. He was the last and best of us. Nadine thought it might be a good idea to come here and wait someplace that didn't remind us of a thousand things that are gone."

"Wait for what?" Rose asked.

"For me to get sick. Rose, do you believe in ghosts?"

"I don't know. No, I don't think so."

Gordon nodded. "I didn't either, before. I do now. They talk to me sometimes, my dead friends. And the thing is, it's so good to hear them again. I miss them all so much."

"Do they talk to you up here? In Hubbard, I mean? Or just in California?"

"No, here, too," Gordon said.

"What do they say?"

Gordon smiled. "Everything. Nothing. They remind me to buy milk, to pour Nadine another cup of coffee, to look around without bitterness, to get on with things. A million unimportant reminders. I feel ridiculous having told you."

"No," Rose said, suddenly chuckling. "You're lucky to have friends like that. If Petie ever haunts me, it's going to be unbearable."

TEN YEARS ago, two months before she died of lung cancer, Eula Coolbaugh gave Petie a Crock-Pot. It was nothing very special, just a cheap one out of the Sears catalog, but it had a pretty floral pattern going around its middle, and inside Eula had packed some of her own kitchen things: a carrot peeler, some tin measuring spoons, a dish towel, two matching pot holders, some turkey trusses, three little egg cups and a coffee scoop, all of them well used.

I know it's not usual to give old things to a bride, she'd written in a note to Petie, *but you know we don't have much. Well, hell, even if we did, I'd want you to have these things. They've been in my kitchen for twenty-eight years, some of them, all the time I was raising my family, and they helped me cook many a fine meal. My table was always a happy one, and I'm hoping that all that accumulated love will somehow seep out of these things like groundwater into everything of yours they touch. You be happy, honey. Eula.*

P.S. Love my boy but make him stick to his promises. It's how I raised him, but he's always been weak that way.

Eula was a plain-faced woman, thin as a wire even before her cancer; a woman who understood that not everyone good had reason to be proud. She was the only one in the world Petie had told, really told, about Old Man. And Eula had heard her out, had poured her cup after cup of good country coffee, not fancy like Nadine's but hot and strong, and patted her hand and gone right on putting clean shelf paper in her cupboards like she did every spring, even this one when she could so easily have kept herself busy dying.

Petie had sat at the kitchen table—the honest old thick-legged farm table she now had in her kitchen—and, picking at the fake slubs in the fake linen of Eula's yellow plastic tablecloth, let it all come out, all that poison, all the years of living in the twelve-foot camp trailer with no privacy and nowhere to go when Old Man came home.

"Some things can't be undone," Eula had said when Petie was through, "though the good Lord knows there are times when nothing else would be just. All the same, you and Old Man, you're pretty well stuck with each other now, aren't you? You can never escape your family. The damn fool, I'll bet he'd cut his own heart out if he thought he could undo sober the misery he's committed drunk."

"You're wrong," Petie said. "The only thing he's felt remorse for in his whole life was letting my mother die in that hospital over in Salem. It turns out there was a hospice place just starting up over in Sawyer, only no one told him in time. He figured if he'd known, it would've saved him maybe twenty-five thousand dollars."

"That's just talk."

Petie snorted. "You know what he said about my mother one time? He said, *Aw, hell, you know how some things are. They're pretty enough when they're new but they don't hold up worth a damn after you get a couple miles on them.* He and old Charlie Lutie had a good laugh over that one."

"Charlie Lutie drinks too much."

"Old Man drinks too much."

Eula had sighed. "I remember him when he was little. He had

cowlicks all over his head and they always made him look a little crazy. The whole time he was in school he got picked on more than anyone else, I couldn't tell you why. He just had a look about him. All his life, people never liked him much. He knew it. How could he not know it? Except for your mother, Lord bless her soul."

"She never liked him, she was scared of him. He hit her sometimes. Well, he hit a lot of people sometimes. But he hit her in sneaky ways, like he'd go after the backs of her thighs with his overall straps, the buckle ends, where no one would see the marks. Did you ever notice how she sat on a chair so straight, so proper, never leaned back? That's because he hit her right where the seat would cut into her legs if she sat back. Then he'd call her prissy. In front of people. He'd tell her, *Sit back there, Paula, take a load off, you're nothing special.* And she'd have to scootch back in her chair, let the edge dig in, and try to smile so he'd leave her alone and she could ease forward again and it would start all over. Eula, you know I'm not making this up."

"I know, honey," Eula said softly, sitting across from Petie at the table with her dustrag quiet in her hands. "I remember the way she used to sit."

"You know what she loved? She loved being in the hospital. I think it's one of the reasons she hung on so long. Everyone *did* things for her, she said. People she'd never even met before, and they were always *doing* things that the only reason for doing them was to make her feel better, since everyone knew nothing they did was going to save her. She couldn't get over that. The first time they rubbed lotion on her back she cried because it felt so good but she was afraid we'd have to pay extra for it. I guess she'd heard somewhere about people who give massages, that they were real expensive, so she thought Old Man would find out and get back at her. She was afraid he'd make her come home."

Eula spit on her thumb and rubbed a spot from the tablecloth. "She was a pretty woman, your mother. Maybe it was fear that made her go so plain so fast; she started getting plain before you were even born. We used to wonder, but we just figured the women in that family bloomed early and then faded. None of us knew much about her folks. She came down to town for school every day from Camp Twelve, you know the old logging camp back there over Peach Tree Hill? Even then they hadn't logged back there in years, but a few families stayed in the camp and tried to homestead. She was real poor, I know that, because I remember her clothes. Not that any of us had much. She told me once she was grateful to your daddy for getting her away from all that."

"Jesus Christ."

"That depends, honey."

"On what?"

"Did she ever tell you anything about what she came from?"

"No."

"Well."

It was true that they rarely saw any of her mother's family, although Petie had a grandfather and two uncles; her grandmother had died of pneumonia a few years before Petie was born. The uncles, skinny men with bad skin, blue-black hair and tiny eyes, sometimes came and talked to Petie's mother at the front door, occasionally came all the way into the kitchen in their heavy boots. Sometimes Petie's mother argued with them about money, but mostly she just listened and then tried to get rid of them before Old Man came home. It sounded to Petie like the uncles talked most about Petie's grandfather, who she didn't even see until she was six or seven. She and Paula had gone to the feed store in Sawyer to get some more young tomato plants that year after year her mother nursed into bearing hard green tomatoes that never ripened because Hubbard was too cold. Petie had been examining a box of smelly chicks when she heard her mother make a noise of surprise, or distress, or possibly fear; it had been nothing more than a sharply drawn breath, really. When Petie turned she saw her mother holding her purse tightly before her in both hands. Blocking her way was a big bearded man, the darkest man Petie had ever seen although his hair and beard were mostly gray. He had a gut that hung slack over his belt, and a look like a murderer, and he'd stood in her mother's path staring for a long time before leaving without speaking a word. Paula stayed where she was, then rubbed her hands one at a time down the front of her skirt. Petie had said, *Who was that?* and her mother had said, *No one, a bad man. No one. If you ever see him again, you walk away. He looked like you,* Petie had said. *Well,* her mother had said. *That can't be helped.*

AT THE end of that afternoon in the Coolbaugh kitchen, with clean shelf paper lining all the cupboards and Eula slumped pale and exhausted at the table sipping coffee spiked with Jim Beam against the pain, Petie had asked her what she should do. About Old Man, about the truth, about all the things she'd unloaded onto Eula's thin, tough shoulders. "Just go on," Eula had told her. "One day by one day, just like you've been doing. Marry Eddie. Have some babies. Grow older. Don't look too hard for joy. Don't stay too long where there's sorrow. Love whenever you're able."

And over the years Petie had tried to do what Eula said, and mostly it had worked. Old Man had come around sometimes, especially at the end of the month when his Social Security was gone, and Petie didn't talk to him much but she let him stay to eat if he was reasonably sober, because the boys didn't have any other old family and because they were boys, not girls. He sat on a tree stump in the yard and picked his ears and smelled of cigarettes and old beer and age, and they didn't really like him much but they didn't bother to dislike him, either, because they didn't pay enough attention.

And then Old Man had died. Together Petie and Rose had gone up to the twelve-foot trailer up there in the woods next to state land. The trailer was beige and aqua, filthy with blown pine needles and dirt and rust, round-shouldered, squat, hunkered down like a crazy old hermit between a couple of big spruce trees. In the six years since Petie had set foot inside, the trailer had started returning to the earth. Pill bugs inched their way across the floor, balled up and died on the little table and on the sleeping platform. The wood floor was rotten, and pushed up black and soft between cracks in the linoleum. The place stank. Petie had only stayed long enough to find and retrieve a rusty fishing tackle box holding forty-two dollars and twelve cents. Rose found under the mattress an old pair of work pants, three socks, a brown plaid shirt with no elbows and four Marlboros in a plastic bag. They also found one spoon, a can opener, a pot, a jar of instant coffee, a can of pork and beans, a can of roast beef hash and twenty-four empty bottles of beer. There was nothing else. They closed the door and walked away, and as far as Petie knew, the trailer was sitting there still.

She wondered how anyone could live so long and come to so little, and not just in material ways. At his funeral and at the Wayside after-wards, where most of Hubbard's old guard went in his honor, no one could remember much. Had he ever been a Lion, an Elk, active with the VFW, helped with the annual salmon bake, any of the kinds of clean civic things you tried to remember about somebody at his funeral? No. John Stewart Tyler had been born and raised in Hubbard, never a resident of anywhere else except for three years during the war, and no one could remember shit. But that was because they were thinking in the wrong places. As they drank a few beers on Petie's forty-two-dollar-and-twelve-cent tab, they started telling the honest stories, the ones about Old Man drunk, swearing at the tourists butchering bottomfish down at the charter boat tables; about him falling asleep and snoring through every single city council meeting for the last nine years. And the favorite of them all, the one everyone knew, about Old Man's eye. He had lost his right eye in an accident years ago, before Petie was even born, and had been fitted with a glass eye. But he used to remove it from time to time, and at some point had dropped it and knocked a chip out of the white part. Even before Petie's mother got sick he'd been cheap, so he'd never bothered to replace the thing, just stuck it back in, chip and all, so that it glinted sometimes in the light. When he got really and deeply drunk, he would rub the eye absently with his shirt cuff until it was pointed some-where crazy, straight up at the ceiling like he was witnessing God de-scending, maybe, or into the bridge of his own nose like a lunatic. For years old Boyce, who'd tended bar at the Wayside until Roy took over six years ago, would tap Old Man on the shoulder when it got too bad, or when someone from out of town wandered in and stood to be frightened. "Eye," Boyce would tell him, and Old Man would feel around with his thick cracked fingers until he'd located the chip, and then he'd twirl the eye around until it was right again.

By the end of the evening it was the kind of funeral party Old Man himself would have liked, with everyone getting a little toasted, telling stories and eventually wandering on home feeling sentimental and kindly about the deceased, now that the pain in the ass was no longer around. And Petie hadn't been sorry to have him gone, not by a long shot, but she hadn't been joyful either, not the way she'd always thought she'd feel.

Petie wondered what Eula would think of them now—did think of them, if she was in fact up there floating above their heads like she always threatened Eddie she'd be. What kind of stock would Eula take of him, with his great new job driving a Pepsi truck, wearing a little blue-and-white-striped uniform shirt with *Eddie* stitched in fancy script over his breast pocket, goofing with the clerks and checkers in the markets and restaurants from ten miles south of Sawyer to thirty-five miles north of Hubbard, flashing his little clipboard and smiling, smiling? And yet, never mind Jeannie Fontineau, never mind the other places he'd driven into with that hood ornament of his. He did work, even though it never lasted, even though he didn't like to very much and wasn't very good at anything he'd tried. He wasn't like old Dooley Burden, who hadn't held a job since he lost his boat to the bank in 1983, who let his sister Connie support him by working the early morning shift at the Anchor, hoisting and lofting those trays even with bursitis so bad she couldn't tie her own apron in back. Eula would likely say Eddie was doing all right, although it was nerve-wracking as all hell being along with him for the ride. And she might say Petie didn't make things easy, and she would be right—especially now with Ron Schiffen.

And what about Ryan? Would he be turning out any better if he had Eula to run to on a bad day, when Petie was edgy and Loose was picking on him and Eddie was nowhere to be found? Eula would have welcomed the boy into her kitchen and made him a cup of sweet hot cocoa, served up in one of her thick chipped blue-and-white-striped mugs. She would have sat him at her table and told him something practical: *Hon, the problem with you is, you register every little gust and breeze that blows by. It's no wonder you're always spinning around. What we're going to do is, we're going to toughen you into a sturdier tree.* And then she'd give him projects he could succeed at, preferably intricate ones that would take him a long time, distract him from his latest failure. Taking apart the egg timer, rewrapping all the pans under the stove burners in tinfoil, tracing all the dead ivy trailers back to the main vine and clipping them. Projects Petie rarely had the energy or time to invent, and never within a haven like Eula's kitchen.

Then there was Loose, who was beginning to show not just a temper but a mean streak. It was true he picked on weaker older boys like Ryan, but he was starting to pick on younger ones, too. She had had another call from school, had been advised to set up an appointment for him with a counselor except she hadn't gotten to it yet. The thought filled her with dread. Wasn't it good that he was gutsy, that he could stick up for himself? Wouldn't the rest even out after a while—wouldn't he learn to use all that energy for something better? And yet, who would teach him, Eddie Coolbaugh? Eddie knew hurdling and dirt bikes and women, and that wasn't enough, not nearly enough to fill up someone like Loose. Could it possibly be that, even with the little contact he and Loose had had, across the yard and while he had apparently swayed and dozed, some of Old Man had rubbed off?

And what would Eula have thought of Petie herself? It seemed to her that as most women got softer with age—Rose, for instance, got lovelier every year with her pretty bosom, her hands that looked as plump and young as they had in high school—she, Petie, got harder, stringier, tougher. When she looked in the mirror she thought she looked stunted and sexless, like Peter Pan, only meaner. A tough, bandy little person, a scrapper; someone who, when cornered, would bite. Surely not the sort of person—sort of *woman*—who would, in two hours, be slipping off to Sawyer to meet Ron Schiffen for lunch.

Chapter 5

WHEN THE people of Sawyer tucked into a meal or a snack, seventy-two percent selected a Pepsi product to go with it. Their consumption of Ocean Spray drinks and bottled Lipton teas was also rising sharply, and it was all Schiff's doing. When you helped yourself to a 20-ounce cup at the Quik Stop's fountain service, when you wheeled your shopping cart around the handsome pillars of alternating Pepsi/Diet Pepsi/Pepsi cases at the end of Safeway aisle 8B, you were enjoying a little piece of Schiff's handiwork. Right now, just this week, he was sponsoring two grand openings (banners, cups, special discount on 24-ounce servings), two high school ball fields (painted signs behind the infields, portable Pepsi cart at home games) and a special two-day building supplies exhibition (portable Pepsi cart, disposable Pepsi painter's caps to the first fifty people). Schiff's profile had never been higher. In Harrison County, anyway, Pepsi was king.

But Ron Schiffen hadn't always been so lucky, not by a long shot. His mother's term of endearment for him when he was growing up had been Dumb Stuff. *Jeez, it's a good thing you've got looks*, she'd tell him, *because you haven't got a hell of a lot else working for you, do you, kid.*

It was true that Schiff had done badly in school from the get-go. He'd been hungry, for one thing. He'd never been sure if that was because they didn't have any money or because his mother was lazy and never bought or cooked enough for them. Her name was Delia and she worked as a bartender at the Elks Lodge in Rose Briar, Arizona, and she slept all day when other mothers shopped and cooked. It didn't matter that much; school had bored him. You had to sit still for long periods of time, and you had to pay attention, two things Schiff wasn't very good at. So he and his brother, Howard, had scavenged food, backed each other up in school yard fights, and beat feet out of town just as soon as they were old enough—eighteen, for Schiff, nineteen for Howard, who had waited for him. They both went into the army. Schiff did three tours in Vietnam—*three tours*—and lived. Howard did six and a half weeks in Stuttgart, Germany, and was run over by a truck. All these years later, Schiff still missed him.

Once, before he and Howard took off, they were sitting in a lopsided little piece-of-shit tavern twenty miles or so from home. They were big boys, Howard especially, and no one messed with them about IDs or any of that. They were putting down a couple of cold ones when an old man, dusty and dry as a summer ditch, came in and sat down with them. They got to talking—not Howard, Howard didn't talk, but Schiff and the old guy—and the old man told the boys he'd been witching for water, thought he'd probably found some just before dark. Water was more precious than gold in that part of the country, and much scarcer. Said he thought he'd found a big underground feeder, might be the one that would open up that part of the desert. Boys want to go in on it with him? Nah, Schiff had said. They were only weeks away from enlisting out of that hellhole, and besides they didn't have money. *Too bad*, the old man said. *Missing a big one, boys.* And Howard had sat over the bar, rubbing water beads off his beer bottle with his thumb, and after the old fellow had downed a beer and gone he'd said, *I got a feeling. We should have given him what we have.*

Nothing is what we have, Schiff said. *Your car. My pay from the grocery. Anyway, he was a loser, didn't you see his eyes? Squirrelly, Howard, squirrelly as they come.*

Yeah, Howard had said. *But a good witcher. I heard of him.*

Schiff had laughed, but now that part of Arizona, that *exact spot*, was covered by an eighteen-hole golf course, condos, foo-foo clubhouse, and fancy light posts and shit. Development as far as you could see. The old man had probably spent his last days gumming his food in the best nursing home money could buy.

No, Schiff hadn't always been lucky.

But today, dreamy-eyed with prosperity and expectation, Schiff propped his boots up on his execu-desk in his private office in one corner of his snappy red-white-and-blue corrugated steel Pepsi distributorship and surveyed a dangler. Danglers were little cardboard and string constructions that suspended soda cups over fountain services so everyone could see them and the coupons or promotional deals they advertised. This one was a honey, tying into Seton County's sesquicentennial. Classy. Covered wagons and pioneers circled the cup and plodded on across the dangler. People were going to love it. He'd order an extra fifty thousand cups from Portland when he got back from lunch.

Calling over his shoulder to his secretary Bev, Schiff left the distributorship and dragged his soles cheerfully through the gravel he'd had refreshed just that week. He pulled his truck keys from his pocket, but only through habit; it would be better to arrive at The Recess on foot. His truck was a big studly silver thing, the only one like it in either Sawyer or Hubbard, and under certain circumstances that could be a liability. Eddie Coolbaugh, he knew, was up north where Schiff had sent him, but he couldn't so precisely pinpoint Carla's whereabouts, although he'd given her a friendly call at the Wayside ten minutes ago to be safe. And of course there was always Randi the Makeup Queen, who was supposed to be in school, but who knew?

The Recess was a block away from the county courthouse, and catered to the legal and paralegal crowd—one of the few circles left in which Schiff was relatively unknown. The restaurant, which did not use Pepsi products, wasn't his kind of place—all ferns and little watercolor paintings and drawings and shit where you couldn't even get breakfast after nine-thirty—but he hadn't chosen the place for the food or the atmosphere. He scanned the gloom for Petie, but he was ten minutes early—he prided himself on being punctual—and she hadn't arrived yet. She'd come, though.

He chose a table in a back corner, where the traffic would be light and the lighting would be nil. No sense in adding to Petie's skittishness, plus he wasn't as fond of a risk as he used to be. In fact, it had been a very long time since he'd taken any, much as his reputation had it otherwise. He didn't really know why that was. He wasn't nearly the cad women seemed to want him to be, hadn't been in a long time. There must be something about the look of him, despite the little gut he carried now. He did have a mouth, he'd grant you that. But he didn't mean anything by it; these days, talking dirty was just something to pass the time.

Suddenly Schiff heard a woman talking about penises. He was sure of it. She was talking quietly, but Schiff had excellent hearing and knew how to use it. She sat two tables away from Schiff's, with a very young man whose back was turned.

"No, no, a plethysmograph. A penile meter. They put it on the defendant's penis and then show him pictures to see what gets him aroused." Schiff saw the edges of the young man's ears get pink. A penile meter, for Christ's sake.

Then they started talking about something else, something about law school, and Schiff got bored and stopped listening. He hated lawyers, anyway. All they wanted was money. Then again, sometimes he thought maybe he'd become a lawyer himself, so he could sit around all day fast-talking for big bucks. He'd never met a lawyer yet he thought was any smarter than he was. A penile meter—who thought up shit like that? He actually felt sorry for anybody who was perhaps at that very minute hunched miserably in some dingy courthouse room with his poor middle-aged dick stuck up some kind of tube or encircled by a tape measure or something. On the other hand, he had no use whatsoever for people who messed with kids. Schiff had woken up one night when he was nine or ten to find one of his mother's boyfriends working his hand under Schiff's covers while Schiff slept. Schiff had kicked him in the chin and the guy had beaten the crap out of him. But he'd never tried anything again, not with him or with Howard. For a long time after that Schiff had slept with scissors under his pillow.

A waitress approached Schiff's table with water and silverware. Lemon slices floated around inside the water pitcher like pond scum; no ice. The waitress had on a long droopy black dress, black canvas kung fu shoes and a leather thong that looked like it had been around her neck since sometime in the late sixties. She wore a bleary, stoned expression. "And how am I today?" Schiff asked her as she poured him a cloudy-looking glass of water.

"Fine—what? Oh." She looked annoyed and walked away shaking her head. Schiff loved that line, he really did. It threw them every time. He grinned and relaxed back in his chair to wait.

PETIE CIRCLED the block three times before she pulled the car up to the curb outside The Recess and punched down the door locks. As though anyone would steal the poor thing, especially a half a block from the courthouse. Still, Eddie had put in a new radio only a couple of weeks ago, celebrating the first payday on his new job, and she'd hate to have it ripped off before they'd even made the first payment. She got out of the car, stamped twice to get her jeans seated over the instep of her boots, and shouldered her purse. She'd eat lunch, she'd go home. People did it all the time.

Inside, she paused by an old washstand set up as a hostess station, to let her eyes adjust to the gloom. She'd never been here before. Rose would like it, because of all the plants. Petie didn't think much of it herself. The chest of drawers beside her had an old lace doily on it, like you were supposed to be eating lunch in someone's grandmother's bedroom; desserts were displayed on a pie safe and a couple of rickety tea carts. Petie didn't see the charm in old things. All they meant was you couldn't afford new ones.

She scanned the room mechanically, without hope. Schiff's truck hadn't been parked outside: the asshole wasn't even here yet, and it was already five minutes after they were supposed to meet. Plenty of people were looking her way, too. She was the only person in the place wearing jeans. The men were all in coats and ties; the women wore little skirts and blouses and scarves and shit. Everyone but Petie was wearing cologne. Petie smelled like onions. They'd been making jambalaya. She clamped her old purse under her armpit and hung her thumbs over her belt buckle—well, Eddie Coolbaugh's belt buckle, silver plate, big as a saucer, with a fancy brass *C* right in the middle; a belt buckle that on Petie's small frame said *Screw you*.

Suddenly, from the far back of the room, a big easy smile reached her like a perfectly shot arrow. Schiff was slouching like a lazy old tomcat at a table that looked much too small. Despite the heat of the place he was wearing his Pepsi jacket, and in front of him was a glass of milk.

"Hey," he said after he'd watched her walk every inch of the way across the room and sit down across from him.

"Hey, Schiff."

"Happy to see me?"

"Give me a break."

"You don't like me much, do you?"

"No, not much," Petie acknowledged.

"Is it because I'm supposed to be a womanizer?"

"Are you?"

"A womanizer? Hell, if I did half the things I'm supposed to be doing, I'd be smiling a lot more."

"Then why did you ask me over here? Is it about Eddie, did he do something wrong already? We can't afford for him to lose this job, Schiff. Was it something he did on purpose, or was it an accident?"

"Neither."

Petie looked at him warily.

"I just thought, you know, it would be nice to talk."

"You've got to be kidding."

"I'm not kidding."

"You mean it would be nice if I slept with you."

"That *would* be nice—" Schiff lifted a slow eyebrow.

"You can just go and *fuck* yourself," Petie hissed.

"—but the fact is, I couldn't sleep with you right now, because Carla would kill me and I've already been divorced and wiped out once and

Carla wouldn't just wipe me out, she'd ruin me. Carla doesn't like me much, either. I miss having someone to talk to. So I thought, you know, I could tell you some things and you could pretend to listen."

Petie reached for a glass. "Is that my water?"

"Careful, I might have spit in it."

"Who do you remind me of?" Petie said. "Maybe my youngest son. Except he's mature for his age." She drank around the wilted lemon slice for something to do. The waitress came to take their order for hamburgers, looked hostilely at Schiff and stayed on Petie's side of the table.

"For instance," Schiff continued once she had gone, "one thing we could talk about is, I got an offer from someone for one of my dirt bikes. A good offer."

"Was it Eddie?"

"Well, it might have been," Schiff mused. "Or, it might not. You know, a good salesman never gives away his prospects."

"So what was the offer?"

"Two hundred even. Nothing down, four equal payments to be made monthly, with possession after a hundred."

"So it's a good bike."

"A very good bike."

"Then why are you selling it?"

"I'm tired of getting mud in my teeth. I'm thinking of getting a road bike."

"We're just getting back on our feet, Schiff. What do you want me to say?"

"Well, there could be another buyer approaching me with another good offer."

"Is there?"

"If it would help," Schiff said.

"He really wants the bike. He talks about it with Loose all the time. Would it last, is it sturdy?"

"Sturdy enough."

Petie sighed.

"Or," Schiff said, watching Petie closely, "I could change the terms."

"What do you mean?"

"Well, let's say I lowered the asking price to, say, thirty-five a month for four months. Eddie still gives me fifty, but I return fifteen a month to you when I see you. Which I would do, say, every now and then. To talk." Without looking away he tore open a paper packet of sugar and up-ended it into his mouth, neatly tapping out the last several granules.

Petie stared back, and the two of them bore down on each other like oncoming trains. Schiff palmed another packet of sugar.

"Son of a bitch," Petie whispered.

"Look," he said, leaning towards her abruptly over the tabletop. "I know you don't trust me, I know you think I only want to jump your bones. Not that I wouldn't like to, don't get me wrong. They're very, very nice bones." She could feel his feet and legs burning away, reaching towards her under the table. "But that's not it. Okay? Think about it. If I'd wanted to find someone to play with, I would've picked someone easier. Not to mention someone whose other half doesn't work for me."

Petie regarded him frankly. "Are you done?"

"Yes."

"You're a piece of work." But she'd started smiling.

"So are you," Schiff said, grinning. "So are you."

Petie's cheeks were in high color as she accepted her plate from the waitress. Schiff could almost feel the heat coming off them, heat radiating through the thick shiny Indian hair pulled away from her face with a rolled-up bandanna. He could imagine what it would feel like on his bare chest. He'd always liked long hair, liked it dark, too. He wondered if she'd start getting gray soon. Old Man had been grizzled by the time he was forty-two, Schiff had heard; but there was the mother. He'd never heard much about the mother, not from Petie or Old Man or anyone. She had a few years on her already, Petie did, but she looked good to him. Damn good. He drained the rest of his milk.

"So," Petie said when the waitress was gone. "Do you come here often?"

"Not too often."

"I mean, God, Schiff, the place looks like where old lawyers go with their secretaries when they die. See that guy over there? I think he's the one that nailed Old Man on his last DUI. Mr. Leather Suspenders and Fancy Pen. Guy probably kicks butt all morning and then comes in here to scarf down a Lawburger or something before he has to go pick up his dry cleaning."

"He sure was plowed," Schiff said.

"Who?"

"Old Man." Schiff had been the first one to discover Old Man blindly trying to drive his way out of a ten-foot-deep ditch by the side of the road one night. No one ever figured out how he got in there in the first place, his truck and himself being in nearly perfect shape for two old beaters, not a fresh brush-nick or roll-mark on either of them. Old Man never got his license back after that; people just stopped and gave him a lift if they saw him walking along in the rain or cold. Some kid from Sawyer eventually bought his truck for a hundred and twenty-five bucks and a tow.

"Hell, he drove like that all the time," Petie said. "There was a bunch of people used to pull over whenever they saw him coming. When I was little, he and my mother used to really go at it about his driving when he was stewed. The drunker he was, the more he wouldn't let her drive. When he was really wasted, he wouldn't even let her sit up front with him. She'd climb in beside me in the back and hold my hand."

"I've never heard much about your mother."

Petie shrugged. "She died. It was a long time ago."

"Was she pretty?"

"No."

"Car accident?"

"Cancer."

Schiff nodded. "My father supposedly died of cancer."

"Supposedly?"

"That's my mother's story."

"You don't think so?"

Schiff shrugged. "I never met him." He pressed a few sugar granules onto his fingertip from the tabletop and brushed them into the ashtray.

"That's too bad."

"It certainly didn't stop me from turning out wonderful."

"So where's your mother now?"

"Delia? Beats hell out of me. We don't talk."

"Ever?"

"Not since 1968."

"What happened in 1968?"

"Me and my brother Howard left home. It's a long story. Maybe I'll tell you sometime."

"Now's good."

"Mmmm." Schiff raised an eyebrow.

"For the *story*."

"No." He pushed back his cuff and checked his watch, pulled out a Pepsi credit card and picked up the check. "Meet me next week and I'll tell you then."

Petie slung her old purse over her shoulder. She stood up and reached across the table, brushing his cheek lightly with her fingertips. He neither flinched nor ducked.

"Nice try," she said.

IT WAS only once she was in her car that she allowed herself to slip off her denim jacket. She had soaked her shirt completely through. She must be in worse shape than she'd thought, to be thrown so badly. But there was something about the man, besides simple gall. He had a sleepy, feral look, cool as cool, unblinking, sure, in no hurry. No one had looked at her that way for years. Hell, no one looked at her much of any way at all anymore. She and Rose didn't so much see as breathe each other, and Eddie Coolbaugh—well, God, Eddie Coolbaugh. Who knew what Eddie saw anymore. Eddie didn't see, really; things just got blown into his eyes and stuck there for a while. Jeannie Fontineau, and so on.

Quickly, before Schiff could come out, she cranked over the engine, rolled down all the car windows and headed for the Crestline

Apartments a few blocks away, where she had promised Rose she'd drop off an envelope with Gordon.

In her rearview mirror as she pulled out she saw Schiff amble out of the restaurant, set a toothpick between his teeth, bury his hands deep in his pockets and watch her drive away.

AT THE Crestline Petie pulled up beside Gordon's Peugeot—what the hell kind of car was that, anyway, a Peugeot?—reached under the seat and pulled out the fat envelope Rose had given her that morning. More cookbook pages. Rose was spending every free minute working on the damn thing. For no money. It wasn't the first time Rose had been taken advantage of. Petie had tried to talk her out of the project, especially now that Christie was back, but Rose had turned stubborn, which was rare with her. She just said that she liked doing it, and that Gordon was being very encouraging.

"Then they should pay you," Petie had muttered.

"You know they would, Petie, if they could. Don't you think they're good people?"

"They're all right."

And Petie meant it: they were all right. They were honest and they worked hard and they had given her and Rose jobs. But they were taking advantage of Rose, getting her to do all that work and not paying her, and Petie didn't like that.

It took a long time for Gordon to answer the door. When he did, Petie recognized one of Rose's crocheted afghans around his shoulders, and he wore a pair of burgundy suede slippers on his feet. From within, a vaporizer hissed. He was very pale, and looked like the boys did after a bad bout of the flu: rabbit-eyed, clammy-handed, fuggy from too much bed rest and fever.

"Rose called and said you'd be dropping some pages by," he said. He spoke thickly. Rose had said something about there being fungus in his mouth. "Do you want to come in?"

"That's okay. I've got to get back."

"Wait. I've got some proofs I want Rose to see. Can I send them with you? Would you mind?"

"Sure."

Petie stepped inside and looked around. She had never been here before. Along one wall there was a slender-slatted bench; the other furniture was pretty, upholstered in chintzes of salmon and green. On the walls were several pencil sketches of men, small things in thick wooden frames; one a face, another a nude—a *man*—lying on his side. A whole wall of books, plants; an electronic keyboard of some kind. Some tall brass candlesticks with salmon-colored candles. It was beautiful and immaculate and no other man Petie had ever known would have been caught dead there.

On his desk a computer showed a page of Rose's book on the screen. Gordon did a few things and the page changed.

"Take a look at this." He motioned Petie over. "Remember the cabbage and chorizo soup? Here's the spread we're doing on it. It's good, isn't it?"

Petie looked, but it was just a recipe to her, except that it had a longer explanation beside it than she'd have wanted to read. Rose had always been the reader, not her.

"Rose has a strong, earthy voice," Gordon said, rapidly flipping other pages onto and then off the screen. A printer began dragging paper through itself in the corner. "It's very unusual, very clear. I think we're going to be able to find a regional publisher for her. Think of it. You two will be famous."

"Not me. Just Rose."

"She includes you in everything she's writing. Haven't you read any of it?"

"Nah. She's talked about some of the recipes with me, you know, double-checking things, but I'll read it when it's done."

Gordon nodded and tapped the new papers into order, put them in an envelope and handed it to Petie. She took it and headed for the door, but before she got there she could hear Gordon clearing his throat, a thick, painful sound. "Petie."

"Hmmm?"

Gordon draped the afghan over the back of his chair and set his feet carefully. "Has Rose talked to you about me?"

"Sure."

"So you know I don't have the flu."

"Yes."

"Are you okay with it?"

"No," said Petie. "Are you?"

Gordon smiled. "No."

"Look, I'm not afraid of you, if that's what you mean. I'm not thrilled, either. Okay? You're my boss. I work for you and Nadine. I like my job, and I'm not planning on going anywhere else. Is that what you wanted to know? The rest is none of my business."

Gordon nodded and colored.

"Hey," she said more softly. "I say what I mean, but it comes out hard sometimes. It's awful, what's happening to you. And I'm sorry. Look. Rose is the nice one of us two. You make sure she knows if there's anything we can do. Anything. Okay?" She crossed the room and picked the top off the vaporizer, took it into the apartment's tiny kitchen and filled the well, then hooked it back up again in the living room. "You're not leaving this on overnight, are you?"

"No."

"Well, if you do just make sure you fill it up real good."

Gordon smiled a little, shivered and readjusted Rose's afghan over his shoulders. Petie picked up the envelope again.

"Petie."

She turned around at the door.

"Thanks."

"Yeah." Quietly she pulled the door shut behind her and sighed.

IT HAD always seemed like a mistake that, of the two of them, Petie had been the one to have two children—her, on whose reluctant shoulders children had fallen like a sack of cats. Rose had spent a tranquil, besotted pregnancy rubbing her belly and dreaming, while

Petie had spent both of hers fighting back, prodding at the kicking babies with a ruler, a pencil, a spoon, her thumb. All three children responded to them the same way. They brought Petie their anger and outrage, but when they were hurt, especially Loose, they went to Rose. And so there was nothing really new in Petie's turning over Gordon to Rose as she so often turned over the boys.

"Maybe you could just look in on him," she told Rose back in Hubbard as she handed her Gordon's envelope. "I mean, if you're going over there anyway. He seemed to want something."

"You mean like food?"

"No, no, nothing like that, he's got Nadine for that stuff. No, more like someone to talk to, maybe. I don't know. He wanted to know if I knew what he had."

"So?"

"Well, I do. So I said so."

"God."

"I don't know, he seemed relieved he didn't have to tell me."

Rose shook her head. "It's awful."

"I know. So I told him to tell you anytime he needed anything we could help with."

Rose nodded.

"I thought I'd better let you know."

"Okay." Rose began to slip the new pages out of the envelope.

"I had lunch over in Sawyer with Schiff."

"What?"

"Yeah."

"Why?"

"I don't know. He asked. I thought he wanted to tell me something about Eddie, some fuckup."

"Did he?"

"No. Eddie made some deal with him for some dirt bike, though. He wanted my okay."

"Oh." Petie opened the front door, but Rose called out, "Hey! I nearly forgot. Barb Dumphy called. She thought you might be over here cooking. Something about setting up an appointment to talk to you about Ryan."

"Shit." Barb Dumphy was Ryan's fourth-grade teacher.

"You're supposed to call her back between three-thirty and four. Or she said she might try you."

Sure enough, the telephone was ringing when she got home. Like a fool, she picked it up. "Mrs. Coolbaugh? This is Barb Dumphy at school. Ryan's teacher? I'm glad I managed to find you. I'm calling because I'd like to set up an appointment to talk with you and Mr. Coolbaugh about Ryan."

"Is he crying at recess again?"

"Actually, I'd rather not talk about it over the phone. What I was wondering was, could you and Mr. Coolbaugh come to school tomorrow afternoon, maybe at three-thirty?"

The woman sounded nervous. Son of a *bitch*. Petie hoped they didn't owe anyone money. With a dish towel she whacked at a late-fall fly dying on the windowsill. "I could probably come. My husband has to work."

"Well, that's fine, even just one of you. Do you know which is Ryan's classroom?"

"Yes."

"All right, Mrs. Coolbaugh. We'll see you at three-thirty tomorrow. Bye, now."

Petie kept the receiver to her ear as the connection was broken and then replaced by a dial tone. By the kitchen clock the boys would be home in ten minutes, and the sink was piled with dishes Petie had turned her back on to meet Schiff. She looked at them with anger; she hated dirty dishes in any sink. Old Man had always left crusty plates around, and old juice glasses with a film of beer still on them. The trailer had stunk of them all the time, even when Petie cleaned them the minute Old Man turned his back. Not that there was much of a way to clean anything in twelve feet of no kitchen and just a dishpan of water to wash in, another for rinsing, poured from the jerry cans she filled three or four times a week at the spigot outside the First Church of God.

Old Man never got water. Hell, he would have kept on peeing out the window if Petie and Eddie hadn't built an outhouse for them. That had been eighteen years ago, when she hardly knew him except that he'd watch her in class sometimes, two years older than the rest of the students and still flunking algebra. One day out of the blue, he turned up whistling in a place where no one would normally go—they were squatting on state land, so the trailer was a good fifty feet off the petered-out end of Chollum Road. The day Eddie showed up, Petie had been struggling to get some scavenged boards anchored to a two-by-four. It was October, and cold, and she didn't have much of a hammer.

"Hey," Eddie Coolbaugh had said. He had a hammer in his hand. At the time he seemed as unlikely to be there as Santa and his reindeer. Maybe someone had told him she'd been scavenging wood from the landfill. "You could use a better hammer." He extended his and Petie took it.

"You have any nails?" she said.

"Those nails are all right."

"They bend pretty easy."

"Because you were using a tack hammer. You try that one, they won't bend. Hit it square, though. You got to hit it real square or you'll bend any nail."

He watched her pound a couple of nails, all of them true. "Big wall or little?"

"Who said it was a wall?"

"It's either that or a fence, and this doesn't look like a place for a fence. Big?"

"I don't know. I guess not. I don't have much wood."

Eddie sorted through the pile she'd collected and lined pieces up on the ground and sawed them even while Petie hammered. Between them they made four walls and a doorframe by dark. Eddie sank a post-hole or two in the loamy ground, against which the walls could be raised and then anchored. He still had not asked what they were building, nor shown any particular curiosity. Out of the corner of her eye Petie watched him work, and there was something about his profound lack of interest she liked. And the fact that he had no smell, none whatsoever.

When the light was gone, Eddie had said, "We better do the roof to-morrow. Supposed to be rain coming in."

Petie let nothing show. "Yeah."

Eddie brushed off his clothes, ran his fingers through his hair to tidy himself.

"Why'd you come up here, anyway?"

Eddie had shrugged. "There wasn't anywhere else better. You want a ride back into town? It's getting late."

"Nah. My dad and I, we'll probably camp out here tonight. He's supposed to meet me."

"Yeah?" Eddie looked at her blandly through the gathering darkness.

"I'm building an outhouse," Petie had said flatly. "We live here."

"Yeah," said Eddie. "I heard that."

Next day he'd come back with lumber and a toilet seat and it had been that way between them ever since.

Chapter 6

For nearly as long as Ryan could remember, Rose had kept a scrap bag in her bedroom closet. It was a plain muslin sack filled with the leftover bits from sewing projects stretching back years: baby quilts she'd made for all of them, smocks and rompers for Carissa, skirts and blouses and dresses for herself. The two of them used to pore over the contents like two kings in a countinghouse. Rose loved rich colors and fine naps, and inside the plain bag were whole seasons: a springtime garden of pinks and yellows and blues, smoky autumn afternoons of grays and golds and fading greens.

Ryan sat in the narrow entrance to Rose's closet with the bag open at his feet, cloth carefully unfurled and transforming his legs and feet and lap into a fine landscape: a vast blue velveteen sea, green-checked fields, brown-striped mountains spiking from his toes. Deployed across the folds at the foot of the mountain range but not far from the sea were several Pilgrims and an Indian. The Pilgrims were begging the Indians to give them food, since they lacked the skills to take care of themselves in the New World. Ryan's class was learning about the early settlers and Thanksgiving in social studies. Ryan was deeply interested in the Pilgrims' plight. He himself felt unprepared most of the time, and knew the shame and terror it caused.

Ryan loved being at Rose's, even with Jim Christie there. Christie rarely spoke, which was all right with Ryan because he understood that

Christie was shy. When Ryan and Loose had walked in after school today, he had simply nodded to them both, flipped a faded ball cap onto his head, pulled it low and gone outside. Loose had trailed after him, hoping for mechanical revelations—Christie was known as a first-rate auto mechanic, better even than Eddie Coolbaugh. Ryan had Rose and the house to himself until Carissa came home from Sawyer on the school bus.

Rose poked her head into the room. "Sweetie, are you going to want a brownie?"

"Okay."

"Oh, look!" Rose cried, seeing the scrap bag. "All the beautiful things! It's been a long time since any of us got into my scrap bag, hasn't it? When you were little you used to take stuff out one by one and rub them against your cheek."

"I don't do that anymore," Ryan lied. He had stroked his cheek with every cloth he'd withdrawn. It was one of his rituals. He had a lot of rituals. In his pocket was a little satin scrap he'd stolen because he liked the way his fingernail felt scraping across it. He would bring it home and put it under his pillow, where he could scratch it as he fell asleep. The thought made him shiver a little with pleasure.

"What are the Q-tips for?" Rose had come in to take a closer look.

"They're not Q-tips. They're Pilgrims."

"Oh! Is it Thanksgiving?"

"No, because they need to find a turkey first. They're all starving to death, except the ones who are dying of mosquito bites."

"Yuck."

"So they're walking to the mountains to try and find an Indian who could give them a turkey."

"You have the wildest imagination. You know, you could watch cartoons if you want to. Loose is outside with Jim working on my car. You could choose whatever show you want."

"Maybe in a little while."

"All right, sweetie. Just clean up in here when you're done." Rose turned to leave.

"Rose?"

"Hmmm?"

"Why did my mom have to go to school?" Ryan tried not to sound nervous, but he'd worried all day. Maybe they thought he had done something wrong. Sometimes he could feel Mrs. Dumphy looking at him, especially lately, when he wasn't playing with the other kids at recess. He was sculpting a hole under the fir tree with the knot on the trunk. He'd been perfecting it for a week, a round, smooth hole the size of an upside-down helmet.

Rose turned back in the doorway. "She went to see Mrs. Dumphy, sweetie, that's all I know."

"Oh."

"Is there something wrong?"

Ryan shrugged miserably.

"Do you want to talk about it?" Rose came back into the room and sat on the bed.

Ryan shook his head.

Rose put her arm around the boy's shoulders, his bones insubstantial as a bird's. "All right, sweetie. Come out when you're ready and I'll have your brownie waiting. Don't be too long, though, because they're some of Carissa's best and someone else might not be able to restrain themselves."

"Okay."

Impulsively Rose came back into the room and gave Ryan a noisy kiss on the top of his head. "I don't get to see enough of you anymore. You need to come and visit me more often," she told him. His head smelled like paints; he had worn home an Indian headdress of construction paper. It had been meticulously painted, the spine of each feather detailed, the feathers themselves intricately rendered and beautiful. Ryan had worn it with great dignity.

Rose closed the door to her bedroom behind her quietly. Ryan was one of the most difficult children she had ever known, but also one of the sweetest. God or whatever had just dealt him a difficult nature and there was not a thing he or anybody else could do about it. Loud noises had always startled him, even when he knew they were coming; the vacuum cleaner still made him tremble when it was run over a hard floor. As a baby he'd only been at ease in motion, and his happiest times were when Petie pushed him in the Sea View housekeeping cart, wedged tightly between piles of starchy white towels and linens. On her off nights Petie had spent hours in the dingy laundry room of her apartment building dozing in a plastic chair while Ryan rode the dryer in his car seat, soothed by the hum and the heat and vibration. Later there had been the periods when he couldn't bear any wrinkles in his socks, when the color orange made him cry, when he was afraid of spiders that weren't there. Then Loose had come along, a tough, roly-poly, manly baby, a bottle-slinger, a nipple-chewer, surefooted and fearless but with none of Ryan's sensitivity or sweetness. Rose and Ryan and Carissa had become a trio for a while, while Petie regained her footing. Now Rose worried that she was losing touch with him. He seemed skittish to her, and quick to startle, but then he always suffered when things went bad between Petie and Eddie Coolbaugh. At least Eddie was working again.

Rose spaded brownies out of a deep pan, licking her fingers. Carissa in middle school, Loose in first grade: how could it be that these children were growing up when she didn't feel old herself? She still had her pretty breasts, her sense of peace, her talent for delight. Christie was home safely—riches!—and she had this cookbook, hers and Gordon's. Blessed man, and so sick. She would see him tomorrow, after she and Petie had made their Souperior's run. How awful, to be dying. She couldn't picture a man loving another man, didn't want to, but whose business was it, anyway? Everyone needed to love something and maybe Gordon, like Ryan, had simply been dealt a bum hand. Maybe he didn't want to love other men; undoubtedly Ryan didn't like minding the wrinkles in his socks when everyone else could just put on their shoes and go. You couldn't blame people for what wasn't theirs to choose.

So she'd write a good book for him. That might make him happy.

The front door opened and Rose looked up, thinking it was Carissa home from school, but instead it was Petie.

"Is Ryan in here?" She tossed her purse behind the couch and threw herself full-length onto the slippery old brocade cushions. "I saw Loose outside with Christie."

"He's playing in my room. He smells like paint."

"Not on his clothes."

"No, just a little in his hair. He made an Indian headdress in school and wore it home. You'll want to take a look at it—he did a really good job. Is he okay? He's worried about something, but he didn't want to talk about it."

"He scored a 158 on an IQ test."

"Is that good?" Rose asked.

"It's off the fucking charts. Mrs. Dumphy's sitting there saying Ryan could be the next Einstein, and I'm saying they've got the wrong kid."

"Oh, Petie. You know he's smart."

"I know he's odd, is what I know. She said he's working way below the level she'd expect of a kid with that IQ. She wanted to know if there were any problems at home that might be distracting him." Petie ran her hands through her hair. "Fuck, I'm not going to go into my personal life with her. I said everything was fine. Which it pretty much is, now. Do you have any beer?"

"Better—wine coolers. Ice, or no?"

"No."

Rose pressed Petie's small shoulder as she walked by. There was always something. There always had been. As she poured their coolers into glasses she heard Petie go to the bedroom and look in on Ryan, then after a long minute close the door softly without speaking and come back to the living room.

Rose handed her the glass without the chip in the rim.

"He's got fabric spread all over the room," Petie said.

"That's because he's in New England or Virginia or somewhere. He's making up a game about the Pilgrims."

"Huh."

"He's got a great imagination."

"No kidding. Half the time it seems like he's on Mars."

"He's very talented, Petie, you know that. You should see the headdress he brought home from school. The feathers look real, I swear. If you get tired of him, just send him over to me."

"Don't say it too loud."

"I'm serious. I'd take him for a few days anytime, you know that."

"I know. He's a good kid, though. Plus I'm tough as an old shoe." Petie took a long drink of her cooler.

"Was Carissa out there when you came in?" Rose asked.

"Yeah. She and Loose were with Jim. He's a nice guy. They're hanging all over him, and he's just going on with his business. For a man who doesn't talk, he sure has a way with kids."

"He's very patient. I worry about what Carissa will do when he leaves again."

"Maybe he won't."

Rose smiled. Of course he'd leave again. The front door banged and in ambled first Loose, then Carissa.

"Hey," Petie said.

"Hi," said Carissa. Her cheeks were pink from the cool fall air, her eyes bright.

Loose said nothing. He dragged one toe behind him across the carpet, leaving a thin trail of mud. Rose frowned at him. "You. Shoes off."

Loose paused, unfazed, and kicked his shoes halfway across the room. He was a big child, with Eddie's good-natured, uninquisitive face. Rose shook her finger at him. He had always been a physical child, but Rose had also seen him labor over mechanical projects for hours. He was capable of that kind of concentration.

Loose threw himself onto the sofa next to her.

"Where's Jim?" she said, pulling him into her side with a strong arm. "You wear him out?"

Loose let Rose pull him in, but only for a minute and then he squirmed out of range. "He said he was going to the Wayside."

"But he's coming home for dinner," Carissa called quickly from the kitchen, where she was scraping brownie crumbs from the bottom of the pan with the spatula.

"Are you cooking again?" Petie called back.

"Yup. Meat loaf."

Petie let her head fall way back on the sofa. "I wish you'd come over to our house sometime and make us meat loaf. We're doing boxed macaroni and cheese. God, but I hate to cook at night. I dream about cooking. I'm not kidding. I dream about every little step. Some nights all I do is *peel* the carrots and then *peel* the potatoes and then *cut* the onions up into tiny pieces, perfect pieces all the same size, and then I do the celery and by then it's three o'clock in the morning and I'm about ready to kill myself. I mean, it's bad enough to do that stuff day after day, but to have to do it all night, too—"

Rose was laughing, and Petie started laughing, too. Ryan came out to see what was going on, and Petie hoisted herself up, draining the last sip of her wine cooler. "Hey, kiddo," she said to Ryan. "You were so quiet in there I thought maybe you'd escaped out the window and gone on home."

Ryan shrugged and wandered towards Rose.

"Did they find someone to give them a turkey?" she asked.

"One. I don't think it was enough, though."

"Enough for what?" Petie said.

"To eat."

"What happened to them, then?" Rose asked. "Did someone tell them about squash, or give them some corn?"

"No." Ryan put his hands on Rose's knees, leaned in until he was two inches from her face, and whispered, "They all starved to death."

Petie shuddered. "God, Ryan."

"But it's only make-believe, isn't it," Rose whispered back to the boy. "Anything can be done and undone in make-believe." She held out her wing, and Ryan slipped silently under it.

"Stories like that give me the willies," Petie said, and shook herself.

"You could stay for dinner," Carissa said from the kitchen doorway. She had an apron of Rose's tied carefully over her school clothes.

"Oh, thanks, sweetie," Petie said. "But Eddie's probably sitting at home right now wondering where we are. C'mon, boys, before I get too tired to get up. Loose, your shoes. Your shoes. Your *shoes*. You can't go out in just your socks, dodo-head."

Petie shooed the boys into their coats and out the front door. "Say hi to Christie for me."

"Okay." Rose made a sign to Petie: *Chin up.* "See you in the morning. Curried lemon rice."

"Sounds disgusting. Whose is it?"

"Nadine's."

"Figures."

"It might be all right."

"C'mon, Mom," Loose said, butting his knee into the back of Petie's knee.

"Okay, okay." Petie put her hand on Ryan's back and in another minute, in a haze of exhaust fumes, they disappeared down the road towards home.

For dinner along with meat loaf Carissa made green beans, scalloped potatoes, and a Jell-O mold for dessert. She set the table with gay cloth napkins she'd made herself; put out a leaf and twig centerpiece that, when her back was turned, Rose tried to prevent from leaking tiny ants all over the tablecloth. She put out a cold beer for Christie and a glass of Diet Pepsi for Rose and milk for herself and then she sat down to wait.

"Honey, he may not come home in time," Rose said gently after a little while. "It's such a beautiful dinner, it deserves to be eaten when it's at its best. Let's go ahead and start."

"I could call him," Carissa said.

"You could fix him up a nice plate and he can microwave it when he comes home."

"Why can't I call him?"

Gently Rose said, "Carissa, men like Christie, they're used to living their own way. If you press them, if you hem them in, they just fly away."

Carissa's face drooped with disappointment, then brightened. "But if he just forgot, it'd be okay to call."

Rose sighed and stood. Why should Carissa understand, at thirteen, what it had taken her years of Pogo to learn? "Sweetie, it'll embarrass him if you call him there. He knows what time dinner is. Let's fix him a plate. You can use Great-grandma's flowered one with the gold edge. It'll look real nice."

Carissa finally gave in, and Rose reached down her great-grandmother's flowered plate, the one they normally used only for Thanksgiving and Christmas, the only piece of a fifty-piece set to arrive intact over the Oregon Trail.

"Do you think he doesn't like me anymore?" Carissa asked as they finally sat down to their own tepid plates. "He asks me to do things with him, but then it's like he's angry with me."

"Angry?" Rose had never seen Christie angry with anyone.

"Well, not angry exactly. But, you know, distant."

"Oh." Rose was relieved. "That's just his way, sweetie. He doesn't mean anything by it. It's just a trick he's learned, so he can be alone on a boat even when there are people next to him twenty-four hours a day."

Carissa looked doubtful.

"Your father was the same way. He couldn't stand having people get too near him."

"But he wasn't a fisherman."

"No, he wasn't a fisherman."

Carissa frowned and then shrugged. She had always liked hearing about Pogo, good or bad, but lately she'd lost interest. Pogo was an old picture in an album. Jim, though, Jim was real.

"Well, anyway," Carissa remembered, lighting up, "he told me this afternoon he'd let me come out on the *Blue Devil* the next time there's a weekend charter that isn't filled." The *Blue Devil* was the sportfishing boat Jim was skippering for a few days so Mikey Farley could take his wife Mavis to Arizona for a while to get some relief from her arthritis.

"You could come with us," Carissa said, and started to clear the table. It was a safe offer: Rose got profoundly seasick.

"No thanks, sweetie. But it was nice of you to ask."

"Sure."

Rose poked Carissa suddenly in the ribs at the kitchen sink. "Do you think he's cute?"

"*Mom*. He's old."

Rose laughed. "Well, I do. I think he looks nice."

Carissa finished the dishes and then her homework, and by the time Christie came in she was fast asleep. He was not drunk; he was not a drinker. In the whole of the evening he had probably had only one or two beers. Stepping quietly in his worn boots, he hung his battered jacket in the closet and put his cap on a little table near the door, next to Carissa's schoolbooks. He had picked up some weight since his return, and some of the weather lines in his face had smoothed out. But there was still something elemental there, something primitive and solitary, something irreconcilable with houses and kitchens and home-cooked meals.

"She thought you'd be coming home," Rose said carefully from the kitchen, heating the plate.

"I thought I might."

"She wanted to call you."

Christie nodded and accepted the food Rose handed him. "She could've called me."

"I didn't think you'd want her to."

"No, she could've."

"She said she thought she made you angry sometimes."

"Angry?" Christie looked up from the slow, careful work he was making of his dinner. "She said I was angry?"

"Are you?"

He lowered his eyes to his plate. "She's a good girl. Why would she make me angry?"

"If she's crowding you, Jim, all you have to do is tell her. She can take it. It would be a kindness, really."

"She's not crowding me."

"Well, if she was, though."

"She's not crowding me."

"All right. I'm glad. It's just, I wouldn't want to see her hurt."

While Christie ate his dinner Rose padded around the kitchen in her slippers, getting things ready for tomorrow's soups, laying out ingredients, pots, utensils. She always moved fluidly through the lateness and the dark, as though some extra measure of grace was bestowed upon her in the vulnerable small hours of the morning. Christie finished his meal, stacked his plates and utensils neatly and brought them to the sink to wash. Rose dried them and stored them away. When they were done Christie lifted his hands to Rose's shoulders and repeated in a low voice, "She's a good girl. I wouldn't hurt her."

"I know."

"It was a fine dinner."

He pulled Rose close, and when he kissed her he smelled like salt air and rough clothing and the day's work. She breathed him in as she put her arms around his neck, and he lifted her as though she was no more than air. He took her standing in the kitchen, very carefully and in absolute silence. When she closed her eyes the only thing that communicated pleasure was the quickened rhythm of his breathing.

WHEN CARISSA woke up for school the next morning Christie had breakfast waiting for her: juice, pancakes and sausage patties, prepared on an electric skillet in the living room so he wouldn't get in the way of the day's soups in the kitchen. Carissa gave a happy cry of pleasure, her disappointment of the night before completely erased by the sight of the breakfast he had made just for her.

"Aren't you taking the *Blue Devil* out?" she asked, eagerly accepting the plate he served her.

"Nah. Rainy Tuesday in November, nobody in their right mind's wanting to go out."

"Yeah. Plus they all barf anyway in the winter, don't they?"

"Lot of them do."

Carissa nodded knowingly. "Did you eat the meat loaf?"

"It was real good."

"We thought you'd be home." Carissa pressed up syrup and bits of sausage patty with the back of her fork.

Christie nodded. "I couldn't be, though."

"Oh, that's all right," Carissa said breezily. "Sometimes my mom just gets worried, that's all."

"Does she?"

"Well, just sometimes."

"She shouldn't," Christie said. "You tell her that."

"Okay. But she's probably listening, anyway."

"I am not," Rose protested from the kitchen. Pot lids clashed.

As soon as Petie and Rose had made the morning delivery to Souperior's, Rose headed over to Sawyer with her final batch of pages for Gordon. She'd never been to his apartment before, and had been looking forward to seeing it since Petie had described it to her. But now, climbing the stairs, she had a sudden feeling of dread. She didn't know much about AIDS; as far as she knew, no one in Hubbard had ever had it, or even known anyone who'd had it. Were there rules about what you should touch and not touch? Were there certain things she shouldn't say or do? Would he mind her being there? He had become her tutor, her mentor, her guide. She didn't want to see him diminished, and most of all she didn't want to be repulsed.

He met her at the door wearing maroon suede slippers, black sweatpants and a gray sweatshirt—sick clothes, at-home clothes. He was pale and had lost weight in the two weeks since Rose had seen him, but he was fundamentally himself. She thought all over again that his was one of the gentlest faces she knew. Where hardship had made Petie tough, it had beaten Gordon instead into a soft and supple leather.

"It's beautiful," she said, looking around his apartment from the doorway. "Petie had said it was."

"Thank you. Come on in."

Rose walked admiringly through the living room. It was just the way Petie had described it: the plants, the chintz, the pictures on the walls.

There was also a box of latex medical gloves on the coffee table, partially obscured by a maidenhair fern, although Gordon wore nothing on his own hands. Was she supposed to put on a pair? In the air, along with the smell of good coffee and cinnamon, was something bleachy.

"Gordon, do I—" She gestured towards the gloves and held up her hands.

He smiled a tight little smile. "No, they're for Nadine, mostly. In case she has to touch certain things I've used."

"Oh."

He set a fresh cup of coffee in front of Rose and sat down across from her, in an armchair. "It's just a precaution. Do you understand that you're not in danger here? You can drink that safely."

"Yes, I know," said Rose, although she hadn't until he said so. "How are you? Are you beginning to be better?"

"Not just yet."

"Nadine wants you to move over."

"She's talked with you about that?"

"Yes."

"I wish she wouldn't."

"She needs a friend. She was just thinking aloud."

"It's only a sinus infection. It's treatable."

"But we're all over there, and you're here. It would be so much easier. Less lonely, too. If you were over there with us we could see you more."

"I don't need to be taken care of. You understand that."

"Yes."

"I don't want to be taken care of."

"I wasn't thinking that, Gordon. But if you won't come into the cafe—"

"You know I can't come into the cafe." Three weeks ago, just two days after he and Nadine had talked her into working on *Local Flavor*, a purple lesion the size of a cat's eye had appeared on the inside of Gordon's left wrist. Kaposi's sarcoma, Nadine had told her. The gay cancer. Having a KS lesion was just like wearing a big A on your chest, she'd said.

In L.A. it could clear out a bus seat in seconds flat. Rose had never heard of it before, much less been able to identify one inside the underside of somebody's shirt cuff, but Nadine said Gordon was insistent: if anyone experienced caught sight of the lesion, there wouldn't be a customer to be had for hundreds of miles around.

"Well, if you won't come to the cafe, then no one gets to see you except for a few minutes when we can get over here. It seems lonely, that's all. Plus Nadine misses you. I'd miss you, too, but I've been too busy writing for you."

"What have you brought today?"

Rose sighed and reached for her big envelope. "Will you at least think about it?"

"I'll think about it. Now show me what you've brought."

"All of it."

"The rest?"

"Everything."

Gordon grinned, the first honest smile of the visit. "Then let's get to work."

For the next two hours they pored over recipe spreads and edited copy on Gordon's computer, excising a word here, a sentence there, to make everything fit. Rose was mesmerized by the ease with which he manipulated the pages; she had never been close to a computer before, except in the school office or the Department of Motor Vehicles, and had never seen books built on anything at all. The more polished the pages became, the less familiar her words looked. If she'd had any idea what she was agreeing to when she said yes to Nadine and Gordon, she'd never have had the nerve.

"It's going to fly, Rose, I know it," Gordon said after he had printed out the last page. "I've got a friend in California I've already talked to about this, and he's very interested in seeing what we've got. We'll send it off tomorrow and then we'll just have to wait and see." He let Rose retrieve the whole set of pages from the printer and watched her tap them into order. She realized suddenly how ill and drawn he looked. They had worked too long. Without laying a hand on him it was obvious he was running a fever.

"Oh God, look at you," she cried, getting up and hurriedly putting her chair back at the kitchen table, where it had come from. "Why didn't you say something?"

"Because it was fun."

"Well, lie down on the sofa and let me fix you something. I've got half an hour before I go get Carissa at school. Hot or cold?"

"Nothing."

"You need to take some aspirin, and if you're taking aspirin you need to keep food in your stomach. Hot or cold?"

"Cold."

"Good. Let's see what we've got to work with."

Gordon made his way to the sofa, stretching out and pulling Rose's afghan around him. He stayed where he could see her as she puttered, probing his refrigerator, freezer and cupboards.

"Why did you smile when I said you needed to keep food in your stomach?" she asked from the kitchen.

"I wasn't smiling at that. I was just remembering how I used to take aspirin for things and it would actually make them better. It seems so simplistic."

"Don't you take aspirin?"

Gordon smiled gently and closed his eyes. "Yes. I take aspirin."

Rose nodded uncertainly and went back to her explorations. "Ice cream, milk, chocolate syrup, half a banana, a scoop of peanut butter, a dribble of vanilla. Okay. I need a blender. Do you have one?"

"There's a food processor. Second shelf."

Rose hauled it out, scooped, sliced, squeezed and poured. "Big noise," she called in the habitual warning she'd developed for Ryan so many years before, when he still startled so badly. When the milk shake was foamy she poured it into a tumbler and brought it into the living room. Gordon was asleep, a pen still absently caught between his fingers.

Setting the tumbler on the coffee table, Rose secured the afghan under his shoulders so it wouldn't slide off and put her hand very gently, very briefly, to his forehead. Hot, but not incandescent. She should wake him for the aspirin, but she didn't have the heart. Bending over him as she had over Carissa and Loose and Ryan so often, she could see straight back to the young boy he must have been, moon pale and shy, a stammerer, wanting to please, damned for being smarter than everyone, doomed to years of speech therapy. Impulsively she put her lips to his forehead in a fever check, a mother's kiss, a prayer to will away all harm. Then, on tip-toe, she let herself out the door and closed it soundlessly behind her.

R<small>OSE AND</small> Carissa stopped at Souperior's on the way home. The cafe was deserted except for Nadine, who sat alone in one of the booths by the windows, folding napkins and watching a thin rain forming on the panes as though the air itself was weeping. Carissa went straight into the cafe's kitchen to make a cup of hot chocolate with the espresso machine, the way Nadine had taught her. Rose slipped into the booth and backed her coat off her shoulders.

"We finished," she said. "All the pages are done. He was really pleased."

"He's so excited about this, you have no idea."

"He said he had a friend who might publish it."

"Not just a friend. An editor at a very important regional publishing house. He and Gordon have known each other for a long time." Nadine neglected to say that this man, too, was living an AIDS countdown, and a certain amount of his responsiveness came from the fact that he had nothing to lose. "If he's still interested once he's looked at the manu-script, Gordon wants to go down there to talk with him. Gordon should be better by then."

"I think you should call him in a little while," Rose said.

"Why?"

"It's okay," Rose soothed. "But he was running a fever. No more than a hundred, probably, hundred-point-five. But he fell asleep before he took any aspirin. I was fixing him a milk shake, but he conked out before he could drink any of it, and I didn't wake him up."

In the kitchen, the steamer on the espresso machine hissed and spat furiously before succumbing to Carissa's pitcher of milk. "How long ago was that?" Nadine asked. In the muted light of a Souperior's evening, her face looked pale and tired, her overbite pronounced. Gordon wasn't the only one who'd been losing weight. She'd tied a bright rag in her hair, but it wasn't fooling anybody.

"Half an hour, forty minutes ago. I stayed as long as I could. Carissa was waiting for me."

"I'm going to call tomorrow morning and *make* them switch him to a different antibiotic. Oh, I *wish* he'd move over here. He won't even let me find us a bigger apartment we could share in Sawyer. As it is I don't get over there to his place until eight-thirty or nine, and half the time he hasn't eaten any dinner yet. I almost never get back over here before midnight."

Rose looked at Nadine sympathetically. She'd had no idea. Petie still made fun of Nadine for her naïveté and convictions, and was outspoken in her certainty that she and Gordon would go broke by the end of the winter—if they were lucky and lasted that long. Looking across the table in the gloomy twilight, Rose thought Nadine looked almost as ill as Gordon, hunched over her coffee mug, picking absently at a blemish in the crockery. She leaned across the table and touched Nadine's hand. It was icy. "Look. Let me come down here and do dinner and close up for you for a while. Then you could get over there earlier. Petie could probably even take a couple of nights a week."

With an extraordinary effort, Nadine smiled. Her eyes were wet. "Thank you, Rose. No. You've got families. Your boyfriend is home."

"They wouldn't mind. And Carissa could help me. She'd love it."

"I can't afford to pay you," Nadine said flatly. "You've already been great about the book, all that time and work. We're very grateful. No. I'm thinking of closing the cafe for dinner except for maybe Friday, Saturday and Sunday, at least during the winter. Business is so bad it won't matter much, and that way I could get home earlier."

Carissa emerged from the kitchen and crossed the room on long colt legs. "She's beautiful," said Nadine absently, watching her. "Have I said that before?"

"No."

"Well. Nothing needs to be decided right now. They'll change his antibiotic and he'll get better again and we'll have some more time to think about it. If you hear of anything over here, though, a nice bright apartment or even a little house if it's clean, would you let me know?"

"I'll let you know."

"Thanks, Rose." Nadine slid out of the booth and straightened the tablecloth after herself. "Maybe, just for tonight, though, I'll close a little early."

Rose shrugged her coat on and gathered purse and keys. "Hey," she called from the door. "If you're late coming in tomorrow, I'll just go ahead and open for you." And she and Carissa ducked out into the evening.

Alone again, Nadine pulled out a SOUP'S ON TOMORROW sign—she and Gordon didn't like CLOSED—propped it in the window, then went back into the kitchen to close up. The pitcher Carissa had used for her steamed milk was clean, set upside down next to the sink to dry; the cocoa had been put away and the counter wiped down. A good girl, Nadine thought, who showed every promise of carrying on her mother's uncomplicated warm nature. She and Gordon had been lucky to find Rose, would be doubly lucky to keep her once she knew Nadine was going to let Petie go at the end of the week. It was a decision she had only reached yesterday; she hadn't even told Gordon yet. But they had no choice. What had seemed to them like a gutsy adventure—moving to Oregon and opening a cafe, being their own bosses and reaping the benefits and challenges all for themselves—now seemed like sheer burden and folly, an endless drain on time and resources they did not have.

Finished in the kitchen, Nadine stacked several containers of soups and salads on a table—dinner for her and Gordon, at least she didn't have to cook—and poured herself a last mug of coffee against the drive to Sawyer and back. She slid down the length of a pew and settled back, making herself tick off the "pro" side of the list. Petie's husband was working again. The Coolbaughs would be all right, and besides, if Petie pushed, Nadine would still contract with her for bread. Rose loved to cook, and seemed fond of Gordon: she would stay. Nadine would have her cut down her quantities and they'd violate at last the policy Petie had always picked on: no more different fresh soups every day. They'd freeze, they'd recycle. They'd get by.

And hopefully *Local Flavor* would still pull for them, although it was now mid-November and Gordon, so excited that he might have discovered someone, wasn't even talking about self-publishing anymore but thinking sugarplum thoughts of rave reviews in the *L.A. Times.*

Gordon.

Whenever she thought of him after a respite of a minute or two, Nadine's stomach did a little jeté of anxiety. She knew he was deeply frightened. They both were. When the purple lesion on his wrist had appeared it had only been one, and small, and although it was ominous, of course, it had been somehow too modest to really frighten them once they got over the initial shock. Didn't he still feel well, except for the perpetually swollen lymph glands, the occasional bouts of fatigue and diarrhea? And hadn't the chemo techniques gotten better and better? And who really, *really* knew about the witch-away powers of AZT? Hadn't he managed to stay clear of the host of opportunistic infections that plagued all the other AIDS people they had known in L.A.? All this brittle hopefulness they had conjured in the face of what they knew to be statistically true: he had nowhere left to go but down, and probably within two years or less. But mostly they'd remained perky—or mired in denial—as long as he had been feeling well. Now he was sick in earnest and the vigil had finally begun. They'd learn how to live this way, too, but it was going to take time.

Nadine stirred her cool cup of coffee, her chin in her hand, ruminating. Outside it was completely dark, and all she could see at the windows was herself and Souperior's reflected back again, interrupted in streaks by the tears of the rain.

Chapter 7

PETIE WAS laid off at the beginning of the week. Poor Nadine had kept going around and around, explaining that business had been slower than they'd expected while their overhead had been higher, and if it was slow in November it was going to be everything they could do to stay open come January. She had blushed and stammered and finally Petie had decided to put her out of her misery. She put her hand on Nadine's forearm—they were stalled in the kitchen doorway—and said, not unkindly, "Hey. It's okay. I'd have chosen Rose, too." Nadine had nearly wept with relief and gratitude.

On impulse when she left, Petie turned the snout of her little car northward. The Sea View Motel was a single-story horseshoe perched on top of a little hill on the east side of the highway, its office tucked between units six and seven like a mother hen guarding her brood. Each of the twelve guest rooms had floral curtains and spreads made by Marge; each had a screen door protected by aluminum swirls from getting punched in by careless guests; each had shag carpeting, green for the even-numbered rooms, orange for the odd, installed when Marge and Larry bought the place in 1979 and still shampooed by Larry every four months, even in the off season. The Sea View was tidy inside and out, and tended to attract young honeymooners driving festooned pickups, older people taking a break from their RVs, families with young children visiting the beach: decent people. Larry had been known to turn away potential guests he thought looked like trouble. *Shoot,* he'd tell them. *Ain't that* NO VACANCY *sign lit up out there? No? Must have forgot to turn it on again. Old people, you know, we'd forget our names if they wasn't on our Social Security checks. Sorry, folks. You try the Bailey Courts down south of town. They have a real nice place.*

Petie pulled up to the Sea View office and got out without taking the keys from the ignition. Through the window she could see Larry behind the desk, working on a wall clock. He was thick and jug-eared and he wielded a screwdriver with the delicacy of a surgical tool. He'd been a diesel mechanic for thirty years, until he'd had a heart attack and his shop had canned him. That had been in Albany, over in the Valley. He had only been fifty-nine and anyway he couldn't stand being still, so he and Marge had decided to sell everything and buy the Sea View for cheap from the previous owner's widow. The place had been a dump then, but look at it now.

"Well, look who's here!" Larry said when he heard the harness bells on the doorknob ring. "Why, Marge was just saying the other day how you were getting to be a stranger." He came around the desk and gave Petie a crushing one-armed hug. "It's good to see you, honey. You're looking real good. Let me find Marge and tell her you're here. I think she's in number four, putting in some clean towels. That Rhonda. Well, I'll let Marge tell you."

Larry called Marge on the phone and in a minute she came bustling in the door, breathing hard, soft and warm and generous as an old sofa cushion, thirty pounds overweight, freshly permed, lightly emphysemic. She was smiling so hard Petie could see the edge of her upper plate. "Oh, honey, what a nice surprise!" She folded Petie in a big, honest, country hug. "We were just talking about you, weren't we, Larry. That Rhonda. Shoot. We miss you around here."

Marge poured Petie a mug of coffee from the perpetual pot behind the desk. Neither she nor Larry drank it, because of her nerves and his heart, but they always kept a pot on for the guests. Petie flopped down on the soft old couch by the window, and Marge heaved herself down, too, patting the back of Petie's hand.

"So what's going on with Rhonda?" Petie said. "She still drinking?"

Marge sighed. "Well, sure, but it's not just that. You know she's been seeing that Clayton See fellow, he comes down here from Tillamook all the time. The good Lord must know what he does for a living, but Larry and me, we sure can't figure it out. Anyway, it was last Wednesday and we'd had some people in number twelve, a young couple married one year exactly, real nice kids from over by Silverton, expecting their first baby next March. Larry'd just checked them out—honey, you sure you don't want to tell this story, it's going to embarrass me to death—and I'd sent Rhonda down there to clean up. Well, it gets later and later and I need her to run over to the laundry and fetch me my linens back, you know how we do in the winter when we don't use enough for them to do deliveries. Anyway, I look out the window and see Clayton's truck out there and I put two and two together. I was getting real mad, wasn't I honey, so I go down there to twelve and I knock on the door but I don't hear anything. So I knock again and I still don't hear anything, so I'm thinking maybe she really did finish in there and moved on, except we didn't have any other guests that night to clean up after. I know, honey, I'm making this a long story, I never could tell a decent story, jokes, either, but I'm almost to the end, I swear. Anyway, I get my master key, you know, just to be sure, and I open up the door, and there they are rolling around buck naked, and *on clean sheets*."

Marge's face was bright with indignation. She put a hand to her chest to catch her breath. "Well, I was so angry I took one of those dirty pillowcases she'd dumped by the door and I started hitting them with it, I mean really whaling." Suddenly she broke down and started giggling, and Petie and Larry did, too, big helpless belly laughs. After a few minutes Marge wiped her eyes and sighed. "Shoot," she said. "I wasn't in my right mind, I'll tell you."

"She's just lucky Clayton didn't drag out a gun," Larry said, getting back to his clock. "That boy's a bad one."

Marge snickered and slapped Petie's knee lightly. "He didn't exactly have nowhere to hide one, now did he, honey?"

Larry shook his head.

"You better be real careful with him," Petie said, sobering. "He runs drugs, and I hear he's pretty good at it, too. Rhonda never was too smart about men. Well, she never was too smart, period."

"I don't know. The real truth of it is, she just don't fit in here with Larry and me," Marge said. "We've about decided to let her go."

"When?" said Petie.

"Well, we were going to do it right away, but we really want to see the grandkids at Christmas, you know, like we do, and we need someone back here."

"I keep telling her we could just close, but she won't do it," Larry told Petie.

"That's a good week for us, Christmas to New Year's," Marge protested. "He knows it is, too. So we'll probably wait until we come back. We worry about it, though. We haven't completely decided."

"What if I take care of it for you?" Petie said.

"Oh, that's so nice of you, honey." Marge reached over and squeezed Petie's hand. "But you've got your family and your new job."

"Not by then I won't."

"Uh-oh," Marge said.

"I just got laid off. I've only got a week left."

"Oh, honey!" Marge cried. "Now, that's a shame. And you thought they were good people, too."

"They're okay. They waited until Eddie was solid with Pepsi before they did anything. And they're keeping Rose on."

Marge looked unconvinced.

"So you're really thinking you could come back with us?" Larry said.

"Well, I was thinking of it. If you needed any help."

"Why, honey, that's wonderful! Isn't it, Larry? Petie coming back here?"

"*Hell*, yes," Larry said quietly. "We couldn't pay you more, though, Petie. You know that."

"I know," Petie said. "It's okay."

Marge's eyes grew bright. Her Christmases with her three kids and seven grandkids meant more to her than anything else all year. She pressed Petie's hand, and then kept it in her own. "We'll be so glad to have you back. You just don't know."

Petie stood and patted Marge's hand. "That's okay. Listen, I've got to go."

"Listen to us going on and I haven't even asked you about the babies yet," Marge cried.

"They're okay. Ryan's Ryan, you know, and Loose's having a little trouble in school, but they're okay," Petie said, pouring her leftover coffee down the little sink in the Pullman kitchen at the back of the office. She rinsed and dried the mug and hung it up on its peg. "Okay, you two, I better go."

"Okay, honey," Larry said, one-arming her again as she passed by. "We love you."

"Oh! Wait just one more minute," Marge said, heaving herself out of the sofa. "I have something for you to take for the boys, just something little. Just wait right here, they're back in the back room."

Petie shrugged into her jacket and Larry shared an amused look and head shake with Petie. That Marge.

She came out in a minute, puffing, and held out to Petie two net bags holding plastic beach pail sets shaped like turtles. "Here. Aren't these just darling? I was going to give them to the grandbabies, but what are they going to do with beach toys in Tempe? A salesman brought them around last week and we kept a few just to be polite."

Petie tucked the pails under one arm and gave Marge a quick hug. "Thanks. I really better go. You talk to Rhonda and let me know when you want me to start. Anytime after a week from tomorrow."

"All right, hon. Bye-bye."

Side by side, Marge and Larry watched her get into her car and waved until Petie had turned onto the highway. She waved back as she pulled away. The plastic beach toys clashed together on the floorboards. Neither of the boys would be caught dead with them, but it didn't matter. She'd treasure them for a while and then sell them at her next yard sale.

·   ·   ·

From a distance, the hills east of Sawyer seemed to roll away pristine and virginal as schoolgirls, but this was an illusion. In fact, on acre after acre, switchbacks teetered along the ridgetops, balanced there by cat skinners who drove the big timber company Caterpillars with the delicacy and surefootedness of mountain goats. These roads had no names, no mileposts, no directional signs and no shoulders, just mile after single-lane mile of decaying track threading in and out of new and recently planted clear-cuts.

Petie knew most of the roads well. So did Schiff. So, of course, did two-thirds of Hubbard, but who else was going to be out there jouncing around seven miles east of Sawyer at one o'clock on a wet Wednesday afternoon in November? They hadn't seen another vehicle since they'd turned off the highway. Schiff's muscle-bound truck took the ruts and potholes stiffly. Petie rode with her legs tucked up Indian-style, watching out the window. She wore no expression whatsoever. Her hands were out of view, stuffed into the pockets of her old denim battle jacket, which she wore tightly buttoned. Inside her pocket she toyed with fifteen new crisp dollars.

Schiff sat more easily, even athletically, behind the wheel, one arm resting on the door, the other riding the top of the steering wheel. Inside his beard he was smiling. It had been twenty minutes since he'd picked Petie up at her car on a back street in Sawyer, and she was still nervous as a cat. To guard herself any more tightly she'd have to be wearing a padlock.

Schiff had no idea what Petie was going to do, what either one of them would do. When he first turned off the highway onto the logging roads he half expected her to jump out of the truck and run away. But Petie had just stared out the window. She smelled faintly of soup—bean and sausage, Schiff guessed. She always smelled of some kind of soup or bread. It was better than any perfume. He had always loved the smell of food on a woman. He wished she'd say something, though. He didn't enjoy silence, although he could use it effectively enough when he put his mind to it. He was easier with talk, though, being a talker himself.

To see if he could shake her up, he steered the truck through a few unnecessary potholes and grinned. Petie shot him a look that said she knew what he was up to. Eddie always said she was real smart. Was she? Smarter than Schiff? He'd gone out with a smart girl once after he left the carnival; a college girl, rich girl, she'd worn a little string of pearls that were worth a couple of months of Schiff's fleabag rent if he'd stolen them, which he prided himself on not doing, broke as he was. Her father had run a bank. The father had hated him. Schiff was screwing the girl every chance he got, often in her little pink bedroom just down the hall from the family room where the father read the newspaper, so who could blame the guy? Certainly not Schiff, who had sympathized completely and tried to stay out of his way. Not that Schiff had been the girl's first, but the father wouldn't know that, and anyway the others had undoubtedly been pretty boys, college boys the father wouldn't have been afraid of. Even then Schiff had understood that he was scary; now he looked back at the pictures from those years—the squirrelly eyes, the dazzling fuck-you, walk-in-front-of-trains smile—and marveled that he had not even once been shot by one of the fathers, boyfriends, brothers. Not that there hadn't been some close calls. At any rate, the girl had thought Schiff was romantic because he had shrapnel buried like a hundred peppercorns under the skin of his shoulders, and because he'd been in a lot of trouble in the last couple of years. The girl had liked to brush his hair—he had had more of it back then, brown and glossy as a girl's, and he'd grown it long—and she gave him money sometimes; twice she bought him books he pretended to read. Once she took him to a fancy restaurant and he tried very hard not to embarrass her. She had been nice and gentle and earnest, and she'd been pretty good in the sack, too, but she'd started closing in on him just the same, and then she'd begun crying a lot. Surely something had happened at the end, but Schiff had no recollection of what.

Sitting on the seat beside him, Petie still wasn't talking, and it was starting to annoy him. It wasn't like he'd forced her to meet him, although there'd been that tiny financial incentive; he had been sure she'd come for the company. When he pictured the two of them together—

something he'd been doing lately—she didn't look like this little sparrow, all puffed up against bad weather. In his imagination they were in bed together, but, oddly, not during sex. Instead they were cuddled together among big white pillows and crisp white sheets, Petie's head on his bare shoulder, that black hair spread out and glossy. Carla hated to cuddle. Schiff had too, when he was young, had actually taken pride in it: here was a man who couldn't be held, who was nothing but a sweet strong wind blowing through. Well, he'd been younger then, he hadn't needed the shelter; or maybe he just hadn't minded the elements as much.

He eased the truck over the smoothest parts of the road, steering carefully. "Eddie said you were laid off," he said.

"Yeah."

"So what will you do?"

Petie shrugged, not looking at him. He could just make out the hard little edge of her shoulder through her denim jacket. "I don't know. I can keep doing the bread, if I want."

"What's it pay?"

"Couple of bucks a loaf for twelve loaves. Not enough."

"Jesus. I'll say."

"It's probably more than she can afford, though."

"Yeah, right. Two hotshots cash out everything and move up from L.A.? They're both younger than I am, plus the guy doesn't seem to work at all. C'mon. There's a lot of bucks there. They just want you to think they're broke so you'll work real cheap."

Petie shrugged noncommittally and squinted through the windshield as they drove into a little squall of rain. "I'll probably go back to the Sea View," she said.

"You think they'd take you back?"

"Yeah. Business is lousy but they're not real happy with Rhonda. Marge's been talking about letting her go and filling in herself, but they want to go down to Tempe and see their grandkids for Christmas."

"Didn't they get new beds in a few months ago?" Schiff cocked a suggestive eyebrow, but Petie was focused on something else.

"Listen," she said. "How solid is Eddie with you?"

Schiff frowned. He didn't joke about business. "He's solid if he don't screw up. He's a good driver, and my customers like him."

"Screw up like how?"

"I don't know. Drive the truck into a ditch, deliver the wrong orders, forget to come to work. Steal. Stupid stuff."

"He wouldn't do those things."

"Nah," Schiff agreed, although privately he wasn't so sure. How many jobs had Eddie Coolbaugh had just since Schiff came to town seven years ago? The guy was nice but he was a loser just the same, the purest one Schiff had met in a long time.

"So, good," Petie said. Suddenly she looked better. Seeing her brighten, Schiff pulled the truck off the road into a recent clear-cut, nothing for miles around but stumps and rubble. The ground bogged slightly under the tires, but it would hold, and if it didn't he could always winch himself out. He loved his truck. In it, he was capable of greatness.

"So, let's get to it," he said. He switched off the engine and settled himself against the door, his arm reaching her way across the seat back. Petie narrowed her eyes at him; inside her jacket pockets he could see her hands ball up. She was plenty capable of decking him. God, he loved this; it reminded him of high school. He smiled at her good-naturedly, let a few beats go by. "Lunch." He gestured towards her bag on the floor.

Petie colored, crossed her legs tightly from ankle to thigh and pulled up a paper bag, setting it between them. There was plenty of room; the seat was wide as a bed, unyielding as a pew. Deftly she spread out between them five peanut butter and jelly sandwiches, two Hostess Ding Dongs, two boxes of apple-raspberry juice. The sandwiches were tiny, hardly larger than cigarette packs, and were made on anadama bread Petie had baked for Souperior's that morning.

"Has Carla ever worked except at the Anchor?" Petie said, leaning lightly on the name, divvying up the sandwiches: one for her, four for Schiff. A Ding Dong and juice box apiece.

Schiff eyed the little sandwiches skeptically. He was going to go back to work hungry, he could tell. "Nah. And the Anchor's just for beer money. I've told her she doesn't have to work."

"She and Rose sure never got along too well."

"Carla don't get along too well with anyone, especially women. She's mean."

"She's okay."

Schiff shrugged, and popped half a sandwich in his mouth. He didn't really want to be talking about Carla, it was depressing. He chewed, swallowed, looked out the window and suddenly said, "Sometimes I wonder how the hell it happened, you know? God, when I first met her she was sweet all the time, and she looked so good you could watch her walk away forever." He felt Petie next to him, listening. "She still looks good walking away, only she keeps on coming back, you know what I mean?" He cracked a thin smile, polished off the other sandwich half, subsided pensively. Carla had been fun once, too. Back then, that high thin whinny of hers hadn't sounded witchy when she laughed. And she had long beautiful fingers she liked to run lightly over his arms and chest as she got sleepy, which made him break out all over in ecstatic goose bumps. Hers were the fingers of a goddess, a queen, a courtesan. A trickster. She hadn't touched him voluntarily, except for show, in years. God almighty, how was he supposed to have known she'd turn out to be so awful?

He pulled himself together. "Nah," he said, "Carla, she's okay. She just gets bored. I mean, that's the thing about Carla, now that Randi's growing up. When Randi was little they were always doing stuff together, sewing and baking and shit. Carla, she thought Randi would always be her best friend. But then Randi left her in the dust a couple years ago, and Carla didn't see it coming. And it isn't just that Randi's got other stuff to do, you know, it's that she dumped Carla because Carla's old. You know how kids are. Carla can't stand that. So now she goes to the Wayside and plays video poker all afternoon."

"I heard she was down there a lot."

"Yeah, well, she's cutting back, though."

"That's good."

"Yeah. I don't know. I don't know what the fuck difference it makes, really."

"Well."

They both sat quietly for a minute.

"So, I didn't think we'd be out here talking about Carla," Schiff said.

"What did you think we'd be talking about?"

"Sex?" Schiff said hopefully.

"Give me a break. So why do you stay, anyway?"

Schiff shrugged. "Maybe I'm just too old to get cleaned out again," he said. He didn't feel like talking about it anymore. He polished off the last of his sandwiches, popped an entire Ding Dong in his mouth, took a sip from his ridiculous juice box, wiped his beard neatly with his fingertips. "So how's Christie doing?" he said. "He settled in?"

"He's fixing up Rose's car. He told her he's going to have a surprise at Christmas. Maybe he's going to turn it into some kind of low-rider. Wouldn't that be something? He could do it. He's a good body man."

"He's not the only one." Schiff leered absently while he watched Petie put away the plastic produce bag in which she'd brought their sandwiches. She smoothed it flat with her quick little hands, then folded it in half, then in half again, then tucked it inside her purse. Schiff wouldn't let Carla reuse anything, not even Ziploc bags. His mother, slovenly in so many ways, had been obsessive about husbanding kitchen materials. He and Howard had had to wash out plastic wrap, save margarine tubs, reuse paper bags until they were soft as felt. Delia had cuffed their heads hard if they threw out any reusable piece of aluminum foil bigger than an index card. He still couldn't stand the rotten feel of reused foil.

Frowning a little with concentration, Petie stowed the last bits of their trash in her paper bag and set it on the seat between them. She held out her hand and Schiff passed over his empty juice box obediently. He pictured her moving around her house that way, quick and commanding, absorbed in tasks, all her toughness evaporated into the safety of home. And now, for an instant, here, too. Schiff liked that.

"So what was the deal with your first wife?" Petie asked, settling back again on the seat, not quite as far away as she had been.

He considered the question. "Mary. She was mean, too, meaner than Carla by a mile, meanest woman I ever met. She was an Indian girl, Nez Perce, but small, even smaller than you, and beautiful, she looked just like a doll. She stabbed me one time for coming home from work late. That was down in Klamath Falls, when I was working for a mill. They call a union meeting, I stay, and bam! I come home and she stabs me in the arm with a meat fork. Said she knew it wasn't a union meeting, said I'd been out with some girl from the A&W down there. I told her if I was going to step out on her, for Christ sake, I wouldn't be stupid enough to stop for a quickie on my way home from work. I told her if I ever decided to fool around, she'd never know about it."

"Did you?"

"Did I what?"

"Fool around on her."

"What do you think?"

"I don't know."

"Well, I'll tell you, *she* did," Schiff said, looking out the window. "I get all these nice letters from her in Vietnam because she figures what the hell, I'm probably going to die over there anyway. Then I get home and find out she's got a *kid*. She's been humping my best buddy my whole last tour. Says it wasn't her fault, because I'd been away so long and didn't come home on leave. It's *my* fault." Schiff flipped the wind-shield wipers on, switched them off. "So, you know, some homecoming. My first night back I drove my car through the front window of my buddy's gas station. Broke one of my kneecaps in four pieces, dislocated the other one. He drove me to the hospital. It was good to see him."

"You're kidding."

Schiff cracked his window open. Petie was turned to him, her eyes bright and sharp. He ran his fingers absently through his beard. When was the last time someone had listened to him? "I ended up going back with her for a while—a year and a half. The kid turned out to be great. Her name was Angela, except everyone called her Angel. She looked like one of those kids in the paintings with the big eyes. We were buds, I took her everywhere. I'd put her way up on my shoulders and she'd hold on to my hair with both hands, never said a word, eyes as big as baseballs. The day I left she just stood there in the window watching me. I still dream about that sometimes. Neither of us had told her anything, but kids, they know what's going on. I could tell Mary was trying to make her come away from the window, but Angel, she just stood there. I left a thousand bucks in a savings account for her but Mary probably spent it all on herself the first month. I heard Mary married some rancher out in eastern Oregon after a while. Couple of years ago I thought about looking for the girl, but Carla didn't like it. Hell, she's probably already married by now with her own kid."

"I guess she hasn't tried to find you."

"Nah."

"So why didn't you come back when you got leave over there?"

"There were some things I had to see."

"Like what?"

"Singapore. Thailand. They were the most beautiful places I've ever been."

For a while it was quiet in the truck.

"If I'd known," Schiff said softly, "I never would have come back."

"Known what?"

He looked at her almost tenderly. He could have wept. He cleared his throat instead, switched on the ignition and put the car in gear. "That you wouldn't sleep with me," he said, and turned the truck around for home. Neither of them spoke again until they reached the outskirts of Sawyer.

"They really don't have any money," Petie said then, as though there had been no lapse in the conversation.

"Who doesn't?"

"Nadine and Gordon. They really don't. The only thing that'll keep them from going under is if they get more local business."

"So?"

"Well, Rose would be out of a job, for one thing. Plus I like them. They're weird, especially Nadine, but they're good people. I mean, they're trying hard. It would be real good, Schiff, if they could keep the place."

"I've never heard anyone say they were that great."

"I'm saying it."

"They canned you."

"They should have done it a month ago."

Schiff pulled the truck alongside Petie's car. "So, what are you saying?"

Petie gathered up her purse and her junk and opened the door halfway. "I'm saying you know a lot of people. Just talk the place up. You could do that. Hell, take Carla and Randi there for dinner one night. Or maybe the dirt bike club could meet there this month. You know Rose is a good cook, so no one's going to get poisoned or anything, and it would help. It really would."

"Jesus." Schiff held up his hands. "All right. I'll see what I can do."

Petie gave a curt little nod and hopped out. She was so small she disappeared from view completely once she'd slammed the door. Schiff was just about to pull away when the door was yanked open again.

"Hey," Petie said. "Thanks."

"Yeah."

Just as she reached the outskirts of Hubbard the storm that had been building over the horizon for the past hour broke through like a bad head cold. Hailstones big as BBs stalked down the highway, dogged by rain. The boys would be just about to start walking home. Petie turned the nose of the car into the squall; the car hesitated, coughed and began favoring its bad wiper.

Petie had heard that turkeys were so stupid they drowned by opening their mouths during rainstorms. Most children, in her opinion, weren't a whole lot better off. As she pulled up to the curb they poured

out of the elementary school in the usual states of joyful unreadiness—
no jackets at all, or jackets without hoods. All winter the school smelled
muggy and sour from so many soggy children.

The crowd thinned, but neither Ryan nor Loose appeared. When the
last straggler had emerged, Petie switched off the engine and sprinted
inside the school's front door, where all the smells reached out and
seized her, as they always did. This had been her school, too, hers and
Rose's, and it had looked and smelled pretty much the same then as it
did now, except for newer desks and chalkboards: the same uneven,
well-worn fir floors, the same construction-paper alphabet circling the
ceiling, the same cheap Pilgrim and Indian and turkey cutouts taped on
the walls. You could almost see their ghosts sitting in the second row of
the first-grade classroom, sweet-faced Rose still years away from her
pretty breasts; scrawny Petie full of ribs and knees and elbows sharp as
hairpins, friends at first through an arbitrary seat assignment. It was the
last year they were too young to pick out who was poor, whose mother
was a slut, whose father was drinking, who was getting hit. But even
through fourth grade they were happy years of hot school lunches and
Dixie cups of stale ice cream you ate with flat wooden spoons and
pennies-for-Unicef boxes Old Man raided and gave back to Petie half
full, to turn in on the morning after Halloween. Turkey years. Then
Petie's mother had died.

No one was in the first-grade classroom, but Petie could hear voices
down the hall, from the gym. She was drifting that way, woozy from sen-
sory flashbacks, when suddenly a small boy burst past her, a first or second grader, in tears. An instant later a woman appeared in the doorway,
put her hands on her hips and sighed. The child disappeared into the
boys' bathroom. Seeing Petie, the teacher pressed her lips together and
shook her head. Petie didn't recognize her.

"We have *got* to get more supervision in here, we've just got to," she
said, as though someone had been arguing with her. "Do you have children in Latchkey?"

"No, but sometimes they hang around until I come pick them up,
when the weather's bad."

"Well, it's a fiasco, plain and simple. Good Lord, look in there! We don't have a program anymore, we have bedlam. Two-thirds of our students can't go home after school, and they don't have anywhere else to go so they're staying right here. We're not set up for this. Ten kids, *maybe* fifteen, yes. Forty, no way." The woman suddenly stopped and then smiled ruefully at Petie. "Wow. Sorry. It's not like it's your fault."

"It's okay."

"I should go after that child, but I'm the only one in here and I'm afraid to leave them alone."

"I could watch them for a minute."

"I wish, but I don't think it would be legal. You could check on the boy, though. That would be great. His name is Harry Reilly. He's one of our smallest boys, so he gets picked on."

"Okay. Just tell my kids I'm here, if they start to leave. I'm Petie Coolbaugh—Loose and Ryan's mom."

"Oh. Yes, I know them. Well, thanks. Try and get Harry to come back to the gym with you. Tell him he can't stay in the bathroom for the whole afternoon."

Petie found the boy sitting beneath the row of small sinks, his knees pulled up under his chin. He was frail, like Ryan had been when he was six and he had the same shocky, hunted look.

"Hey," said Petie, easing herself under the sinks near Harry. She smoothed out the wrinkles in her jeans, retied her shoes. "Want a Life Saver?" She fished around in her purse and brought out a linty roll she always kept on hand in case she needed to bribe the boys into submission. The child nodded, and Petie peeled down the paper. "Red or pineapple?"

"Red."

Petie handed it to him. "I never liked the pineapple ones, either. Let's throw it away. It's got fuzz on it, anyway." Petie gave the Life Saver a free throw into the metal trash container on the far wall. It rebounded off the tile wall and dropped in. "All *right*."

The boy watched her doubtfully, sucking prodigiously on his Life Saver. He'd probably used a pacifier until he was four. He had the overbite for it. Petie stowed the Life Savers back in her bag. The boy stared at his feet.

"So what happened in there? Did some kids gang up on you?"

Harry shook his head.

"Someone hit you?"

He shook his head again.

"Did you get called a bad name?"

No.

"Did they tell you not to tell?"

Yes.

"Was it a bunch of people? Just one? What grade, third? Second? First? First. Oh, no. Let me guess. Was it Loose Coolbaugh? It was. It was Loose, wasn't it?"

Harry punched the end of his shoelace in and out of the eyelets in his sneakers. The corners of his mouth trembled.

"I'm sorry, sweetie," Petie said. "He doesn't mean to be such a shit." She retrieved the Life Savers and offered the boy another one. He popped it in his mouth.

"What exactly did he do?" Petie asked. "If I knew, I could try to make sure it doesn't happen again. It's okay. I won't tell on you, cross my heart." Petie crossed her heart.

The boy's answer came out in a whisper. "He touched my weenie." He worked his shoelace in and out.

"Your—oh."

"I don't like it. I don't want him to do it anymore."

"Has he done that to you before?"

The boy nodded miserably.

Jesus.

Petie patted the boy's matchstick arm. "Come on. I've got to take you back to the gym now, your teacher needs to know where you are. Okay? I'll make sure that child never lays a hand on you again. I promise."

She pushed herself out into the room, and reluctantly the boy emerged from under the sinks, too. She took Harry's sticky hand and walked him back to the gym. The teacher saw them, and looked at Petie inquiringly.

"He's fine," Petie said, handing him over. "He didn't want to talk about it. Have you seen my kids?"

The teacher stood Harry in front of her and put her hands on his shoulders. "I think they're over there. Well, Loose is. I don't see—"

Petie put two fingers to her mouth and blew an ear-shattering whistle. The entire gym froze. Loose turned reluctantly from a little knot of boys across the room and shuffled Petie's way, Ryan emerged from beneath a set of risers, and the room broke up again into a kaleidoscope of children.

"Time to go home." Petie took Loose roughly by the arm and steered him out of the gym. Ryan trailed after.

In the car, Petie slapped the back of Loose's head hard with her open hand. "Why did you pick on that poor little kid? Jesus fucking Christ, Loose, he's about half your size and he was scared to death."

"It wasn't me, it was some other kids," Loose lied hopefully.

"Bullshit. *Bullshit*."

The three of them were silent the rest of the way home. Both boys got out of the car as quickly as possible and walked ahead, jackets zipped tight.

"Get out of my sight," Petie hissed at Loose once they were inside. "I mean it. You stay away from me." They stared at each other in the middle of the kitchen. Petie took in the crewcut head, round as shot, the honey-colored eyes underslung with bags, as though prematurely debauched.

She whispered, "God almighty, you look just like your grandfather."

Loose ran from the room.

"The son of a bitch."

She stood alone in the kitchen, an incipient migraine clamped onto her temples like the furious red-hot hand of God.

Chapter 8

EVER SINCE she went back to work at the Sea View, Petie had been keeping her thoughts to herself. Rose didn't press; it went that way with Petie sometimes. When Petie bleached out her hair she'd also stopped talking for five days. That had passed. This would pass. The thing with Petie was, you couldn't expect to understand all the time. Sometimes you just had to settle back and catch a glimpse of whatever you could from the passenger side.

And then, Rose had been busy. For a week she had taken over at Souperior's in the afternoons so Nadine could go check in with Gordon and then come back by five. When Gordon had finally begun to improve, Nadine invited Rose to stay on for a few more afternoons to learn the simple bookkeeping and purchasing systems, in case they ever needed her to take over. Rose's life was gliding by in a lovely blur of good soup and purposeful days and warm uncomplicated nights with Christie. A good life.

Once, a long time ago in Doggett, Rose had lain beside Pogo and said, *How do you think this will end?* It had been a hot rich sweet night, full of growing things within and without, ten o'clock and just dark, the kind of night through which it was best to lie beside someone. Carissa had been two months from being born. Rose had been lying on her back, hands clasped contentedly around her belly, breathing in the fragrances and thinking about a miniseries installment she and Pogo were watching on TV. She'd turned her head on the pillow and said, *How do you think it's going to end?*

And Pogo had said softly into the darkness, *I don't know, darlin'. Probably one day I'll just go.*

Less than a year later Pogo was gone, but from it Rose had learned that by anticipating neither misery nor joy, she might attain serenity. Christie would go back to Alaska again one day soon; Gordon would get sicker. But not right now. None of those things was going to happen right now, or even, probably, tomorrow.

On Petie's last day with Souperior's they decided to make one of their favorite soups, a creation that had had no name until Gordon dubbed it Crab Pot Chaos for *Local Flavor*. Crab season wouldn't start for another two weeks, but Rose had sweet-talked Dooley Burden into setting a couple of crab rings off the docks yesterday in exchange for a couple of rounds at the Wayside. That night Jim Christie had brought home twelve pounds of prime Dungeness and the report that Dooley had been drunk by nine.

By eight-fifteen the next morning Rose's house reeked of crab, and Carissa, Rose and Petie were all bellied up to Rose's kitchen table, picking. In the center was a growing mound of crabmeat sweet as butter; everywhere else, shells. On a nearby counter a box of Band-Aids stood at the ready. Rose always cut herself to pieces on the shells once her hands turned cold and slippery. No matter; she liked picking anyway. Like crafts, it freed the mind. Better than crafts, good food came out at the end of it. Perfect work.

"Cute outfit," Petie said to Carissa. She blew a puff of air at her bangs to get them out of her eyes; the rest of her hair was pulled back in a messy French braid, the first hairdo of any kind Rose had seen on her in years.

"Thanks." Carissa smiled with delight. She was wearing a short flippy skirt with a big sweater, striped tights and huge thick-soled shoes. "Mom made the skirt yesterday, I think it's so cool. Pay Less had this great fabric sale last week."

"We made her a cute top to go with it," Rose said. "We got some fabric for a pair of leggings, too. It's this funny tropical print."

"Mom says she's going to put the monkey over my butt. There's this one monkey in the print, peeking out from behind a big bunch of bananas." Carissa giggled.

"It would just be our little joke," Rose explained. "No one sees anyone's butt anymore, anyway, with all the big sweaters and shirts you guys wear."

"You're lucky you've got the mother you do," Petie told Carissa. "God obviously had a plan when he gave me boys. I can sew shirts like nobody's business but I couldn't give fashion advice to a cow."

Petie's small quick hands broke open a crab body and, with a crab claw, flicked out the yellow intestines, green liver and other muck, ripped off the gills and broke open the cartilage compartments for the succulent lump meat. She had picked crabs all one winter at a processing plant over in Sawyer and she was twice as fast as anyone else at the table. By long-standing agreement, she did all the bodies because the guts made Rose queasy, and Rose did all the legs because Petie didn't have the patience. It was a good system. They both passed body parts to Carissa whenever she ran short.

Rose told Petie, "I like your hair that way. It's real pretty."

"It's pretty ratty, you mean," Petie said. "I would have done better if I'd had more arms."

Carissa giggled.

"You should put some makeup on," Carissa said. Rose had recently let her buy her first cosmetics.

"Sweetie, if I went to a makeup counter they'd take one look at me and say, Oh, *please*."

"You used to wear makeup," Rose said.

"Well, yeah, like a racoon, but that was before."

For a few minutes the only sounds were the cracking of shells and cartilage and the sucking wet sound of meat being extracted. Rose wished she hadn't said anything about Petie's hair. She'd probably scared her off, now, and it had been so long since Petie had taken any interest in herself. Years ago, way back in high school, Petie had worn rings of black eyeliner and mascara around her eyes, plus pearl lipstick and shiny eye shadow, all applied from a shoe box stowed under Rose's bed. Petie and Old Man had been up in the trailer by then, and Petie came to Rose's house every morning and used the shower. She had had her own house key, her own towel, her own place in Rose's closet for some of her clothes. Rose and her mother had lived in the tiny old cottage off Third then: four rooms, nine hundred square feet total including the crawl spaces, the whole house saggy and faded as an old shirtwaist and powdery with dry rot. Rose's father had left them when Rose was two years old, and her mother supported them by doing dress alterations and custom sewing, often enlisting Rose's help and even sometimes Petie's for the big jobs like the Sawyer High cheerleader uniforms and, once, uniforms for the entire high school band. She was a proud, brittle woman who brooked no disagreement with Rose over the fact that, while she liked Petie, Petie was still trash. Eight years ago, just before she died, she told Rose that Petie had been her greatest act of Christian charity. Small wonder Petie hadn't been able to stand her. Still, Petie had come every morning, doing her makeup in a broken wall mirror she'd found and given to Rose so they could see what they were doing.

Rose bore down and cracked a claw. "Mama used to say you had hair like a Chinaman," she said. "Remember her saying that? *From the back Petie looks just like one of those Chinamen I saw down in San Francisco*, she'd say. *Small and with that hair.*" When she was eighteen Rose's mother had gone to San Francisco for a week with her father, and she never let anyone forget it.

Petie nodded. "She was always so afraid I was going to rub off on you."

"Well."

"Her worst fear was that I'd somehow infect you and you'd end up spending your life in a twelve-foot camp trailer somewhere. You know that's true," Petie said.

"Well, she worried about the same thing for you."

"No, she expected that for me. What she worried about was that I'd take you along."

Rose chuckled. "Well, then she's up there feeling stupid right now, isn't she? Seeing Eddie with his good job, and you finally being able to ease up a little."

"Who are you guys talking about, anyway?" Carissa said.

"Grandma."

"Oh." Carissa wrinkled her nose. "She always smelled like mothballs. I don't remember her much."

"I do," said Petie. "On the other hand, she was good to me."

Rose sighed and swept over a new pile of legs Petie had separated from the bodies. "Nadine was sure pleased for you about your being able to go back to the Sea View."

Petie smiled. "No kidding. I thought she was going to start crying when she laid me off."

Rose laughed softly. Poor Nadine. She still had hopes that one day Petie would at least like her from a distance. Nadine deserved to be liked.

"Did you hear that Rhonda's run off with Clayton See?" Petie said. "I give it five weeks, six at the outside. Jesus, I mean he's even stupider than she is."

"Well," Rose said idly, and sucked on the first bad cut of the morning, one on the ball of her thumb. Outside a little wind sprang up out of nowhere, knocking hard little pinecones out of the trees and down onto the flatish roof of her double-wide. They sounded like chipmunks bowling. It was probably rough out on the water, where Jim was. Boats were lost this time of year, even when they weren't crabbing. Last year the *San Pedro* had gone down in plain sight of the jetty. Cal Hansen hadn't washed in for four days and another crewman whose name Rose couldn't remember—a Sawyer boy, college kid on semester break—had never been found at all.

"Hey, how's Gordon?" Petie asked. "Is he feeling better?"

"Yes. He thinks he's over the worst of it. They gave him some new antibiotics that cost ten dollars a tablet."

"Whoa," Petie said. "What did you think of his apartment?"

"I thought it was beautiful. You'd never know you were in Sawyer at all."

"I liked the drawings," Carissa said, watching out of the corner of her eye to see what Petie or Rose might say.

"You let her see those?" Petie said to Rose. "Carissa, you're too young to see pictures of naked men."

"I thought they were beautiful," Carissa said. "The man in the pictures was Gordon's lover. His name was Johnny and he was twenty-nine, and he died of HIV. That's why Gordon and Nadine came up here. Gordon said all his friends had died, that Johnny was the last one. He said he wanted to die someplace where it didn't surprise him to be alone. I think he meant except for Nadine."

"Jesus," Petie said. "So you told her about Gordon?"

"She knows she has to keep it a secret," Rose said. "Right?"

Carissa nodded vigorously. "I know how to keep a secret."

The table grew quiet again. Petie picked the meat from the body of the last crab and absently started stacking backs, one shell on top of the other like Yertle the Turtle.

"Carissa, get the popcorn bowl for Petie to put the crabmeat in, okay, and then put all the newspaper and shells in one of those Hefty bags Jim keeps by the back door. I'll get him to take it up to the dump tonight so the house doesn't stink."

"It already stinks," Carissa said.

"So it doesn't stink worse. Please, hon."

As soon as Carissa left the room Rose said to Petie, "What's going on with you? Something's happened."

Petie blew out a breath. "Loose's been grabbing some little kid's dick at school."

"What?"

Irritably Petie snatched the elastic band from her French braid and shook out her hair. "Just what I said. He's been cornering some littler kid and grabbing his dick."

"Well, maybe it's just a phase. I mean, Loose has always been such a physical kid, and kids their age play doctor all the time. We used to."

"It's not the same thing. The kid's name is Harry, he's a runt and he definitely was not playing doctor."

Rose stared across the table with concern.

Petie said, very low, "I look at that child and he makes me sick."

"What are you going to do?"

"I told him if I ever hear of him doing that shit again I'm going to beat him senseless."

Rose looked at her hands. Several of her fingers were bloody; all of them stung.

"No one does shit like that around me," Petie hissed. Her face was pinched and white. "No one."

LATER THAT day, along with a final paycheck, Nadine presented Petie with a small blank book made of beach grass paper. All of it—the paper itself, the binding, the pen-and-ink cover illustration of a steaming soup pot—was done by Gordon. Inside, on the front page, he'd calligraphed *Thanks for the warm memories. Nadine and Gordon Latimer*. It was very beautiful, although God only knew what Petie would make of it. They held a long-standing position that a gift must be something in which the giver as well as the recipient could invest. Otherwise, it put the material exchange above the mutual emotional bond the gift was meant to express. The integrity of the emotional exchange was the thing; otherwise, why not just give Petie a six-pack of Bud or some hunting socks and be done with it?

In the midst of Nadine's ruminations Petie had arrived with the final delivery of soup—just ten minutes before the cafe was due to open. Nadine had gotten over worrying about it. Petie and Rose hadn't failed her once, and besides, it wasn't as though there were customers lined up along the sidewalk waiting for her to unlock the doors. Although, bizarrely, business had picked up. About a week ago a large party of local people had come in unannounced for dinner—some kind of motorcycle club, Nadine gathered. Fortuitously, Rose and Petie had fixed a couple of their most sturdy soups that day and Petie had baked one of her plainer breads. The surprise audition had turned out to be a success, and now other Hubbard people had begun dropping by for lunch.

Between them, Petie and Nadine wrestled the two vats into the kitchen—chowder plus Crab Pot Chaos. Nadine let out a little cry of pleasure when she peeked under the lid, although her menu had called for navy bean.

"Our favorite!" she said. "I'll bring some home to Gordon after lunch, he'd never forgive me if I didn't."

"Twelve crabs, and we have the cuts to prove it," Petie said, holding out her hands. "How's he doing?"

"Better. He's better."

"Good." Petie nodded curtly and turned and walked out of the cafe to get the bread. Nadine accepted a tray from the car's backseat.

"We're going to miss this," Nadine said, holding the cafe door open for Petie with her hip. "I only committed to the Riseria for two weeks, you know, in case you change your mind."

"Never happen." Laden with the other tray, Petie led the way back to the kitchen. Nadine had envisioned them lingering there for a minute or two, sentimentally, but after Petie put her tray down she headed straight back out through the cafe and to the front door. At the door she turned— Nadine jumped—and clapped Nadine lightly on the shoulder. "So, good luck," she said. She hitched her purse up on her shoulder and stood there, small and fierce and somehow slightly menacing. "Were you going to pay me now, or do you need me to stop back?"

"What? Oh! No. I've got it right here. And this is something from Gordon and me. Just to say thank you." It was then that she handed over the little book. Her hand trembled slightly as she held it out.

Petie pocketed the check and gift with barely a glance, and that had been it. Nadine would have to make up something more graceful for Gordon. It was the first present either of them had given since Johnny's birthday, two months before he died. *Get what you like,* Johnny had insisted to Gordon. *I mean, it's going to be willed back to you anyway, sweetie, so you might as well go for something with carryover.* Blind from cytomegalovirus by then, and too frail to leave their home except for appointments at the medical center, Johnny announced that he had become nothing but two ears and an asshole, and the one gave him life and the other took it away. So Gordon and Nadine had fed him as well as they knew how with Puccini and chants and Peruvian flute music and Paul Horn at the Taj Mahal and, for his final birthday, the best portable CD system they could find, so he could have it with him in the hospital. The last music he asked for on the day he died was *Fanfare for the Common Man*. If there was a piece in the world that could have been more terrible to hear bursting like false hope into that room, Nadine couldn't imagine it.

The CD system and all its music still mourned in a box in Gordon's apartment. One day soon it would be resurrected, a homely old attendant, to preside over Gordon's dying. His last T-cell count had been 42. He had two new KS lesions. On the other hand, his sinus infection was gone, the thrush was under control and he had so far been spared the wasting diarrhea that had stripped Johnny so vengefully to the bone. So he would go on. In fact he was flying to L.A. tomorrow morning, the first trip for either of them since coming to Oregon. Gordon had a meeting set up with his publisher friend Paul to discuss *Local Flavor*. Paul had been very enthusiastic about the project over the phone. Nadine would have liked to go, too. She missed the city desperately, although she'd never let on to Gordon. She didn't miss any one thing in particular, or even all the predictable things like good coffee and art and movies and the one or two close relationships she'd left behind. What she really missed was being understood. Half the time when she talked to them, Rose and Petie glazed over. It wasn't the subject matter, either; they simply didn't understand her vocabulary. She was learning to speak in synonyms as well as body language, offering two choices whenever possible to raise the odds of word recognition. Just for a day or two, it would have been a relief not to feel like the last surviving member of her species.

. . .

Jɪᴍ ᴄʜʀɪsᴛɪᴇ sat alone at a table at the Wayside, nursing a beer and staring with no particular impatience at Scruffy Johnson's signature carved into the tabletop like a terrier's yip. He'd crewed with Scruffy one year, stringy little fellow with a high voice and low motivation, one of the few people Christie'd ever really disliked. It took a lot. Mostly he didn't pay enough attention. You had to be pretty easy to get along on the boats. You had to know when to climb down inside yourself, way down where it was quiet, and just wait until the weather went by. Coming up wasn't always easy, but all in all it was a useful secret most people didn't seem to have learned.

Eddie Coolbaugh brought the rain in on his back. "Blowing like a son of a bitch, too," he said cheerfully, obliterating Scruffy Johnson with two fresh bottles of Henry's Private Reserve. "Coast Guard was just posting a storm warning when I came through town." He removed his Pepsi jacket, shook off the rain and draped the jacket tenderly over the back of his chair. He looked spruce these days, walking high on the balls of his feet, ballpoint pens hooked jauntily over his breast pocket, his name stitched there in suave blue script. Christie had heard from Rose that he was making good money. It sounded like a dog's life, driving that truck up and down the coast all day delivering crap, but then Eddie had never liked boat work.

"Two more fronts right behind it," Christie said. "Cold ones, too, coming down from Kodiak. Could be a tough year for crabbing."

"Every year's a tough year for crabbing."

"Got that right." Crab season went from December 1 to January 31, the roughest seas of the year. Boats went down. Christie'd never needed money bad enough to go out on a crabber, never would. You had to ride the ocean on your own terms.

"Schiff tell you I'm buying his bike?" Eddie said.

"I heard it somewhere."

"Good price, too. Damn good price. I figure I'll get it by Christmas. You need to come out sometime."

"I never had much of an appetite for bikes."

"Yeah. Well, you're missing something, though, I can tell you. We got some great new trails in there back of Chollum Road."

"Well," Christie said, and lifted his beer. He liked that Henry's. It went down cold and clean as ice water.

"So how's the car going?" Eddie asked.

"Good. It's going good."

"Loosey came home real excited that day he was over at your place. Petie said you might be doing something fancy. Big secret or something, she said."

"Nah. Just fixing it up. I might sell it, get Rose something newer."

"Yeah? You got something special in mind to buy? I heard old Dooley was wanting to sell that little Chevy Nova his sister used to drive before she passed away."

"I heard there was rust," Christie said.

"That right?"

Christie shrugged. "It's what I heard."

The door blew open, and a couple of men Christie recognized but didn't know came in slapping rain from their chests with their bare hands. Eddie waved them over. Christie downed the last of his Henry's, nodded at the men, slapped Eddie's shoulder and headed out into the rain.

It was five-thirty in the afternoon and dark and slick-looking as creosote, the same weather they'd had for a week solid. As Christie drove through town he looked inside Souperior's and saw Rose with her back turned, looking west into the rain—or, more likely, into her own reflection. Her hands were clasped behind her and she wore her hair in a soft loose ponytail. Christie slowed down, drank her in, drove on. It didn't occur to him to stop and go in. He didn't feel right in there; it wasn't a place for him, with all the ferns and church pews and women's touches.

When he got to the house Carissa was in the living room watching TV. She had stretched out on the sofa, but when he came in she sat up and quickly fixed her skirt and her hair.

"Hi," she said, and clicked off the television.

Christie nodded and hung his coat in the coat closet. "Your mother closing up for them?"

"Yeah. Nadine is driving Gordon to Portland tonight so he doesn't have to get up so early tomorrow to catch his plane. He's going to Los Angeles to talk about Mom's book. It's so exciting."

Christie nodded. He was suspicious of Gordon's soft voice and soft clothes and apparent dislike of work, but he knew Carissa had taken a liking to him so he kept his mouth shut.

"Does that bag outside have the crab shells in it? She said she left me some to take to the dump tonight."

"Yeah. There's soup for you, too. I could get it for you if you're hungry."

"Nah." Christie went into the kitchen and drank a big glass of water from the tap. Then he came back out and put on his coat again.

"Are you going out again? Why are you going out again already?" said Carissa.

"To dump those shells."

"Well, I could go with you."

"No."

"But I did all my homework. Look." She picked up a school notebook and stood close to show him three or four neatly printed pages. "It's a book report on *The Yearling*. It's for extra points. I finished everything else on the bus."

Christie gave in. While he waited, Carissa grabbed one of Rose's coats from the closet. She had gotten to be as tall as Rose, but her long legs and heart-shaped face were not Rose's. And then there was that extraordinary skin, fair and buttery and new, unblemished, unaged, unmarred. Christie was a little afraid of her. He had never seen anything he wanted to touch more than her pinkening cheek.

He turned and walked out the door.

"Wait up. Do you have a key?"

"Yes."

Carissa slammed the house door shut behind her. Christie slung the garbage bag into the truck bed, then hoisted himself in behind the wheel, opening Carissa's door from the inside as she struggled with the bad hinge. He had to shove some salvaged auto parts away to make room for her; he never had passengers, didn't like them.

"Don't sit there," he said. Carissa paused uncertainly halfway into the cab. He scrabbled under the seat for a towel and spread it over the grease left behind by the car parts.

Carissa arranged her skirt precisely and sat. Then she fluffed up her hair.

Christie turned over the key and pumped hard until the ignition rasped and caught.

The dump was an unmanned landfill north of town. No one paid the dump fees administered on the honor system; people drove up at all hours and heaved into a ravine their household rubbish, old Christmas trees, corrugated sheeting, doomed appliances. Christie drove there in silence, gripping the smooth old steering wheel with concentration. He'd have to replace the wipers one day soon. The old truck could use some work, once Rose's car was done. A couple more weeks, if his luck with parts held.

When they turned onto the landfill access road Christie took a series of potholes hard. Carissa squealed and bounced a few inches to the left, a few inches to the right. Perfume—Rose's perfume—wafted through the disturbances she left in the air. Christie leaned into the windshield.

"You got some mail today," Carissa said, holding on to the dashboard. "Did you see?"

"No."

"Well, it was some real estate thing. We didn't open it or anything, it was just a postcard. It's for some weekend at the Bachelor Butte over in Bend. Mom said it's like they give you two nights for free and all you have to do is let them show you a movie and talk to you for a little while or something. And you could even win a TV or an electric knife or something. Me and Mom think you should take us. Mom said she heard it was real nice over there."

Christie shook his head in the dark. Fool property deals. He knew people from the boats who played the real estate market like cards, owned a condo in Anchorage, a place in Seattle, time-shares. Always trying to figure out which one to go to, which one to rent out, which to unload. What did he want with property?

"So?" said Carissa.

"Go if you want to."

"But we want you to go, too."

"Nah."

"But it's free."

"Don't matter."

Christie bounced the truck into the landfill, fighting the wheel.

"But there are Jacuzzis," Carissa cried.

"Let it go, girl."

Carissa crossed her arms and sulked.

Christie stomped on the emergency brake, jumped out and strong-armed the garbage from the truck over the brink into the darkness. He heard the crab shells clash feebly as they landed. He kicked after them a couple of pieces of twisted sheet metal lying by his feet. The place was a hazard. He imagined that if he stayed quiet enough he'd be able to hear a thousand small animals at work down there breaking into all the Hefty trash bags. It made him shudder. Animals in the wild were one thing; he was okay with that. But animals in men's places, on the boats and around the docks, was a thing he couldn't abide. There were no rats on any boat he worked because he couldn't sleep right until he'd gotten rid of them all. Once, when he was young and working a stinking heap of a boat that sank a few years later from sheer rot, he'd woken up when a rat stepped on his eye.

As Christie got back in the truck the rain started picking up. Exposed in the truck bed was a new Coleman lantern he'd bought in Sawyer that afternoon. He'd nearly forgotten about it. He turned the truck up Chollum Road. Carissa looked at him inquiringly in the darkness, but said nothing; wherever he was taking her, she was game.

At the very top of Chollum Road, where every year another foot of asphalt was reclaimed by ferns and undergrowth, Christie stopped, turned off the engine and left the headlights on.

"What are we doing here?" said Carissa.

"Nothing. Stay here." Christie opened his door.

"But where are you going?"

"Just stay here. I'll be back in a minute." He slammed the door and hauled from the truck bed the soggy lantern box. Hopefully the mantle hadn't gotten ruined. He hurried into the woods with the box, following the headlight beams breaking up among the trees. Although it was overgrown there was a well-defined path, and in a minute he reached a humpbacked little trailer. He pushed open the door—there was no lock, now or when he'd found the place a few weeks ago—and felt inside for the big utility flashlight he'd left there last time. He turned it on, set it down and wrestled the box through the narrow door.

Inside the air was strong and spicy. Two days ago he'd cut ten or twelve noble fir boughs, scored the branches and piled them in the middle of the floor. Now the astringent fir sap cut the loamier smells of dereliction and decay—nature's room deodorizer. He'd clean the branches out tomorrow. Christie set the wet box down on the only piece of furniture in the trailer, a cane-bottomed chair he'd found at the Twice Around in Sawyer last week. A two-burner gas camp stove and a wall barometer sat on a warped fold-down table built into the trailer wall. Except for Christie's sleeping bag rolled up on the wood platform where a bed was supposed to be, there was nothing else.

"Is this yours?"

Christie turned around sharply. He hadn't heard the door open. Carissa was standing outside peering in. "I told you to stay in the truck," Christie said.

"I got scared waiting out there."

"Go on back."

Carissa edged past Christie to get inside. She touched the barometer, fiddled with the knobs of the camp stove, looked around. "Is it yours?"

"For now," Christie said. "Go on, now."

"But where did it come from?"

"It was here. I found it. It was empty."

"It's kind of nasty, isn't it."

"Suits me." Resigned, Christie worked on the cardboard box for a minute, lifted the lantern gently from its packing and set it on the little fold-down table. The mantle looked fine.

"I bet this used to be Old Man Tyler's trailer," Carissa said. She sat on the sleeping platform beside Christie's sleeping bag and leaned on it with her elbow. "Petie's father. I heard Petie used to live up here somewheres a long time ago. I never saw it because we weren't allowed."

"Well, whoever it was, it's empty now."

"He died."

Christie nodded and pulled a kitchen match from his pocket. He always carried a few with him, a habit that had come in handy more than once. The lantern mantle caught, flared and expired into a fragile incandescent net of ash enclosing the flame. Christie lowered the glass chimney into place, and the hiss and pop of bottled propane filled the small space. In the white light the trailer walls were covered with mold.

"Aren't you going to live with us anymore?" Carissa said quietly.

"I am." Christie hung the lantern on a hook he'd found overhead. It swayed as he backed away to the opposite end of the trailer. He'd have to replace the floor with a fresh sheet of three-quarter-inch plywood. "But a man needs a place of his own to come to sometimes."

Carissa looked around doubtfully. "But it smells," she said.

"It won't after a while."

"Are you going to sleep here?"

"Don't know."

"Does Mom know?"

"Nah."

"If you let me come up here with you sometimes I won't say anything. It could be a secret."

Rain beat down harder on the metal roof. A thin rivulet ran down one of the metal seams. Caulking would fix that.

"Time to go," Christie said, and shut down the lantern. He held the

utility flashlight so she could see as she stepped lightly off the bed platform and picked her way around the pile of boughs to the door. As she
passed Christie, Carissa placed her hand briefly but firmly on his chest.
She might have been steadying herself. Then she stepped out into the
darkness.

Chapter 9

OLD MAN didn't have a service for Petie's mother when she died; he didn't even bring her home from Salem. He said he couldn't afford a funeral, plus who were her friends, anyway? So he had her cremated someplace near the hospital while they waited and collected her ashes in a cardboard box. When Old Man opened it to see what his money had bought, there was only a plastic bag inside, no different than the bags in which bulk chicken parts are packed and about the same weight, fastened with a similar metal clip. Old Man handed the bag over to Petie, and in her hands the ashes felt warm and pliant and dense, like a living weight. Some of the ashes—fine, gray, greasy—had sifted out of the bag, or been carelessly packed to begin with, so that a film covered the outside. When Petie put the bag down on the seat beside her, some of the ashes came away on her skin. She screamed. Old Man had made her hold the bag—gritty with little bits of bone and teeth—on her lap all the way back to Hubbard.

The next day Old Man took Petie and the bag over a maze of logging roads to Camp Twelve, where Petie had never been before and where her mother, she knew, had been afraid to go. Camp Twelve was in a clearing in the middle of nowhere at all. Old Man steered the truck slowly between two rows of falling-down cabins that faced off across a mud road, ten cabins in all, and all alike. Someone had once made an effort with them, building them with quaint, steeply peaked roofs, front doors centered between paned windows and tiny front porches just big enough to hold a chair or two on a nice evening. But that had been a long time ago. Most of the cabins had been derelict for twenty years and more; the window-panes were broken out or taken, the front doors missing, the porches rotten and separating, the stairs gone. Near the ground, termites had eaten ragged holes in the rough clapboard siding, and animals of all kinds slunk in, in the night, and nested. The difference between these cabins and Petie's grandfather's cabin, when Old Man pulled up in front, was little more than curtains at the windows, a rusting junk heap out front and the presence of a front door. The curtains were too old to be any color, and hung out of the broken panes like shirttails, pushing against some plastic that had been nailed up on the outside. The front door stuck. Old Man told Petie to stay in the truck, but she was scared of being alone with the ashes and bones and teeth so she followed him anyway, leaving the heavy box on the seat.

Inside, the cabin was mean and dark. There was no stove and no fireplace; the only heat came from a propane heater in the corner. Against one wall was a crude bed, a chest of drawers and a lantern. At a table, bent over a two-burner propane camp stove, was the big dark man Petie had seen with her mother in the feed store four years ago. The bad man, Petie's grandfather. He didn't look so big now, though. Behind his beard his face was wasting, and the circles under his eyes were yellowy gray. His eyes were a deep yellow, too, almost tobacco-colored, and so were the palms of his hands. He had no gut now; his overalls hung slack around him. He nodded at Old Man, and then his eyes rested on Petie. She moved a little closer to Old Man and set her feet. After a minute her grandfather grunted and said, "Sure looks like her, don't she." He moved around the rough table and sat down in the cabin's one chair.

"I came up here to tell you she's gone," Old Man said, standing where he was. "She passed yesterday. We brought her ashes, thought they belonged here. She wasn't no part of Hubbard."

The old man passed his hand over his face once and Petie saw something in his eyes that might have been sadness, might have been anger. He grunted. "What she die of?"

"Female cancer. They kept her going a while, but it didn't do any good." Old Man pulled a cigarette from a pack in his pocket and lit it by striking a match on the zipper of his pants.

"You got another of those?"

Old Man fetched up another and handed it over. Petie's grandfather gestured impatiently for Old Man's cigarette, and used it to light his own. The smell of the two cigarettes plus of the men themselves—Petie's grandfather smelled sour and strong, like something spoiling, and Old Man's clothes were stiff with wear—turned Petie's stomach.

"What's your name again?" her grandfather said to her.

"Petie."

"Not much of a name for a girl. What do they call you that for?"

"I don't know." Petie had always been called Petie. It had never occurred to her to wonder why.

"Paula, she called her that ever since she was a baby," Old Man said. Petie hardly ever heard him use her mother's name. Usually he just said Her, or She. Old Man flicked his cigarette butt out the front door into the dirt yard, shook out a fresh one and lit it. Her grandfather took the pot he'd been stirring off the camp stove, set it down on the rude table in front of him and started spooning soup. He didn't offer any to them.

"You bring anything to drink?" he demanded of Old Man.

"I might have a bottle in the truck."

"Well, go see."

Petie followed Old Man outside so she wouldn't have to be alone with her grandfather. She knew there was a bottle; they'd stopped to buy one on their way through Sawyer.

"You stay out here now," Old Man told her, dragging the bottle out the truck window. "Play."

It was mid-November, and a light rain had started to fall. Petie only had a sweatshirt on; her jacket had gotten too small while her mother was in the hospital. "It's cold," she said.

"Stay in the truck, then." Old Man hurried back into the cabin with the bottle cradled in his arm, leaving the door slightly ajar.

Petie looked with dread at the cardboard box on the seat of the truck.

The plastic bag inside, she thought, would still feel warm. She couldn't stay in there with that. From the cabin she could hear the squeaky release of a cork. That meant they'd be drinking whiskey and it would be a long time before Old Man had had enough. Until she got sick Petie's mother used to take her out for walks when Old Man drank whiskey. They'd walk anywhere their feet took them, down to the docks if the weather was fine, or to Howrey's Market, or to the gift shops, where they'd watch people spend their money on little ceramic spoon rests and indoor/outdoor thermometers and plates you could hang on the wall.

Once, on a warm summer day, they'd dared to go into a gift shop they'd never entered before because her mother thought it was too fancy for people like them. Its shelves were full of teacups covered in tiny floral prints, and dozens of matching teapots fancier than anything Petie had ever seen. She wondered if anyone actually used them. They looked so fragile, just like eggshells. She and Paula had been standing near the front door watching one of the saleswomen help a customer when the saleswoman slipped and dropped a cup onto the glass display case. Paula and Petie both gasped, appalled to see a porcelain chip the size of a dime fly off. Paula's hand tightened around Petie's wrist, as though they could somehow be blamed, but the saleswoman simply moved the damaged cup to one side, replaced it with one that was undamaged, wrapped the entire purchase in layers of pale yellow tissue paper and cheerfully told the customer goodbye. Seeing Petie standing so still, the saleswoman winked at her and beckoned her over. Paula stayed where she was, but gave Petie a little push.

"Have you ever seen anyone so clumsy?" the woman said.

Petie stood mute.

"Which is your favorite pattern, honey?" she asked, no doubt taking in Petie's cheap clothes, her patched sweater with the button missing. Petie pointed to a blue and white cup with little yellow rosebuds all over it. It was the same pattern as the one on the broken cup.

"Is that right?" the woman said. "You know, I think that one's my favorite, too. It's a very old pattern."

Petie nodded and looked back at Paula, who was standing near the door trying not to call attention to herself. Petie turned to go.

"Wait, hon," the woman said. Pulling up several leaves of tissue paper, she wrapped up the chipped cup with the broken piece placed inside it. "You take this home and I'll bet you can fix it with just a little bit of glue."

Petie could see Paula near the door, putting both hands to her mouth. The saleswoman said, "Now, don't you worry, honey, this cup would be tossed out otherwise, and think of what a waste that would be." She pulled up another couple of sheets of tissue paper, this time placing on them a saucer with the same pattern. "You take this, too," she told Petie. "There's nothing in this world as lonely as a saucer without a cup." They were the most beautiful things Petie and Paula had ever had. Paula had put them on a special shelf where she and Petie could admire them anytime they wanted.

Now Petie crouched alone by the truck, in the lee of the rain, but she got wet anyway, and her teeth started to chatter. She could hear voices, rasping and uneven, inside the cabin; she didn't want to go there, not even to get warm. Instead she found an oily tarp on the floor of the truck to wrap up in, and scavenged a candy bar from the glove compartment. Old Man had bought two of them from the hospital vending machines a couple of days ago, one for him and one for Petie, except that he forgot to eat his. Under the candy bar was a book of matches and Petie took that, too.

Keeping the tarp over her head, Petie looked into the cabins one by one. No one had lived in any of them for a long time; not even an old chair had been left behind in the first three. In the fourth she saw a bench, a rickety thing but at least she could sit on it, and the cabin itself was dry inside, although doorless. From there she could still see Old Man's truck, so he wouldn't be able to leave without her when he was finished.

The bench was wobbly but it held. Petie hunkered down beneath the tarp and unwrapped the candy bar—a Baby Ruth, her favorite. By sucking all the chocolate off, then picking out the peanuts one at a time with her front teeth, then eating the nougat, she made it last a long time, and for a few minutes the pleasure of the candy made her forget how cold she was. She hardly ever got to eat candy bars except when Rose brought one to school in her lunch and shared it. Rose liked Hershey bars best, so this was only the third Baby Ruth Petie had ever had. As soon as it was gone Petie began to shiver. Old Man came out of the cabin, but only to pee by the side of the truck and get a fresh pack of cigarettes from his toolbox. When he went back inside he struggled a little, but got the door to the cabin all the way closed.

In a corner of Petie's cabin there was a small pile of twigs and grass and leaves and down from seedpods. It had once been a nest, now abandoned. When she looked at it more closely Petie found mixed in a bright blue button, a bottle cap, a pop-top ring, two pennies and a piece of foil. The nest had belonged to a pack rat. Carefully Petie picked out and moved the pack rat's treasure to safety, then found other bits of twigs and splintered lumber around the cabin's foundations, where it was still dry. She piled them carefully on the dusty nest and struck a match.

The little pile caught and burned with the speed and abruptness of a breath suddenly drawn. As quickly as she could, Petie found other bits and pieces to feed the fire, laid them on one by one and watched them burn. In the sudden warmth her hands began to tingle, and she leaned closer to see their translucency against the fire, admiring the color, soothed by the heat. They were small, pretty hands, dainty hands, her mother's hands. She bowed low to give a careful breath of encouragement to the fire, and a corner of the tarp she was wrapped in erupted in flames.

Petie cried out. Old Man would beat her if she ruined the tarp, especially since she had taken it from the truck without his permission. She flung it to the floor, but the oil made it burn faster. She folded the tarp quickly over itself, but the top layer instantly caught. There was nothing else to do. Petie raised her foot and brought it straight down into the flames, again and again until finally the tarp lay stinking and dead.

Unnoticed, the little fire on the floor guttered and went out.

Petie must have screamed.

The men came running from the other cabin, stumbling over ruts and tree roots. Petie's grandfather had an old rifle; Old Man brandished the nearly empty whiskey bottle by its neck. They burst into the cabin bellowing and stinking drunk, expecting a bear or a cougar. Instead they found Petie sitting on the floor vomiting.

"Jesus Christ," Old Man yelled, seeing her foot and leg. "What have you been doing, girl?"

"Well, get her off the floor," her grandfather barked. "Lift her up, boy, and get her back to my place."

"For Chrissakes," Old Man swore. He hoisted Petie roughly and weaved out of the cabin and across the track. It had begun raining in earnest, and he slipped twice in the deepening mud.

Inside, Petie's grandfather pointed to the narrow bed along the cabin wall. It was covered with a battered quilt, not clean. Old Man dropped Petie the final eight inches and she passed out briefly as she hit.

"Butter? Ice? Baking soda?" Old Man was saying when she came to.

"Don't have none of that," her grandfather grumbled.

"Then get me some ashes. Some ashes and some water." Then Old Man ripped away what was left of Petie's melted shoe and she passed out for real. The cardboard box was gone from the truck when Petie came to, halfway home, and her foot and lower leg had been packed in a thick poultice of ashes and water. The ashes they put on her foot that day might or might not have been her mother. She never asked Old Man, and on his own he never said.

The burn healed slow, but it healed. Her mother would have seen to that, Petie thought. It wasn't the same as goodbye, but it was something.

Chapter 10

After PAULA TYLER died and Old Man was served his eviction notice, the women of Hubbard descended upon the saggy little house on Chollum Road. They came knowing there was no way they would be here at this place if there hadn't been a death. They didn't like Old Man, never had, not since they were all kids together. No, they came out of respect for Paula Tyler, who they knew to be a poor soul who hadn't been given a single break in her whole life. They remembered when she first came down out of the hills, way back when they were all young and pretty and every one of them thought they'd turn out different, turn out lucky. Even then, when all of them still looked so good, you could tell that Paula wasn't lucky. And it wasn't just her ending up with Old Man. There had been rumors about some bad thing that had happened to her, something no one would exactly put a name to; something that made her walk in that slidey way she had, like she was trying to be invisible, like she was maybe trying to walk and keep her legs together at the same time. Some of the girls swore she had a smell about her, a sweet smell like something going bad, but most of them didn't believe that. Most of them just thought she was a poor, sad, going-nowhere girl who deserved their pity if not exactly their friendship. So now five women tied on bandannas and unpacked their mops and brooms and cleaning supplies and clucked over the dirty front room, the foodless kitchen, preparing to pack the place up while thanking God both privately and out loud that none of this had happened to them or their kids.

Only Eula Coolbaugh sought Petie out. "Hon, you okay?" she asked, still from a distance. Even at nine Petie was nobody's darling. She had disconnected, shocky eyes, everything about her stuffed way down out of sight. Even her shadow was like weak tea. She was a ghost moving around the house as the women moved, crouching just out of their view. She tried again. "I'm Eula Coolbaugh. I'm so sorry about your mama, hon. I knew her real well once. We all feel bad about her passing."

The dead had livelier eyes.

"Is there anything you'd like to know, hon, about what we're doing?"

She didn't move, could have been deaf except that as Eula was about to turn away the girl whispered, "Why did he burn her?"

"What?"

"Why did he have her burned?" Petie said.

Eula turned around. "Lord, Petie, what a question. I don't know. Some people don't like the idea of being buried. Maybe she asked your daddy to have her cremated. No matter what, she didn't feel anything, hon. She was already in heaven."

The child stared at her with unblinking eyes. "He made her burn in hell."

"Oh, honey, even your daddy can't make hell." Eula Coolbaugh squatted in front of her. "Hell is everlasting fire that can't be made on this earth," she said. "Listen to me. I knew your mother—I knew her for a real long time, and she was a good woman. I know for a fact that she's in heaven right now sitting beside God, safe and glad and peaceful."

For just a moment Eula reached out and touched that small and terrible head in the faintest benediction, the merest offering, a futile appeal to the angels she knew damn well had never once come to watch over this child. But shrinking from her touch, the girl slipped away. Eula had heard rumors about the accident up at Camp Twelve, about the poultice Old Man had made with Paula's ashes. What do you say to a child who has to live with something like that? What do you do when you know that whatever she'd suffered was nothing compared with what was probably yet to come? Not having an answer, Eula Coolbaugh did what she always did. She set her shoulders, took up her bucket and broom, and got to work.

WHEN PETIE thought she was no longer being watched, she crept into the back bedroom and removed a small bundle wrapped in dirty tissue paper. She slipped down the back steps with it, into the chill, and crouched beneath a weather-beaten old coastal pine. She didn't believe what Eula Coolbaugh had told her. If angels were watching over her mother, they wouldn't have let her get sick and die in the first place. They wouldn't have let Old Man burn her in hellfire so hot all that was left behind was ashes and teeth. And now that Petie had also been touched by fire, and her mother's ashes had been mixed with her own burned skin, she would surely be going to hell one day, too. All this she knew; what was less clear was what would happen to Old Man. Would he be there, too? Or would she and her mama finally be left alone, even if it was to burn in everlasting fire?

From beneath the tree, Petie watched the women begin to load their cleaning supplies into their cars.

"Where's the girl?" one of them said.

"She must be out here somewhere. She's a strange little thing, isn't she? What do you make of a child like that? I sure wouldn't want my kids around her much. There's something wild about her—something feral."

Eula Coolbaugh broke away and squished towards Petie across the sodden yard. "We're all done, honey," she called. "You can tell your daddy the place's been put right and your mama's things are in a box by the bureau." She reached Petie and scribbled something on a piece of paper. "If you need anything, hon, you call me. This is my phone number." Petie allowed the paper to be tucked into the pocket of her jeans but she didn't speak or move.

When all the women had finally driven away Petie brought out a broken spade she'd found once by the side of the road and dug a hole. She dug it wide and deep and smooth and clean and then she unwrapped the shreds of tissue paper and took out the chipped teacup and its saucer. *There's nothing in this world as lonely as a saucer without a cup. You take it, too, honey. They belong together.*

She closed her eyes and turned the cup in her hands, knowing that if God had bones they would surely feel like this, so smooth and cool and strong. She placed the saucer in the ground first, packing dirt beneath and around it, and then nested the teacup in its circle. She buried them together, perfectly paired and cradled in an everlasting embrace, marked by nothing but a smooth, clean place in the dirt beneath the tree. When she was done she turned her back on the house for the last time, crossed her thin arms over her chest and walked up Chollum Road. At its end, it became nothing but a dirt trail into the woods. And there, under the dripping trees, was the little cripple-backed trailer.

Old Man was already inside, sitting on a rickety cot smoking a cigarette and nursing a beer. A sleeping bag had been thrown down on the narrow sleeping platform across from him. "That's yours," he told Petie, jutting his chin in that direction. "Drawers are underneath. Your clothes are in there. Bucket's out back—you use that as a toilet. Dump it out and bury it when you've finished your business, then hang the bucket back on the tree. Water's in that jug out the door. Clean yourself when you need to. There's a towel somewhere around here. If you get cold, deal with it. We're not going to be using a bunch of propane every time. Heater's only for evening, and only when I tell you. Same with that lantern—don't you be using it unless I give you permission. I know you skinny kids, you're always cold, always wanting to turn the damn heat up."

Petie sat on the sleeping platform.

"What are you staring at?" Old Man said. "You and her, you're both always staring at me like I'm some piece of trash someone drug in. Don't you go staring at me, girl."

Petie dropped her eyes. "Is there food?"

Old Man pointed his beer bottle towards an old Igloo cooler and, on top of it, a beat-up camp stove like the one Petie had seen at Camp Twelve. She moved it to the floor and lifted the cooler lid. Inside were six bottles of beer, a package of hot dogs and a package of American cheese.

"You do all the cooking now," Old Man told her. "Your mama must have taught you something about it, not that she could cook worth a damn—God almighty but that woman *could not cook*. I never had worse food in my life. Hell, it's probably what gave her that cancer. First woman on earth to die of her own cooking. What d'you think?"

Old Man snorted at his own little joke, taking a long pull on the beer that Petie judged to be his third or fourth bottle. Fewer than that and he didn't ask questions; more than that and he didn't want answers, though Petie generally had them in her head. For instance, she knew that her mother's cooking was bad because you can't make good food when you're in a sustained state of terror. Old Man was always ugliest to her at mealtimes, baiting her, bumping her so she'd put her hand on the hot pans to keep from falling. The finest cream would curdle in a kitchen like that. Petie knew this as surely as she knew that Old Man had put her mama in hell. It wasn't just that he'd had her cremated. It was that he'd told her, over and over, "Paula, you will never get away from me, not even in your deepest dreams. You're mine in this world and I'll see you in hell when it's done." That's what Petie hadn't told Eula Coolbaugh back there in the old house. "I'm onto you, Paula," she'd heard him hiss. "I can read your thoughts, I can see clear into your mind. You will burn in hell forever and there's not a goddamn thing you can do about it."

Old Man tossed a few crumpled dollars in her direction. "Tomorrow you take this and go to the store, buy what we need. You have to make that last. Don't be expecting me to give you money all the time, because I won't."

Petie tucked the money into the pocket of her jeans and felt the forgotten slip of paper on which Eula Coolbaugh had written her phone number. Eula Coolbaugh had had a kind face, a good face, the face of a lesser angel. Petie wadded the slip of paper into a ball, lit the stove and fed it to the sickly flame.

NADINE SAT in her car at the Sawyer airfield and chewed a hangnail. Gordon was supposed to have arrived already, and in the rain, of course; the coastal rain she'd come to take personally, dripping and blowing without end like a bad cold. He had been gone for five days, and good God, how she'd missed him. In his absence she saw them as they truly were: a forty-one-year-old woman who fifty years earlier would have been called a spinster lady, and a forty-one-year-old bachelor known for keeping to himself except on the rare occasions when he was seen with attractive young men in the city.

Ten years ago each of them had had a good life, a life each had every reason to expect would last forever. Nadine, with her master's in English literature, managed a bookstore, a small shop specializing in important literature and select first editions. She had few friends, but those she did have, she loved. Gordon had just met Johnny and when they were together the two of them glowed like the sunrise. Shy Gordon, shy Johnny, avowed lovers for keeps, lovers forever, only who knew that forever could possibly end so soon? It was still a good time to be a gay man in love. No one was dying, no one had died, no one feared the prospect of death. Old age still meant your seventies, not your thirties. It seemed like such an impossibly long time ago. Nadine and Gordon, smart and kind and to whom the easy way never seemed to apply. Johnny would die in Gordon's arms, just as Gordon would one day die in Nadine's. And here they were, waiting, brother and sister clinging together in the hell-blast of terminal illness and irrelevant dreams.

The airplane appeared at last, a tiny thing fighting its way free of clouds as sticky as cotton candy. As Nadine watched, the plane seemed to be simultaneously blown sideways and down, making heart-stopping contact with the runway. Nadine whispered quiet thanks to whatever deity might be listening inside her car and turned up the heat.

When the airplane door opened, Gordon didn't so much step out of the plane as bore his way into the solid face of oncoming rain and wind. Nadine dashed out to meet him, wrapped a raincoat around him and hurried him back to the car. She hurled his bag into the trunk and, panting, the two of them slammed their doors in unison.

"Jesus," Gordon said. "Did it stop raining at all while I was gone?"

Nadine shot him a baleful look.

"Did you know that it's actually *not* raining someplace in the world?" Gordon extended a bag of bagels, the single thing she'd asked him to bring back from Los Angeles.

"I've heard, but I don't believe it." Nadine dug into the bagel bag as she swung out onto the coastal highway. "Tell me everything."

There had been movies and sunshine and good food eaten in the presence of pleasant company. There were the greetings extended to her by acquaintances and former neighbors. Nadine listened to it all, chewing thoughtfully until he'd finished. "And Paul?" He hadn't said a word about *Local Flavor*.

Gordon looked out the window, milking the moment but failing to suppress a grin. "He liked the book. No. He *loved* the book. Apparently the press has been kicking around the idea of starting a line of Pacific Northwest books for a long time—travel, history, field guides, light-houses, that kind of thing."

"And cooking," Nadine guessed.

"*And* cooking."

"Was he willing to commit to the manuscript?"

"Yes, and here's the thing: he wasn't the only one. His whole editorial board has bought in. They love Rose's voice. They're willing to give her a decent advance and pay me to edit the rest of the manuscript. They like what we've got, but they want about half again as many recipes."

"Can she come up with them, do you think?"

"I think between her and Petie they can. If not, we'll revive the rest of the contest recipes. Oh, and they want the book illustrated. Pen-and-ink drawings, watercolor washes, maybe woodcuts, of bread, veg-etables. Folk art, primitives. They're leaving it open until we've found an artist."

"Will they look for someone in L.A.?"

"They'd prefer to hire someone up here so the writer/illustrator team are really from the Pacific Northwest. Publishing integrity and all that. I agree with them."

"We could run another contest, just around here to see what we come up with," Nadine said doubtfully.

"I thought I'd ask Rose. She already knows everyone within a hundred-mile radius."

Nadine chuckled. He was right, of course. How she loved him, her last remaining family, her greatest fan and supporter, the one person alive who loved her unconditionally. She reached over, squeezed his forearm and piloted their tiny ship into the less than safe harbor that was Hubbard. Although she parked in front of Souperior's and turned off the car, she made no effort to get out. "Is Paul doing all right?"

Gordon sighed. "He's holding his own. He had pneumocystis a few months ago, but they pulled him out of it. You'll enjoy this. He says HIV has made him a professional maverick, a guerrilla editor. 'Baby,' he said to me, 'I back what I believe in now. What the hell can happen to me if I'm wrong? And here's the thing: I never *am* wrong now. God must reserve a special privilege for the dying.' "

"Well, they could fire him," Nadine said.

"That's not what he meant."

"I know it's not what he meant."

Nadine drove in silence for a moment before asking the question they had been avoiding since leaving the airfield. "What about you?" Gordon had seen his doctor while he was away.

"I seem to be okay."

"No new lesions?"

"No."

"T cells?"

Gordon shrugged. "A few less. Not many."

Nadine scrutinized him. He was telling the truth.

"Okay?" he said.

"Okay."

They went into Souperior's together, two and a half months to the day after Gordon had imposed his own exile. At the kitchen door Nadine could feel him draw a deep breath and let it out the way a connoisseur might reluctantly part with the smoke from a prized cigar. Rose was checking on a pot of soup—chicken and wild rice with tarragon. The minute she saw them she put down her spoon and gave Gordon a hug.

"Oh, welcome home!" she said, holding him by the elbows for a minute to get a look at him. Whatever she saw apparently satisfied her. She took up her spoon again and stirred. "Did you have a good trip?"

"Yes, I did."

"I'm glad." She stirred, sipped, added a bit of pepper, stirred, sipped again and covered the pot.

"Aren't you going to ask me anything?" Gordon said.

"I did."

"I mean anything else."

Rose wiped her hands on her apron. "I assumed it was private."

"Private?" Gordon said.

"Your doctor visit. I hope they had good news for you."

"Oh! No, that's not what I was thinking. I mean, yes, my doctor had relatively good news for me—I'm doing okay. But I was thinking about the book. I thought you'd want to know what the publisher said about the book."

"And what *did* he say?"

"Sit." Gordon led her to a booth in the empty restaurant. "Nadine, do you want coffee?"

"I'll get it. You two talk." Nadine disappeared into the kitchen.

Rose regarded Gordon mildly. "Well? What did your friend say?"

How could the woman be so serene? The source of such equanimity must be genetic—there was simply no other explanation. They watched a couple come in and find a table near the windows overlooking the bay. Nadine, hearing them, came from the kitchen, set mugs of coffee in front of Rose and Gordon, and handed menus to the couple. Gordon had missed the place, missed the atmosphere of quiet purpose these women had created.

"He wants to publish your book, Rose."

"Oh." She raised her hands to her mouth. "Oh!"

Gordon reached over and pressed her wrist with both hands. "He loved it. He loved your voice—the way you talk through your writing. His whole staff did. They want the book to come out next fall. Which will be a push, I'm warning you, because there's a lot of work left to do. But they've sent me back with a contract. Two, really—one for me as editor of the book, the other for you as its writer."

"I don't know what to say. I hope they haven't made a mistake. I'm no writer, Gordon, you know that. I'm not even a cook. Petie and me, we've been making soup for years because it's what you make when you don't have any money and there won't be any coming in till the end of the week. You've got to give your kids something. You and Nadine treat it like it's gourmet food but it's not."

"Sometimes the ones who aren't writers are the best of all," Gordon said. "Your voice comes through like a clear bell. But since you won't believe me, let's talk about your contract instead." Gordon reviewed the terms, the amount Rose would receive as an advance, what rights they were buying and which ones Rose retained, what percentage of each sale she would receive and how many additional recipes they wanted her to come up with.

"And Rose, there's one more thing. They want the book illustrated," Gordon said when he was done. "Would you happen to know anyone? They'll want one cover illustration, eight or so large illustrations and a couple dozen small accent drawings—a bunch of carrots, a bowl and whisk, that sort of thing. There won't be much money in it, but he'll have quite a bit of artistic freedom. It will be a beautiful book."

Rose immediately said, "I know—and oh, it'll be perfect!"

"You know someone? Of course you know someone. I never cease to marvel. Who is it?"

"Petie, Gordon! Petie could do it."

"Petie?" Gordon said doubtfully.

"Oh, I'm *so sure* of it. You probably haven't ever seen her drawings."

"No," Gordon said with growing alarm.

"Well, she doesn't show her things to people."

"Then what makes you think she'd draw for us, for this book?"

"She needs the money."

"Ah." Gordon sighed. "Look, isn't there someone else who might be more, ah, more reliable? Someone who's had experience?"

"No," Rose said flatly.

Gordon watched her for a long minute. She fairly vibrated with conviction.

"Look," he said. "Go ahead and talk to her about it, and if she's interested bring me some samples of her work. But I can't make any
promises, Rose. You'll both need to understand that. I don't want any of
us to be put in an awkward position, but I can't compromise my judgment."

"Well, you're already in an awkward position, aren't you," Rose said,
smiling gently. "I know you, I know exactly what you're thinking. You're
thinking that Petie can't draw but I don't know it, or that I *do* know it but
hope you won't. It's not like that, Gordon. She's good. She's very good.
It's very personal for her, though, very private. I'm not sure she'll even
let me bring you anything, but if she does I want you to consider her.
That's all I'm asking."

"Fair enough." The cafe door was thrown open and a family blew in
with the rain. Rose stood to greet them and fetch menus. As she left, she
touched his wrist, where the little purple lesion was still faintly visible.
"Gordon," she said.

"Hmmm?"

"Thank you."

. . .

HUMP DAY SOUP

*We like to make this soup on Hump Day, Wednesday, to celebrate half
the week being over with. It is a cheerful meal and kids like it a lot, or
at least ours do. Think of macaroni and cheese, only soupier. Start
with a block of cheddar cheese if you can afford one, or the cheese
pack from boxed macaroni and cheese if you can't—it will be good either way.*

Rose stopped reading aloud from a yellow legal tablet and sipped ru-
minatively at her diet cola. "Do you think we can use it?" she asked
Petie, who was up to her elbows in flour and yeast. "I mean, do you think
anyone but us would ever want to make it?"

"We made it, didn't we? Hell, Ryan and Loose still ask for it some-times."

"I know, but they're kids, they don't know any better. Would some-one want it who'd actually pay for a cookbook?"

"We've bought cookbooks. Hell, I know for a *fact* that I once bought a cookbook for a quarter at Connie Neary's yard sale. I'll probably be getting around to reading it soon. In my free time, which I don't have any of."

"I think I'm going to leave it out."

"Don't leave it out."

"It's out." Rose tore the recipe in half, and in half again. "I want to ask you about something."

"I did *not* drink three beers at the Wayside last Friday, if that's what you want to know. Did Schiff tell you I did? He wasn't even there most of the time."

"You were at the Wayside last Friday with Schiff?"

"No, I was at the Wayside last Friday with Eddie. Schiff showed up, Eddie took off before I'd finished my second beer, so Schiff gave me a ride home."

"You better be careful," Rose warned. "You know how Carla is. Remember that time when she thought Lee Ann Hafner was trying to start something with Schiff, so she ran Lee Ann off the road at the state park and made her swear on a Bible that she wouldn't ever again so much as look at Schiff, so help her, okay, God? It scared the crap out of her, and all she'd been doing was talking to him about getting Pepsi at a dis-count for the Cub Scout jamboree."

Petie snorted. "Don't you just wonder what Carla was doing with that Bible in her car in the first place? She's the most unholy person I know, honest to God. So, what? Does she pray on the Bible for a lucky streak at video poker? Maybe she reads psalms over her fourth wine cooler. Shit, Carla Schiffen's nothing but spare parts and she has been for years."

"Well, you ought to be scared of her," Rose said. "Hell, even *Schiff's* scared of her. She's one of the most vengeful people I've ever heard of. I'm just saying you need to be careful."

Petie scowled.

"All right, we'll talk about that another time. What I wanted to ask you about has to do with the book."

"They're not paying you enough. I've said it before, and I'll say it again."

"They're paying me plenty, Petie, for God's sake. I have no idea what I'm doing, half the recipes aren't really ours and the other half we made up out of leftovers. But I don't want to talk about the money."

"Do you need me to test the last couple of recipes?"

"No—"

"Because I'm not going to test Jeannie Fontaineau's beef barley, I haven't changed my mind about that."

"Will you shut up? My *God* you're twitchy. Anyway, this isn't even about soup. They want someone to draw pictures to go with the book. I think it should be you."

Petie stopped kneading. "What?"

"I want you to illustrate the book. Gordon said they need someone to do a drawing for the cover and a bunch of smaller things for inside."

"What makes you think I can do it?"

"I know you can do it. What I don't know is whether you *will* do it. Think about it—*us*, you and me, making a book. Wouldn't that just be something, though?"

Petie slapped a ball of flabby dough onto the breadboard.

"Listen," Rose said. "You know Gordon's sick. Well, his friend who's going to publish the book has AIDS, too. I don't think they have a lot of time. We're going to have to work pretty fast."

"Gordon said that?"

"Of course not."

"So what do they want—pretty little flowers and cottages and happy people and shit?"

Rose snorted. "No. At least, I don't think so. Gordon said a lot would be left up to the artist. You could talk to him about it, at least. He said he'd love to see your work."

"You already volunteered me? I can't believe you fucking *volunteered* me."

"I didn't volunteer you, exactly, I just asked if you could apply for the job. That's all." Rose stood and pulled on her coat. It was time to go home and start supper. Christie liked his meals early and regular.

"Well, you shouldn't have," Petie said.

Rose sighed. "They'll pay you fifteen hundred dollars."

"You're kidding."

"I'm not kidding." Rose wrapped a scarf around her throat.

"Whoa." Petie let out a long, low whistle.

"So come up with maybe ten or so sketches and drawings to show Gordon. If you do it soon—soon like tomorrow—you won't have anyone competing against you. I want you to do this with me, Petie. I want both our names on the cover."

"When would they pay?"

"Maybe some up front, then the rest when you turn in all the work. That's what they're doing with me. So think about it. And next time I see you I expect you to tell me everything about the Wayside on Friday. Something is definitely up with you."

"Nothing is up."

"I want to hear everything."

"*Nothing* is—" The door slammed shut and all that was left of Rose was a gust of cold wet air.

"Shit."

Several years ago they had sworn that neither one of them would smoke a cigarette except when they were with each other. They might get cancer, but if they did, at least they were going to get it together. Petie cheated sometimes; she assumed that Rose cheated sometimes, too. She tapped a fresh cigarette out of the pack and lit it.

Last Friday, long before seeing him at the Wayside, Petie had had lunch with Schiff again. They had driven in Schiff's pickup to an old county landfill where no one ever went except to make out or dispose of a body or an old beat-to-shit appliance.

"I had coffee at the Hot Pot this morning, me and Bob Harle," he told Petie after he'd parked the truck under some dripping trees and Petie had divvied up the sandwiches. "We're just sitting there talking and this family comes in—overweight woman, balding guy, teenage daughter, you know, nothing special, a farm family. They sit right near us, keep looking at us, and then after a few minutes the girl comes up to me and says, *Are you Ron Schiffen?* So I say yes. She says, *We stopped at the Pepsi place and they said you might be here. We were looking for you.*"

Petie chewed, watching him through her bangs, that silky Indian hair Schiff sometimes found himself thinking about when he shouldn't; that hair and her small tough body. No one had ever watched him like that before. "So who were they?"

"Wait. So she says, *Are you Ron Schiffen?* And I say yes, and then she says, *Well, I'm Angel.*"

"Oh my God, Schiff."

He was breathing quickly, remembering. "I didn't even recognize Mary. I could've walked right into her and said excuse me and walked away again without ever realizing she was someone I knew. She was just sort of, I don't know, faded, nothing special. And she used to be a *goddess.*"

"But what about the girl?"

Schiff tapped his fingernail on the dashboard. "That child was beautiful. When I left her she was *beautiful*, like an honest-to-God angel—I used to swear that if you looked at her with the lights out she would glow like a goddamn candle." He wiped his mouth with care on the napkin Petie had brought, folded the napkin in half and in half again, and then unfolded it and smoothed it over his knee. "But the thing was," he said, "she wasn't beautiful at all. Nice girl—pretty hair, braces. Ordinary; hell, not half as pretty as Randi. She'll probably be pregnant in another year. I used to think her and her mom hung the moon and stars, and then I run into them and I don't even know who they are. Even once she *told* me who she was, I couldn't see it."

He looked at Petie with the dumb eyes of a field animal. "I just couldn't see it."

"So then what?"

"Then they left."

"Just like that?"

"Well, you know, she said it was good to meet me, and I asked about how she was doing in school and shit. I got her address." He fished a Post-it out of his shirt pocket and looked at it with amazement, like it had revealed the face of Jesus, maybe, or glowed with a heavenly light. "She was the closest thing I ever had to my own kid and I tell her to, you know, take care, be good, and I cannot think of *another single goddamn thing* to say. Her mom and me, we didn't even talk."

"So, what, they burst your bubble?"

Schiff frowned at her. "What bubble?"

"The one where you're the cowboy and they're the helpless woman and child you left behind. The one where everyone adores you and they never grow up and they never change and none of it's your fault."

"I knew Mary would change," he said hotly, and then subsided. "Jesus, though, not *that* much."

Petie looked out her window, as though she could actually see through all the breath fog. "You tell Carla about it yet?"

Schiff sighed heavily. "She won't like it. Carla, she doesn't want to talk about other people. Anyway, I never told her about Mary and Angel."

"You're kidding."

Schiff shrugged. "She don't like to know about things that happened before her."

Petie ate in silence, drank her Pepsi. Schiff watched her out of the corner of his eye. "Aren't you afraid I might take advantage of you, out here where no one's watching?" He leered halfheartedly. "An attractive woman like you?"

"You don't have to do that, Schiff."

"Do what?"

"Proposition me. Do the macho sex thing."

"Is that what I'm doing?"

"It wasn't until now," said Petie.

"Then what *was* I doing?"

"Telling a story, Schiff. You were just telling a story."

"And what were you doing?"

"Listening," Petie said.

"Is that okay?"

"Yes."

"Okay."

Petie gathered the odds and ends of their lunch things and stowed them by her feet. "Are you ready to go back?" she asked.

"No," he said, turning the key in the ignition and easing the truck into gear.

Now, THREE days later in the middle of her kitchen, Petie stubbed out the last cigarette and listened for noise. She found Loose right away by following the sounds of two pieces of wood being knocked together out in the side yard where he often played, oblivious of the rain and cold, a tough child at home. It was harder to locate Ryan, but at the foot of the stairs Petie could hear the low murmur of a child reading out loud to hear the music of his own voice wrapped around the taste of someone else's words. Unobserved, Petie picked up the phone and dialed.

Bev Houghton answered at the Pepsi distributorship in Sawyer. "Hi!" she greeted Petie when she heard her voice. "You want to talk with Eddie? He's up north, but I could give you his voice mail."

"Thanks, but I actually need to talk with Schiff for a minute."

"Oh! I think he's in. While I've got you, though, are you coming to the company Christmas dinner next week?"

"Sure," Petie said. "I never miss the chance to attend some dinner where you hold a disintegrating paper plate in one hand and a beer in the—"

"A Pepsi," Bev interrupted.

"What?"

"Where you hold a disintegrating paper plate in one hand and a *Pepsi* in the other—" Bev said helpfully.

"—until the plate disappears and you're wearing your food on your shoes," Petie said. "Count me in. Me and Eddie. Can kids come?"

"Of course."

"My two kids, too, then."

"Okeydoke. You ready for me to put you through to Eddie's voice mail?"

"Schiff," Petie said through clenched teeth. "I needed to talk to Schiff."

"Oh, that's right, I forgot. I'm sorry, hon," Bev cooed—and she a woman who Petie knew damned well could tell you the color of the toilet paper she wiped herself with two days ago. "Nice talking to you, Petie."

"Sure," Petie said, and then mouthed into the receiver, "My ass." God save her from fat Bev and the death grip of her memory, which was puny only when compared with the size of her big mouth.

On the other end the phone rang for the third time. Thank God. Maybe Petie wouldn't get through but could still tell Schiff she'd tried.

"Hiya, princess," Ron Schiffen suddenly murmured in her ear. Bev must have told him it was Petie on the line. Of course she had.

"*Fuck* the princess," she hissed, feeling herself slipping into the unreal and tireless world of Schiff's knee-jerk seductions.

"That would be nice."

"Don't you ever stop?"

"No," Schiff said sadly. "Not that it gets me anywhere. Still, miracles do sometimes happen."

"And if you were granted one miracle, what would it be?"

"It has to do with you and a hotel—"

"I'm serious, Schiff."

"Me, too, princess."

"Look, why did you call me earlier?" He had left a very careful, neutral message on her phone, presumably in case something went wrong and Eddie checked the machine instead of Petie.

"I wanted to see if you would have lunch with me."

"I've had lunch with you."

"Some people eat lunch every day."

"We're talking every day as it is. Why is that?"

"I like you," Schiff said simply.

"I don't think lunch is a good idea."

"Why?"

"Why? Carla is why. You're the one with the wife."

Schiff was silent.

"Okay," Petie said. "You can call me. Let's leave it at that."

"How can I seduce you if I never see you?"

"You said it, bucko, not me."

"Eddie's got a south county run the day after tomorrow. Have lunch with me then. You can choose where."

"I'll talk to you tomorrow, Schiff. You can call me tomorrow." Through her own loud breathing, Petie heard his voice still talking as she hung up the phone. She couldn't explain this to Rose even if she wanted to. Here, in the middle of winter's pall on the dripping Oregon coast, unseen among people she'd known and been known by all her life, she had found something more dangerous than gunshots, more threatening than sex, and for which there were no words of explanation or retraction. Here, when she didn't even know she'd been looking, in a man she'd never liked, she had found love.

Chapter 11

JIM CHRISTIE sat watching girls stream out of Sawyer Middle School like liquid sin. He hadn't noticed girls like these when he was their age, but he noticed them now all right, the way their skin fit so perfectly over their muscles and bones, the way they were so taut and elastic, too good to be real except they *were* real. Right here, right in front of him, surging all around his pickup like he was no more than a stone in the river. An old man, an invisible man, with his faded hair and worn-out eyes and years of wrinkles from looking into the jaws of bad weather. A quiet man who *looked* with great potency.

Jim Christie wasn't like most of the men on the boats in Alaska, who took whatever form of woman came along as soon as they hit port. He knew how to wait and what he was waiting for. Sex was a deep, warm, dark place and he wasn't about to spoil it in a randy moment. He could wait—did wait—for Rose, with her generous hips and her soft luminous hair and the way she hummed when she took pleasure. She was strong drink, turning his head around, making him forget to keep things hidden that were best left concealed—his longing to stay in a place he was desperate to leave; his certainty that he would die in the next fishing season; the knowledge that he would go north to Alaska anyway.

"Hey!" The top of a blond head just showed above the window on the passenger side of his truck. "Open the door!"

Christie reached across a wasteland of mechanical parts and cracked the door. Carissa elbowed it open and tossed in an armload of books and notebooks, then heaved herself onto the seat after them. "Whew! I'm glad you're here. I thought Mom was coming for me."

"She had to work." Christie turned over the ignition and steered his old truck into the crush of beater cars and school buses clogging the road.

Carissa raked her loose hair back and then let it fall in a tumble, Rose's mannerism eerily reenacted. Christie kept his eyes on the traffic.

"What do you want for dinner?" she asked. "I could make that tuna casserole you like."

"That'd be fine," Christie said.

"Or we could have meat loaf."

Christie shrugged. "Whatever you want."

"What do *you* want? You never say."

"Don't want anything. If I do, I can fix it myself."

"You never let anyone take care of you. Why won't you let us take care of you?"

Christie reset his ball cap. "Don't need it."

"Well, it'd be nice if you'd let us spoil you sometimes. Mom spends the whole time you're away thinking up things to fix while you're home, and then you don't ever want anything."

"I like everything you fix, your mom, too. She knows that."

Carissa sighed and set her jaw. "Well, it would help if you were a little more demonstrative." Christie cocked an eyebrow. "You know—showed how you feel."

"I know what it means."

They drove the rest of the way to Hubbard in silence. Carissa absently twirled a strand of hair around and around her finger. Christie could just make out the scent of her shampoo overlaid with something else, maybe perfume. He drove with both hands on the wheel.

They drove past Souperior's. "How late is Mom working tonight?"

"Till seven."

"Can we go by your place, then?"

"No."

"Are you still fixing it up?"

"I go there sometimes," Christie said.

"Every day?"

"Depends."

"Do you take Mom?"

"No."

"Does she even know about it?"

"Only if you told her."

"I promised it would be a secret."

"Doesn't need to be."

"Then why haven't you told her?"

"Haven't had any reason to."

Carissa made a sound of exasperation. "Well, I wish you'd let me go back there again. I want to see what you've done."

"Haven't done anything."

"Well, you could, though. Curtains maybe; maybe a rug. A chair."

"I've got what I need."

"Could you take me up there some other time, then?"

"We'll see," said Christie.

"Please?"

Christie set his shoulders and Carissa subsided, crossing her arms over her chest. She perked up again almost immediately, putting her hand on his arm. "I know, I'll make brownies. How about brownies?"

Christie turned into their driveway, leaving the carport empty for Rose when she came home.

"Brownies would be fine," Christie said, and walked away from the girl to the house.

She touched him a lot. It wasn't a good idea.

EDDIE COOLBAUGH had finally found a place for himself that he loved: Pepsi. He wore his snappy uniform with pride, stood a little taller whenever he was wearing it—the neat striped shirt, the blue zip-front jacket, the pants with the smart creases sharp as knives. He hopped from his truck cab with a confident bounce, knowing he was good-looking, knowing he was somebody. The women always held him up at his stops, signing for his delivery slowly, pretending to look things over, making foolish remarks about the weather, about a daughter's wedding coming up, about nothing at all. What they were really saying was that he was a good-looking man of some importance, a man worth noticing, perhaps even worth remembering. For that, Eddie owed Ron Schiffen big-time. Eddie might even take over for him one day, who knew? He would learn the business, maybe get an inside position after a while, warehouseman or bottling plant foreman. He'd be good at that. Not a desk job, though. He'd hate a desk job, unless it was Schiff's and he had a secretary who did all the work while he, Eddie, put his boots up on the desk and talked on the telephone. He'd mentioned his ambitions to Petie, but she just told him to go slow, do the job he had, be satisfied with that. Petie didn't understand the fire in his gut when he thought about his possibilities. Schiff might, though. Eddie would talk to him one day soon, lay things out for him and see what he had to say. Not yet, though. Eddie wasn't ready yet.

He and Petie didn't see things the same way much anymore. Eddie didn't know exactly why that was. He'd cheated on her once or twice, but everyone did that and the women mostly got used to it after a while. He took care of his kids and kept a roof over their heads; he let Petie do pretty much what she wanted to, even when it stank up the house and jacked up their electric bill. He didn't see the point of it, himself, but he wasn't a man who tried to tell people what to do. Now she was digging up little bits of drawings and shit from everywhere because Rose had told her she was an artist. She'd always doodled, from as far back as he could remember. When she lived with them, his mother had always kept paper and pencils around the house. It was probably because of Eula that Petie had shown anyone she could draw in the first place. It was beyond him why someone would pay for her doodling, but if they were willing to, well then, Eddie wasn't going to discourage them. It was just like her and Rose to go off on another wild-goose chase that wouldn't take them anywhere in the end, but hey. If Petie wanted to waste her time, that was her lookout, not his. He wasn't a man who kept too tight a rein on things, plus Petie got mean when she was cornered. He'd learned a long time ago to swing wide.

Her beater Colt was already in the parking lot at Hubbard Elementary when Eddie pulled in with his Pepsi truck. He ran a deft comb through his hair, straightened the lay of his jacket and ducked into the school. Petie and Mrs. Hendrik were already in the first-grade classroom there, seated at a ridiculously small desk with a folder opened between them. Mrs. Hendrik—a twenty-four-year-old do-gooder he couldn't stand and neither could Petie—jumped up, scraped over another chair made for dolls or midgets, and urged him to sit down.

"Mr. Coolbaugh, your wife and I have been talking about Loose. As you know, I thought it would be a good idea for us to get together."

"Yeah," Eddie said, looking around the room at the bulletin board cutouts of parrots and monkeys and jungle crap. Jesus, he'd hated school.

"Mr. Coolbaugh, I believe Loose is having some problems."

Petie stiffened almost imperceptibly in her chair. "He hasn't been doing anything wrong with the other kids, has he?"

"Excuse me?" said Mrs. Hendrik.

Eddie could see Petie's hands fist up, never a good sign with her. "He was picking on another boy a week or two ago, a smaller boy."

"Well, he can be aggressive. We have had to discipline him several times, Mrs. Coolbaugh, as you know. But that's not what I wanted to discuss with you both."

"No?" Petie said.

"No. Loose is having some trouble with his reading."

"Reading?"

"He doesn't seem to be, well, getting it. The other children are reading whole sentences, but Loose can't. I think we may want to have him evaluated."

Petie leaned forward over the tiny desk. "You mean, he's not in trouble for doing things to other kids?"

"Oh, no, Mrs. Coolbaugh. Loose is a physical boy and he can be rough sometimes on the playground, but that's normal in a child with his temperament. No, what I'm concerned about is whether Loose has some mild disabilities that are getting in the way of his learning."

Eddie squinted. "What exactly are you talking about, Mrs.—ah—?"

"Hendrik." The young woman colored. "You can call me Nan."

"Well, then, Nan, are you saying there's something wrong with my boy?"

"Eddie," Petie warned.

"No, I want to hear this. Are you saying my boy isn't normal?" Fucking teachers—God, but he hated teachers.

"Oh, no," the teacher said. She looked frightened. "No, what I'm saying is that it's possible—just possible, Mr. Coolbaugh—that he may have a learning disability of some kind, or an attention deficit disorder. Has anyone ever discussed this with you?"

"No," Eddie said flatly.

"Eddie is dyslexic," Petie said.

"Oh! Well, that might give us some clues, then," Nan Hendrik said.

"Loose is not stupid," Eddie said.

"No one's saying he's stupid, Eddie."

"Just the opposite, Mr. Coolbaugh. Loose is very bright, and he seems to have a rare mechanical gift. He says he helps you fix things."

"We work on cars, dirt bikes."

"Well, that's very impressive."

"So what do you want us to do?" Petie said. "We don't have money, Mrs. Hendrik, for special counseling."

"Oh! No, none of it costs money—the school district provides testing and assessment. If we find anything we think will require more specialized help, we'll talk about it then."

"And if you find something wrong with my boy?" Eddie said.

The teacher pressed the palms of her hands together. "We don't think of learning challenges—disabilities—as *wrong*, Mr. Coolbaugh. We know a lot more now than we did when you were in grade school yourself. Early intervention can make all the difference. And we might not find anything at all. I simply want to be thorough. A diagnosis at his age can make all the difference in helping him with lifelong learning skills and self-esteem issues."

"Mrs. Hendrik—forgive me, Nan—let's cut through the shit," said Eddie. "You think he's not measuring up. You want to know if there's a reason he's stupid. Well, I can understand that. I'll even take your advice. But I want to make one thing clear. I don't want him being called special or slow, you understand me? I don't ever want to hear of somebody's saying that. And I don't want any of the other kids to know about this."

The teacher colored. *Jesus,* but he hated teachers. They always knew more than you did, and they never admitted it to your face. "You might have been singled out, Mr. Coolbaugh, but Loose won't be. There are two other boys in his class right now who are being evaluated, too."

"Who?" Eddie said.

"I'm sorry, Mr. Coolbaugh, but that's confidential, just the way Loose's evaluation will be kept confidential."

"I'll bet one of them is that Crowley kid." Eddie turned to Petie. "He's the one who was still crapping in his pants—"

"Eddie," Petie warned.

"Come on, Petie, he's a slow kid—Dooley Burden used to think he was retarded, remember that? Loose is nothing like that kid."

Mrs. Hendrik looked desperately at Petie.

"It's okay," Petie told her. "He's sensitive about this stuff. He had a tough time. Voc Ed, three years of Algebra I, that kind of thing."

"Shut up, Petie."

"So what now?" Petie asked the teacher.

"Well, with your permission I'll set up some evaluative testing for Loose in the next couple of weeks. When we've got the results, I'll contact you so we can go over them."

"Yeah, yeah," Eddie said.

"Do what you need to do," said Petie.

"Oh, thank you, Mrs. Coolbaugh. I'm so glad. You have no idea how important this may turn out to be."

Petie got out of her tiny chair and pushed it under the tiny desk. Eddie got up and left his chair as it was. Mrs. Hendrik rose, too, and held out her hand.

"Thank you, Mrs. Coolbaugh."

Petie pressed the teacher's wrist lightly. "It's okay."

"And you, Mr. Coolbaugh." Eddie ignored the hand outstretched in his direction and turned for the door.

"Yeah, yeah," he said, and was gone.

Yᴏᴜ'ʀᴇ *ꜱᴜᴄʜ* a piece of shit, Eddie," Petie said when she caught up with him in the parking lot. "You really are. That poor girl was scared to death of you and all she was trying to do was make sure Loose doesn't have to go through what you did. What the fuck is wrong with you?"

"My kid's not stupid."

"Did anyone say that? I didn't hear *anyone* say that."

"Not yet," Eddie said. "But they will."

"You listen to me," Petie hissed. "You know who his grandfather was. You know what I've been thinking every night at two in the morning for weeks, when you're snoring away? I've been worrying about whether that child's becoming a pervert just like Old Man. *That's* what I've been thinking. And hey, guess what? He's not a pervert. At least he's not a pervert yet. He isn't stupid either. Get your fucking priorities straight, Eddie."

"My kid isn't a pervert."

"No, he isn't a pervert. But he *could* have been a pervert."

Eddie leaned on the door of his Pepsi delivery truck. "Jesus, Petie. Did you really think that?"

"Yes. So I'm thinking this other is good news. Hell, you don't get put in prison for failing to learn."

"Yeah, well, okay, so I might have been a little hard on her."

"Hard on her? Shit, wild Indians with bows and arrows would have been less intimidating."

Eddie wasn't listening. "You know what's funny? If one of the boys is going to have problems, I figure it should be Ryan."

"Why? He's always been a good student."

"Why? Because he's a goddamn wimp, that's why. I mean, what other kid do you know who's afraid of goats?" Ryan had an inexplicable fear of a large goat that lived a couple of blocks down the street from them. He said its pupils went the wrong way. It was, admittedly, a thin reason.

"He's a bright boy," Petie said. "He just has his ways."

"Yeah, well, some damned weird ways. Like what was that thing with always having to wear the same hooded sweatshirt? Remember that? The damned thing nearly fell apart before he'd give it up. What the hell was that? All I'm saying is that I would've been less surprised if it had been Ryan having trouble."

"He's a good boy, Eddie."

"Yeah, well. Nan Goody Two-Shoes there will figure out what's going on with Loose and we'll deal with it. I'm not going to let them put him in Voc Ed, though, I'll tell you that right now." Eddie had been tracked into Voc Ed for years. They called it Talent then—how cruel was that?

"They don't do Voc Ed like they used to anymore, anyway. Everybody's in the same class, and they just give special attention to the kids who need it. It's different now."

"It fucking better be."

And that was that. Eddie buckled himself in, revved up his truck and was out of the parking lot before Petie had even gotten her key into the ignition. What Eddie minded was that Ryan was not a manly boy, but whose fault was that? Deep down, Eddie had never been able to stand being around him. A difficult baby had grown into a difficult child who cried too easily, trembled uncontrollably when Eddie rabbit-punched him for fun, missed Petie the few nights he'd consented to spend away from home. The only other adult he trusted was Rose, and Eddie knew it. There were some things you couldn't change.

Petie pulled out onto the highway, headed for Souperior's. First school and now this. Against her better judgment she had some of her

drawings and watercolors in the backseat that she was going to show to
Gordon. Rose promised to meet her there, in case she lost her nerve.

You think you're something special, girlie? You think you're some kind of
artist? Old Man used to jeer at her. *If you think I'm going to buy you paper*
or pencils, you're wrong. If you want to doodle, the school can damn well give
you supplies. I pay for them with my tax money, don't I? Ask the school. Ask
them!

All Petie's paintings and drawings were tiny, most of them smaller
than a postcard, the only size that even in the damp trailer was guaran-
teed to dry before Old Man came back and tore them up. Rose had made
Petie a special decoupaged cigar box where she could store her pictures
until the next morning, when she'd bring them to Rose's house.

Rose was already waiting at a table by the streaming windows when
Petie arrived. Petie could hear the blood in her veins.

"So?" Rose said.

"Good news. He probably has a learning disability."

"So it didn't have anything to do with that little boy?"

"No—she didn't even know what I was talking about."

"Thank God," said Rose.

"Thank God."

"So what did Eddie think?"

"He's pissed. He thinks it should have been Ryan."

"No."

Petie shrugged. "So where's Gordon?"

"Not here yet. You want a cup of coffee?"

"Not as much as I want a cigarette. I'll be outside if he shows up."

"You shouldn't."

"Don't cross me," Petie said darkly.

Rose held up her hands in mock surrender and tossed Petie a disposable lighter and a pack of Merits she had put in her purse this morning, figuring one of them might need one. Petie left the decoupaged box
on the banquette seat. There were so many mornings when Petie had
shown up with that little box tucked under one arm. Rose always looked

through it while Petie was showering, and what she often found were pictures of the most unlikely things: a composition of beer bottles in the rain, a ball of tinfoil on a slice of American cheese, five buttons and a cigarette pack. No people; there were never any people.

Now, waiting for Gordon, Rose peeked again into the same little box and found it filled this time with tiny sketches and watercolors of sun-soaked fruits and vegetables, feather bouquets, loaves of bread, wheels of cheese. Tiny things, still; splendor in miniature, thimbles of magnificence.

Petie and Gordon came to Rose's table at the same time, Petie from the kitchen, Gordon through the street entrance. Both wore beaded caps of rain. Gordon looked good, stronger than he'd looked for several months. He wore an air of quiet dread, presumably born of worry about the degree of Petie's incompetence and his ability to deal with it kindly.

Petie pushed the box across the table towards Gordon without a word and turned away to look over Hubbard Bay. Gordon lifted the lid and for an eternity, without a word, reviewed the whole stack once, turned it over and examined it again. Petie never looked at him and Rose never looked away, resisting the urge to gnaw a nail only through the purest self-control. Finally he tapped the pictures into order, looked at Rose and frowned, clearing his throat several times.

Petie's hand tightened just perceptibly around her coffee mug. Her focus on the streaming windowpane never wavered. A wisp of hair, silhouetted against the window, pulsed with a vein at her temple. "It's okay," she said. "Rose wanted me to do it. I did it."

"Oh my God, imagine my relief!" Gordon burst out, failing to keep up the sham of his disappointment any longer. He grinned crazily at Rose, who colored with pleasure from her bosom to her hairline. "Oh, my dear, these are wonderful, *wonderful*. I'll need to send one or two down to L.A. so Paul can see the quality, but I'll recommend Petie absolutely and without reservation. I think this work, her style, is just exactly right. Petie, if they ask you to come up with new pictures, say, a bunch of carrots, a steaming soup bowl, that sort of thing, how would you feel?"

"Fine," Petie said to the windowpane. Gordon looked at Rose. What was up?

"Petie?" Rose said.

Petie rose, pressing her hands flat on the tabletop. When she took them away again, there was blood on the tablecloth. She had put her fingernails through her palms.

She walked out of Souperior's without another word.

In the center of the table the pictures remained, mute and deafening.

"Will she come back?" Gordon asked, disconcerted.

"Oh yes," said Rose, her eyes brilliant. "Oh yes."

WHEN ROSE got home, only Jim Christie was there, watching the news on television. When he was out on the boats, he read, read all kinds of things like studies in quantum physics and volumes of poetry from the 1920s, and works by Upton Sinclair and John Steinbeck. He never discussed these books with anyone or read the same thing twice. But when he was home, he was a news fanatic, avid to catch up on the things he'd missed while he was away. Rose found him absorbed in a TV clip about Halston's newest line, introduced that day on the irrelevant runways of Paris.

Rose told him about Petie and the pictures. "I wish you could have been there," she said. "You could have cut the air it was so thick. And then he loved them. He *loved* them!"

"Good."

Rose shook her head. "You know, all these years and I *still* fall for her act sometimes, that she doesn't care a bit. She cares. She cares so *much*."

Rose kicked off her shoes and tucked her feet up under her skirt, snuggling against Christie. He snaked a hand underneath to cup her calf. "My mother gave her gifts every Christmas—little things, you know, because we didn't have any money, either. Usually it was something she sewed or knitted, a dress or a sweater, maybe. And Petie would have to keep it at our house because one time Old Man saw a new pair of jeans Petie had saved up for months to buy, and he cut them, took a scissors and cut them right up the front of the leg, so even if she fixed them it would always show. He was drunk, of course, but that was Old Man, *Jesus* he was mean. Anyway, so my mother let her keep things in my closet. And Petie always treated those Christmas gifts like they were made of solid gold. Every year she would give my mother one of her little pictures because she couldn't afford to buy us anything, but my mom never put them up on the walls."

"Sounds like your mother treated her good, though," he said.

"Oh, yes and no. She never invited Petie to go with us when we went anywhere, like to visit relatives in the Valley. Petie could act pretty rough, and I think Mother was afraid Petie would embarrass her. Petie knew it, too. She'd never talk about it with me, but she knew all right. No, my mother was a good Christian woman who considered Petie a poor lost lamb who'd strayed from the Lord's protecting gaze. The one thing she did invite Petie to was church, but she never would go with us. She used to say people like her and Old Man didn't belong in a church, not even on a visiting basis. She told me she figured that if either of them actually set foot over the threshold, lightning and hellfire would come in straight through the roof." Rose chuckled, and then said quietly, "God. Petie."

"Lucky thing she's got you."

"Ummh." Under her skirt, Christie's hand moved from calf to thigh, the rough skin of his fingers brushing the softness of hers.

"Where's Carissa?" Rose said.

"Neighbors. She's spending the night."

"Ah," said Rose.

"Uh-huh," said Christie.

And then there was no more talking, not for a long time. Rose loved all of Christie, loved the taste and smell and feel of him, loved his few words and intellectual appetite and sexual generosity. He touched her in exactly the ways she needed to be touched. Sometimes it seemed to her

that their entire relationship was as simple as that. She touched his
sleeping hand and thought that Pogo, the only husband she would probably ever have, had had neither time nor generosity. He'd thrust himself
into her before she was ready and be done before she was ready, and
then he'd get dressed and go out. He'd given her Carissa, though, and for
that she would always be grateful.

Rose had asked Jim Christie once if he'd ever wanted children and
he'd said, *Nope. Don't think I could've been around enough to be a good father, and I don't have the guts to be a bad one. Kids need what they need, and
if they don't get it from you, they'll find it someplace else, or die deep down in
their spirit. Those deaths are silent; you don't even hear them happen, they
just do. One day a kid wakes up broken in ways he can't fix. That's the way it
is,* Christie had said. *The wrong thing isn't being childless; it's having children you can't fill up.*

Maybe that's what was wrong with Ryan; maybe he was waiting for
the neverness of Eddie Coolbaugh to fill him up. Petie and Rose had
poured and poured their love into him, but it wasn't ever enough. His
Thanksgiving Pilgrims died, his playground courage failed him. It was
as though Ryan had been born with Petie's empty places built right in.
And yet, Ryan had a father who lived with them and always had, while
Carissa didn't remember Pogo at all; and of the two children, it was Ryan
who suffered. Why was that? Rose's mother used to say that the Lord
moved in mysterious ways, His wonders to perform. Rose didn't know
about the wonders part. Ryan's yawning needs, Loose's and Eddie's troubles learning, Petie's life—these were not Rose's ideas of wonders, unless
the Lord had a pretty damn peculiar sense of humor. Could He? After
good people like her mother spent their lives celebrating His goodness,
could He really be nothing but a prankster playing with the unfortunate
of His earthly congregation, who made little kids like Ryan with skins
too thin and too porous to keep out fears and troubles, just to see how
much they could take? Her mother had often said that the Lord never
gave his chosen more than they could bear, but Rose thought that was
garbage.

She snuggled deeper beside Jim Christie, fitting her curves into his contours like an interlocking puzzle. She had no answers, but tonight, for her, it was enough simply to know that she and all those she loved were safe and warm and under the shelter of some cover, no matter how inadequate.

Chapter 12

Ron schiffen had a bad feeling, and he wasn't a man generally given to bad feelings. He scraped the end of a bent paper clip across the soles of his boots and listened to Bev on the phone outside his office door. She was talking to someone in the snotty I-know-what-you're-up-to-missy-so-don't-think-I-don't tone she'd begun using lately when Petie called. A moment later, the intercom buzzed. "It's Petie for you," she said. "Eddie Coolbaugh's wife."

"My *God*, I hate that woman," Petie's furious little voice came to him through the receiver. "Is she awful to everyone, or just to me?"

"Just you," Schiff admitted.

"She makes you want to take a shower, like she's dripped slime all over you."

"Ooh," said Schiff.

"Oh, *screw* you—"

"That would be nice."

"I'm hanging up."

"No, no! No. Don't." Schiff sat up straighter and put both soles flat on the floor. He could hear Bev outside, rattling drawers in the file cabinet nearest his office, her regular listening post.

"I have to cancel lunch," Petie said.

"No you don't."

"Yes I do. I'm sorry. Marge had to take Larry to the hospital this morning. I said I'd watch the office."

"When?"

"Right now. I'm already here. Look, call me when Bev's at lunch."

Schiff listened to the familiar sound of Petie hanging up on him. To the dead receiver he said loudly, "I'll let Eddie know when he gets back. I hope it's nothing serious."

"Someone we know in Hubbard's got heart problems," he said once he'd hung up, for Bev's sake.

"I'll bet," he heard her mutter.

There might come a time when he'd have to fire that woman.

Now he wouldn't be seeing Petie at lunch, which he'd been looking forward to for days. He could call her when Bev went to lunch—if she went to lunch, which she probably wouldn't do today just to gall him. He could at least hear Petie's voice. Or he could make up some Pepsi business in Hubbard, maybe pretend to inquire about an outstanding invoice at the Quik Stop and swing by the motel on the way. Except that everyone knew his rig, and if he parked at the motel, or even at the Quik Stop, there would be talk about why he'd come to Hubbard in the middle of the day, which he never did, and without even letting Carla know. Worse, Carla herself might drive by, see his truck, go into one of her jealous rages and come busting in demanding to know what he was doing at the Sea View Motel with Petie Coolbaugh. And what was he supposed to say? That he was just talking to her, because he liked talking to her better than anything else he could think of, even knowing she would never sleep with him? Who would believe that? Hell, even *he* wouldn't believe that. And it would make no difference at all that it was the truth.

So he bided his time until fat Bev finally went to lunch at almost one o'clock, when the other office staff would be coming back. By his reckoning, he had somewhere between five and ten minutes of listener-free time. He dialed the Sea View's number. Petie answered on the second ring.

"Sea View Motel," she said.

Schiff put on a cornball voice. "Is this the Sea View Motel?"

"I just said it was."

"Well, do you have a honeymoon suite with a Jacuzzi?"

"No. Check with the Whaler, or the Spindrift. Do you want their phone numbers?"

"Nah," Schiff said, dropping the act. "I'd only want one if you were part of the package."

"Give me a break," Petie said.

"Does that mean no?"

"Don't fuck with me today, Schiff. Not today."

"You're no fun. How's Larry?"

"I haven't heard from Marge yet. He looked awful, though, when I got here. He was all sweaty and gray—you know the look people have when they're real sick. It shouldn't happen to them. Larry's a good man."

"Bad things happen to good people too, you know," Schiff said.

"Well, they shouldn't."

"I don't know what world you grew up in," Schiff said, "but where I come from bad things happened to good people all the time."

"Then we must come from the same place."

"You want me to bring you something to eat?"

"Why? Where are you? Are you here?"

"No."

"So what if I said yes?"

"I'd bring you something to eat."

"Really?"

"Yep," Schiff said, realizing it was true.

"That's the nicest thing anyone's said to me all day," Petie said.

"Must not be a very good day."

"No, not very."

A car door slammed in the Pepsi distributorship parking lot. "Sorry, princess," Schiff said. "Gotta go."

"Okay."

"Be good," he said.

"What's the point?"

"Ooh," he said, but only after he was sure Petie had hung up.

. . .

SHE STOOD by the plate-glass window in the motel office for a long time, watching the squalls stalk across the bay. The last time she'd been alone in this office was when Ryan was an infant lying in a bin beneath the counter. Nothing had changed since then except the year on the Craftsman tool wall calendar. Like a time machine, the toothpick cup and cut-glass candy dish, the green sculpted carpeting and wood-look paneling hurtled her backwards at the speed of thought. If it were possible would she choose to hear Ryan's baby wail one more time? Maybe so, maybe just for a few minutes. She had loved the smell of his skin, the feeble flailing of arms and legs as frail as chicken wings. He had been—still was—a difficult child, but secretly dearer to her by far than big-headed Loose who, let's face it, looked too damn much like Old Man. Ryan was everything lost and afraid that Petie had ever felt but fought, as though her troubles had come back to fall, redoubled, on Ryan's fragile head.

And what of fear, really? Had she ever been more afraid of anything than she was of the all-seeing eyes of that baby, whose booties were smaller than oysters, whose dependence on her goodness was absolute? Her abiding terror for years was of fucking up, of boiling the boy, of pushing him into oncoming traffic, of hurting him in any of a hundred other ways. It was her legacy, her inheritance, her hand-me-down junk from generations of Old Man's people, and Paula's, too. Even now she marveled that so many years had gone by and for all his fragility Ryan had come to no harm at her hand. There in the lobby of the Sea View Motel, the ghosts of Paula Tyler, of Petie's terrible grandfather, of Old Man himself swarmed overhead with the beating of soiled wings.

AFTER THEIR eviction Petie and Old Man lived in the little humpbacked trailer in the woods off and on for four years. The Adult and Family Services people had contacted Old Man once, a couple of years after Paula died, about a report that he was providing substandard living conditions for Petie. Old Man had sidestepped it all somehow, which was okay with Petie. She was on her own most of the time by then, anyway, bringing herself up with Rose's help. Old Man had a job sometimes as a night security guard down at the docks, and even though everyone knew he was nothing but a drunk, they gave him a flashlight and a jacket and told him to keep an eye on the boats and call if he saw something suspicious—which of course he never did, since he was the most suspicious person for miles around. Petie always knew when he came in, reeking of beer or whiskey, in the early morning. She'd pretend to be asleep while he peed out the trailer door, stumbled into his rickety cot and passed out cold.

Then came a night when he was less drunk than usual, but more addled. He shook her by the shoulder. She hit him hard in the solar plexus with her elbow, lit the Coleman lantern and sat up, shivering. He was crouching on the trailer floor holding his head in his hands and making peculiar noises, not quite human. His mouth hung slack on one side, and he kept saying something she couldn't understand. Then, with prodigious effort, he managed the last coherent word Petie would hear him utter for five months. *Scared*. It was probably the only thing that saved him.

Petie put a blanket over his shoulders and told him to stay where he was until she brought help. He kept his eyes on her face like a lifeline. She could hear him keening as she got into his truck. It was the awful sound of a bad man reckoning with his own wrongdoing and coming smack up against the knowledge that he could rightfully claim no slack and no mercy, not from God and certainly not from her.

Petie had been driving down to the docks and the Wayside for years to haul Old Man home. She took the wheel now with a deadly calm, pulling into the Coast Guard station at the mouth of the bay.

"My father is sick," she told the duty officer. "We need help."

"Did you call 911?"

"We don't have a phone."

"I can call for you."

"We don't live in a house."

The duty officer slung on his coat. "Where is he now?"

Petie led the officer back to the trailer. Old Man was lying on the floor, uncovered and unconscious, lying in a small pool of vomit. The Coast Guard officer called for an ambulance and monitored Old Man's breathing and pulse while they waited. Petie rode with the team to the hospital over in Sawyer. Her talk with the emergency room people was blunt.

"He's a drunk," she told them. "He's always been a drunk. I don't know what you'll be doing to him, but you're going to have to dry him out first."

She saw the nurses look at each other. One of them, a tired man with a gentle face, said, "We were told about the, ah, conditions your father was found in. Do just the two of you live there?"

"Yes."

"What about your mother, where is she?"

"Dunno. She's dead, though."

Four eyebrows went up; two mouths turned down.

"Oh?"

"Yeah."

The male nurse noticed two linear wounds on Old Man's arm and shoulder, each a couple of inches long, still healing, apparently deep but very clean, almost surgical.

"What's this?" he asked Petie.

"He must have cut himself," she said blandly.

"Oh?"

"Yeah."

"Sweetie, let's be honest," the nurse said. "Those aren't ordinary cuts, and they weren't self-inflicted."

"Really?"

"Really. So you don't know anything about them?"

Petie waited a beat, looking the nurse straight in the eye. "Sometimes he spends time with the wrong people."

"Ah. Well, they appear to be healing," said the nurse, still frowning at Petie. "Do you have any older brothers or sisters, an aunt or an uncle maybe, someone you can stay with?"

"No."

"How old are you, honey?" the second nurse, a woman, asked her.

"I just turned fourteen."

More side glances all around. Finally the male nurse said, "I think the hospital is obligated to contact Adult and Family Services about you. You can't go back there alone."

Petie was surprised. "Why? It'll be better than living there with him."

"How long have the two of you been living there? The ambulance people made it sound very, ah, primitive."

"Four years, two months, three weeks and a day. Except once for two months and once for three, when he fooled somebody into renting us some piece-of-shit house."

More frowns. An administrator was called in, a whispered consultation held behind a curtain, and the woman finally approached Petie. She cleared her throat and said, "Patricia, I understand that you have no friends or family in the area whom we can call for you. And we can't let you go back to your—well, back. From what the doctor has told me, your father has had a rather serious stroke. He will have to stay here for at least several days while we stabilize and evaluate him, and then he'll have to go through some sort of rehabilitation. There's no way of telling right now how long that might take, but it could be months."

Petie nodded.

"Look, I'll be frank," said the administrator. "We have a bit of a dilemma here. Legally we can't let you leave without knowing you're in the care of a responsible adult. If you don't have any friends or family members you can stay with, we'll have to call Adult and Family Services to request a foster home for you."

"I'm not going to a foster home."

The male nurse shook his head. "Then give them an alternative, kiddo. They can't just let you go. You know that."

"Give me a few minutes," she asked the administrator, who frowned but agreed.

"I'm trusting you not to leave here, Patricia, without our permission. If you run, we can't help you."

Petie thought hard. Rose's mother wouldn't take her in, she knew, and if she called anyway she'd only get Rose in trouble. But there was no way in hell she was going to some snake-pit foster home. She approached the administrator. "Do you have a phone book?"

"A local one?"

Petie nodded.

"Of course," the hospital administrator said, leading Petie down a short hall to her office and taking a phone book from a shelf above her desk.

Petie drew a deep breath. "Look in the *C*'s," she said. "Look for Coolbaugh. Eula Coolbaugh."

WITH AN effort Petie tore herself away from the window and the quicksand of her memory. She dialed the Pepsi distributorship. When Bev put her through, she said, "Schiff, look. I need you to do something for me."

"Shoot."

"My skin is crawling. Will you call the hospital and ask about Larry? I have a bad feeling."

"I know," he said. "I've had one all day."

Petie hung up and then reconnected, this time calling Rose. She explained the situation and asked Rose to pick up Ryan and Loose and take them home with her. The minute she hung up the phone rang again.

"Hi," Schiff said. "He's not doing well. He had a torn aorta. They were afraid he wouldn't make it to Portland, so they operated on him here. He came out an hour ago."

"Did you talk to Marge?"

"Yeah, for just a minute." Schiff cleared his throat. "Look, princess, there's a good chance he won't make it. He probably had a stroke on the table, and now he's going into renal failure. His system's just not up to this."

The line was silent.

"Petie?" Schiff said.

"Yeah. I should call their kids."

"Already done. They'll get here as soon as they can."

"You called them?"

"Yes."

"Why?"

"Because Marge couldn't. Look, it's the middle of winter, no one's going to check in. Switch on the NO VACANCY sign and get out of there."

"Yeah. I'll come over and sit with Marge until her kids get here. Will you let Eddie know what's going on? Rose is going to pick up the boys and keep them until he gets home."

"No problem." Schiff could hear in her voice that she was a million miles away. "Hey, Petie," he said.

"What?"

"Drive carefully."

PETIE CLICKED on the NO VACANCY sign, jumped in her car and headed for Sawyer Samaritan Hospital. Larry and Marge. There was never just Larry or just Marge; like salt and pepper shakers, or egg white and yolk, they were a matched pair, a nested set, a unit indivisible. Petie couldn't imagine one of them without the other. They had brought up three kids, gone to church every Sunday for forty-five years, lain in bed side by side through head colds and stomach flu and pregnancy. They had chosen sheets and shopped for groceries and buried parents and decorated Christmas trees together. They were aging and dumpy and jug-eared and failing in a dozen small ways and they still looked at each other like they were all by themselves in a fairy tale. When walking any distance, they always held hands. Maybe Jim Christie held Rose's hand sometimes. Eddie Coolbaugh and Petie never did, never had. But then, they hadn't started that way. Petie couldn't even remember when it had occurred to her that she was in love with Eddie.

She pulled into the hospital parking lot. To her surprise, Schiff's truck was also just pulling in. "I gave Eddie the rest of the day off," Schiff said in greeting. "Did you pass him on the headland?"

"I don't know. I wasn't paying much attention. Has anything changed?"

"With Larry? I don't know, I haven't called again. I decided to just come down."

They walked into the hospital lobby in silence and made straight for the second-floor waiting room. Everyone who'd lived in Hubbard for long had been inside the small hospital for a birth, an operation, a false alarm, a visit. Old Man had died there. Ryan and Loose had been born in the three-bed obstetrics ward, and there had been countless visits since for stitches. Now the elevator stopped on the second floor and Petie and Schiff turned left without missing a beat. Alone in the tiny waiting room at the end of the hall, Marge sat with her back to them, looking out the window.

Petie put her hand softly on Marge's shoulder as she came around the ugly plastic couch.

"Oh, honey," Marge said, showing the full wreckage of her face. "You wouldn't believe what's happened."

Petie pulled up a chair opposite Marge, and put one hand on Marge's knee. "I know. Schiff told me. He's called DeeDee and Frank and Bobby. They're on their way."

"You know, I believe he's going to be all right. They aren't saying that, of course, but I believe it anyway. Me and Larry, we know things about each other. Honey, he's fighting, I can feel it. Can't you feel it?"

Petie looked Marge full in the face. "No," she said. "But I don't have to, as long as you can."

Marge patted Petie's knee absently, deafened by the din inside her own head. "You know, when he was in the hospital over in the Valley, when he had his first heart attack, they thought he would die then, but Larry, he fooled them. He showed them then, didn't he?" She looked beseechingly at Petie and Schiff, who stood behind Petie's chair. "It's not his time yet. If it was, I'd know. Wouldn't I?"

"Let me get you something to eat," Petie said. "Can you think of anything you'd like?"

"Oh, no, honey, I couldn't eat a thing."

"Coffee, then. Or tea. You need to keep up your strength."

Schiff leaned over to Petie. "I'll go. You stay here."

"Why, isn't that nice of him," Marge said, watching Schiff walk away. She leaned in closer to Petie and said, "He's always been a little *forward* for me, if you know what I mean, but I'm glad he's here just the same." She sat back and ran a fluttering hand over her hair. "I must look so bad, honey. I didn't even shower this morning. Larry, he said to me he wasn't feeling good and I know him, he doesn't say that unless it's serious. That's when I called you, honey. He passed out coming over the cape, did I tell you? I was so scared. I was just so *scared*. Oh, honey." She started to cry. "The doctors, they don't know if Larry can get through this. They just don't know."

Petie moved over to sit beside Marge so she could put her arm around her shoulder. She had learned very early that there are times when words are as useless as a broken umbrella, and this was one of them. The rain had to fall; the best you could do was huddle together until it passed. In a little while Marge gathered herself and pushed off from Petie to sit up on her own. "I'm sorry, honey," she said.

"Do you want me to talk to the doctors for you?" Petie said.

"Oh, no. I know they're real busy with Larry. They'll come see us after a while. Do you know they won't let me see him except for fifteen minutes an hour? Now, I don't see the point of that." She looked indignantly at Petie. "I might just try to walk in there and see if they'll make me leave. Larry has no secrets from me."

"I don't think it's secrets they're worried about. I think they just want him to have all the quiet he needs to get his strength back," Petie soothed. "Once he's stronger, they'll let you stay with him more, I'm sure."

"Well," Marge said, and drifted away on a current of thought.

Petie sat quietly for a minute or two, but when it became unbearable she stood and paced. There was no sign of Schiff. She walked down the hall to the nurses' station and got the attention of a nurse she didn't recognize. "Excuse me," she said quietly. "I'm a friend of Marge and Larry Hopkins. I'll stay here with Marge until their kids get here from Arizona and California. How is Larry doing?"

"You're a close family friend?"

"Yes."

"Then I'll be blunt. Mr. Hopkins had a stroke during surgery, and there's been extensive damage. His kidneys have also begun to fail."

Petie nodded. "Is there any possibility of his pulling out of this?"

The nurse looked at Petie kindly. "I'm sorry. It's really only a question of how quickly he'll die."

"Have the doctors told Marge that?"

"Yes, but I don't believe she heard them."

"No," Petie said. "I could tell that. Is Larry in any pain? Does he know what's happening?"

The nurse shook her head. "He's in no pain, we're making sure of that. As far as how aware he is, that's harder to answer. He's in a deep coma, and there's been extensive brain injury. I would encourage you and Mrs. Hopkins to talk to him when you're with him, in case it brings him comfort, but frankly, I think he's already gone."

"Do you know how much time he has?"

"No. Maybe one day, maybe several. He's on life support now, so how quickly he passes away will be partly up to the family. There should be enough time to say goodbye."

"But there's no hope."

"I'm sorry."

"Thank you," Petie said, and turned away and muttered under her breath, "Jesus *Christ*."

At the other end of the hall, Schiff had returned and was sitting with Marge, encouraging her to drink the coffee he'd brought up in foam cups. Petie caught his eye. He stood and came over to her, where they could talk out of range. Marge didn't seem to notice.

"He's dying," Petie said.

"Does she know?"

"They've told her, but no, she doesn't know."

Schiff nodded. "Look. Why don't you go back to Hubbard and pack some things for her? They'll let her sleep here tonight if there's an empty room. I'll stay with her until you get back."

"Can you do that? Don't you have to get back to work?"

"I'm the boss," Schiff said. "I've given myself the afternoon off."

"You don't even really know these people. You don't have to do this."

"Get going."

"Hey, Schiff?"

"Go. *Go*. Shoo." He turned his back on her and returned to the waiting room at the end of the hall. It was as great an act of courage as Petie had ever seen.

PETIE MADE the drive over the headland and into Hubbard in record time, preparing a mental packing list: medicines, hairbrush, toothbrush and other toiletries; a pair of knit slacks and a matching top; a change of shoes and socks; a jacket, nightgown, robe and slippers. It was only when she got back to the hospital that she realized she hadn't made even a token effort to bring anything for Larry. She'd pretend to Marge that his things were in the trunk of her car until he needed them.

Schiff must have seen her drive up. He met her at the second-floor elevator and lightly laid his hand on the small of her back. "Breathe deep," he said. "She's starting to get it."

"Uh-oh."

"Uh-huh. It's not pretty. They've sedated her a little to keep her together, but it's been touch-and-go a couple times. Screaming, sobbing, like that." Schiff ran his fingers through his thinning hair.

"How's Larry? Has anything changed?"

"No. Look, I should take care of one or two things in the office, but I'll come back as soon as I can."

"No, don't come back. I can stay now until their kids start showing up. What time is it? DeeDee should be here in another few hours. Has Marge eaten anything? If they're drugging her I've got to get her to eat."

Schiff shook his keys free of the change in his pocket. "Okay, look. I'll be near the phone if you need anything. If I don't pick up, tell Bev to get my ass out of the bathroom. I won't be any farther away than that. After five just call me at home."

Petie lifted an eyebrow. "Oh, right."

"Look, I'll explain the situation to Carla."

"Hell will freeze over before I'd ever call you at home," Petie said. "Call me in the morning and I'll fill you in."

"Jesus, princess, you're a scrappy little thing, aren't you?"

"That's me," said Petie, turning on her heel and walking away.

PETIE SET the suitcase with Marge's things beside the sofa in the waiting room. Marge herself was gone, so Petie walked back down the hall and looked through the door into the intensive care unit. At the end of the ward, partially obscured by a curtain, she could see Marge standing beside what must be Larry's bed. Petie couldn't hear her, but she could see that Marge was talking a mile a minute. *That Marge, she's a talker,* Larry liked to say. *Don't matter if she has anything to tell you or not—hell, she can spend half an hour telling you there's nothing new.* Then he'd pat her arm lovingly, and she would blush and dimple even though she'd heard him say the same thing a million times.

The nurse Petie had talked to earlier spotted her at the door and, misunderstanding, beckoned her inside. When Petie reached her, she whispered, "I'll let you go in, but just for a few minutes. We've given Mrs. Hopkins a mild sedative, by the way, to see if we can keep her calm. She'd been getting agitated, and that's no help to anyone."

"I don't really need to see him."

"No, go ahead. Just don't stay long."

With dread Petie approached in silence. She could hear Marge saying, "Darlin', you do what you have to do. I'd keep you here forever and ever, you know that, but if the good Lord is asking you back to His table for supper, why, that's an honor you can't turn down. You go on ahead, honey, and I'll be there as soon as I can. You just ask Him to keep my dinner warm."

Petie willed herself to walk the last few steps, willed her face to take on a gentle expression instead of the horror she felt. When she touched Marge on the shoulder, Marge twitched away, and Petie backed up again. Larry looked like a wax effigy, a botched job with lips too narrow and eyes too deep and ears the size of saucers. Beneath the light sheet covering him she knew he'd been laid open from breastbone to navel, but there was no evidence of pain or spoilage. On the other hand, there was also no evidence of life.

The nurse swept by Petie and stood at Marge's side. "Why don't you get off the ward for a few minutes, Mrs. Hopkins? I have some nursing things to do for your husband. Your friend is here now, and it would do you good to walk a little. We'll page you if anything changes."

"It's a good idea, Marge," Petie said. "Come downstairs with me and let me find you something to eat. Larry would never forgive me if I let you go hungry."

Marge turned her ruined face to Petie and nodded. "All right, honey," she said. "All right." She allowed Petie to steer her downstairs to the tiny cafeteria and buy a club sandwich that she doctored with mayonnaise and abandoned. They were back on the ward in ten minutes flat, and that only because Petie had done her best to stall.

DeeDee, Larry and Marge's daughter, swept onto the ward half an hour later, while Marge was at Larry's bedside. Petie recognized her instantly. She was bosomy and moon-faced and loud, and Petie had only met her once before, when she brought her husband and two kids up from Tempe and they all got food poisoning at the Snack Shack. That had been two years ago, and in Petie's opinion DeeDee looked even worse now than she had after vomiting for twenty-four hours.

"Oh Lord," she said to Petie in greeting, "I cannot believe what's happening. I get a call at work from some man I've never heard of, and the next thing I know I've stuck my kids with the neighbor and I'm sobbing on a damn airplane. I'm surprised I didn't drive into a tree on the way down here from Portland. Look at my eyes! They're going to be swollen completely shut by morning."

"They might have Murine down at the gift shop," Petie said.

DeeDee waved away the problem. "Tell me first about Mother. Is she all right?"

"No, but they've given her a mild tranquilizer and she's managing. It'll be easier for her now that you're here."

"And Daddy?"

"Look, DeeDee, I don't do these things well, so I'll just say it. He's in a coma. His kidneys are shutting down. The nurse on duty told me that it's the way a lot of doctors want to die, because it doesn't hurt. You just slip away."

"Does Mother know that?"

"Yes."

"Where is she now?"

"With Larry." Petie led her to Larry's bedside, where Marge and DeeDee clung together in something between a bear hug and mutual collapse. Finally Marge held her daughter at arm's length and looked her over.

"Oh, your poor eyes! Baby, they'll be swollen shut by morning. We'll have to get you some Murine. They probably have things like that in the gift shop downstairs."

DeeDee smiled wanly and nodded in Petie's direction. "That's exactly what she said."

"She's allergic to her own tears," Marge explained to Petie. "Always has been, poor thing." To DeeDee she said, "You remember Petie, honey, who helps Daddy and me out sometimes at the motel?"

DeeDee nodded, but her thoughts had clearly moved on. "Isn't there something else they can do? I have to say, Mother, that he'd be much better off in Portland at a real hospital."

"There wasn't any time, honey. And now it's too late." Marge drew a shaky breath. "You know Daddy's only holding on to say goodbye to you all."

"I don't believe this," DeeDee said.

"Do you know when your brothers will get here?" Petie asked her.

"Sometime this evening. They were catching the same flight out of San Francisco."

Petie touched Marge's arm. "Now that DeeDee's here and the others are on the way, it's time for me to go home. I'd like to say goodbye to Larry before I go, if that's all right with you."

"Of course, honey, he'd never forgive you if you didn't. You go on ahead. DeeDee and me will just be down the hall."

When Petie approached Larry's bed it seemed to her that Larry had diminished, was actually, measurably, smaller than he'd been just a few hours ago—as though by morning he might dwindle away completely, not so much in death as through evaporation. She laid her hand on his lightly, outside the covers, and his eyes moved under the lids for a minute. She turned and walked away without saying a word. Her back was straight, her gaze steady, and she remained dry-eyed all the way to Hubbard. She hadn't wept for either Paula Tyler or Old Man, and she didn't intend to weep now. Instead, without having planned it, she pulled into the Wayside, bellied up to the bar and ordered a beer. To her relief, the place was empty except for a young couple she didn't recognize and Dooley Burden sitting in the corner doing a crosstik. Roy was bartending.

"Hey, Petie," he said in greeting. "We heard about Larry."

"Yeah," Petie said.

"Any chance of him pulling out of it?"

"No."

Roy shook his head and polished up a glass. "So how's Marge?"

Petie shrugged. "Better than she's going to be in a few days. Her kids are coming in, though."

"Shit," Roy said sympathetically.

"Yeah. Has Schiff been in?"

Roy's eyebrows went up but he kept his expression neutral. "Haven't seen him."

Petie ran her thumb over the old bar, all the cuts and nicks and fork bites Hubbard's finest had been laying down in that oak slab for more than thirty years. Old Man, alone, had been responsible for a set of knife cuts twelve inches long and nearly half an inch deep at a stretch of the bar he'd held up from the time he was old enough to order his first beer to the day he died.

"Well, speak of the devil," Roy said to Petie, and lifted his chin in their direction as Schiff and Carla walked through the Wayside door. Carla was dressed in a tarty dress with little X's and O's all over it and had the long jaw and beaky nose of a born nag. She glared at Petie and chose a corner table as far from her as she could get. Schiff came and stood by Petie's barstool with his back to Carla, though it may not have been intentional.

"I called the hospital a few minutes ago but they wouldn't tell me anything," he said. "How's Larry?"

Petie ran her hand over her face to quiet her heart. God, but it had been a long day. She felt suddenly like her skin had been peeled away. "No change. DeeDee got there about an hour ago. The other two are due in this evening."

"And Marge?"

Petie looked at Schiff. When she spoke, it came out as a sob. "She told him"—she faltered, and drew a deep breath—"she told him if the Lord was calling him home, it was okay for him to go."

"Jesus," he said, but Carla was waiting and the Wayside was all ears. "Look, Petie. You take care."

And he turned and walked away.

Later they heard that the whole family had assembled at Larry's bedside by mid-evening. They stayed with him until he died peacefully at five forty-five the next afternoon—recalled, as Marge would tell it, to the gracious table of our Lord.

Chapter 13

EULA COOLBAUGH always said there was something happy about lemons, their cheerful color and their firm, tidy shape. Petie had never seen a lemon close up until she moved to Eula's house, where there were always lemons in a wire basket hanging over the sink. *Honey, to me a lemon is like a pretty girl who believes she's plain,* she used to say to Petie. *The lemon doesn't make a lot of fuss the way a mango or a papaya does, flashing all those cheap bright colors around for everyone to see. But when you gussy her up with a little sugar, why you realize she's a beauty. You and that lemon, honey, you have an awful lot in common.*

Even so many years later, Petie could remember word for word the conversation between the hospital administrator and Eula Coolbaugh that morning at Sawyer Samaritan after Old Man had his stroke. The hospital administrator had dialed the phone, briefly introduced herself and described Petie's situation. It was only seven o'clock in the morning, but Eula Coolbaugh gave no indication that she was taken aback either by the early hour or the astonishing nature of the call. The administrator handed the phone to Petie.

"Hi, Petie," Eula had said, as though they spoke all the time instead of just once, years before. "I was hoping I'd have a reason to come to Sawyer today. Now I do. I'll be there in twenty minutes, hon. Is that okay with you?"

To her eternal mortification, Petie started to cry, nodding as though Eula could see her over the telephone.

"Hon? Look, you just sit right there in the lobby. I've got my car keys in my hand. You watch for me, and before you know it I'll be there." And she had been. Like an avenging angel she had descended on Sawyer Samaritan Hospital, folded Petie in her substantial wings and lifted her up to heaven.

A room of her own, with clean linens and a handmade quilt.

A closet.

A bathroom with running water.

"Why don't we go pick up your things, hon, once you've had some breakfast," Eula had said while Petie sat at her kitchen table for the first time, wolfing cereal.

"I don't have any things."

"You must have clothes."

"A few. My friend Rose's mother lets me keep them in the closet at her house."

"Hairbrush, toothbrush?"

"I keep them in my backpack." Petie could feel Eula Coolbaugh watching her as she drank the dregs of cereal milk from her bowl.

"More?" Eula asked her.

"Yes. Yes, please."

Eula had set the cereal box and jug of milk in front of Petie and stroked her hair, just once, as though it wasn't skunk-colored, poorly cut and not quite clean; softly, the way Paula had once done. Petie had forgotten about that. She hoped Eula would do it again, but Eula had gone back to the sink and was washing dishes. Then Petie heard footsteps on the stairs.

"That'll be Eddie," Eula said. "Running late like he always does."

Eddie came into the room tucking in his shirt, apparently unsurprised to find Petie Tyler sitting at his kitchen table. "Morning, sweetie," Eula said to him. "Petie Tyler's going to be staying with us for a while. Her dad is sick."

Eddie nodded, but his attention was entirely on his breakfast.

"Hon," she said to Petie, "I'm assuming you won't want to go to school today, since you were up most of the night with your dad and all."

"Oh, I always go to school." Petie hadn't missed a day of school in three years, mainly because it was warm and dry at school, and there was food at lunchtime—Rose's extras, if she'd brought enough, cafeteria leftovers if not, scavenged for her by Dooley Burden, who was the school custodian then and who knew Old Man from way back when they were growing up together.

"Well, you go if you want to, hon," Eula said, surprised. "But I think it would do you good to stay home."

"Home?"

"Here."

"Oh." And so she had, staying warm and dry in Eula Coolbaugh's kitchen for the next four years. Now she sat at Eula's table in her own kitchen, looking hard at a basket holding six lemons, two limes and a tangerine. At Gordon's suggestion she was trying pen and ink with a watercolor wash, a technique that was as new to her as it was unforgiving. On the floor beneath her chair were five discarded attempts, soon to be joined by a sixth as, with a small roar, she lost control of her brush again. At the same moment Eddie Coolbaugh threw open the kitchen door and blew inside on the shoulders of the wind.

"Jesus!" he said, slapping his Pepsi cap against his hand to knock off the rain. "Coast Guard's put up storm warnings again."

Petie pushed her watercolors and paper aside. "They closing the bar?" she said. A sandbar at the mouth of the bay made passing into the open ocean dangerous even on a good day. On a bad one, it could sink a fishing boat in minutes.

"Not yet. I heard there's another front coming in after this one, too." Eddie slouched against the doorjamb between the kitchen and living room, listing slightly with the uneven pitch of the floor. "How many of those things do you still have to do?" he said, nodding towards her still life.

"I don't know. Seven maybe, maybe more, depending on whether I can get it right or not. I've only got eight that are keepers, maybe six others I could live with if Gordon can."

"The money's good, though."

"Yeah."

"You hear anything from Marge?"

"No, not yet." Marge had been down in Tempe with DeeDee ever since the day after they held a memorial service for Larry at the First Church of God. Marge and Larry's children had wanted to have the service in the Valley, but Marge said Hubbard was their home and the people there were like family, so three weeks ago more than two hundred people had crammed into the little church to say goodbye. Marge had held up pretty well, all in all. Afterwards she'd whispered to Petie, *Honey, I'd be screaming right now if it wasn't for the drugs they're giving me.* The motel was closed indefinitely. It didn't make any money in winter, anyway.

"So I talked to Schiff today," Eddie said.

"Did you?"

"I laid it out for him, about how I could be a real good assistant manager if he'd train me. I told him I wanted to move up in the company, you know, and I'd do whatever he thought it would take."

"So what did he say?"

"He was interested. He said that right now it would mean keeping me out of Sawyer and Hubbard more, so I could learn all the territory, not just up north. I might go to Portland, too, to regional meetings in Schiff's place sometimes. I'm telling you, it was like he'd already thought about some of this stuff, I mean without my having brought it up."

"You know Schiff," Petie said. "He's always looking for the angles."

"Well, and he likes me, I know he does. He trusts me to not fuck up, you know? Sales on my route are up twenty percent since I started, did I tell you that? No shit. Twenty percent."

"Well, that's something."

"Damn right. I tell you, I've got a future with this company. I could be big—hell, bigger than Schiff, maybe. I mean, you know how he pisses people off. I get along with everyone; I know how to make people comfortable—well, you know how I do. I'm no fuckup."

"Good thing, too, because I'm going to be unemployed again as soon as I finish these drawings. I don't see Marge ever coming back here, do you?"

"Why not?"

"Without Larry? Come on."

Eddie shrugged. "Well sure, she'd need someone to handle the maintenance part, but she could probably hire Dooley cheap."

Petie snorted. "Dooley can't hammer a nail straight."

"Yeah, well, she'd have to watch him."

"Anyway, that's not what I meant. They did everything together. I think she'll miss him too much."

"Tell you the truth, I don't know how two people could spend so much time together."

"I thought it was sweet," Petie said.

"Admit it. If we spent that much time together we'd kill each other."

"So what does that say about us?"

"We're independent."

"We don't have anything in common," Petie said.

"What? We have two kids, that's about as in common as you can get. We go camping in the summer and, you know, like that."

"What else?"

"What do you mean, what else?" Eddie said. "There are the holidays, Christmas and Thanksgiving and shit."

"Yeah."

"Well, okay then." Having proven his point, Eddie went into the living room and turned on the television. Petie set a fresh piece of paper in front of her and picked up her brush.

"Wait," Eddie yelled from the other room. "There's also coffee. We both like coffee."

"Yeah," Petie said, and she thought again what she'd been thinking since that day at the hospital with Marge: that she was going to make a great widow. It would be real tough on the kids if Eddie were to die before they were grown, and there would be times when she would miss him, too. But all in all, she doubted her heart would skip too many beats.

She had mentioned this to Rose a couple of days ago, and Rose said it was the worst thing she'd ever heard, worse even than anything she'd had to say about Pogo. Petie didn't think so. She thought the worst thing she'd ever heard was what Old Man had said about Paula after her death. *I could've saved twenty-five thousand dollars, maybe, if someone had just told me there was a damned hospice near here.*

Petie took up her pen and ink again, but it was hopeless—her hand simply could not find its place on the paper. She put the basket of fruit in the refrigerator and yelled to Eddie that she was going to Rose's house to pick up the boys. Carissa had been baby-sitting them for a few hours so Petie could draw. Not that it had amounted to anything.

She drove the ten blocks to Rose's house in her sleep, thinking about Marge and being left behind in a cold and empty place. She hadn't mourned for Paula, or for Old Man, or for herself as one and then the other left her behind. Eula's passing had been different, awful, like surgery without anesthetic where the pain went on and on. But it hadn't been what Marge was experiencing; nothing Petie could imagine could equal what Marge must be experiencing. Petie shuddered as she turned into Rose's driveway. Christie's truck was gone, and so was Rose's newly spiffed-up Ford, the family's main Christmas present from Christie.

"Helloooo!" Petie hollered as she let herself in Rose's front door. The boys made shushing and hiding noises Petie wasn't supposed to hear in a game nearly as old as they were. Petie clapped her hand over her eyes and played along, searching the house until one by one they gave themselves away by giggling or, in Ryan's case, shivering in nervous anticipation so strong it shook the hangers in the closet where he was hiding. Once Petie had found all three, they bunched up together in the front hall.

"Where's your mom?" Petie asked Carissa.

"Work."

"Where's Jim?"

Carissa shrugged. "Dunno. He goes out a lot anymore. He doesn't tell us where."

"The Wayside, probably," Petie said.

"Nah, he always tells us when he's going there, in case Mom wants to meet him when she's done working."

Petie put one arm around the shoulders of each boy. "So where else could he go? There's no place else to go to. Well, the Anchor, maybe."

Carissa looked away. "Oh, I think he has someplace he goes to when he wants to be by himself."

"What, a cave?" Petie teased. "There isn't anyplace you can go in Hubbard and be by yourself."

Carissa lifted her shoulders. "Well, there might be someplace." Like Rose, she would have pretty breasts one day. Petie could already see Rose's lovely bones, the full, creamy chest. Every time Petie saw her, the girl seemed to have aged another year, but she still had her same sweet face.

"Well, thanks for looking after the boys," Petie said. "Now that you're over in Sawyer every day, we miss seeing you."

"Yeah," Carissa said.

"C'mon, guys," Petie said, shepherding them to the door. "Daddy's waiting for his dinner."

"Bye, 'rissa," the boys bellowed as they went out the door, in another old ritual.

"Do you want to come back with us?" Petie asked. "You don't have to stay here by yourself."

"Oh, no thanks," Carissa said, coloring deeply. "I'll be fine here. There's stuff on TV."

"Okay. But you call if you need anything," Petie said, and backed out quickly into the rain.

THIS TIME Carissa waited to hear Petie's noisy little car disappear down the hill before rooting around in the coat closet again and pulling out one of Rose's slickers, her own rubber boots and a big flashlight. She took a plate of sandwiches out of the refrigerator, and from a cabinet brought out a Tupperware container of homemade chocolate chip cookies she had strong-armed the boys into helping her make right after school. She quickly stowed all these things in a water-proof backpack.

She had debated all day whether to ride her bicycle or walk the twelve blocks, finally deciding to walk because she wanted to look good when she arrived. She had braided her hair into a thick, glossy plait that hung straight down her back, and had changed into a new pair of jeans while the cookies were baking. Now she zipped her slicker up to her throat, lifted her hood into place, slung the backpack over one arm and stepped out into the wet blackness that was nighttime on the Oregon coast in winter.

By her calculations, she had two hours before Rose would get home from work. The walk to the top of Chollum Road took fifteen minutes. When she got there she saw Jim Christie's truck parked beside the hunchbacked trailer. A faint light glowed through the little window.

She walked right up to the door and rattled the handle. She could hear a sudden scuffle of boots, and the thump of something being dropped. Christie opened the door and Carissa hopped up and inside.

"It's so cold," she said to him, hugging herself.

"What are you doing here, girl?" Christie looked angry, but Carissa had been prepared for that. She lifted the plate of sandwiches and the cookies out of her pack. "I thought you might be hungry. I brought you dinner." She looked around and saw that what Christie had dropped was a large hardbound book. He'd been sitting in a folding camp chair, reading by the light of the same Coleman lantern he'd brought the last time she was here. The air was fusty and sweet with the smell of a pipe he'd been smoking, now burning feebly in an ashtray beside the lantern.

"I didn't know you smoked a pipe," she said brightly. "Do you like it better than cigarettes?" She took off her slicker and folded it carefully, laying it on the floor. The trailer was warmer than it had been outside. All the mold was gone from the walls, and a new floor had been laid down.

"You shouldn't be here," Christie said, still standing.

"It's okay," she assured him.

"It isn't."

"Well, at least eat something before I go. It took me fifteen minutes to walk here, and I made the cookies just for you."

Christie took a sandwich with a shaking hand and, still standing, ate it in four bites. Carissa watched, crestfallen. "Why are you so angry all the time? Last summer you used to talk to me but now you don't. You're hardly ever at the house anymore."

"You're real young," Christie said.

"I'll be fourteen next month."

"Yeah."

"That's not young."

"It's young," he said harshly, and then softened his voice. "You could get in trouble here, girl. You could get me in trouble."

"How?"

"Put your coat on. I'll take you home."

"I don't want to go home. No one's there." Carissa began to cry. "I made these sandwiches and cookies and I thought you'd be glad to see me. I've been looking forward to it all day. Why are you like this? You're not like this with Mom."

"Me and your mother are different." Christie took up the lantern and, stooping carefully, stepped out the trailer door. Carissa flung on her coat and followed, sniffling. "Don't you like me?"

"You need to leave me alone," Christie said.

"I think you're awful," Carissa said, and ran out of the woods onto Chollum Road.

❚T TOOK a block and a half for Christie to persuade the girl to get in the truck so he could drive her home. By the time he reached across the seat to shove her door open, his shirt was soaked with sweat. He'd felt safer in full-force storms at sea. Her face, when she climbed in, was all pink and white like a rosebud, and clouded with unhappiness.

"You hate me."

Christie tightened his grip on the steering wheel. "That's not it."

"You'd rather be in that crummy trailer than at home with me."

He pulled into their driveway. Rose wasn't home yet.

"Well, I think there's something wrong with you," Carissa said, slamming her door.

"Maybe so," said Christie, though Carissa had already disappeared inside the house. "Maybe so."

• • •

HALIBUT LEEK AND POTATO

We are very fond of halibut, a fish that goes well with everything from tomatoes to heavy cream. Its sturdy meat keeps to itself instead of falling to pieces and disappearing into the body of a soup the way sole or flounder do. We like using it with leeks and potatoes, which are other modest foods that do well in team efforts.

It had been a desperately quiet night at Souperior's—one couple and a small family, and that was it, total take under forty dollars—but Rose had been able to write. She had five recipes still to go, and barely a week in which to write them. She'd used up all of her and Petie's soups, and now she was either adapting other contestants' recipes or making them up herself. Cheddar shrimp with broccoli. Potato corn chowder. Scallop and oyster stew with biscuits.

She checked her watch and was stunned to find it was seven forty-five, nearly closing time. The kitchen wouldn't take much cleanup. After closing she'd promised to swing by Petie's to see her latest illustrations. Petie had been in a very odd frame of mind lately, and Rose was worried about her. She disappeared sometimes during the day, and she was even more distracted and short than normal. Rose wanted to have a talk with her, but somehow they were never alone together anymore. It looked like this evening would be no different. When she arrived at Petie's house the boys were arguing about which TV channel to watch and Eddie was yelling at both of them to shut up, goddamn it. Petie rolled her eyes and put a bottle of beer in front of Rose at the table.

"Look at these," she said, and handed Rose a stack of pictures: a steaming bowl of soup, a bouquet of rosemary and thyme, a still life with carrots, celery and shallots; a close-up of two potatoes and a yam.

"They're really good," Rose said after she'd looked at each one twice. "They're *really* good. Don't you think so?"

Petie shrugged. "I can live with most of them. I'm hoping Gordon can, too. I worked for an hour tonight and turned out nothing but crap."

"Well, I think these are great." Rose tapped them into a stack and set them carefully in front of Petie. "So tell me about Loose. Didn't you go see Mrs. Hendrik yesterday?"

"Yeah. She said Loose is dyslexic like Eddie, but maybe not as bad. She said they didn't find anything else, no behavior problems. No behavior problems, my ass! I could show them behavior problems all right." Petie chuckled and took a swig of beer.

"So what do they want you to do now?"

"Nothing. They have a Voc Ed person who'll work with him three times a week. They said there was more intensive stuff they can do, too, if that's not enough."

"That sounds okay, doesn't it?"

"Yeah."

"What did Eddie think?"

"Well, you know, this is Eddie we're talking about. He says it's a pile of shit. But he's also the one who wanted Loose to get Voc Ed help as many times a week as they could arrange it. I know it was hard on Eddie back when we were all in school but, you know, he never talked about it, never does now. Eula used to bring it up at dinner sometimes, about how he should never confuse learning problems with basic smarts, because he was just as smart as the next guy, maybe smarter. I don't think he ever believed her, though. He'd always get mad at her for bringing up his problems in front of me. That house was tiny, though. There wasn't any way to talk about anything privately unless you sent everyone out for beer or something."

"So have you told Loose?"

"Oh, kind of. We've told him that he learns in a special way and so does his daddy. He knows he'll get teaching time with someone who knows how he learns and can help him."

"Is he okay with that?"

"Who knows. This is Loose we're talking about, bead of water on a hot skillet. You never know what's getting through and what's not, never mind what'll stick."

"He's a good kid, you know. You should believe in him more."

"Yeah, well," Petie said. "Hey, is Gordon okay?"

"I don't know. He has a new cancer sore on the back of one hand. Nadine's pretty down in the dumps. When we finish the stuff for the book next week he's going to hand-carry it to L.A. and Nadine's going with him this time. I said I'd take care of the cafe for them. I think she needs a break real bad."

"I bet."

Rose pushed herself up from the table, drank the last of her beer and put on her coat. "I need to get home."

"Hey, how late is Christie staying this year? He still waiting until March?"

"It looks like it," Rose said. "We're just loving having him back. If it was up to me, he'd never leave again."

"Think you could talk him into it?"

"No, but I might try anyway."

W**HEN ROSE** got home she found Carissa bundled up in a nightgown and fuzzy robe watching, of all things, a basketball game on television. She looked flushed and miserable, like she was getting sick.

"Good game?" Rose asked her, crossing the room to kiss her on the forehead. No fever.

"What?"

"The basketball game. Who's winning?"

"I don't know," Carissa said dully. "I don't even know who's playing."

"Ah," Rose said, running her hand over Carissa's cheek. "You look like you don't feel well."

"I'm okay."

"Huh. Where's Jim? Have you been here alone all this time?"

Carissa shrugged. "I don't know where he is. He went out someplace. He's always going out when you're not here."

"Well, then it'll just be me and you." Rose kicked off her shoes and sat down on the sofa, tucking up her feet. She put her arm around Carissa and pulled her close.

"Did Daddy like me?" Carissa asked.

"What?"

"Daddy. Did he like spending time with me?"

"What an odd question. Of course Daddy liked you. He liked you better than he liked me, when you get right down to it. He hasn't called, has he?"

"No."

Rose twirled a strand of Carissa's hair around her finger thoughtfully. "When you were born, he said you were the most beautiful ugly thing he'd ever seen."

"There's no such thing as being beautiful *and* ugly."

"Of course there is. Pogo was very perceptive that way. When you were little and trying out your walking legs for the first time, he used to say you walked like a Martian would walk if they suddenly landed on earth."

Carissa smiled. "He said that?"

Rose smiled, too. "Many times." She hugged Carissa close. "What's making you think about Pogo?"

"I don't know. I just wonder sometimes what it would have been like if he'd stayed."

"Oh, honeybun, I can't imagine. Pogo wasn't much of a family man even when he was trying. He had walkin' feet. That's what he used to say—*Rosalie, my feet are only good for one thing, and that's walkin'. They've never been worth a damn for putting up on a couch every night in time for the news.*"

"I bet he just didn't want to stay. He probably didn't love us at all," Carissa said.

"Well, you might think that, but it wasn't so simple. It was an odd thing about Pogo, but he always told the truth, even when it wasn't pretty, or when it wasn't anything you'd want to hear. He was an honest man who never got the knack of staying put."

"How come he's never called or come by?"

"Scared to, would be my guess. And the longer he stays away, the more scared he'll be."

"Scared of what?"

"Could be a lot of things. What I'd say. What you'd say. What we *wouldn't* say, but would think. What he'd do if he liked us enough to maybe stay."

"Do you think he would?"

"Stay?"

"Uh-huh."

"No. Only as long as his walkin' feet would let him, sweetie. Only that long."

"I don't think Jim likes me."

"Oh, that again. Why?"

"He looks at me funny."

"How?"

"I don't know. He just gets this weird look on his face, and then he goes someplace else."

"Hon, I know he likes you," Rose said. "I don't know how I can prove that to you, but he does. Only he's not a family man, you know? He has a life of his own and sometimes he shares it with us, but then he needs to get away from us sometimes, too. It's Jim, sweetie, not us, that's the reason for his doing things or not."

"Do you really think so?"

"Yes, I do, hon, from the bottom of my heart."

"Well, I hope he leaves soon," Carissa blurted out.

"That's a harsh thing to say."

"I don't care."

Rose sighed. "Well, you'll probably be getting your wish sometime soon. He's always gone by March, you know that. And he hasn't said this year will be any different."

"That'll be okay with me. Just us two again, like we used to be."

Rose rested her cheek on the top of Carissa's head. "Yes. Just us two. You know, I can think of worse ways of living than that."

THE NEXT day, Rose went to Sawyer, bringing the final *Local Flavor* manuscript to Gordon. It was 225 pages of double-spaced recipes and text, more words than Rose would have thought she knew how to put together. Petie's pictures were finished, too, except for two more small illustrations they'd send by UPS when they were done. Rose wondered if she'd miss it, once the work was finished. Who knew? Maybe she and Petie would think of something else to write about— seafood? maybe a seafood cookbook?—that Paul would like. Or maybe they could write a traveler's guide. They could call it *Off the Beaten Path in Oregon*. It might work. She and Petie, between them, could find enough to talk about, she was sure, especially if they drove back into the valleys on logging roads. Petie knew a lot of them, and they could explore the rest using U.S. Forest Service maps. She could write it, and Petie could illustrate it. She'd ask Gordon about it. Maybe he could help.

Rose knocked on his apartment door and waited for the muffled call to come in. Instead of the usual cheerful shout, though, Gordon simply opened the door. A deep purple lesion climbed from just above his left eye to his hairline. He looked pale and ill and for the first time since Rose had known him, she understood that he would die. How Nadine would deal with that Rose couldn't begin to imagine. Nadine was as close to Gordon, in many ways, as Marge had been to Larry, and look how that was turning out. Petie had gotten a call from DeeDee just yesterday say- ing that Marge didn't have the heart to come back to Hubbard knowing Larry wasn't there, so she'd decided to stay in Tempe for a while, rent a little place of her own near DeeDee and the kids and see what happened.

DeeDee had asked if Petie wanted to run the Sea View Motel for her, keeping everything for herself over and above the bank loan payment. If Petie didn't want to do it, they'd understand, DeeDee had said, but in that case they'd have to sell the place, and at almost the worst time of year. Petie had promised to give her an answer in the next few days.

Gordon and Rose sat down across from each other at his kitchen table. She set the stack of pages in front of him, put a cardboard portfolio filled with Petie's drawings beside it, and smiled. Gordon smiled back.

"Look what you've done," he said. "You've written a book. A *good* book. Who'd have ever thunk."

Rose wasn't sure what that meant, but she blushed at the gist of the compliment. "I can't believe it's done. Really, I can't believe it. I don't know how to thank you for believing in me."

"You and Petie are a couple of the strongest people I've ever met," Gordon said. "I think—listen, because I mean this—I think you both could do absolutely anything you wanted to, if you set your minds to it."

"I've been thinking—" Rose said, and laid out for him her ideas for a cookbook or travel book.

"I don't know that Paul would be interested in another cookbook, at least not right now," Gordon said carefully, "but I think the idea of a guide to the lesser-known back roads of Oregon could be fantastic. Especially if it included stories about the people who actually homesteaded here. You and Petie could scout the area and go to the county historical society for information. Plus the county courthouse will have birth and death records, property deeds, that sort of thing." Rose watched as he lit up, fueled by this new idea. Then, abruptly, he moved the manuscript and drawings to one side, lining up their edges carefully. "Listen, there's something I should probably tell you," he said. "Nadine and I may not be coming back. Well, we'll come back to pack things up, but we've decided to move back to Los Angeles."

"Why?"

Gordon sighed. "It's not that we don't like it here, please understand that. It's just that we don't really fit in, do we, and it's been lonely for

Nadine. She has you, thank God, but she's tired and she worries too much about money on top of worrying too much about me. She thinks she can get a job in L.A. that might be less stressful, which is funny since that's why we *left* L.A. in the first place. I don't know, things never work out quite the way we expect them to, do they? I'm going to be sick enough soon that it'll be hard for her to take care of me up here without an HIV clinic or program of some kind. Paul and I actually talked about living together when I was down there last time, though who knows what Nadine will think of that. Still, it would keep costs down. Paul's lover—" Gordon broke off and looked at Rose. "Is it okay if I talk like this?"

"I think so."

"Paul had a lover who died of HIV just like my partner Johnny did. We know what we're facing, is what I mean. It's easier to get through it if you don't try to get through it alone. Most of Paul's friends have died, and so have most of mine. I don't say that to be dramatic. It's just the fact."

"I can't even imagine your not being here," Rose said. "I understand, but it's awful. Do they let unsophisticated country girls visit Los Angeles?"

Gordon grinned. "All the time, Rose."

She smiled back a little tearfully. "Then I guess it'll be all right."

Chapter 14

SCHIFF HAD had another one of his dreams about the redheaded farm girl he met at the fair. He was at a fair in his dream, too, but instead of being safety-chained to a ride, he'd been shackled to Carla. The girl had been taunting him, daring him to cut himself loose. *Go ahead, Skip,* she kept saying. *Betcha can't do it. Betcha won't.*

The problem, as Schiff kept trying to explain to her, was that they were at the top of the ride and cutting the chain would mean he'd free-fall fifty feet or more. That made no difference to the girl, who'd simply said, *You don't have it, Skippy, you do not have what it takes to do something about that woman.*

What woman? he'd asked.

The awful one. You know the one I'm talking about.

But Schiff knew a number of awful women—his two wives, for example.

In his dream he reached for the chain-cutters the girl held out to him, but he woke up before he could do anything with them, and that pissed him off. He'd done a lot of hard things in his life, don't think he hadn't. Look at his feet. They were all scarred up, especially the soles, and do you know why? Because he'd used them to stamp out the flames of a buddy who was burning in Vietnam. Schiff hadn't been able to walk for a month. But the girl didn't let him tell her that story. She was too busy ragging on him about *not* doing stuff. *I know you,* she said in his dreams. *You have a million reasons why you won't do something, but the fact is, you won't do it because you don't want to do it. That's the real reason. You know it, Skippy, and I know it, too.*

So he'd woken up slick with sweat, wondering why he hadn't cut that chain, why he hadn't stayed with Petie Coolbaugh at the Wayside the other night and let Carla sit by herself. There'd been a time when he would have. Why not now? Was it Carla, did he really love her in a way he'd kept a secret even from himself for years? Did he stay out of some higher moral commitment to her and Randi the Makeup Queen? Or did he simply lack the balls to go? He knew what the girl would say to that, and it wouldn't be pretty. But it wasn't that simple, not anymore, not at his age. He was forty-two. He couldn't afford to be financially wiped out. And make no mistake: Carla would hunt him to the ends of the earth before she'd let him get away with so much as one penny more than his share. She was the most vengeful woman he'd ever met. Petie had even more at stake than he had, with her kids and Eddie Coolbaugh's good job and Marge closing up the Sea View and all. So really, you could say he was giving her up out of concern for her own greater welfare.

Oh, Skippy, that's rich. That's the best one yet.

There were times when he couldn't stand that girl.

Schiff got a tighter grip on the steering wheel as he crested the cape and pierced the gummy fog at the top. He had never dreamed a single dream about Petie Coolbaugh, even though when he was awake she was like a light acid burning away under his skin.

He flipped down his visor briefly to make sure the postcard was still there. It was an offer he had received in the mail yesterday for a free weekend at Bachelor Butte, a resort over in Bend, if he'd simply agree to listen to an hour-long sales presentation. Usually Carla was all over the mail, but yesterday she was playing Bunko with some girlfriends at mail time. Normally they played Bunko on Thursday nights, but Tootie had gotten sick, so they'd rescheduled it. Normally Schiff wouldn't have been home that early, but he'd had a headache and left work early. It was awfully coincidental unless it was a sign from God that he was meant to go—and

Petie, too. He tucked the postcard into his shirt pocket. Maybe he'd go ahead and mention it to her if he could get her on the phone. Two nights, three days at Bachelor Butte Resort in Bend. Him and Petie. Yowzah.

Truth was, he hadn't seen Petie for over a week. She'd gone squirrelly on him since he and Carla had looked for her at the Wayside the day Larry went into the hospital. Not that Carla had any idea she was chaperoning. He'd never wanted anything as bad as he'd wanted to hitch up a barstool beside little Petie Coolbaugh. That walk to Carla in the corner had taken him miles through a wilderness.

He'd call Petie when he got to work. With Eddie Coolbaugh hot for promotion, Schiff had been sending him all up and down the coast from Garibaldi to Winchester Bay, and Eddie had thanked him for it. Handy, since Petie would at least still answer his phone calls.

At work he waited until fat Bev went to the restroom, and then he dialed, taking the postcard out of his pocket so he could read it to her.

"Yeah," Petie said on the third ring. He'd never met anyone less friendly on the telephone.

"Hi, beautiful," he said.

"Uh-huh."

"I'm sitting here looking at something. Can you guess what?"

"Yeah, and you better put it away. They arrest people for that, and next thing you know you're listed in the weekly police report in the *Sawyer News-Tribune*."

"Jesus, Petie."

"What."

"I try to be nice and you get all nasty on me."

"Turnabout's fair play, bud."

"Meet me somewhere. Say yes before Bev comes back."

"No."

"Yes. It's a small word. Some people use it all the time. Say it. Yes."

"No."

"You're damn tough, you know?"

"Don't think I don't work at it, though," Petie said.

Bev had come back. Schiff could hear her lower her broad haunches onto her squeaky desk chair.

"Gotta go, muffin," he said.

Petie hung up on him without a word.

"That Randi," Schiff said to the air. "Who would have ever guessed she'd turn out to be such a good kid."

PETIE SAT back and regarded her latest creation, a line drawing of a spoon, a whisk and a double boiler. She only had two more illustrations left before she was done. It astonished her that she could be paid for doing something she'd do anyway for the love of it alone. Rose was trying to convince her to go see Pico Talco and show him her work. He owned a successful art gallery down on the south end of town.

She picked up the phone and dialed the Pepsi distributorship. Mercifully, Schiff answered the phone himself.

"Yes," she said.

"What?"

"Yes. When and where?"

"The reservoir in half an hour?"

"Bye."

Another crime committed.

THE RESERVOIR was way back in a valley outside the Sawyer city limits, a place that was used like a park in the summer but deserted in the winter except for the fishing line, bobbers and lures that festooned the overhead power lines like bunting. Petie drove to a spot she and Schiff had found where they weren't especially visible from the road and had a view of the water—as though the surroundings were what they came here for. Schiff arrived while she was shutting off her car engine.

"Hi, peaches," he said, throwing open his passenger door for her. "Hop in."

She dragged with her a bag of peanut butter and jelly sandwiches. He had a six-pack of cold Pepsi. "What made you call?" he said.

"I don't know."

"My magnetic personality."

"I don't think so."

"*Your* magnetic personality?"

"Give me a break," Petie said.

"Anyway, I'm glad you did."

"Yeah."

They ate in silence, listening to each other swallow.

"Did you ever want something you were pretty sure you weren't supposed to have?" Petie said after a while.

"You," said Schiff.

"No, I mean it."

"So do I."

Petie shot him a look out of the corner of her eye. "I want to try making money painting."

"That shouldn't be too hard. Paul knows a painting contractor over in—"

"No, I mean painting pictures. Illustrations. Like I'm doing for Rose's cookbook."

"I didn't know you did that."

"Gordon's paying me for it. I'm nearly done."

"So find another book."

"I don't know how."

"Maybe Gordon knows someone else."

"Yeah," Petie said, chewing thoughtfully. "When you were young, when you were a kid, did anyone tell you that you could be president?"

"No one even told me I could graduate high school," Schiff said.

"I don't believe that."

"My mother's nickname for me was Dumb Stuff."

"That's awful."

"She was an awful person."

"Mine wasn't. She just died too soon," Petie said.

"Of cancer."

"Of cancer, of misery, of hopelessness. It's hard to know. I used to think she left me on purpose, because she seemed so glad to be going. The only time I can remember her being happy was the last two months she was dying, when she looked so bad Old Man finally gave up and left her alone."

"My mother's probably still out there someplace, drinking. Drinking and screwing guys for a few bucks left on the bar."

"Did she keep men around when you were growing up?" Petie asked.

"You mean the ones who came more than once or twice? A couple. One was a deadbeat, Leroy—used to steal tips out of my mother's purse when she was sleeping off a long night. We never had enough to eat, I mean *never*, and this jerk was rolling in cigarettes and beer, plenty to go around and then some." Schiff chewed reflectively.

"Who was the other one?" Petie asked.

"What other one?"

"I don't know. You said there were two."

"Yeah, well, he was a prick, that one. Herbert Parr, Pastor Herb to you—a man of God. Christ, there's a joke. My brother damn near killed him one night."

"Why?"

"Let's just say he had a pair of hands," Schiff said.

"Hands?"

"Yeah. Wandering hands. Wandered my way one night when I was twelve or so, Jesus, I woke up and there he was, the fucker—pardon me, *Pastor* Herb. He used to call me 'my son' if you can believe *that*. No one, princess, *no one*, should ever wake up like that."

"I woke up like that," Petie said.

"You?"

Petie cleared her throat. "I was fourteen and Old Man and I were going on four years living in that piece-of-shit trailer up in the woods. He worked down on the docks most nights, but this one night he came back early because he'd lost his beer money on some stupid-ass gamble about who'd bring in a bigger catch, the *Lenny Hector* or the *Seabird*. Anyway, he was pissed off and sober, and there I was, sleeping like I always did in about three old sleeping bags to stay warm, which you could never do no matter if you had a pile of a thousand blankets, Jesus, I've never been as cold as I got in that fucking trailer, I didn't know you could *get* that cold and still wake up in the morning. Anyway, Old Man must have been looking for someone to take his bad luck out on, and it turned out to be me. He put his hand—"

"Wait."

"He put his hand under the blankets—"

"Wait."

"—and he slid it down real slow and real nasty until he got between my legs and that's how I woke up, to the feel of a little hangnail he'd been picking at all day scratching the inside of my thigh. The thing about it was, I had a knife all ready."

"Jesus," Schiff said respectfully.

"I got him in the arm first, deep, but he was a tough old bastard and it just made him mad. He came back at me and grabbed. I stuck the knife into his shoulder that time, right up to the handle, and I heard somebody yelling, yelling real loud, and it was me, and then he started screaming, too, and I got out and ran. I ran as hard as I could but here was the worst part, the *worst part*. I couldn't figure out anyplace to run to. I went to Rose's house but it was only three in the morning and they didn't wake up. You know, it's not that easy to wake people up when they have a good place to sleep at night."

"So where did you go?"

"No place. A tree. I went to a tree in the yard of a house we lived in once, a tree I'd buried something under a long time ago. I held on to that tree until daylight, thinking that God Himself, if He was just, would come down out of the heavens for me and take me home, but He didn't. He didn't do a goddamn thing. It got light after a while and I just got up and walked to Rose's house like it was any other day. No one noticed anything. After school that day I went home with Rose and peroxided a white stripe down the middle of my hair like a skunk. I don't know why. Old Man beat hell out of me for it, but he never tried anything else again. A couple of months later I went to live with the Coolbaughs."

"Jesus."

"You know something else? He healed right up, the son of a bitch, all neat and sanitary just like surgery. The only people who ever suspected anything were the nurses at the emergency room the night Old Man had his stroke. They guessed, at least I think one of them did, but there wasn't anything he could do about it even if he'd wanted to, which I don't think he did."

"Aw, princess. Jesus."

Petie shrugged. "No one knows. I told Eula the summer before she died. Now you know."

"Rose?"

"Just you."

"You won't have to kill me now, will you?"

Petie cracked the smallest hint of a smile.

"Why me?"

Petie's hands gripped each other in her lap. "Don't you ever get tired?"

"Of what?"

"Of carrying it all."

Schiff blew out a long slow breath. "All the time, princess," he said softly. "All the time."

Rain began drumming lightly on the truck's windshield. Paula had once told Petie that raindrops were the Lord's tears when someone told a lie. She'd never believed it until now. She hadn't lied, exactly, but she'd left out some things. There was the part about having to pretend she had her period all the time so she could get excused from gym class, because if she'd undressed in public the bruises would have shown. There were the back-of-the-leg-with-an-ax-handle bruises and their cousins, the broom-handle bruises. Old Man especially liked to lay them down when Petie hadn't kept dinner warm for him until he came in just after last call at the Wayside. Man had a right to his dinner, he'd bawl at Petie, and it never mattered that it was one o'clock in the morning, or that she'd spent most of the evening huddled over a little fire in the woods because Old Man had forgotten to buy propane again.

And there were the buttocks bruises, same weapons, different crimes—failing to keep beer in the cooler for him, failing to wash his clothes, failing to look at him with the right combination of fear and obedience.

But though these were the brightest bruises, they were not the deepest. Those were the ones Old Man left when he lay on her back with his hand across her mouth, pushing into her. She had made the rape sound like it had only happened once, but that wasn't true. For two years he had laid down on her like that. She wore choking amounts of perfume she had found in a thrift shop over in Sawyer, but it didn't make much difference. Every day that she lived in that trailer she wore Old Man's stink like a robe. At Rose's on bad mornings she rubbed herself raw with Comet cleanser. Once she tried gargling with diluted bleach. And of course there was the peroxide with which she'd ruined the hair he used like reins, pulling back so hard sometimes she was sure her neck would snap. He'd beaten her bloody for that.

She didn't remember exactly when she'd come upon the little hunting knife in the woods, her savior and salvation. She'd seen the glimmer of steel under leaves near the dirt bike path and uncovered it. The knife was a pretty thing, new and brilliant, and the blade folded smoothly into a handle made of horn or bone. Petie had drawn the blade thoughtfully across the ball of her thumb to test its edge, and watched with approval as blood sprang into the cut the knife laid open like a scalpel.

For two weeks she'd slept with that knife under her pillow.

She would never forget the perfect contact of steel on bone when she buried the blade in Old Man's shoulder—a shoulder he would never regain full use of. God may not have lifted her up in her hour of need, but He had done the next best thing by bringing her that surgical blade and the ferocity to use it.

·   ·   ·

SCHIFF FLIPPED down his visor and removed the post-card. "Run away with me," he said, holding it out.

"Where to?"

"Bend. Two nights, three days free." He pointed to a happy couple holding hands and walking on a perfectly manicured golf course. "This could be us."

"That could never be us."

"Why not?"

"We're damaged goods. There's not a resort on earth desperate enough to use people like us in their sales brochure." Petie took the postcard from Schiff and examined it more carefully. "Jim Christie got one of these a couple of months ago."

"They going?"

"Nah. You know him. He's only half tame. Make him go to a place like that and he'd chew off his own foot to get away. He said we could use it, though. Rose and me and the kids."

"Not Eddie?"

Petie shrugged.

"Go with me, then," Schiff said.

"Would you ask if you thought there was even the slightest chance I'd accept?" she asked.

"No."

"Well, God love you for an honest man."

"Don't tell anyone. It'd spoil my reputation."

HONEY, EULA COOLBAUGH used to tell Petie, *I always wanted a daughter and all I got were sons, so you must be my reward for putting up with those boys. I wouldn't have missed you for the world.*

Petie kept her room spotless, did her own laundry (a washer, a dryer!) and cleaned up every night after dinner (a sink! running water!). She was given a desk for doing schoolwork, but she always sat at the kitchen table instead, that island of warmth and safety from which she could keep Eula firmly in her sights in case, like smoke, she began to thin and fade.

Eula told her what she knew about Paula Tyler's family.

"Oh, they were a big clan once, way back in the hills, everyone knew about them. Rumor was, they'd even found silver once and had a mine that was all camouflaged, 'course no one's ever found it," she said, sitting at the table across from Petie on winter afternoons, nursing a cup of coffee. "They homesteaded that land. They were supposed to have been good blood once, but by the time they got to your mama's generation I guess they'd curdled. We all heard the stories.

"Your mama had seven brothers, big dark men, drinkers and fighters. Some of them died logging and some of them went up to Anacortes to fish and never came back. I don't know what happened to your grandmother. Some people say she died after having a baby, a stillborn one, but I don't know anything about that. At any rate, your mama was the last living child and the only girl. I met her when she was fifteen. She was a year older than me, but much smaller. She reminded me of a bird, small-boned that way, smaller than you are now."

"Why'd she come to Hubbard?"

Eula squinted at Petie closely through the smoke from her cigarette. "We never really knew, hon, but there were stories. Some people said she got pregnant up in those hills, that she had a baby before she ever came to town for high school, but I don't know about that, either."

"A baby?"

"That's what people said."

"A *baby*?"

"Your mama never talked about it. Probably wasn't a baby at all, at least not here in town. Your mama came to Hubbard by herself and people make up stories."

"So why'd she marry Old Man?"

Eula shook her head. "Maybe because he'd have her. What with all those stories about her, not many people would have much to do with her. She lived in a little room at the Mosebys'—you wouldn't know them, they're all gone now—and she waitressed for rent money at a place that used to be down by the docks. It wasn't much, but it was all she was ever going to have, on her own." Eula lit a fresh cigarette and blew out a thin, ruminative stream of smoke. "You know those seal pups that wash up orphaned in fall, the way they look when night's coming on and their mamas haven't been back for them? Paula was like that from the day I met her. I think maybe it's God's way to numb His creatures when there's nothing left for them but how long it'll take them to die." Eula patted Petie's hand. "She didn't have your spirit, hon. She didn't have your fire."

"She would duck her head and let Old Man punch her. I never saw her fight back, she just let him do it."

"Did he ever hit you?"

"While she was alive? No."

Eula smiled gently. "That's why she didn't stand up to him, hon. She took those punches because as long as she did, you wouldn't have to. There wasn't a lot else she could give you, but she could do that one thing." Eula sighed and stubbed out her cigarette in the cracked custard dish she used for an ashtray. "Your mama did her best, but she was broken, hon, as surely as any starved horse."

"She never said goodbye."

"I don't think she could bear to."

"She could have stayed if she'd wanted to—"

"Oh, hon."

"—and then she could have kept Old Man away from me."

Eula looked at her and said quietly, "I know where you've been. I've watched that same scenery go by my window for years. I never stopped there myself, but I recognize it when I see it."

"You know what he's done to me?"

"One day you can tell me."

"Then what am I supposed to do now?"

"Leave it by the side of the road and drive away, honey. Just drive away. One day it'll be just another little spot on the map where you visited once, a long time ago."

. . .

PETIE LET Schiff drive out ahead of her, falling back so they wouldn't appear together at the intersection. All she'd need was to have Carla drive by at that exact moment. Her life had been a straight and unwavering line for a long time, but now she could feel it buckling beneath her feet, had been feeling it off and on for days.

On a sudden impulse, she steered her little car down a logging road. She felt all ripped open, maybe from remembering things she thought she'd put away a long time ago. She'd never even told Eula Coolbaugh about those last months in the trailer, where her words echoed off the dripping walls every night: *If you lay a hand on me, if you even think about it, I'll know. I'll know, and I'll wait you out and I will kill you.*

Old Man had wept, cringing over his wounds. He claimed he'd never meant any harm, but what was a man supposed to do without a wife, caring all alone for a teenage girl? It wasn't right, he said; God Himself would understand that. It just wasn't right. And him without any money, without any prospects, down on his luck in a down-on-luck town where the best you could hope for was money enough for beer. And Paula never had been worth a damn as far as wives went; never would have him when he asked, and then afterwards she'd cry. The woman cried all the time like a goddamn leaky faucet, said it *hurt*, now what kind of a thing was that? It was against nature, that's what it was, and he didn't believe it, thought it was just her way out of what she didn't want to do—and then she'd found out about the cancer. How was he supposed to have known, when she'd cried from the first day he'd had her, some honeymoon, especially since she hadn't been fresh to begin with? But he'd put up with her, hadn't he, and put up with her family (all this pouring out of him after four years of grunts and nods), those terrible brothers who appeared at night out of the rain like pure evil, wanting money, wanting food, as though Old Man had any to spare, except he was afraid of what they'd do if he didn't. And now Petie, his own daughter, was threatening him the same way, was that any way to treat family, to treat him, her only known living relation?

And sometimes, during these last nights, his speech would become thick and his gait lopsided and Petie blamed it on cowardice and beer, not blood clots. He cringed before her, whining on until she dozed in her sleeping bags with the knife held tight in her fist.

When he came out of rehab five months after the stroke, he came to Eula Coolbaugh's first, holding his ball cap in his hand, hangdog and shaky. Petie was there, listening from another room. "Eula," he said, "I'm grateful to you for taking in my daughter. We've had tough times, I expect you know that, but I'm better now and I can take her back."

"I don't think so," said Eula.

"No?"

"No."

"Well, I expect she's talked about me to you," he said, his voice catching. "I expect she's told you some things."

"Yes, she has told me some things," Eula said evenly.

"A lot of things?" he said.

"Quite a few, John."

"Well, she's always had a burr up her butt where I'm concerned. She lies, you probably found that out already. She lies all the time. That's why I had my stroke, you know. Trying to figure out all those lies."

"I've never heard Petie lie," Eula said.

"Well, she's a clever girl, probably been real careful with you, real nice so you'd let her stay. She's not nice to me. How long was I in that place, and the hospital before that, and she never brought me nothing. That's the kind of girl she is, takes after her mother's family, shifty values. Well, you probably remember that from when we were kids, Eula, all that talk."

"That was a long time ago, too long ago to mean anything. Now you listen to me, John. I don't care how repentant you are, I don't even care if you've sworn to God Himself that you'll behave. That child is not going anywhere with you, and if you fight me or lay a hand on her, I'll get a lawyer. There are a few things a judge might not be real thrilled to hear about you, you understand me?"

"That's no way to talk. I don't deserve that kind of talk, I come to your house real nice."

"And I appreciate that, John. I know you'll leave the same way."

And, nonplussed, he had.

In a town the size of Hubbard, it was inevitable that he and Petie would run across each other now and then. He always asked her for money and she always gave him what she had, figuring it was well worth it if he just stayed away from her the rest of the time. She'd married Eddie right out of high school, and then Old Man had nothing on her anymore. But by then it didn't really matter: she hated him less as the fire of her anger died, and she saw in him the sick, smelly old man he'd become. She had no intention of going out of her way to see him, but she didn't avoid him anymore, either. More than a few times, she drove down to pick him up at the Wayside when Roy called to tell her he'd fallen dead asleep on the bar.

Hating just took too much energy.

Petie bumped and lurched along the potholed logging road for half an hour, lost in both thought and actuality. As she was beginning to consider turning around and driving all the way back to the reservoir, she saw the siding of a house or shed briefly through the trees—a flash of aqua and it was gone. She rounded one more bend and found herself emerging from the woods at the top of Chollum Road. The aqua she'd seen was the side of Old Man's trailer, still where she and Rose had left it years ago, only cleaner.

Beside the trailer was Jim Christie's truck.

And from the trailer itself, as she neared it, Petie first saw Carissa step out, and then Jim Christie himself. Startled, Petie met Christie's eyes through the windshield.

He didn't look away.

Chapter 15

WAIT IN the truck," Jim Christie told Carissa. He didn't take his eyes off Petie Coolbaugh again or offer her the advantage of his turned back. Once Carissa had closed the truck door, she took a step or two closer to him. "What are you doing?" she said. Her voice was tight and low.

He set his feet. "I come up here sometimes."

"Why?"

"It's quiet."

"Isn't it quiet at the house?"

"Man needs his own place sometimes."

"Is this your place?"

"I use it sometimes. Never seen anybody else here." He watched Petie's chest rise and fall, rise and fall.

"So what do you do here when it's quiet?"

"Smoke. Read."

She looked over his shoulder at Carissa, hunkered down in the truck. "Doesn't look to me like you were reading."

"She comes up sometimes. She knows she's not supposed to, but she does it anyway. Nothing I can do to stop her."

"Does Rose know?"

"You think I'm doing something wrong, you'd better just say it." Christie had seen polar she-bears with the same look when they thought their cubs were in danger. There was nothing you could do to reason with a she-bear when she had her blood up, and it looked like the same thing with this scrappy little woman. She'd think what she'd think; nothing he could say would change that. And he didn't especially care for the thing she was thinking. Young girl like Carissa with an old fisherman like him, barely tame.

She said, "I don't know what you were doing. But it doesn't look good to me, I've got to tell you. It doesn't look good."

"You saying I did something to her?"

"It happens."

"You saying it happened with me?"

"I'm saying I hope to God it didn't," Petie said. She approached the truck, rapped on the passenger window and gestured to Carissa. The girl slipped out of the truck, meekly following Petie to her car. They drove off without a word.

Christ.

Christie wrenched open the creaky passenger door of his truck and rooted around until he found a fresh pack of cigarettes, then ducked inside the cripple-backed trailer as hailstones began ricocheting like grapeshot off the aluminum. He shook off his cap, reseated it on his head and sat down in his camp chair sucking smoke.

The wind was picking up, another storm front on the way, a spring storm. Three more weeks, four at the outside, and he'd need to be back in Dutch Harbor looking for a boat to crew. Some of the men at the Wayside were already heading up. You could tell who they were by how nice they were being to their wives and girlfriends, buying them sudden foolishness like perfume and cheap gold rings to make up for another three, four months of being dumped. Christie himself had courted that way once when he was still a young man. He had a woman named Tina Bea Martin he liked well enough, met her up in Anacortes, Washington—small town, tightly packed and full of fishermen. Tina Bea had been trying to get him to anchor himself in her harbor and nearly succeeded, got him as far as buying her a Black Hills gold earring and pendant set at the jewelry store closest to the harbor, the one he'd been told favored fishermen. The jewelry was in the shape of a whale and he thought she'd like it, not that he knew anything. Hell, he'd been afraid to even touch it, it looked so fragile, like spiderwebs on a sunny day. *Someone's getting something special*, the salesgirl had teased him in a voice that made him break into a light sweat. *Lucky her.*

And Tina Bea had liked them just fine, too, but somehow he'd never gone back to Anacortes. He heard in Dutch Harbor that Tina Bea had married a skipper the next year, captain of the *Flying Dutchman*. Christie knew him: good skipper, good man. As for Christie, he didn't have a special woman again until he met Rose. He'd come down to Hubbard with a deckhand from the *Phoebe K.*, nice kid who was swept overboard the following year, never found. They'd made it as far as Hubbard and stopped at the Anchor Inn for lunch. Rose had served them, with her pretty smile, sweet round hips, bosom like perfection. She'd asked where they were from and where they were headed and Christie had said, *Here. We were headed here.* When the kid pulled out of town an hour later, he pulled out alone. Christie took a job on a charter boat and stayed until the following March. Slept in a campground on the outskirts of town for the first week, at Rose's after that.

It frightened him sometimes, how good she looked to him. She sucked the air out of a place, made him light-headed and stupid, same thing drinking had done when he was young and still a heavy drinker. Drunk, he could take on the world if he had to; sober, he was nothing but a tired man who just wanted to get out of the season alive and without owing. And when he did get out the last two years, money in his pocket and a month of sleep coming to him, he hitched a ride down Hubbard way and dreamed of Rose.

And yet, he'd been able to quit drinking.

P ETIE DROVE Carissa home in silence. The girl kept her head down, examining her fingernails. In the driveway Petie turned off the ignition and turned to face her. "Do you know about that trailer?"

"Is it the one you used to live in?"

"Yes."

"We didn't hurt it or anything."

"You couldn't hurt that trailer if you hit it with a ball peen hammer."

"Why are you mad, then?"

"Am I mad? I'm not mad."

"Yes you are."

Petie sighed. "Why were you up there, 'Rissa?"

Carissa shrugged miserably. "I don't know."

"Did you walk there on your own?"

"Yes."

"Do you go there often?"

"I go there sometimes."

"Why?"

"I like Jim," the girl whispered.

"I know you like him. Does he like you?"

"I don't know. I think sometimes he does."

"How does he show it?" Petie asked.

"I don't know."

"Does he give you compliments, maybe tell you you're growing up, tell you you're pretty? Does he touch you?"

The girl turned a deep crimson and bolted from the car.

PETIE DROVE her little car straight into the teeth of the latest squall, driving blindly. She needed time to think. The wind was already strong enough to be pushing gobs of spindrift across the road, and night was coming on, black as a blindfold. Out of habit she looked at the Wayside parking lot as she passed it and saw Schiff's pickup. For the first time in weeks, she had no desire whatsoever to see him. Some of the other Wayside regulars were there, too: Dooley Burden, Connie, a couple of others. Not Jim Christie.

What in hell was she supposed to do about Jim Christie? What did Rose know? For that matter, what did Petie know? Maybe nothing; maybe something. She turned her car around and drove back to Rose's house. The lights were all dark, and there was a note on the kitchen table telling

Rose that Carissa had gone next door. Beside it was another note, written on a piece of paper torn out of one of Carissa's school notebooks.

Rose,
I've gone north. Don't know what boat I'll be on or where I'll be stay-
ing, but I'll send word when I can. You're a real nice lady and the
only woman I ever really felt for. I want you to know that, no matter
what you hear about me and in case I don't come back. You and
Carissa, you stay safe. Maybe you could think about me sometimes.

Jim Christie

Petie left the notes where they were and ran back to her car. At the top of Chollum Road she set off through the trees. But this time there was nobody there, not even ghosts.

I DON'T understand," Rose kept saying the next morning across Petie's kitchen table. Her eyes were swollen from crying, and she was still wearing yesterday's clothes. She'd sat up all night hoping Christie would come home, but he hadn't. There wasn't so much as a sock left in the house to show he'd ever been there. He'd up and disappeared like the thinnest smoke. "Why would he just leave like that? Tell me again what you saw."

And Petie explained again, with great patience, the moment when Jim Christie and Carissa had stepped out of the trailer together, and what had happened afterwards.

"But that doesn't *mean* anything!" Rose cried.

And Petie said what she'd already said over and over. "If it didn't mean anything, then why did he leave?"

"I just can't believe that. I can't. He always took such care with her, like he was afraid she could break. Carissa said nothing happened between them. I asked her very carefully, Petie, and she said *nothing ever happened between them.* Why would she say that if—"

"I always said that about Old Man," Petie said.

"Old Man?"

"I always told you we were doing okay."

"Oh, what's that supposed to mean?" Rose cried.

"It means that girls don't always tell the truth when they think the truth is rancid meat."

"What?"

"Things weren't fine then. They might not be fine now."

Rose began to cry. "I don't understand you. I don't understand what you're talking about, or why you said what you did to him."

Petie sat rooted to her chair, twisting around her finger the cheap wedding band Eddie had given her so many years ago. "Can you listen?"

Rose blew her nose on a soggy square of toilet paper.

Petie took a deep breath. "Old Man fucked me two or three nights a week for two years. And every morning I came to your house and every morning you didn't know a thing."

Rose watched her with horror. "Jesus Christ, Petie."

"What I'm saying is, some things can't be said, not even if they're true and not even if you're honest."

"Oh my God."

"Two years. *Two years,*" Petie hissed. "Do you remember the day I bleached my hair?"

Rose nodded.

"The night before, I stabbed him."

"What?"

"I had a knife and when the bastard tried to get on me I stabbed him."

Rose stood up and walked to the kitchen window, looking out as though she could see something through the streaming panes. "I can't think," she said.

"The point I'm trying to make is that Carissa may or may not be telling the truth."

"But why?"

"Because she loves him. Because if something did happen, even something awful, she would think it was her fault."

"Did you?"

"Yes."

"But I'd know if he was capable of doing something like that. Wouldn't I know?"

"Maybe."

Rose crossed her arms tightly over her chest. "So what should I do?"

"I don't know."

"And what am I supposed to tell Carissa? She thinks she's the one who made him leave. She feels responsible. What am I supposed to say to her?"

Petie sighed and swirled the half inch of coffee left in the bottom of her cup. "Just walk away. Help her walk away, too."

"I don't *want* to walk away," Rose cried. "Why should I? Nothing's changed."

"What's your other choice? The man left."

Rose hung her head. "I know."

"So? How much did he love you if he could do that?"

"I hate the things you're saying."

"I know that, but you need to hear them. Has it ever occurred to you that he might not be the man you thought he was? Carissa may need help."

"Or maybe not. She's not you, Petie. She isn't you, and Jim isn't Old Man."

"I know that," Petie said softly. "Don't you think I know that?"

Rose abruptly picked up her coat and purse. "I can't stay anymore. I'm sorry, Petie, but I can't. Yesterday everything was fine, and now it's all gone. If what you're saying is true, I should be grateful to you, but I'm not."

Petie set her jaw and watched Rose go. When the noise of her car faded away, she grabbed the phone and dialed the Pepsi distributorship. Talking fast, she left a message, then grabbed her purse and car keys, rounded up all the money in the house—twelve dollars and a fistful of change—and bolted out the door.

. . .

SCHIFF PULLED his truck off the reservoir road and waited. Petie arrived in less than five minutes. He hopped out of his truck with a sheaf of maps and spread them out on the hood of her car: Oregon, Washington, British Columbia, Alaska. He'd marked the way to Anacortes, Dutch Harbor and Kodiak with a highlighter—all the places Christie might be headed for.

"You know this is a bad idea, princess," Schiff said.

She waved him away. "Did you get hold of Eddie?"

"Yeah. He'll pick up your kids at three-fifteen, just like you asked."

"And you told him I was going to be home late?"

"Honey, going to Alaska isn't exactly coming home late," Schiff said.

"I'm not planning to go to Alaska. I'll find him before then."

"You're not going to find dick by driving the interstates," Schiff said.

"What the hell else am I supposed to do, Schiff? You tell me what I'm supposed to do, and I'll do it."

Schiff put his arm around her. "I don't know, princess."

Petie shrugged him away impatiently.

"Do you have any idea what you'll do if you find him?" Schiff asked.

"No."

"Look—"

"I've got to go," Petie said. "If I don't go now I might never go, and if I don't go, I'll never get over it."

Schiff stepped aside wordlessly and let Petie pass around to the driver's side of her car. The muffler was going, the fan belt squeaked and the car favored a bad wiper. Not a car meant for long distances. Schiff said, "Listen, princess. There's a Motel 6 right off I-5 in Portland. If you don't find Christie first, check in there for the night. I'll make a reservation for you there as soon as I get back to work."

"You don't need to do that."

"Just do it, okay?"

. . .

PETIE LIT a cigarette just north of Hubbard and didn't stop smoking until she got to Portland three hours later. At that rate, if she didn't find Christie she'd come back with emphysema.

She and Rose had never been at odds before. It was like having her skin ripped off. She didn't know what had gone on between Carissa and Christie—knew less and less as she replayed those few minutes again and again. What she did know was that Rose's heart was broken, and she was the reason why. If she could find Christie and coax him back home, she would make things right between her and Rose again. She had to.

She'd only been to Portland once before, when she went with Eula Coolbaugh to a doctor's appointment. Pete had been living with the Coolbaughs for nearly four years when Eula got sick. Petie had long since outgrown her skunk-colored hair, but the bliss of sitting in Eula's kitchen had never faded. If anything, at eighteen she was more possessive of Eula than she had been at fourteen. When Eula developed a dry cough that never seemed to go away, Petie took a proprietary view of it and dogged her into going to see a doctor over in Sawyer. The doctor had sent her on to another doctor in Portland. *That* doctor had sent her to see a colleague, and then, in the final lightning moment of Petie's delusion that bad things had finally stopped happening, the colleague sent Eula on to an oncologist. Eula Coolbaugh had lung cancer, too advanced to do much about except to keep her comfortable and slow it down a little with chemotherapy if she chose. It might buy a few months, the oncologist explained, but it wouldn't change the outcome by more than that.

Petie and Eddie Coolbaugh were engaged by then, as only seemed natural when Petie had been a part of the household for so long, familiar as an old boot, impossible to imagine the family without—she who kept the calendar of birthdays, labeled the Christmas ornament boxes, set out Eula's Easter, Halloween, Thanksgiving and Christmas decorations with reverential care. She and Eddie had been planning a summer wedding and high school graduation celebration, all in one, with a reception at the Anchor Inn. Eula refused to hear of a change in plans that would allow for a quiet, private wedding at home as soon as possible. *Your wedding puts you square on a path you'll be walking the rest of your lives,* Eula told them. *You will not start this marriage in sorrow. You plan the wedding you want, honey, and I will be there smiling.*

And so she had. She gave Petie gifts of wisdom, cookery and clean kitchen shelves, and Petie often thought afterwards that that was more than most people could hope to receive in a lifetime. The morning Eula died, Petie had sat by her bed in a rush-bottomed chair, alone, holding Eula's hand. Old Man hadn't let her see Paula at the end. Had she looked like this woman whom Petie loved so fiercely, this weathered rock against which Petie's tree had leaned for shelter? Paula Tyler had cast no cool shadow, buffered no winds. As Petie sat in her pauper's chair in that bedroom with its lemon-and-white-painted walls, she felt a change and glanced over to find Eula looking at her. She hadn't spoken much in the last several days as she fought for every breath, but she spoke to Petie now and her voice, though ravaged, was loud with conviction. *Let it go, honey,* she said, *and like the phoenix you will rise up whole*. They were the last words Eula would ever speak to anyone. She died at two o'clock that afternoon with Petie by her side along with Eddie and his two brothers, flown in from Alaska and Idaho only hours before.

Petie gathered clothes and jewelry for Eula to be buried in, but she did not attend the funeral or memorial reception. Instead she went to her tree. Sitting beneath it, right on the bare ground, she watched the clouds that would bring winter one day soon and wondered why people believed in God. She had given Him every opportunity to show Himself; had pleaded for His revelation, His mercy, His simple decency. She had been as near to bankruptcy as it was possible to get and still leave the house in the morning, yet there was no miracle, no divine presence in her home or heart, nothing but nothingness—a stillness, a silence that was absolute. She sat beneath that godforsaken tree for two hours, and when she rose, it was not as the phoenix. She lived with Eddie in their mouse-turd apartment and had coffee at the Anchor Inn every morning; gave birth to Ryan and then to Loose; had jobs, lost and regained them;

and she *never once felt a thing*. She had become a marvel of nature, capable of slipping a red-hot poker through her own heart.

PETIE DROVE with one eye on the road and the other scanning every rest stop, convenience store and fast-food restaurant she passed. She knew the look of Christie's truck as well as she knew her children's faces, but in nearly three hours of driving, she didn't see anything that was even close.

By the time she reached the outskirts of Portland it was dusk and she was locked in rush-hour traffic. She couldn't believe how densely the cars were packed together on the freeways, slowing to a crawl as on-ramps merged and lanes closed down and branched off to other roads. In the car beside her at one point she saw a man reading the newspaper as he drove. Other people sang or talked into tiny tape recorders or huge car phones that looked capable of killing someone. What would it be like, living in a place like this? Who would know you; who would ask you how you were and mean it? On the other hand, no one would know your business; no one would even know your name. You could be a perfect stranger as long as you wanted. You would have no sins, no baggage, nobody wanting you to fail. Hell, you could run away without ever leaving town.

By the time she reached the far side of Portland it was dark. There was no chance of finding Christie's truck until it got light again. Reluctantly Petie found the Motel 6 right at the bottom of an off-ramp.

"Evening," said the clerk, a young man with a mended harelip and blank expression.

"My name is Coolbaugh. I should have a reservation."

"Uh-huh." The clerk flipped through some papers on the counter. "Here we go. Patricia?"

"Yup."

"You're in number 105," the clerk said. "Double, smoking."

"I don't need a double," Petie said.

"Says right here, one double, one night. Is that correct?"

"One *single*, one night."

"I'm sorry, ma'am, but we don't have a single. We're full up."

"How much more is the double?"

"Ten dollars."

"Ten dollars? How much is the room?"

"Forty-five, plus tax. The total comes to fifty-three dollars. Do you want to keep it on this credit card?"

"What credit card?"

The clerk sighed. "Ma'am, you gave us a credit card number when you called in your reservation."

"Ah," said Petie. Damned Schiff.

"Shall we keep it on this card?"

"Oh, let's," Petie said sweetly. "Since I don't know what the card is to begin with, what the fuck, huh?"

The clerk tightened his lips almost imperceptibly and that was all. Christ, they must put them through a hell of a training program, to have them stand up that straight and polite when some asshole like her came in. "Look, I'm sorry," Petie said. "It's been a long day."

"It's okay, ma'am."

"I work in a motel, too. Back on the coast, in Hubbard."

"Yeah?"

"It's called the Sea View. Sea View Motel. You might have heard of it."

"Uh, no," the kid said. He handed her a piece of plastic in a paper sleeve.

"What's this?" Petie turned the plastic card over and back.

"It's a key."

"Doesn't look like a key."

The clerk sighed. "You put it in the slot in your door. When the light turns green, just open the door and remove the key."

"No shit," Petie said.

The clerk smiled at her weakly. "That's right, ma'am."

"And to think that back in Hubbard we just use the metal kind."

"Well," said the clerk.

"Yeah," said Petie. "Well."

There didn't seem to be anything left to say.

The room was just a few doors down from the office, and the key worked, improbable as it looked. Two queen beds, little soap for your face, bigger soap for the bath. Thin white face towel, tiny washcloth, tiny bath towel, no-slip rubber bath mat with suckers like an octopus. Tired foam pillow, television bolted to the bureau. Fifty-three dollars. Shit.

Petie sat on the bed for a few minutes, turned on the TV, turned off the TV. You dream of being away from everyone and then once it happens you can't think of a thing to do. She picked up the phone and called home, collect.

"Where the hell are you?" Eddie said.

"I'm in Portland. I won't be home for a few days."

"What?"

"It's a long story, Eddie, but something happened. Christie's gone and Rose is real upset and it's my fault. I'm trying to find him and get him to come back. You haven't seen him, have you?"

"No. What the hell are you talking about?"

"I'm talking about that I don't know how long I'll be gone."

"Well, you better tell this to the boys, 'cause I'm sure as hell not."

"Look, Eddie, help me with this, okay? I can't explain it all right now, but it's important."

On the other end of the line there was silence.

"Hello?"

"So what am I supposed to do with the boys, huh? I've got a job."

"I heard that."

"So what am I supposed to do?"

"Put them in Latchkey after school. They'll take them."

"So when do you plan on coming back?" Eddie said.

"I don't know. I'll be back when I find Christie. I'll call you when I know. Let me talk to Ryan."

The phone receiver was dropped and Petie could hear Eddie receding into the background shouting for Ryan. A couple of minutes later the receiver was knocked around and then picked up again.

"Mommy?"

The boy sounded like a four-year-old. His voice was high and quivery. Petie was going to have to shore him up. "Hi, sweetie. How was school today?"

"We're doing a play about Lewis and Clark."

"No kidding? So who will you be? An Indian scout, maybe?"

"A horse—I'm one of their horses. The people get lots of fleas in their clothes and stuff. Can horses get fleas?"

"I don't know. You could probably go and ask one."

"A horse?"

"Well, or a flea."

Ryan giggled.

"Guess where I'm calling from," Petie said. "I'm in Portland."

"When are you coming home? Daddy yells at us," Ryan said. His voice had dropped so low that Petie had trouble hearing him.

"I'm not sure, sweetie. I've got to find someone."

"Who?"

"Jim Christie. He left and it's making Rose sad."

"I like him," Ryan said simply.

"I know, hon. So does Rose. So I need to find him for her."

"He's real quiet."

"Well, he's shy, kind of like you are."

"Uh-huh. He gives me money for candy sometimes."

"He does?" Petie said, surprised.

"One time we split a PayDay."

"Ah. Well, I've got to find him and then I can come home."

"Why did he leave?"

Leave it to children to ask the tough questions. "I said something he didn't like."

"What?"

Petie sighed heavily. "I can't explain it right now, sweetie, I just did. So now I'm looking for him to apologize."

"Oh."

"Okay. Listen, if you see Rose will you be extra nice to her? She's upset right now."

"Do you think I should make her something?"

"Like what?"

"I could make her a picture," Ryan said.

"Oh, you know how much she likes your pictures. I'm sure that would make her feel better."

"I could draw Lewis and Clark."

"With fleas?" The boy giggled. "Sweetie, I've got to go. You be good and do what Daddy says. I love you."

"I wish you were home."

"I know, sweetie. I do too. I'll be there just as soon as I can. Okay?"

"Okay."

The boy hung up the phone before Petie even said goodbye. She considered calling right back to talk with Loose and then decided Ryan would pass on whatever he thought was important. She'd talk with Loose tomorrow. She realized she hadn't eaten since morning and she was starving. She picked up the phone again and dialed the front desk. The same kid answered. "Can you tell me where to find a restaurant?"

"There's an Elmer's a block away."

"I was thinking of something cheaper. I only have twelve dollars."

"There's a McDonald's two blocks from here. Make a right when you leave the parking lot."

Petie ate French fries all the way back to the motel. Out of habit she scanned the lot for Christie's truck. She didn't find it, of course, but she did find something else, a big truck with plenty of chrome and special accessories. Mud from the reservoir road was still lodged in its wheel wells.

Nearly deafened by her pounding heart, she opened the door to her room. There, sitting on one of the beds, was Ron Schiffen, arms behind his head, his old house-slipper boots crossed neatly at the ankle.

"Hiya, princess," he said.

Chapter 16

GOOD GOD, the look on Petie Coolbaugh's face—something between horror and joy, or possibly both. It had been worth the three-hour drive up from Hubbard just to see it.

Should he have chosen someplace fancier than the Motel 6? But he didn't know anyplace fancier, and besides, in his imagination he hadn't been thinking about the damned decor. His daydreams had been filled with other delicacies, small canapés of kisses, entrées of passion, desserts of the sweetest culmination. The fact was, life had begun to be worth living again, and it was mostly thanks to this small edgy woman.

"I can hardly wait to hear what you told them back home," Petie said. Her face was flushed a deep red and Schiff watched with satisfaction as she hoisted herself onto the cheesy bureau top clear on the other side of the room and dug a pack of cigarettes from her rat's-nest purse.

"Think you can sit any farther away?" Schiff said.

"If I could, I'd already be there. What did you tell them?"

"I'm meeting with my regional manager first thing in the morning," Schiff said, crossing his arms behind his head with satisfaction. But after all, it had been an easy scam. "His office is in Portland."

"Ah. And the double room?"

"I thought you'd be more comfortable."

"More comfortable than what?"

Schiff lifted an eyebrow.

"No way—there is *no way* you're staying with me," Petie snapped.

"I'd love to, princess, but I already have a room of my own."

Petie stared at him. "You son of a bitch."

Schiff smiled modestly.

"Why are you here, then?"

"To help," Schiff said.

"What makes you think I need help?"

"You didn't do too well on your own yesterday, now did you?"

Petie flushed. Her hands, Schiff was pleased to note, were balled into fists. "What's really going on here?" she said.

"What do you want to be going on?"

"Nothing. I want nothing at all to be going on, because I'm having trouble dealing with what I've already *got* going on and I don't need you to be dishing out any more."

"Look, muffin, you've got some things on your mind that I'm guessing are making you a dangerous driver, huh? So I'll be the driver. I'll be the one who remembers to stop at stoplights and gets in the turn lane and shit. Okay? I'm here to keep you safe. Think of me as your goddamned angel. That's all."

Petie put her head in her hands, pressing them hard against her eyes.

"So fill me in on your game plan, princess," he said more softly. "You didn't give me a hell of a lot to go on this morning. Do you really expect to find him?"

"Yes."

"Does Rose know you're doing this?"

"No, not unless Eddie told her."

"And what do you plan to do with Christie when you find him? Drug him? Hypnotize him? Beat him with a tire iron and toss him in the trunk?"

Petie scowled. "I haven't gotten that far yet."

"Exactly how far *have* you gotten, princess?"

"I've gotten to the part where I'm sitting in a room at the Motel 6 in Portland."

Schiff swung his legs over the side of the bed. "Well, how about the part where we get something to eat?"

"I ate already. There's a McDonald's near here."

"I saw an Elmer's sign."

Petie set her jaw. "I only have twelve dollars. Well, ten dollars now."

"Who said you'd have to pay? Did I say anything about paying? *Jesus* you're touchy. I'm thinking biscuits and gravy. C'mon, princess."

On his way out he handed over the extra key to her room.

PETIE PICKED at a short stack Schiff insisted she order and watched with something like awe as he neatly put away two biscuits, gravy, two fried eggs, hash browns, link sausages and three large cups of coffee. Except for her lunch with him at The Recess in Sawyer, Petie had never been anywhere alone with a man who wasn't Old Man or Eddie. Under the table she could feel Schiff's booted leg against her calf. His leg had migrated there as soon as they sat down and she had allowed herself to let it stay.

Petie had never wanted anyone before Schiff. She had married Eddie because she couldn't marry Eula. They stayed together because they were already together. Every couple of weeks Eddie would roll towards her across their lumpy mattress and whisper, *Hey, Pete—you wanna fool around?* and they usually did. That was the way it was between them and always had been, consensual sex not being by half the many-splendored thing you saw in movies and diamond commercials. In Petie's experience the best that could be said was that sex was a lot of work that usually went on too often and for too long and, in the end, made a big deal out of a little piece of meat that wasn't much more than a turkey neck even when erect.

"What route were you going to take tomorrow?" Schiff asked her, wiping the last remnants of gravy from his beard and folding his napkin neatly under his plate. Eddie Coolbaugh never used a napkin, though he was neat enough.

"I don't know. I was going to study the map."

"We should probably stick to I-5, at least until we get to Olympia. Have you been on that road lately? There was construction going on, but that was a year ago, no, a year and a half, probably."

"I don't know. I've never been there."

"So how do you go when you go to Spokane?"

"I don't."

"Yakima?"

"Not there, either. I've never been out of Oregon."

"No shit?"

"No shit," Petie said grimly. He'd embarrassed her. "Christ, Schiff, I grew up in a twelve-foot camp trailer. What did you think, that my lifestyle included frequent weekends at a fucking resort?"

"Hey, I'm sorry."

"Yeah, well," Petie subsided.

Schiff paid up and drove them back to the motel. Petie wouldn't let him walk her to her room. It was a bad idea. They would stand close together in the doorway, and then it might just happen that they'd be kissing, and if they kissed they'd have to involve their hands, and if that happened they might just as well go out and buy a megaphone and yell out the window, *We're screwing*. On the other hand, Schiff's reputation was already about as bad as it could get, and Carla believed it all, even about Connie at the Anchor, which was ridiculous because how could Connie lure someone to bed when she had bursitis in her shoulders so bad she couldn't even button the back of her uniform by herself?

Petie was beginning to think that the whole trip was probably a bad idea. Lying in her motel bed, she finally let herself think about what she'd been avoiding thinking about all day: What if she never found Jim Christie? What if she got all the way to stinking Kodiak without seeing any trace of him? The man was feral, knew how to cover his tracks, knew how to slip in and out of towns so no one would even notice he'd been there. He looked like everyone; he sounded like everyone; he drove a beater truck that looked like every other beater truck. If the man walked across a beach barefoot, he'd probably leave no tracks.

And then what in hell was she supposed to say to Rose?

. . .

Iɴ ʜɪs own room, Schiff faced grim reality squarely: through his own doing, he was lying alone in a cheap motel room with nothing to hold but a pillow with the loft of a bowling ball. The soap didn't foam, the toilet paper was single ply, the towels could also be used as handkerchiefs and it was the only motel chain left on earth that didn't give you complimentary shampoo.

And if they didn't come up with Jim Christie by tomorrow night he was going to have to cook up a miracle of a story for Carla. The woman had extra jealousy genes, swear to God. For all the stories swirling around him, Schiff had only cheated on her twice before, neither time recently and both times out of town. Not that she or anyone else would believe him. He wished he had half the stamina he was credited with. The Man of a Thousand Lays.

And then there was the business of missed opportunities. He'd watched Petie run her fingers through that thick shining hair and he'd never wanted a woman so much in his life, or done so much to guarantee that he wouldn't have her. Was it possible—was it just possible—that he was a good man?

He finally fell asleep just before dawn and dreamed of archery tournaments he wasn't allowed to enter.

Aʟʟ ᴛʜᴇ worry was unnecessary, as it turned out. After seven hours of driving the next day they caught up with Jim Christie on the waterfront in Anacortes, in a tavern that might as well have been the Wayside, it felt that familiar. They agreed that Schiff would talk to him first, in case seeing Petie made him bolt. After that, they'd just have to see. When Schiff approached him, Christie was sitting alone at the bar with a beer between his forearms.

"Hey, Jim."

If he was surprised to see Schiff pulling up a barstool, Christie didn't show it. "Hey."

Schiff signaled to the bartender to bring him a beer, and a second for Jim Christie.

"What brings you to Anacortes?" Christie said after a while.

"You. Petie Coolbaugh's been trying to find you. Sounds like there was some trouble."

"No trouble. I just don't like the things she's got to say," Christie said.

Schiff could feel Petie breathing over there at her dark table in the corner. He leaned in close. "Hell, she doesn't mean to hurt anybody. It's just her way. She would have followed you all the way to Kodiak if she'd had to, just to talk to you. Christ, the woman's never even been out of the state before, and here she is trying to track you down. She must want to talk to you pretty bad."

Christie lifted his beer, drank it off in one long, slow draft. "That right?"

"Rose is pretty busted up about you taking off. Petie knows it was her fault, jumping down your throat like she did. Fact is, she's got some history you might not know about, mainly that her father was a certified Grade A pervert. Tried to do things to her when she was about the same age as Rose's girl."

Christie looked at Schiff with those pale weimaraner dog-eyes of his. "Got nothing to do with me," he said.

"Look, I know that. Hell, *she* knows that. But mother hens protect the brood even if no one else hears the fox."

Christie gave a curt nod.

"Talk to her, at least. She's dying over there."

Christie looked around and gave Petie a curt nod, stood up and walked back to the tiny corner table where she'd been waiting, too strung out even to pretend to sip at her beer. When he scraped over a chair, she flinched.

"Hey, Jim."

"Petie."

"Buy you another beer?"

"Nah. Schiffen said you had something to say to me, so I came over to hear it."

"Yeah." Petie shook a cigarette out of her pack and put it between her lips. Her hands were shaking so badly she put out four matches before Christie held out a disposable lighter. When she'd finished with it, Petie set it before him like an offering. "Listen. I probably made a mistake, saying what I did to you."

"Yeah, you made a mistake."

"I'm sorry—look, I'm sorry."

Christie watched her with his bleached-out eyes.

"I forget sometimes that not everyone is bad," she said.

"Yeah."

Abruptly she leaned across the table and said, fast and low, "That trailer is a bad place; bad things happened there—the kind of things that make you think if you ever start screaming you'll never be able to stop." Petie's voice sank until it was nearly inaudible. "I saw you coming out with Carissa and it was like it was happening all over again." Petie drew a deep breath and went on. "Listen, I'm hoping you'll come home. Rose is so angry with me."

"I can't."

"Oh, *why*? I've told you how sorry—"

"Got nothing to do with you," Christie said. "I signed on with the *Gillian* this morning. We're taking her up to Kodiak on the tide tomorrow."

"Can't you meet the boat later, fly up there in a few days, maybe?"

"No. Look," Christie said slowly. "What you said, what you thought I'd been doing with the girl—I used to think about it sometimes. I tried to keep her away from me, but she wouldn't." Petie met his eyes like a head-on collision.

"But you didn't—"

"No," he said. "I wouldn't. But it's better, me leaving." Christie stood, stowing his lighter in his chest pocket and pulling out his wallet. "You need money to get home?"

"No. Use it to call Rose. Use it to have her meet you up there for a couple of days. Use it to say goodbye."

Christie gave her a curt nod, reseated his cap and walked out the door into the gathering twilight.

Petie slumped over the remains of her beer.

How'D IT go, princess?" Schiff said, pulling up a new chair. "You look like crap."

"Thanks."

"Yeah, well. Do you want another beer? Might do you good. Is he coming home?"

"No."

Schiff ran his hand through his thin hair. "Jesus, princess. I'm sorry."

"*Shit,*" Petie said.

"Yeah." Schiff swirled the beer around at the bottom of his bottle. "You want to go home?"

"I don't know. Yeah, I guess."

"Me neither," Schiff said.

"What's the worst thing about going home?"

"Carla," Schiff said instantly. "Definitely Carla."

"But she must love you," Petie said.

Schiff gave her a look.

"No?"

"Hell, I don't know, princess, with her it's hard to tell. I don't think she *likes* me very much. She yells a lot. She gives me the ugliest damn pair of boots you ever saw and then rags on me for not wearing them. *Jesus* I hate those boots."

"Then why do you stay?"

"I don't know. Maybe because it's easier than leaving. I've been thinking about it more lately, though."

"Staying?"

"Leaving."

Petie looked at him in surprise. "Why?"

"I met somebody."

"Oh." Petie dropped her head and flushed. "Come on—there must be something good about home."

"You'll be there."

Petie kept her head down.

"Well, you asked," Schiff said. "What about you, anyway? What's your worst thing?"

Petie blew out a long, slow whistle. "Shit. You mean besides the fact that I don't have a job and my only friend may never speak to me again because I ran off her boyfriend who I unfairly accused of molesting her underage daughter? Gee, give me a minute to think."

"She's not your only friend," Schiff said.

"What?"

"You said Rose was your only friend. She's not."

"Would you be talking about yourself?" Petie looked at him dead-on. "Because I can't speak for you, but I've never wanted to do with a friend the things I'd like to do with you."

"Now, *there's* someplace I'd like to go."

Petie stood. "Take it home with you, cowboy. It'll give you something to think about while you're driving."

THEY SEPARATED, of course, at the Motel 6 parking lot in Portland, where Petie had left her car. She followed Schiff's truck for a long time, but fell behind somewhere in the Coast Range. When she pulled into her own driveway just after daybreak, she nearly ran into Carla's car. Even from the driveway she could hear Carla's voice, high and piercing as a steam whistle.

"Don't tell me you didn't know. How the fuck could you not know? There wasn't any meeting in Portland, Eddie. There was *never* any meeting in Portland. Schiff just rolled home, so she should be here any minute. You should ask her about it. Everyone knows about them but you. *You'd* know if you weren't so goddamn stupid. Why do you think you have such a good job? So you'll keep quiet about him screwing your wife. Jesus, if you haven't figured that out by now you're even stupider than I thought."

Petie opened the front door. Eddie flinched but he did not look away. Petie closed the door behind her and set her purse and keys on the kitchen table without ever breaking eye contact with him.

"Hey, Petie," he said slowly. "Look who's here."

"Yeah."

"She said Schiff just got home, too."

"He probably did. It was a long drive back from Anacortes."

"How long have you been sleeping with my husband?" Carla demanded.

"Look—"

Carla shrieked, "There was no fucking meeting with any fucking boss in Portland. I called. I know."

"Go home, Carla."

Carla took a step towards Petie and leveled a finger at her like a gun. "You're a whore, a pervert. I used to hear about you, about things you did."

"Go home," Petie said.

"If you ever go near my husband again, if you so much as *talk* to him again, I'll have Eddie fired so fast it'll make your head spin."

Petie wheeled around, bearing down on Carla Schiffen like a train wreck. "You stinking sack of shit," she said softly. "You worthless piece of alcoholic trash. You know what the man was doing? He was helping me track down Jim Christie. Christie—you know him, don't you? Rose's boyfriend? You've probably hoisted more than a few with him at the Wayside between all those rounds of video poker. Or—I just thought of this—maybe you were sleeping with him? Tsk, tsk, Carla. Naughty girl, drinking and playing all day while hubby's at work. Or, wait, could it be Roy? Sure, the guy who keeps the beer and booze flowing—you'd be perfect together, you being a drinker and all."

Carla Schiffen's mouth dropped open.

"Go home, Carla," Petie said wearily. "Just get the fuck out of my house."

"Bitch!" Carla shrieked, and bolted out the door into the first tender sunlight of the morning.

Eddie stood there.

Petie dropped into a chair and put her head in her hands.

"What the fuck?" Eddie said.

"Not now," Petie whispered. "Please, not now."

"No, now. You've been keeping things from me, Petie. I know you've been keeping things from me. I want to know what the *fuck* is going on around here."

"Did Schiff tell you anything?"

"He didn't tell me dick. He said Rose was in trouble and you'd gone somewhere to fix it. So I call Rose and she doesn't know what the fuck I'm talking about, you going to fix something. She says Jim is gone, though. Next thing I know, Carla's showing up here at five forty-five chewing my ass. I'm tired of it, Petie. I'm tired of your always being angry and mean to me. Huh? I deserve some respect. I'm working hard, I need to know I'm coming home to someone who's not going to treat me bad."

"Then maybe you shouldn't come home anymore," Petie said. "You know? Maybe you just shouldn't come home."

"Was she right?"

"Was who right?"

"Carla."

"About which part?" Petie said.

"The part about Schiff."

"No."

"So you're not sleeping with him?"

"I'm not sleeping with him. I have never slept with him."

"Then what the fuck were you doing in Portland or Anacortes or wherever the hell you were?"

Petie closed her eyes. It seemed to her that she might spontaneously die, sitting right there at her kitchen table, Eula's table. She was so tired that death didn't even sound like a bad thing. The boys would wake up in less than half an hour.

"I had an argument with Christie. I found him at the trailer, Old Man's trailer. I said some things I shouldn't have, and he took off. That was two days ago. I tried to find him, and Schiff came up to help. I didn't ask him to, he just did. We found Christie in Anacortes, but he wouldn't come home. He signed on with the *Gillian*. They leave this morning for Kodiak. I couldn't stop him. I couldn't do a goddamn thing." She began to cry, not Rose's sad, pretty tears but caustic, bitter ones saved up for years.

Eddie walked back and forth, pleading. "Aw, quit it, Petie, huh? Nah, don't do that now, it's okay, huh? We'll figure it out."

"I can't do it anymore, Eddie. I'm so tired. I'm just so goddamn tired."

Eddie ran a hand through his hair. "What are you talking about, Pete? What—me, the boys? What?"

"Everything," Petie whispered. "I'm talking about everything."

Chapter 17

Rose WAS shocked by how much thinner Gordon looked—thinner, more tired, and the Kaposi's sarcoma lesion on his forehead stood out like blood on a fresh bandage. He saw her as soon as she came in, waving her over to his booth. It was a warm spring morning at Souperior's and there should have been some trace of festivity, of improving spirits, but somehow there wasn't.

When she reached him Rose gave a one-armed hug and pressed her cheek to his. Her lips brushed his forehead unconsciously in a mother's perpetual vigilance for fever, but he was cool. "Does it hurt?" she asked him, slipping into the seat across from him.

Gordon raised a hand and touched the livid patch. "This? No, it doesn't hurt. You look like hell. Has something happened?" In Gordon's eyes she saw love—love for her. How the dying could afford such generosity she couldn't imagine. Her heart contracted for this gentle man who had shined a light into her unseen corners and coaxed from them such accomplishments.

"Rose?" he said.

Rose smiled a little. "Spring. Spring has happened."

"Spring is a happy thing. You don't look happy," Gordon said.

"No. Jim's gone."

"Gone?"

"It happens every spring. He goes back to work. In Alaska."

"You said he wouldn't leave until March."

"No. He and Petie got into an argument about Carissa. She accused him of molesting her."

"You're kidding."

Rose sighed heavily. "It's a long story. Petie's father was a terrible man who molested her when she was younger. I didn't know that until a couple of days ago. So she saw Jim and Carissa coming out of this abandoned trailer up in the woods—the one Petie had lived in with her father—and accused him of abusing Carissa. He disappeared less than an hour later. He left me a note. I never even saw him."

Gordon shook his head. "*Did* he molest her?"

"No."

"You're sure? It sounds odd, his leaving like that."

"It would be, in anyone else. But this is Jim Christie. He gets claustrophobic real easily and I guess maybe Carissa and I crowded him, even though we tried not to. When Petie said those things to him, I think all he heard was, *It's time to go.* He wouldn't do anything to hurt Carissa, he's always so careful with her. And Carissa's so upset, Gordon. She thinks this is all her fault, and I can't think of what to say because in some ways it *was* her fault for pressing herself on him, and Petie's fault for thinking something terrible must be going on instead of something innocent."

"Have you heard from him since he left?"

"No, not directly. As soon as she realized he'd left, Petie went after him, her and Ron Schiffen, which is *another* story. Anyway, they found him in Anacortes, Washington. He said he was on his way to Kodiak aboard the *Gillian*, so I've sent him a couple of letters there but I don't think I'll hear from him, at least not right now. The thing is, I might never hear from him again. Pogo left us, and he was a lot easier to hold down than Jim."

"I can't believe that," Gordon said. "The man seemed to worship you."

"Well." Rose absently stirred her cold coffee.

"So what's with Petie and Ron Schiffen?"

"That's another huge mess. Apparently Schiff decided to meet Petie in Portland and help her track Jim down. He and Petie have gotten to be friends lately, I guess. Now Carla—Schiff's wife, she's awful—is telling anyone who will listen that Petie seduced him. The woman actually took out a half-page ad in the *Sawyer Weekly Standard* saying that Petie had stolen her husband, an upstanding citizen, a moral family man—this is *Schiff* she's referring to—and that they should boycott her. She said Petie comes from degenerate stock—those are her exact words, I swear—and that honest Christian people shouldn't so much as talk to her if they see her on the street or accept her business if they own a store or something. Not that Hubbard has too many upstanding Christian people. She used an old picture of Petie in the ad that someone took at a picnic, one where Petie has this old bandanna tied around her forehead and is holding three bottles of beer. I think Carla's also trying to get Schiff to fire Eddie, but I'm sure Schiff won't do that. He's got a couple of deep rake marks down one side of his face. He said he got them riding a dirt bike through the woods, but everyone knows it was Carla and those long fingernails of hers."

Gordon shook his head. "My God, you go out of town for a few days and look what happens while you're gone."

"It's a small town, Gordon. Things like this happen all the time."

"Not to my friends they don't. Look, Rose, there's something I need to talk to you about. Do you feel like you can listen to some business talk, or should I wait? There's not a lot of time, though."

"Lord, I wish you weren't leaving. You still feel like you have to?"

"Paul and I signed a lease when I was there. Yes, I have to. For Nadine as much as for me."

Rose's eyes teared up. "I feel like I'm losing everyone. You, Nadine, Jim, Petie. And it's all happening so fast."

"Have you lost Petie?"

"I don't know. I was so angry with her. I wish we could go back a week and start over."

"If you went back a week, you'd just repeat the whole thing again."

"Yes, probably." Rose looked out the window over the bay. The *Pixie*, a pig of a sportfishing boat that wallowed even on a calm sea, was just clearing the bar. Today the tourists would be throwing up all over the place. "Anyway, what did you want to talk about?"

"Can I get you anything first? More coffee?"

"No thanks. Go ahead—you're making me nervous."

"Well, here it is, then." Gordon took a deep breath. "Nadine and I have been talking about what to do with this place. We don't want to just close it down, especially after we've gotten this far and people have finally begun to know about it. But we don't really want to sell it, either, not to someone who's going to change it all. So here's what we came up with, that we'd like you to consider. We'd like to turn the place over to you."

"What? Oh my God, Gordon, you can't do that."

"Let me tell you the terms, because you might not even want it when I'm done. We owe ten thousand dollars on a business loan. You would have to assume it and make the rest of the payments—six hundred and twenty-eight dollars a month. We haven't had a month when we couldn't pay it, not even December, so it's doable. If you run the place with maybe just one other person for the summer, you'll be fine—better than fine, we hope. There are some things we can do to help you with visibility, starting with a cookbook signing as soon as *Local Flavor* is released, which Paul thinks may be July, at least that's what we'll shoot for. We'll get book signings in Sawyer, too, not just Hubbard, and maybe even ones in Portland and Eugene. Plus we'll make sure all the newspapers and radio stations get press releases about the book. It might be a good idea to have another cook-off, too, to get people involved again. Anyway, there's time to work out things like that, but the point is, once you've paid off the loan you'll own the place free and clear."

"I don't know what to say. I can't believe you and Nadine are serious about this. What about you? What will you live on?"

"That's the last thing. We'd ask you to pay Nadine five hundred dollars a month until I've died."

Rose shuddered. "Oh, Gordon."

"It will help her in the months at the end, when she may not be able to work regularly if she's looking after me. She'll have plenty of money from my life insurance after I'm gone. So that's pretty much it. We figure you should be able to clear a thousand a month even in winter, and conceivably five or six thousand a month in summer and during spring break."

"I don't know what to say."

"Don't say anything," Gordon said. "Just think it over. And if you decide to say no, we'll certainly understand."

"You know I love this place."

"Yes."

"And you trust me not to fuck it all up?"

"More than I trust Nadine and me, as far as that goes."

"I don't know," Rose said, and wrapped her arms around herself. "God, my heart hurts."

"It's either panic or love," Gordon said, grinning.

Rose smiled, too. "You really think I can do this?"

"No," said Gordon. "I know you can do it. The only question is whether you *will* do it."

PETIE STOOD on the spongy old floor in her laundry room, sorting socks. She liked finding all the mates and marrying them. It appealed to her sense of order; if no sock was left alone at the bottom of the basket, then, at least on some level, all must be well. She remembered Ryan by the socks he wore and how he wore them. First, the tiny elasticized baby socks, white with blue heels and toes, making arcs in the air as he kicked and kicked until, by the time he was a toddler, he had learned to kick them right off so he could walk in his bare feet, small toes fanning and gripping every which way for balance. Within a year he rebelled against socks altogether, unable to bear even the slightest wrinkle inside his shoes. Petie still watched him sometimes when he didn't see her, putting his sneakers on over and over again until each sock inside lay perfectly smooth.

When she and Old Man had lived in the woods, she took their clothes to the laundromat next to the Diary Queen twice a week, soothed by the warmth and dryness, the mindless drone of the dryers, the whoosh and rumble of the wash cycles. Sometimes young women were there, mothers who folded their children's clothes with pride, smoothing and evening and squaring corners in a way Petie never remembered Paula having done. Sometimes fishermen would come in reeking of diesel and guts, heaving mountains of filthy clothes into the commerical-size washers, smoking and flipping through the nickel ads or some NAPA Auto Parts catalog while they waited. None of these people took much notice of Petie, except once when a young woman asked her if her mother would be back soon, or did she need a ride home. Petie had lied and said her mother was just down the street, buying them ice cream sundaes. She'd slipped out the door when the woman wasn't watching, humping her laundry basket the mile home.

Over the noise of the dryer Petie heard the door open. Eddie was supposed to be working and the boys were in school. She heard Rose call, "Hello!"

Her heart made a little jump. It was the first time Rose had sought her out since Christie left and everything turned to crap. She put the rest of the dry clothes back in the dryer and hurried into the kitchen. "Hey," she said.

"I need to talk to you," Rose said, shucking off her raincoat.

"No you don't," Petie said.

"What?"

"You don't need to talk to me, because I know everything you're going to say. About how wrong I was, and how I had no right to say what I did to Christie and how even when I found the man I fucked up and didn't manage to bring him home. Did I get most of it right? Jesus, my hands are shaking. Oh, and if Jim never comes home, I'll have fucked up your entire life."

"Would that be an apology?" Rose asked, starting to grin.

"Yes. Wait, shall I throw myself on the floor at your feet?" Petie said, smiling the first real smile in three days.

"I don't know what I would do without you, and that's a fact," Rose sighed. "Look, I need you to help me think about something."

Petie bowed.

"Get this. Nadine and Gordon want to give me Souperior's." She repeated what Gordon had said while Petie watched her through a rising ribbon of cigarette smoke.

"Whoa," said Petie, and whistled. "It's fairy godmother time. Oops, bad pun, but you know what I mean."

"I'm going to miss him so much." Rose gazed off into space for a minute. "Do you think God plans our friendships, makes sure we meet certain people at certain times?"

"No."

"No, I guess not," Rose said.

"Will you do it, take the restaurant?"

"I don't know. It makes my hands sweat just thinking about it. Feel." Rose held out a palm.

"It's panic," Petie said.

"That's exactly what Gordon said."

"You should do it," Petie said. "Souperior's, I mean. You're already running the place. How hard can it be to own it, too?"

"It can't possibly be that simple."

Petie shrugged. "If you want it to work out, it'll work out. It's not like you'll need to hire a cook. Plus Carissa can help waitress in the summer and on weekends. Hell, Ryan could even be a busboy sometimes."

But Rose's attention had wandered. "Gordon was talking about telling the newspapers and stuff when the book comes out. I didn't understand some of it, but he said we should do a book signing. Hey, Petie, wait a minute—I've got the best idea. You know how the walls at Souperior's have always seemed kind of bare? Let's show your work there. Let's put it up with price tags, so people can buy it right from their tables. It would make the place so much brighter, and it would be a good place for you to start. You wouldn't need Pico Talco or anyone. Doesn't that sound good?"

Petie looked doubtful.

"What," Rose said.

"I have a hard time believing anyone would pay money for one of my pictures."

"Paul did."

"Pretty pictures in a book are much different than hanging by themselves on a wall," Petie said.

"Well, if it doesn't work we'll take them down."

"You're going to do it, aren't you?" Petie said, giving Rose a look. "You're going to own a goddamn restaurant."

"Am I? Yes, I guess I am. Holy shit, huh?"

"No," Petie said, suddenly serious. "It's the best idea I've heard in a long time. If you have to go back to waitressing, you might as well do it at your own place. Hell, maybe we can get Schiff to hold the Kiwanis meeting there every month. Rotary, too. The place is big enough, and everyone's been bitching forever about the crummy food at the Anchor."

"Have you talked to him?"

"Who?"

"Schiff?"

Petie flushed. "No. It seemed like it would be better right now if I didn't."

"Is that okay?"

Petie shrugged. "I don't know."

"It was nice of him to help you find Jim like that."

"It was suicidal. Who would ever have guessed he'd turn out to be a good man. Not to mention an upstanding citizen and moral family man, in case you didn't know that about him already."

"Oh, right," snorted Rose. "I read that someplace."

"Goddamn Carla," Petie hooted.

"Goddamn Carla," Rose shrieked.

They laughed until it hurt.

"Oh, baby," Rose finally said, fighting for breath. "Let's never break up."

"You don't have to worry about me," Petie said, wiping her eyes with the back of her sleeve. "Nobody else on earth would put up with me."

STEPPING OFF the bus at the Greyhound station, Marge opened her arms and drew Petie in, enfolding her in a real hug, a generous hug, a hug you weren't capable of until you were middle-aged and had died once or twice and risen once or twice and learned that what life dealt you wasn't necessarily going to be good.

She had called the day after Petie returned from Anacortes. "Hon, I'm coming north," she'd said, "and I'm scared to death to do it, so if you could keep me company a little I'd sure appreciate it."

"You know I will, but what are you afraid of?"

"That Larry won't be there."

"He's in every loop of carpet and every washcloth and pillowcase. Of course he'll be here."

"I'm counting on that, honey, but it scares me, too, knowing I'll have to lose him all over again when I leave."

"So don't leave."

"DeeDee and the kids, they've fixed up a real nice room for me here."

"How are you getting here?"

"DeeDee's taking me to the Greyhound in the morning. She said I could take her Camry if I wanted, but I'd be scared to. Larry, he was the driver, not me. I drive some in Tempe, but only around the neighborhood, you know—where the kids need to go, and the Safeway and that."

"When's the bus coming in? I'll pick you up."

"Oh, honey, that would be a relief. Just let me look for the ticket—you know, I lose everything now, even when it's right under my nose. I don't know why that is."

Petie heard drawers sliding in and out, and at one point the receiver banged down on something hard and she heard Marge clucking to herself the way she did when she was exasperated. "My Lord," she said breathlessly when she finally picked up the phone again. "Have you ever known anyone so scatterbrained? You know, I think some of it might be the pills they have me taking. I carry a little card in my purse now, honey, with DeeDee and the kids' address on it in case I forget. I probably ought to write my own name on it, too, I'm that bad. Looks like I'm getting in at two-thirty in the afternoon, day after tomorrow."

"All right. Look for me there," Petie said. "Don't give it another thought."

Marge sighed deeply on the other end of the line. "Thank you, honey, I feel easier already knowing you'll be there. You and DeeDee, you've taken real good care of me. Don't think I don't know it."

Now, outside the shabby Greyhound station in Sawyer, she held Petie in her embrace a minute longer than usual and then held her at arm's length. "You look real good, honey." She was dressed in her usual pastel stretchwear and a self collar sweatshirt that said, in sequined letters, *I'm Shelley's Grandma*. "Isn't it the cutest thing?" she puffed as Petie grabbed her suitcase. "She and DeeDee made it for me last Christmas, but it's too warm to wear down in Tempe, so I've been saving it."

Petie led her back to the car, trying not to give away just how bad Marge looked. Her face was thin and the skin seemed to have found new wrinkles and lost most of its color. Larry had always joked that there was just enough of Marge to get a good hold on, but Marge had anguished over those thirty pounds ever since Petie had known her. Now that they were gone she just looked old and baggy. She had used some kind of eye shadow, too, something Petie had never seen her wear before. DeeDee must be working on her. Petie helped her with her seat belt and pulled out onto the highway.

"Ever since Larry passed on," Marge said, "DeeDee and the kids have been real good to me, but I swear to you, honey, I don't know how I've done it."

Then she sat up a little straighter and said brightly, "How are your boys? They're just growing up so fast." Marge had seen them just weeks ago. DeeDee must have instructed her to be cheerful so she wouldn't wear on people.

"Look," Petie said. "You don't have to pretend for me. You don't have to act like you're okay when you're not. Okay?"

Marge dove into her bag for a Kleenex and nodded, overcome. She patted Petie's hand hard and held her Kleenex to her mouth until she'd composed herself and drew a deep, quavery breath. "I'm just not myself right now. Lord, Larry would give me such a talking-to. I miss him, honey." Tears ran down her face. Petie touched her cheek with the back of her hand and brought away a river.

"Don't mind me. Seems like I'm always crying," Marge said, waving her hand. "Sometimes I don't even know it till I've got a lapful of tears. DeeDee and the kids, they've gotten used to me by now. Little Shelley, she just looks at me and says, *There goes Grandma again*, and runs to get me some tissues. I swear I don't know what I'd do without that sweet angel."

"Are we taking you to the Sea View?"

"Yes," Marge said, and put both hands to her mouth. "Look, we're home." Petie drove by the Quik Stop, the Wayside, the Anchor. Marge turned her head away, looking out the window. Petie could feel her tremble.

"Did you remember your car keys?" Petie said. Marge had left her car in the Sea View parking lot when she took off for Tempe.

"I never even took them. They're hanging in the office, right where they always are."

"Okay. Look, I've got a couple of things I need to do, but I want you to come for dinner. Rose and Carissa will be there, too. Rose has been through some tough times lately. I thought we could cheer her up."

"Has she?"

"Well, Jim left."

"Oh, that's too bad, honey. Why, I thought he'd marry that gal for sure, he looked at her like she'd hung the moon, her and that little daughter of hers."

"I guess things didn't work out, at least not for this year. We're hoping he'll come home after the season." Petie pulled into the Sea View. She could feel Marge shiver.

"Look, do you want me to go in with you?"

Marge gave a thin, eerie wail. "Oh! Oh, honey, I keep expecting him to come out the door, you know how he knew the sound of every car. In all the years we lived here I never had to carry a single grocery bag in by myself, he was that thoughtful. And now he's not here," Marge cried. "He's not here at all."

The power of her misery was almost unbearable. The only thing Petie could think to do was to hold Marge's arm firmly in her hand, as though in her grief Marge might fly away instead of sitting arrested and bereft in the passenger seat, her legs out the open door. Marge finally took some deep, shuddering breaths and quieted down. She patted Petie's hand blindly. "I'm okay, honey."

"Bullshit," Petie said. "You aren't okay, you shouldn't be okay, no one *expects* you to be okay, so stop trying to spare me. Just stop."

Marge nodded blindly, mopping at her eyes and nose. "All right, honey."

Petie brought Marge's suitcase up to the apartment she and Larry had built above the office. Marge seemed to have forgotten Petie was there, so she let herself out, saying, "Come over whenever you're ready. Or call me, if you want me to come get you."

The woman looked about as fit to drive as a blind man.

Rose came first, with soup—potato leek, one of her best, in Petie's opinion. Eddie had taken off with Loose to go look at a wrecked dirt bike they were thinking of fixing up, so it was just Ryan and Carissa and the women. Marge would be there any time.

Rose set her pot on the stove and said, "You know, if I'd known it was just going to be us, I'd have invited Nadine, too. They're leaving the day after tomorrow, I can hardly believe it."

"Why don't you call her? Maybe Gordon can close up."

"You know, I think I will—it would be a nice way to say thank you for everything she's done for us, don't you think?" Rose turned on a low heat under the soup pot and smoothed her skirt, a pretty one she'd bought with some of her book-advance money.

Petie handed her the wall phone. "Do you know her number?"

"By heart."

Petie watched Rose cradle the phone between her chin and shoulder. Her hair had silver threads already—her mother had been snow white by thirty-five—and her profile had softened and filled out lately. Petie thought Eve must have looked just like Rose, walking through her garden in Eden humming quietly to herself and snipping a blossom here and there, tidying up a little, doing light housework for the Lord. But Rose would never have fallen for the snake. Rose had a sort of built-in goodness meter that would have picked out the serpent's insincerity in under a minute flat.

"You know how to get here, don't you?" Rose was saying. "Yes, take that last right. We'll wait dinner for you. No, it's not a big deal. Okay? Okay." She hung up the phone. "She'll be here in half an hour," she told Petie. "She was so pleased to be asked. We really could have been nicer to her."

"We were nice to her," Petie protested. "You're always nice to her, and sometimes I was, too."

"We were okay," Rose countered. "Okay is not the same as nice. Anyway Gordon said he'd finish up and close early. They've only had a few customers, anyway."

"Good," Petie said, and turned to Carissa, who was sitting at the table making a friendship bracelet out of embroidery thread. "Would you call upstairs and ask Ryan to come down? I want to talk to you both for a minute before Marge gets here."

When they were all together in the kitchen, Petie said, "You guys know that Marge's husband Larry died a few weeks ago, right?"

Ryan nodded solemnly.

"Well, Marge is real sad right now, she has a big bruise around her heart, and—"

"Did you see it?" Ryan said.

Petie frowned. "Did I see what?"

"The bruise."

Rose smiled. "No, sweetie, it's too deep to see. That's why your mom's talking to you about it."

"Oh," Ryan subsided, clearly disappointed.

Petie started again. "When people miss someone as much as Marge misses Larry, they forget how to be happy for a while, and sometimes it makes them cry even when they're right in the middle of talking to you."

"I like Marge," Ryan said.

"So do I," Petie said. "That's why I want her to come over for supper. It will help. If you have to be as sad as Marge is, it's easier to get through it when you're with people who love you."

"She's probably still going through the five stages of grief," Carissa said.

Petie looked at Rose.

"Anger, denial, bargaining, depression and acceptance," Carissa explained. "Somebody named Elisabeth Kübler-Ross figured that out."

"The child cannot possibly be from my loins," Rose said to Petie.

"We learned about it in Family Sciences."

"What the hell is Family Sciences?" Petie said.

"You learn about how people relate to each other at different stages of life," Carissa said, unruffled by the looks she was getting from Petie and Rose.

"Huh," said Petie. "So anyway, if Marge cries when she's here, I don't want you to worry."

"Hey, Ryan, why don't we make a picture for her?" Carissa said. "It might cheer her up."

The two of them went upstairs to the boys' room. Petie could hear them banging around in the closet. She gave Rose a quick summary of the afternoon, and Rose shook her head. "I feel so badly for her," she said. "You're a brave woman, meeting her at the Greyhound station and having her over."

Petie shrugged. "There haven't been that many people who've loved me, and most of them are dead."

Outside, a car door shut and a minute later Marge puffed in, shaking rain off a plastic rain bonnet. "My Lord," she said. "I was getting used to it being dry in Tempe." She carefully folded her rain bonnet and set it on top of her purse.

"Hi, Marge," Rose said, and approached for a hug.

"Hello, honey," Marge said. "Why, don't you look pretty? Petie said you'd been going through some times lately, but you'd never know it to look at you, hon."

"It's all makeup and bad lighting, but thank you anyway," Rose said. "Can I get you anything? Petie, what do you have?"

"Beer, juice, water. Pepsi, of course."

"I'll just have a glass of water, hon," Marge said.

"Nadine's coming over in another few minutes," Petie told her, "to have dinner with us, too. Girls' night."

"Oh, isn't that nice of you. I always felt sorry for her, to tell you the truth," Marge said, accepting a glass of tap water from Rose. "She seemed like one of those people who has their nose pressed to the glass, watching other people having a nice time, but like it was never going to happen for her. And her brother, what was his name?"

"Gordon," Rose said.

"Yes, Gordon," Marge said. "I never really saw the point to him. He didn't ever seem to do anything."

Rose looked at Petie. "You should tell her," Petie said.

"Tell what?" Marge said.

"Gordon has AIDS," Rose said. "He helps when he can, but he doesn't always feel well enough."

"Why, I had no idea. Is he a fairy?" Marge said.

"Well," Rose said, "he's a homosexual."

Marge nodded thoughtfully. "I can't pretend I understand how people get that way, but Larry and me, we always tried to keep an open mind. There was the nicest boy over in the Valley who cut my hair for years and

years, just the sweetest thing. He'd tell me about his boyfriends sometimes. Will he die?"

"Will who die?" Rose said.

"Gordon. You said he has AIDS. Does that mean he'll die?"

"Yes."

Marge nodded matter-of-factly. "Yes, I thought so. Maybe that's
why Nadine's always looked so sad. I didn't know that, honey. I'm glad
you told me."

A s soon as Nadine arrived, Rose served them all from the
big soup pot. Ryan brought his picture down for Marge, presenting it
with great solemnity. He had drawn a rainbow over the ocean, with a
boat sailing underneath it. Marge was elaborate in her praise. "You're
such a good artist, honey. Look how good you did your colors. Whose
boat is it?"

Ryan tucked his chin gravely. "Larry's."

"Oh, is it? But we didn't have a boat, honey. Larry used to talk about
it, but we just never seemed to get around to doing anything about it."

"It's the boat that's taking him to heaven," Ryan said.

"Oh! Why, that's a beautiful thought, honey." Marge's eyes glis-
tened. "Is the rainbow heaven?"

"I don't know," Ryan said thoughtfully. "But I think it might be. Are
there colors in heaven?"

"I'm sure of it," Marge said. "Do you know, I think God must love
colors, to have made such beautiful rainbows and flowers."

"Yes," Ryan agreed.

"Can I take this picture home?" Marge asked.

Ryan nodded.

"I know just where I'm going to put it," Marge said. "I'm going to put
it smack in the middle of my refrigerator door, where I can see it all day
long." She gave the boy a hug. "You've made an old lady real happy, hon,"
she said.

"Mom told us you might cry."

"Ryan," Petie warned.

"It's okay, honey," Marge said to Petie. To Ryan she said, "I might. I get real sad sometimes. But being here with you I don't feel one bit sad, and that's the truth. Thank you for that, honey."

Carissa and Ryan took their dinner to the living room and turned on the TV. The four women settled around the kitchen table like old campaigners during a lull in the fighting. They ate Rose's good soup and talked quietly about things that didn't matter: the price of early strawberries, the cost of gasoline in Tempe, the five-year prison sentence Billy Wall had been given that morning for abusing those Hubbard boys; Nadine's job at the rare books store in Los Angeles, where she would return to work two weeks from next Tuesday.

Eddie Coolbaugh and Loose came in and disappeared upstairs. After a while Petie went up to check on the boys and Carissa, who'd fallen asleep beside Ryan. When she came out of the boys' bedroom she saw the light on down the hall, in their bedroom. She looked in and found Eddie sitting on the side of the bed with his shirt unbuttoned and one sock off. He was as still as death, as though he'd been beached there for hours, pinned to the mattress by misery.

"Hey, Petie," he said softly when she came in, barely glancing at her.

"Hey, Eddie."

"Boys okay?"

Petie nodded. It was relative.

"I've been thinking, Pete, I've been thinking real hard. Was it something I did?"

"Don't."

"You always seem to know what's going on with me, but I never know what's going on with you, so I figure it was something I did."

"It wasn't anything you did."

"Because I could change it, you know, if you told me. You just tell me, and I swear I won't do it again."

"It's not like that," Petie said.

Eddie looked at her with the terrible, uncomprehending look of an animal being led to slaughter. "You loved me, huh? Didn't you love me?"

"Yes," Petie whispered. "I loved you."

"So where did that go, Pete, huh?"

Petie shook her head. "I don't know."

"You don't just stop loving people," Eddie pleaded. "You love them for keeps."

Petie smiled the slightest smile. "Eula used to say that."

"Well, and she *knew* stuff, didn't she? Didn't she know we were going to get married before we even told her?"

Petie dropped her head, ducked in shame.

"You loved me, huh?" Eddie pressed.

"Yes, I loved you," Petie said. "You and Eula saved my life."

"So isn't that worth something? Isn't it?"

"Yes," Petie whispered. "I'm sorry, Eddie. I'm so sorry."

"Aw, Jesus, Petie." Eddie started to cry. "Jesus. You tell me how to fix it, and I'll fix it, okay? You've always been smarter than me, you always know what to do. You just tell me and I'll do it. C'mon, huh?"

"I'm so sorry."

"Don't just keep saying that, Petie. Goddamn it."

Petie put both hands to her mouth, forcing herself to watch Eddie rise, grab his second sock and bolt from the room. A minute later, she heard the protest of his truck door, and then wheels crunching on gravel.

How do you begin to tell someone they're too thin a meal when they can't even see that you've been starving?

WHEN PETIE returned to the kitchen she found Nadine, Marge and Rose deep in conversation.

"I was twenty-six," Marge was saying, "and we had nothing, not even furniture of our own. Larry's folks let us borrow some things—Lord, there was an old green davenport that Larry always said reminded him of peas and was just about as comfortable to sit on," Marge chuckled softly. "Larry, he was working enough for two jobs, DeeDee was a year old, and then out of the blue the army decides to up and send him to Korea. Well, you can imagine what I had to say about *that*, me with a small baby and Frank on the way. Not that it made a bit of difference what I thought, seeing as how Larry went anyway. I knew a couple of other girls whose husbands were sent overseas, too, but it was still the loneliest time. I'd put DeeDee to bed and turn on the radio real loud so she wouldn't hear me cry. I swear I cried enough tears to fill a bathtub. It was the first time we were ever apart."

"It sounds romantic," Rose said.

"Oh, I don't know about that, honey. You know, some of the boys who went over with Larry were killed, and that was awful, those poor girls hearing from the army that their lives were busted all to pieces—no more husband, no more dreams. And we were all dreamers—we'd spend whole evenings talking about where we'd go for picnics and what we'd bring with us when our husbands came home, what their favorite foods were, what we'd bring for the kids when some of us didn't even have kids yet, just planned to. It sounds silly now, I guess. You girls are so much more independent than we were."

"How long was Larry away?" Rose asked.

"One year and seven months. And those years after he came back to us were the happiest times. He was a good man, my Larry, and he worked real hard to give us a good life, me and the kids."

"Pogo was never like that," Rose said. "He was always taking off and leaving us to figure things out for ourselves."

"All the same, he gave you that beautiful little girl of yours," Marge said.

Nadine said, "My parents used to fight all the time. *You drink too much, you don't help out, you flirted with that girl, you won't amount to anything if you can't keep a job.* For thirty-five years they were locked in mortal combat because neither one of them was willing to be the one who walked out. Funny thing was, my mother died first, and my father fell apart. He died within the year."

"Do you have a boyfriend?" Marge asked her.

"No," Nadine said, coloring. "I'm pretty set in my ways."

"Oh, honey," Marge said, and reached across the table to pat

Nadine's hand sympathetically. "There's a man out there who will worship the ground you walk on, who will look at you and see God because no one else could have made you so perfect. That's what Larry used to tell me, that he looked at me and saw the Lord. If you haven't met that man yet, honey, you just wait for him because he's out there."

"What an extraordinary thought," Nadine said.

"Is it?" Marge said.

"Yes," said Petie and Rose in unison.

Marge reached into her purse and retrieved a postcard. She held it out to Petie. "Here, hon, before I forget, this came in the mail for Larry. It's from Bachelor Butte Resort, that place over in Bend. You get two nights there for free just for listening to their sales presentation. I thought you and the boys could use it."

Petie and Rose both smiled. "Thanks," Petie said, accepting the card. "Every household on the coast must have gotten one of these. The Schiffens got one, and Rose has one that was sent to Jim Christie."

"Well, you use it or not," Marge said. "It sure wasn't doing any good sitting in my mailbox."

Nadine yawned and stood. "I'm sorry to be the poop of the party, but it's been a long day and I've still got packing to do. Petie, thank you for having me over." She slipped into her slicker. "It was a pleasure to meet you, Marge. If you're ever in L.A. please look me up. Petie and Rose will know how to reach me. Rose, I'll see you tomorrow."

"Oh, yes."

When the sound of Nadine's car faded away, Marge said to Petie, "What a nice girl. Honey, you never told me she was nice. Shame on you."

Petie shrugged. "She's more Rose's friend than mine."

"Well, she's nice anyway."

Rose yawned and stretched. "Time for me to go, too, and get Carissa to bed." She went upstairs, roused Carissa and left after a quick hug for Marge.

"Well, honey," Marge said after they'd gone, "that was a real pleasant evening. It made being home easier."

"I'm glad," Petie said. "There haven't been many pleasant evenings here lately."

"You want to talk about it, honey? I've been thinking maybe something was wrong, but I didn't want to press."

"I don't know. I lie in bed at night and I can't sleep for all the noise going on inside my head. There's someone, not Eddie, that I love. There are pictures I want to paint instead of working. I'd like just once to experience joy."

"Honey, there comes a time when staying with a bad life means you're throwing away the chance to make a good one, and God takes great offense at that. He made us in His image, with choices and powers, and if you throw that away and make less of yourself than you could have, you're diminishing what He made with His own hands, and that's a wrong thing, honey. It's plain wrong."

Petie's voice sank until it was barely audible. "Is it wrong to be unhappy?"

Marge leaned forward and squeezed Petie's hand. "Honey, is it wrong to be a broken vase when it's not your fault you fell off the table? You can't always keep things from breaking, hon, but it's not the breaking that God faults us for. It's throwing away the pieces that hurts Him, honey, when He's made perfectly good glue if you'd only take the trouble to use it. Now, you're never going to look brand new again and you can't do anything about that. But you'll hold flowers all the same, even if you're a little stove in on one side. Do you see? The important thing is, you can still be the receptacle for beauty, honey; you can still hold His pretty colors just like you were intended to. Your little Ryan knows that; all children know that. It's only us grown-ups that forget."

Petie sat perfectly still as tears rolled down her cheeks.

Marge went on. "I've heard the stories. You had a bad man for a father, honey, and the Lord took your mama home way too soon. But God gave you a stout heart and a strong mind to make up for it. No one's faulting you for needing time to fix things, honey, as long as you do fix them in the end. It's when you leave yourself broke that you commit a sin. It's not a sin to be unhappy, honey, but it is a sin to *stay* unhappy.

"Now, with me, the Lord took Larry and left me behind with a strong heart and a terrible sorrow. He doesn't fault me for crying, just as long as I do my best to go on. Do you see, honey? He knows I'm a flighty old lady who makes a mess of half the things I try. But I try all the same, honey, I try every day and every hour, and the sadder I feel, the more determined I am to go on. And maybe that's what it all comes down to, honey. Maybe in the end, life is all about going on."

"I love you," Petie said quietly. "I've never told you that before."

"I know you do, honey. You have a gift for loving and you always have, even when it scares the bejeebers out of you."

"I didn't know that."

"Doesn't matter, honey. Everyone else did."

Chapter 18

PETIE CREPT into the kitchen at five-thirty in the morning and dug in her utensil drawer for a set of measuring spoons. They were the ones Eula had given her all those years ago as a wedding present, the present she cherished more than any other gift she and Eddie were given. The house was quiet except for the creak of the trees outside when a gust of wind tangled with them.

She quickly put on a slicker, grabbed her car keys from the counter and drove ten blocks, turned out her headlights half a block away from the old coastal pine and opened her car door with a minimum of squeak. Peering into the darkness, she slipped across the ratty lawn, stepping into the occasional spongy molehill. Beneath the tree she pulled the spoons from one pocket, her broken spade from the other, and crouched under the dripping branches. Her hands shook as she dug the hole and packed the spoons in tight. When she was done, wet through, she crouched there for several minutes, tears mingling with the rain. Her sinuses were nothing but soggy sponges these days, full of snot and tears.

She broke open a clod of dirt and rolled the smaller bits between her fingers, thinking of Eula Coolbaugh, the first woman—the first person—who had loved her without limits. Paula Tyler must have loved her, too, but Petie couldn't summon any memories of it. Paula, in her memory, was a broken woman, a wisp of smoke, hardly ever there at all. Eula, on the other hand, had been substantial, living her life in the wide-open places where Paula had been afraid to go. She had provided for Petie, fought for her, worried over her, urged her to sound her thoughts as loud and clear as trumpets. Eddie Coolbaugh had never had much of Eula in him, but Petie guessed there had been enough to cling to. Now, under the dripping tree, taking in the smell of the loamy earth in great gulps, she could hear Eula's voice, clear and strong: *I'm proud of you, hon. It's long past time to say goodbye, you know it is. Don't you waste what I've given you, all that talk and strength. I love you. Go on, now. Go.*

Petie pressed her palms flat over the grave for several minutes, willing herself to say this worst of goodbyes. In the week since Marge had come home, everything Petie had said was, in some way, a goodbye. In every good-night kiss to Loose there was a farewell; in every cup of coffee she set in front of Eddie Coolbaugh there was a leave-taking. It was even harder than Petie had thought it would be.

She drove home and slipped into the house as quietly as she could, given the desperate state of the old floorboards. Apparently no one heard her, not even when she turned on the shower and gave herself up to the luxury of heat and steam until the hot water ran out.

S CHOOL WAS out for spring vacation, so Petie let the boys sleep. After her shower she filled the car with boxes—clothes, art supplies, a few favorite toys. Just after sunup she drove to the Sea View Motel. Marge must have heard the car because she had the door open before Petie even reached the top of the stairs to her apartment.

"Oh, let me help with those things, honey!" She took a small duffel bag and a box out of Petie's hands and brought them into her bedroom. Petie set down several other boxes and a backpack, and called, "I'm going back down. Don't come—I've only got one more load. I'll be right back."

"All right, honey." Marge appeared in the doorway.

"Do you want me to bring your suitcase down?"

"Why, I guess so. I've been all packed for two days."

"You're still sure you don't want to stay?" Petie said.

"I'm sure, honey. I proved to myself that I could do it, but my heart isn't here anymore. I'm an old woman who wants to spend the rest of her life with family, not with strangers staying for one night."

"All right," Petie said. "You know you can change your mind any-time."

"I know, honey. No, I'll be glad to think of you and Ryan living here now. I know Larry would like that, too. There's lots of love in these walls, honey, all around you like a hug."

Petie descended and brought up her last load. "How are the boys?" Marge said while she put boxes in the bedroom.

"I don't know. They seem okay, mostly. I thought they'd be upset at being separated, but all I'm hearing is griping about why Ryan gets to move to a new house and Loose doesn't." Petie sighed.

"Well, you be brave, honey."

Petie gave Marge a quick hug. "I'll pick you up at two," she said.

"All right, honey, I'll be ready."

The household was stirring when Petie got back. Loose was padding around in Eddie's socks, four times too big. Ryan was completely dressed, including his shoes, and was at the kitchen table eating Cap'n Crunch with chocolate milk, a combination that made Petie feel nauseous just to look at, but then she had no appetite these days. She kissed Ryan on the top of the head.

"Loose, you sure you don't want to come with Ryan and me?" Petie said. "It might be kind of like a treasure hunt."

"What kind of treasure?"

"Well, maybe junk treasure. My grandfather lived up there all his life. I don't know what he might have left behind. No one lives there anymore."

"I want to help Daddy with the dirt bike."

"Okay, as long as you know you have a choice."

Petie pulled mud boots from the closet for her and for Ryan. They'd change into them in the car.

"I'm ready," said Ryan, taking his bowl to the sink and washing it out—something he'd never done before. In the car she asked him why he did it.

He thought for a while. "I don't know."

"I don't know why I do half the things I do, either, but it was thoughtful of you. If you hadn't done it, Daddy or I would've had to."

"Daddy doesn't know how to wash dishes."

"Of course he does." She shot him a look. "What made you say that?"

"You always do them."

"Well, that's mostly true, but you know what? It doesn't take a college education to run a sponge over a dish."

"No," Ryan said doubtfully.

"Are you worried about Daddy?"

Ryan nodded.

"I am too, a little bit, but you know what? Daddy's a grown-up, and grown-ups know how to figure out the most amazing things. If he can figure out how to put a dirt bike back together, sweetie, he can certainly figure out what detergent to use in the washing machine."

Ryan brightened. "Do you think so?"

"I know so," Petie said. "Tell me this, kiddo. Do you think you'll miss Loose?"

"Nope."

"You sure?"

"He beats me up a lot."

"Not so much since he's been taking his medicine," Petie said. Loose had been on Ritalin for two weeks, since they were told he had attention deficit hyperactive disorder along with dyslexia. Petie hadn't wanted to drug him, but even she had to admit it was a big improvement.

The decision to split the boys between them had been Eddie's idea, though she'd never tell Ryan that. Loose was Eddie's sidekick and pal, his shadow, his accomplice. Petie agreed that he would probably do better living with Eddie, at least for now. Ryan, on the other hand, would suffer by staying. He was her son, as Eddie often pointed out in disgust, and she knew that Eddie, with his sarcasm and hurtful jokes, would just make a hard situation harder.

"It's been a long time since I was here," Petie said with undisguised trepidation as they turned onto the logging road that led to Camp Twelve. "It looks gloomier."

"It is kind of spooky," Ryan said.

"Mostly it looks drippy," Petie reassured him. "Did I ever tell you about when I came here?"

Ryan shook his head. Petie decided to tell him the truth. "My mother died when I was your age. My grandfather lived up here, and Old Man figured he ought to know she'd died. So we came here to tell him."

"Was he here?"

"Yes. I think he was the last person who ever lived here."

"Oh."

"You know the scar on my foot?"

Ryan nodded. He'd always been afraid of the rubbery look of the thing.

"Well, this is where I got that scar. My father and my grandfather talked and talked and I got so cold I lit a little fire to stay warm by, except that it spread. I stamped on it to make it go out, but I got burnt. That's why I always tell you and Loose not to play with matches."

"Did it hurt?"

"Holy cow," Petie said. "I couldn't walk on it for three weeks. And you know the odd thing? I never saw my grandfather again. I don't know why."

Ryan looked out the window for a bit. "Will I ever see Daddy again?"

Petie gripped the wheel a little tighter. "Oh, sweetie, of course you'll see Daddy. You'll see him all the time. Sometimes you'll still sleep in your old bed, too, when you stay overnight with him."

Ryan nodded, apparently reassured. Petie had already learned it wouldn't last, that she'd be saying the same thing all over again tomorrow.

They bumped over the increasingly rutted and overgrown road for several miles, until Petie had begun to think they were in the wrong place. Then she saw a clearing ahead, and a minute later spotted the first of the little cabins she always saw so vividly in her dreams.

"There," she said, pointing. "There it is." She steered them into the clearing, though it was smaller than she remembered, and shut off the engine. While they put on their mud boots, Petie made sure her voice was hearty, the voice of an adventurer instead of a coward preparing to face down her past. Ryan went ahead, peering into one tumbledown shack after another. Several that had been standing when Petie was here before had fallen in, undermined by blackberries and rot.

"Look!" Ryan came running up with a battered tin cup. "There's one house with a door!" He pointed at what Petie recognized as her grandfather's house. With considerable dread she pushed open the door. It shrieked but yielded.

"It's creepy," Ryan moaned, standing behind Petie. She had to agree. The interior was still relatively intact, with the crude table and chair she remembered, and the bedstead against the far wall. Pill bugs littered the floor, and part of the roof had fallen in. On the table there was a jar with a brown residue in the bottom. Tobacco spit. There was nothing else, at least not that she could see from the door. She stepped inside, and as her eyes adjusted she saw a mouse nest, a piece of the old curtain, an empty snuff tin, a stub of pencil.

As she stepped the floorboard gave beneath her. Petie cried out, jumping aside as though something living had grabbed her, but it was only rot. Her foot hadn't gone all the way through the board, but had displaced it enough for her to see the tatters of a plastic bag. She reached down and carefully pulled up the floorboard, which came to pieces in her hand like rotten honeycomb. Crouching, she peered into the space beneath, and then quickly ripped up the adjacent floorboard and reached inside.

"Oh my God." She pulled up a plastic bag filled with ashes.

Ryan tugged on her sleeve. Petie said, breathing hard, "Get in the car. It's warmer there. Go."

He scuttled off to the car and shut himself inside.

The bag was completely intact, though there was no sign of the cardboard box that had once held it. She stared at it dumbly, these last abandoned remains of an unmourned life barely lived. Gently she carried the bag outside, putting it in the trunk of her car with shaking hands. Then she climbed into the car beside Ryan and fumbled for the keys.

"You're crying," Ryan said, frowning. "Why are you crying, Mommy?"

"Oh, sweetie." Petie drew a deep, shaky breath. "It's just the cold. It makes my eyes water."

"It's okay." He patted her arm awkwardly and watched her. "Are you sad?"

"Yes," Petie said, wiping the snot from her nose with a limp Kleenex. "I'm sad, but in a good way. I came up here to say goodbye to someone I used to know. I didn't think I'd find her here, but now I have."

"Who?"

"Someone you never met," Petie said, turning the key in the ignition. "Someone I knew a long time ago."

"I didn't see anyone," Ryan said, frowning. "Was she a ghost?"

Petie smiled, drying her face on her sleeve. "No, not a ghost. Maybe more like an angel, sweetie. Well, maybe an assistant angel, because she was very shy, I think, and very afraid, like you get sometimes. She wouldn't have wanted to be an angel herself, having to make decisions like they do."

"What decisions?"

Petie pulled away from the camp, picking her way around the worst ruts. "Oh, there are lots of them, like whether to turn on a rainbow or not, or whether to make the sun come out and shine because someone's done something kind. Like whether to bring a sweet dream to a little boy in the night because he had a hard day."

"Yes," Ryan said solemnly, nodding his approval.

Petie drove in silence until they were clear of the woods and back on a paved road. She had four dollars and fifty-nine cents in her pocket. She said, "I'll tell you what we need. I think we need a Dairy Queen. Don't you think so?"

He did.

· · ·

THEY GOT into Hubbard just in time for Petie to drop Ryan off with Eddie, turn around and pick up Marge, who was waiting for her at the Sea View office door. Petie swept the mud from Ryan's boots out the car door and closed it again once Marge was settled.

"Here you go, honey," Marge said, and put the master key to the Sea View Motel in her hand. "Now you know after spring break's done you can close the place up again if you want."

"I know," Petie said. "I won't, but I know."

"Well," Marge said, watching pensively but dry-eyed as Petie pulled out of the parking lot. "I never expected I'd want to leave this place, honey. But you know he's not here at all. The things he made are here, but he's not anywhere. Do you think it's for the best? Maybe the good Lord spares us the things He knows we can't bear to live with."

"Maybe," Petie said, and reached over to squeeze Marge's hand. "Maybe that's what's happened to me all these years. Maybe I was spared."

"Maybe so, honey. He must have decided you're strong enough, now, and I believe He's right."

Petie had her doubts.

They didn't say much the rest of the way into Sawyer. Marge located and relocated her bus ticket in her purse, and fussed with her various pillboxes and packets of Kleenex and hand lotion. Her mind was already hundreds of miles down the road, running south into Tempe. Her bus was already waiting when they got there. Petie pulled out Marge's suitcase and loaded it into the baggage hold of the bus while Marge presented her ticket. The driver closed and latched the baggage doors the minute Petie backed away.

"Oh!" Marge said, tearing up. "I'm going to be praying for you, honey, I'll pray for you every day. You've got a long road ahead of you, but it's the right one, I know. You let me hear from you sometimes." Petie wept and Marge wept and the bus driver cleared his throat. Marge grasped Petie in one last rib-crushing hug and fierce clap on the back, as though the strength of her conviction and love alone could see Petie through. Petie waved until the bus reached the corner and turned, passing out of sight.

EDDIE WAS waiting for her when she got home. The boys had their suitcase by the door and were arguing bitterly over some toy.

"Jesus, Petie, you sure took your sweet time. It's been like this since you left, they're so keyed up."

Petie walked past him and barked orders. "Loose, go use the bathroom one last time. We've got a long drive. Ryan, you use it after Loose is done." To Eddie she said, "I've left the Bachelor Butte phone number on the refrigerator door. One room's in Schiff's name because it was originally his invitation, and one's in Jim Christie's. We should be home by Sunday night. Will you be home then?"

"Fuck, I don't know," Eddie said bitterly. "What do you care, anyway?"

"Habit," Petie said. "Pretend I never asked."

Loose came out, and then Ryan. Petie ushered them into the car, loading their suitcases and her own into the trunk. "Wave bye to Daddy," she told the boys as they turned around in the driveway. Eddie stood there watching them, his hands jammed into his pockets, lifting his chin at them only at the last minute.

Rose and Carissa were ready when they pulled up. They switched all the luggage into the trunk of Rose's huge Ford, which, thanks to Jim Christie, ran like a Cadillac, though it sucked gas. The boys and Carissa piled into the backseat, with Carissa in the middle so the boys wouldn't start punching and hitting each other an hour into the trip. Rose tucked a picnic cooler under Petie's feet, reeling off the contents. "Pretzels, Oreos, string cheese, Pop Tarts, apple slices and juice boxes, but no one can drink anything yet because if they do they'll have to stop and pee."

Rose pulled down Jim Christie's invitation from the sun visor. "Do you have yours?"

Petie dug it out of her bag. "Got it." She watched Hubbard recede behind them. "Schiff's the only one who's been there. He told me where we should eat. I didn't have the heart to tell him wherever it was, we probably couldn't afford it."

"Do you think he'll be there?" Rose asked.

"No. I asked him to give me some time."

"He knows you and Eddie split, though?"

Petie gave Rose a look. "Is there anyone who *doesn't* know me and Eddie have split?"

Rose frowned. "That's true. You know it seemed easier when Pogo and I went through it. Maybe it was just because we were younger and stupider. Plus Carissa was just a baby. It's so much harder, watching you."

Petie sat quietly looking out the window. "Ryan and I went up to Camp Twelve today."

"Why?"

"I don't know. We just did. It was creepy and sad, like those husks that bugs leave behind when they die."

"No one lives up there anymore?"

"No, not in a long time. I bet my grandfather died pretty soon after I went up there with Old Man."

Rose shuddered. "I remember your poor foot."

"No kidding." The pain had been so bad that at first she'd thought she would die of it. Old Man had made her drink whiskey to deaden it, but the stuff made her vomit. She'd never been able to stand even the smell of whiskey after that.

The sky over the ocean was leaden and boiling, bursting into squalls all the way to the horizon. They were less than a mile from the turnoff that would take them inland to Bend. Petie watched the last of Sawyer disappear in her side mirror. How many times had she driven this way without taking the turnoff, without wondering what lay at the end of that road? Her people—Old Man, Paula, Eula, Eddie, Rose, Petie herself—didn't travel, didn't drive down new roads. They lived and died in a dead-end place where roads ended instead of began, where the skies wept harsh tears and the ocean hemmed them in as surely as any prison wall.

"Look!" Ryan cried from the backseat. Fierce beams of sunlight had shot through a hole in the clouds and lit up the sea like a spotlight. "Someone must have done something nice," he said.

"What made you say that?" said Rose.

"My mom says that's why angels turn on sunshine."

"Have we done anything nice?" Rose asked.

"Not yet," Petie said. "But we're about to. Can you pull over? Just into the park. This'll only take a minute."

"Are you okay?"

"Yes."

Rose pulled into a tiny state park that looked out over the ocean. Theirs was the only car.

"I need something in the trunk," Petie said. "Can I have your keys?"

Rose pulled the keys from the ignition and handed them to Petie, baffled. Petie jumped out of the car, leaving her door open, and circled to the trunk. When she slammed it shut again, she was holding the bag with Paula's ashes.

"You look so weird. What's going on?" Rose said.

"I found these up at Camp Twelve, stuck under the floor of my grandfather's cabin."

"Dust? Why would he have hidden dust?"

"It's not dust. They're Paula's ashes."

"Oh, Petie. How awful."

"She deserves better." Petie walked to the rocks overlooking the ocean, away from Rose and the three children. At the edge, high above the water, she released a handful of the gritty ashes into the wind.

"What's she doing?" Carissa whispered to Rose.

"Those are her mother's ashes. She found them this morning. People scatter the ashes of loved ones out of respect."

"Could we help?"

Rose shuddered but called to Petie, "Can the kids help? They'd like to."

To her surprise, Petie said yes, if she could talk to them first. When they'd all gathered, she set the bag of ashes at her feet. "Did Rose tell you what these are?"

The children all nodded solemnly. "Then you should know a little about her if you're going to help. Ryan and Loose, you, too, since she died way before you were even born. Her name was Paula, and she had dark hair like mine and she didn't smile very much because there were a lot of things she was afraid of. Her favorite meal was banana slices in milk with so much sugar you just about keeled over after you ate them. I don't ever remember her laughing."

The children watched her with sober church faces.

"So here's the thing," Petie said. "If you want to help me scatter her ashes, I want you to do it with a light heart, because that's what she missed out on the most and I think she'd like it. Ryan, you want to go first?"

Ryan approached, and took a fistful of ashes. "Go ahead and throw them up in the air." Petie helped him toss the ashes over his head, into the wind, where some of the heavier particles came down and the rest disappeared in a puff.

"My turn!" said Loose, and flung a handful of ashes in the wrong direction, so that most of them blew back on him and stuck. Appalled, he slapped at his sweatshirt and waited for punishment. Instead, Petie started snorting helplessly. "Oh God, Loosey," she said, and dissolved into laughter. Rose started laughing, too, and then Carissa and Ryan joined in and the only one scowling was Loose. When Petie regained herself she wiped her eyes, put her arm around his shoulders and said, "This time throw the other way."

Loose let go of his next handful and watched it fly away on the wind. Petie whooped and flung more ashes in a high arc. Carissa and then Ryan took a turn and pretty soon everyone was dipping into the bag at once and the air was filled with Paula's ashes, soaring and raining down like confetti.

"Eula used to call those Jesus beams," Petie said to Rose, watching the last shafts of sunlight disappear over the water when they were done. "She used to say if you watched carefully you would see God Himself descending. Do you see anything?"

"No," Rose said doubtfully. "Do you?"

"No." Petie grinned. "Not a damned thing."

They linked arms and walked back to the car without a backwards glance. With luck and light traffic, they'd be in Bend by nightfall, tucking into fresh beds in an unspoiled place. "You know, if God *was* up there watching us," Rose said to Petie as she pulled out onto the highway, "what do you think He'd say?"

Petie knew exactly: they were the same words Eula Coolbaugh had spoken every morning for four years.

It's a brand-new day, honey. Time to rise and shine.

Acknowledgments

DURING THE decade in which I wrote it, *Going to Bend* became not just a book but a lifestyle that I shared with—and in some cases inflicted upon—many. I extend my deepest thanks to Pat Peach, my keen and generous guide into the ways of small towns and the people who live in them; to Bernice Barnett for her excellent legal insights and unwavering encouragement during all those Tuesday lunches; and to Darrell Ward for his love of the craft of writing and his unshakable belief that there is always room in the world for one more good book. My special gratitude also goes to Julie Blake for loving Petie and Rose from the very start; to Beth Basham and Carolyn Hernandez for surviving those ten-pound ring binders; and to my family for plowing through early drafts of *Going to Bend* on their computer monitors—surely one of the greatest known acts of love.

It is with special awe and gratitude that I thank Jennifer Rudolph Walsh for believing in me through all these years; my editor, Deb Futter, for making possible the only thing I've ever really wanted for Christmas; and both of them for their patience, their guidance, and their professional surefootedness.

Lastly, my deepest thanks to my husband, Nolan, for getting it in every way, and to my daughter, Kerry, for sharing this incredible ride with me.

GOING TO BEND

A Reader's Guide

DIANE HAMMOND

A Conversation with Diane Hammond

Q: *Going to Bend* is your first novel. Is there a story behind your writing it?

A: I think of the first half of this book as my graduate school thesis. I wrote it in 1994 and 1995, agonizing over its technical aspects and devices as well as its characters and story line. Craft issues have always loomed large for me. Are the character voices clear enough, consistent enough, revealing enough? How much of the story should I stage, and how much can I just allude to in internal monologues? Is it moving along smoothly? Experienced writers make hundreds of critical decisions by instinct, but most less-experienced writers don't have that luxury. It can be exhausting. In fact, by the exact midway point in the book, I was so worn out from the technical choices and decisions I was making that I was losing my way in the story. This, plus the fact that I had a young child, multiple sclerosis, and a demanding day job, convinced me to put the manuscript down. In fact, I didn't look at it again until 2001, when I was uninspired by whatever work was at hand and instead hauled out the manuscript. By then, thanks to my appallingly bad memory, I had forgotten more about the book than I remembered. This afforded me the luxury of reading the manuscript straight through with relative objectivity, and by the time I was done, I knew exactly where the remaining story was headed, and how to get there. And the craft issues never waylaid me again—I'd graduated. I completed the second half of the book in just six months.

Q: A lot of readers assume that you're from a small Oregon town your-self, because Hubbard is so vividly evoked and its characters are so deeply defined by its limitations. But you were born and raised in sub-urban New York. What's the deal with that?

A: It's true that my background, up until my late twenties, was largely urban. I grew up in Upper Nyack, a suburb of New York City, and later lived in Honolulu and Washington, D.C. But in 1984 I moved to New-port, Oregon, then a coastal town of just under 9,000, and everything changed.

My first job interview—for a secretarial position with the electrical utility serving the central Oregon coast—ended with a stern lecture about the fact that big-city, East Coast ways would not be tolerated here. It was clear that I had two choices: I could maintain my urban identity and spend a lot of time alone and misunderstood, or I could pipe down, listen hard, and learn about a way of life that was completely new to me. It's probably no surprise that my survival instincts led me to choose the latter. On those terms, I was befriended by some extraordinary teachers, skilled storytellers, and sure-footed guides to the insular culture of coastal Oregon. I became an avid solicitor of stories of all kinds, and de-veloped a great respect for the strenuous business of living in a town that offers low-paying jobs, limited educational opportunities, significant isolation, and a whole lot of bad weather.

Q: Yes, the weather on the Oregon coast takes on the aspect of a charac-ter in the book. Why?

A: I think that until you've spent nine months in nearly relentless wind and rain, you can't fully appreciate the effect that such weather has on everything you feel and do. And it's *dynamic* weather, where the rain takes many shapes—teeming, drizzling, blowing, pelting, and pouring straight down, to name a few—and storm fronts come through like con-quering armies. On any given day, damned near everyone I knew could tell you what flags the U.S. Coast Guard was flying over Yaquina Bay to announce the incoming weather. Here's the thing: You lived in all of this, you worked in it, drove in it, carried your groceries inside through it, ferried small children and babies through it, and your moods reflected it even when you thought they didn't. You and the weather become one. So when I began writing *Going to Bend*, it was only natural to cast the weather in a major role.

Q: Let's talk about your characters for a minute. Do you have a favorite?

A: Petie is certainly the character to whom my heart goes out first. She is a woman who's been dealt a bad hand and she refuses to pity herself for it. From that innate pride of self springs everything else about her—her tough exterior, her faith in her own ability to get by, her fierce sense of right and wrong. And yet, her ability to love unconditionally has come through intact. Given her life circumstances, that's a small miracle.

In many ways, *Going to Bend* is a love story. It's about the healing powers of unconditional love. For Petie, finding unconditional love has come at a huge price: Paula's love, though absolute, is insufficient to keep Petie from harm; Rose's love gives her a staunch ally, but also one who offers limited protection. It is only Eula's love that brings with it healing powers, though for far too little time. Even so, these pockets of unconditional love have given her sufficient strength to endure exceptionally difficult circumstances.

Other characters for whom I have a tender spot include Marge and Larry Hopkins, who also have a gift for loving not only each other, but those around them; and Schiff, who is a much better man than he's ever given credit for, either by himself or by those around him.

I'd have to say that Old Man Tyler was the character who presented me with the greatest writing challenge. I'd never created a thoroughly bad character before, someone capable of doing loathsome things. We tend to protect our characters as we do our children, wanting them to be liked and successful. Old Man was neither. And yet, I don't believe he was evil—just incredibly, deeply, cruelly flawed.

Q: How do you approach building a novel? Do you work out a lot of your story ahead of time?

A: I have always envied those writers who can build a story ahead of time, who can pull together a comprehensive road map, the who, what, when, where, how, and why, all very lucidly and methodically set out in advance. It probably says something about the scattershot way in which I create that I am absolutely unable to do this. I really only succeeded in doing it once, and the resulting work was so lifeless that I buried it in a desk drawer.

No, for better or worse I am an impulsive, instinctive, intuitive writer, which means that when I begin writing a book, I know a couple of my key characters, though not well; I have a sense of the feel of the story, though not its specific events; I have a rough timeframe in mind over which the story will take place; and I have a hazy idea of where the main characters will end up. Other than that, I don't know a thing. I invent it, discover it, reveal it—not only to my readers but to myself—in the writing itself. This can be both exhilarating and terrifying; it's a very high-risk creative proposition, in that I'm staking a year or more of my writing life on the bet that I can bring the story—which I don't yet know—home successfully in the end. So far, it's worked, but there isn't a day when I take that outcome for granted. That's why, for me, the process of writing is fraught with danger, a nearly incomprehensible act of the greatest faith in my creative outcomes. I wouldn't wish this writing style on anyone, though on a good day when my characters' voices are flowing and I'm hurrying to get it all down, I wouldn't trade it for anything.

Q: We leave Petie and Rose at a real crossroads, literally and figuratively. Do you plan to write a sequel?

A: I'm often asked that. No, I don't have any plans for a sequel. I feel that I safely guided Petie, Rose, and the rest of Bend's characters through a difficult time, a life-changing time, and at the book's end had safely delivered them not to an ending, but a beginning. I don't believe they need me to take them any further. And wherever they go from here, it will not be with the sort of high drama that makes for a compelling story to read. So, literarily speaking, I've wished them Godspeed and moved on.

I have hung on to the towns of Hubbard and Sawyer, though. My next book, *Homesick Creek,* takes place there, too, though with entirely different and unrelated characters—except for Roy, the bartender at the Wayside, who continues to drift in and out of scenes.

1. Much of the action in *Going to Bend* happens over food preparation. What does soup represent in the lives of Petie and Rose? How is that different than its significance for Nadine and Gordon?

2. Kitchens are also centers for discussion, revelations, and turning points. What key scenes take place in kitchens?

3. As a young man, Schiff meets a redheaded girl at a carnival and, early in the book, vividly remembers the few hours they spent together. Later, he will associate her with Petie. Why? What characteristics and quirks do these characters hold in common—and why does Schiff find them appealing?

4. When Petie is young, she and Paula seek refuge in a gift shop from Old Man's drinking. When a fragile teacup is broken, the shopkeeper gives it and a matching saucer to Petie. What is the significance of these objects to Petie?

5. Old Man Tyler and Petie live in a camp trailer in the woods behind Hubbard. Later, Jim Christie discovers the trailer and uses it for his own purposes. What role does the trailer play in Petie's past and in later causing a disastrous rift between her and Rose?

6. *Going to Bend* explores the different kinds of love that can exist between husbands and wives, fathers and sons, mothers and daughters,

and friends. How did those different kinds of love manifest themselves between the characters in *Going to Bend*?

7. Rose and Gordon become good friends. Why—what do they have in common?

8. In some sense, *Going to Bend* is a story about the effects of isolation—geographical isolation, psychic isolation, and isolation based on shame and secrecy. What are some examples of isolation and its effect on the characters and on their unfolding stories?

9. In the course of the book there is an unfolding tension between Jim Christie and Carissa that will ultimately have tragic results. What's really going on between these two characters?

10. Eula Coolbaugh is one of the most important people in Petie's life. Does Eula's love for Petie differ from Paula Tyler's? If so, how?

11. In a childhood visit to Camp Twelve, Petie is badly burned in a fire, and Old Man applies a poultice of ashes. What do these ashes signify, both then and at the book's end? What role do they play in helping Petie to resolve grief?

12. Eula Coolbaugh may be *Going to Bend*'s only truly wise character. What wisdom does she impart to Petie that has a lasting effect on her life and decisions? Why?

13. The title *Going to Bend* has both a metaphorical and literal meaning. What are they, and how do they relate to the book's main characters?

14. At several key moments in Petie's life, she buries objects beneath a tree. What are the objects, what do they represent, and why does she bury them?

15. Petie and Schiff, both of whom are married, carry on a clandestine relationship through much of the book. What's missing in their respective marriages, and how does this play a role in their unfolding relationship?

16. Jim Christie is an inarticulate man with a severely limited ability to communicate his feelings. How does Rose deal with this throughout the book, and what role does it play in the book's climactic outcome?

17. Work creates tensions throughout the book, and everyone except for Paula Tyler and Eula Coolbaugh has a job. How do the characters regard their respective jobs at the start of the book? At the end? How do they suit each character?

18. Were any of the characters in *Going to Bend* reminiscent of people you've known in your own lives? If so, what were the resemblances?

19. Were there universal truths about people and relationships that were revealed in *Going to Bend*? If so, what were they, and how might they relate to, say, white-collar people living and working in an urban environment?

20. What do you think will happen to Petie and Rose after the book's end? What would you *like* to see happen?

Read on for a sneak preview of the
next novel from Diane Hammond, available
from Doubleday in July 2005.

HOMESICK CREEK

returns to the fictional small town of
Hubbard, Oregon, and captivates us once again
with a cast of vivid characters whose story
is both uplifting and heartbreaking . . .
and completely irresistible.

Chapter One

Mornings come hard and mean on the Oregon coast in winter. Trees on Cape Mano between Hubbard and Sawyer have only lee-side branches, twisted old men with their backs to the sea. More than a few casually built bungalows and cabins are chained to the rocks so gale-force winds won't take them.

Highway 101, Hubbard's only through street, runs north to Canada and south to Mexico, edging along the black basalt shore and over a bridge that spans Hubbard's small harbor. Both sport and commercial fishing vessels are moored there, piloted by the handful of skippers capable of navigating the boiling deep-water channel at the mouth of the harbor. Everyone has a story to tell about a boat that's broken up on the rocks within hailing distance of home. In 1983, eight Realtors on a sport-fishing jaunt drowned in plain sight when their charter boat turned broadside and sank.

For all its tiny size and appearance of sleepiness, Hubbard in 1989 lit its fires early, and nowhere earlier than at the Anchor Grill, which opened every morning at four o'clock sharp. The restaurant was located at the exact center of town, across the street from Devil's Horn, a rocky blowhole through which seawater shot thirty feet in the air when storm seas were running. The Anchor was that rare hybrid, beloved by tourists and residents alike, an easy place with vinyl tuck-and-roll booths, stained carpet and paneled walls, stuffed trophy fish and the everlasting aroma of chowder, fried food, and beer. First light belonged to Hubbard's fishermen and pulp mill workers putting in day shifts fifteen miles away over in Sawyer. From seven a.m. until the reek of fish guts signaled the return of the boats in midafternoon, the place was nothing but tourists with their hair, shoes, and umbrellas in various stages of ruination. By evening, a good-natured polyglot crowd filled the lounge to the accompaniment of Pinky Leonard on the keyboard and owner Nina Doyle playing the bottles.

Bunny Neary had waitressed at the Anchor for twenty-one years, ever since she was nineteen. A couple of months ago old Dr. Bryant had measured a two-and-a-half-inch difference in the height of her shoulders from lifting and carrying trays, but mostly she liked the work well enough. On a good day she could pick up a hundred, hundred and fifty bucks in tips. And from being there so long, she usually got her pick of shifts.

Not today, though. Beth Ann, who normally worked mornings, had called in with strep throat again. This was Bunny's fourth day in a row covering for her, and she was beat. Being on the opening shift meant getting to the Anchor at three thirty—three, if she did the whole list of things she was supposed to do before she opened up at four. She hardly ever did, seeing as how no one came into the place at that hour of the morning but the boys, and the boys didn't give a crap whether the salt and pepper shakers were topped off or the half-and-halfs were iced down or the sugars were filled, just as long as the coffee was fresh and hot. At four o'clock sharp they'd be out there in the back parking lot waiting for her, smelling like Dial soap and cigarettes and yesterday's jeans. They'd slouch in and heave themselves into their booths, slap down the newspaper and call, *Hey, Bunny, where's that coffee?*

The fact was, though, Bunny would have been beat even if she hadn't pulled the morning shift. She hadn't slept worth a damn all night, not after she'd overheard some woman whisper to her husband over the phone, *Just pretend this is about work. Oh, Lord, Hack, do I feel stupid—I didn't think she'd be home.*

She let an extra half-pull of coffee grounds fall into a fresh filter—the boys liked their coffee strong this time of day, weak as tea when they started coming in off the boats around two—and punched the brew button on the coffee maker, touching the waiting pot first. Once, another time she and Hack were on the outs, she'd made a whole pot of decaf without remembering to put a pot underneath and there'd been fresh-brewed coffee everywhere before she figured it out. The boys had razzed her about it for weeks. *Hey, Bunny, did you put a pot under it this time? Ha, ha, ha.* Shit.

Oh, Lord, Hack, do I feel stupid—I didn't think she'd be home. You can't talk with her there, can you. So I'll hang up now. I guess I'll just hang up. Here I go. And she'd hung up. Then Hack had hung up. Then Bunny.

"Hey, Bunny, bring me that maple syrup there, would you?" Dooley Burden called from two tables down. Bunny had known Dooley all her life. He was maybe sixty-four now, and the stringiest thing Bunny had ever seen—he looked like if you were to bite into him, he'd be nothing but tendons and gristle and a little tough meat, like an old dry rooster. When Bunny was little, Dooley had worked a couple of seasons as deck crew for her father, but then it turned out he was epileptic. He managed to keep it a secret until he had a seizure forty miles out, fishing for black cod. He worked down at his brother's fuel dock after that, until he fell a couple of winters ago and pretended he'd been going to retire anyway. Now he just hung around town, razzing all the young fishermen about their joint-venture seasons and their on-board microwaves. The boys let him talk: They'd heard about how he'd flopped around on the deck with the cod and the trash fish so bad they'd finally had to lash him to a hatch cover to keep him from twitching himself clean over the rail with his eyes rolled back in his head. And they knew about how his turd of a brother Carlin never once paid him more than fifty cents above minimum wage in all those thirty-eight years of pumping diesel at three in the morning, while Carlin was busy taking vacations in Hawaii and sailing around the San Juans in his forty-five-foot sailboat, like some kind of goddamn son-of-a-bitch big shot.

Bunny set down a sticky little pitcher of maple syrup on Dooley's paper place mat. The place mat came right back up and stuck when he went to pour syrup on his sausage links, next to his eggs, over his short stack. He'd ordered the exact same breakfast every day for the last twenty-four years.

"What's the deal with Beth Ann?" he asked Bunny, who was so tired she was just standing there watching him. Beth Ann was one of the younger waitresses, twenty-three. The boys liked to send her for more coffee just to watch her walk away. "She got a new boyfriend? She's sure looking nice these days."

"New perm," Bunny said. "Plus she's on that liquid protein diet."

"Aw, I like my women with some meat on them," Dooley said, like he'd even had a date in the last fifteen years. He took a big bite of egg, slid his coffee cup toward Bunny so she'd top it off.

"Well, if you'd just told her that to start with, I'm sure she would have called the whole thing off. You've got a little piece of egg there on your chin," Bunny said, pointing.

Dooley shrugged, flicked the egg off with his finger, drank some coffee. "Hack going to buy that dirt bike he was looking at?" he asked Bunny. "That 250? It's got beans, that bike. It's a good piece of machinery, and the boy was asking a good price. You tell Hack I said so."

"What dirt bike?" Bunny said. "He hasn't said anything about another dirt bike."

"Aw, hell," said Dooley. "Guess I've stepped in it now, huh? You think he's coming by this morning?"

"Doesn't he always come by?"

"He's late, though."

"Yeah," Bunny said. She had tried the house a couple of minutes ago. The line had been busy. Busy, at five fifteen in the morning.

You can't talk with her there, can you.

And now there was some dirt-bike deal he'd never told her about. She set her coffee pot on the table, slid into the booth across from Dooley, and poured herself a cup of coffee.

"You been keeping him up too late?" Dooley said and winked.

"Don't he wish." Bunny drank half the cup down, picked up a fork, and cut a bite out of Dooley's soggy short stack.

"What's the matter, honey?" he said, sucking a tooth.

But Bunny just finished her bite of pancake, sighed, and hoisted herself up from the table. "Nothing. Just tired of getting up at three in the morning to take care of you boys."

Back at the waitress station Bunny threaded her name tag through the little round name-tag eyelets stitched into the blouse of her uniform. *Bunny.* Her real name was Bernadette. Bunny was something Hack had started and gotten almost the whole town to go along with. He used to say he called her Bunny because she had such a nice tail. That was Hack. He'd been a wild one when they first started going together fifteen years ago. She'd met him his second day in Hubbard. It had been a sunny June morning and she and her girlfriend Anita had been sitting on a blanket above the bay, gossiping and keeping an eye on their kids, Anita's Doreen and Bunny's Vanilla—Vinny—both of them almost four years old. Of course, she hadn't been called Vinny then.

Hack had stumbled up, scaring them half to death before he got close enough to show them that easy smile of his. He'd spent the night under the bridge, and he was shivering, still part drunk, and his fatigue jacket was soaked with old fog. He came right up to them and asked Bunny if he could borrow her blanket for a minute—he was about to die of cold, he said, and if there was one thing he hadn't been able to stand, ever since he could remember, it was being cold. That was one of the things he'd liked best about Vietnam—the heat.

He squatted down next to Bunny, and there was something hopeful about him that Bunny liked, as if he was expecting good things to happen any minute. He had the scrappy, take-me-home look of kids who get away from their parents too young. So she gave him the blanket. He'd meant to find a better place to stay than under that bridge, he said while he wrapped up, but he'd closed the last tavern—did she know that one, the Wayside?—and by then it was too late to find anything; plus he hadn't seen the town in daylight to know where to find a room. Wrapped up in her blanket he talked for an hour straight, until the kids started getting hungry and they had to go. Bunny was going to let him keep the blanket, which was just an old flannel one with a hole in the middle, but he gave it back with that slow smile of his and said, *Maybe sometime you could show me some other ways people keep warm around here. If I stick around.*

Oh, Bunny had said over her shoulder. *I bet you'll stick around.*

Hack. He'd been something special to look at with his big rangy body, pretty green eyes, neat brown beard, and a tongue that showed pink as a cat's when he yawned; in fact there'd been something catlike and clean about him all over, even that first time. He'd only been back from Vietnam maybe three months by then, so mixed in with the other things was that half-crazy, what-the-fuck gleam in his eyes you saw in vets a lot in those days. But Bunny had seen that same look all her life in fishermen who'd seen a boat or two go down. Her father had had that look as long as Bunny could remember. In a fishing town, everyone knows men who've walked right up and hung their toes over the edge.

Meantime, Bunny's boyfriend JoJo had already been gone a couple of months and it looked like he wasn't coming back this time. He hadn't left her any money, either, so she and Vinny had to move in with Bunny's folks, which wasn't working out. Her father was always ragging on her that she should have made JoJo marry her after she'd had Vinny. Plus, no Hubbard man would date her because they knew how crazy-mean JoJo would be if he ever came back and found out. And it was true that he'd beat the holy crap out of you if he was in the mood. Bandy little guys like JoJo took up the slack by being twitchy.

Not Hack. Hack was big and slow and agreeable, and Bunny decided right then, on that first day, that he'd be good to have. She knew she had the kind of looks Hack could live with: okay face, better-than-okay figure, and a walk that said Uh-huh. She also knew that even though he still hadn't found the back-home good time he'd promised himself while he was over there in Vietnam, he was ready to rest awhile. And a man like Hack didn't rest alone. So when he started showing up every afternoon at the tavern Bunny went to, with that mouth of his going steady and smooth and her brand of cigarettes stuck in his pocket, she was ready. She let him buy her a beer sometimes but not always, showed up some days but not others, and never explained one way or another. And she ignored him. Nothing drove Hack crazier than being ignored. He'd come sit down next to her and she'd pretend she was busy reading in the newspaper about something going on over there in Poland or Africa or someplace. Pretty soon Hack would start talking, some little pay-attention-to-me foolishness, and when that didn't work he'd bump her barstool or throw little balled-up napkin bits at her, and she'd ignore that, too, until he'd finally grab the paper completely out of her hands and lay half his body across the bar in front of her. He moved her and Vinny into a nice rental with him before the end of the first month.

For a couple of years after that he'd done odd jobs around town, and on weekends he raced stock cars over in the Willamette Valley with some buddies he'd met. He liked to race, but it was mostly so he could be around the cars. He talked to Bunny about them all the time, even though she didn't understand one thing he was saying. He referred to the cars as "she," and if he was anywhere near one he'd stroke and pet its sides and hood and inspect it all over for little hurt places. Bunny had seen him stare at some piece of junk in his hand for an hour trying to figure out a new thing to try, and there would be love in his eyes. She went with him when she could get Anita or someone to watch Vinny, and on the way home they'd usually pull into the Patio Courts or the Hi-Time Motel and screw on the thin scratchy sheets for hours. More than anything, more even than cars, Hack loved to screw. His touch was so good Bunny sometimes thought that if God Himself did it, He would do it like Hack. *Oh, pretty lady,* he used to say to her. *The way you make me feel.*

After a couple of years Hack was still in Hubbard and he let Bunny marry him. He got a steady job managing the service department at Vernon Ford over in Sawyer, until old Marv noticed Hack was a born salesman and tried him out on the used car lot, instead. He did so well they let him sell new cars after only a year. He bought them a house and then a better one. He bought them a sectional sofa and an electric organ. When Vinny's permanent teeth started coming in gray he found a special dentist for her, and when Bunny crashed her car into the back of a motor home that time and they got sued, Hack found an attorney who got them out of it.

But the whole time that was all going on, there was this other thing Bunny knew. Hack had come to Hubbard on his way to someplace else, and he had never meant to stay, just to stop and rest awhile. Right from the start there were times when he got sad, got lost-looking and homesick for someplace he'd never been. The spells hadn't lasted long, and when they were over he'd been glad to be back. But in the last few years the sad times had started coming more often and playing out meaner, and even though Hack still wouldn't talk about them, she knew it was because he was trying to figure out what to do. And whatever he chose, he meant to do alone. One day, Bunny knew, he'd just take her and Vinny and Vernon Ford and everything else about their lives and pitch them over the side and rise up like a big hot-air balloon and be gone. You couldn't keep a man like Hack. The best you could hope for, if you were lucky and you played your cards right, was to get the use of him for a while.

PHOTO: © MARK RAINER

diane hammond has worked as a writer and an editor. She was awarded a literary fellowship by the Oregon Arts Commission, and her writing has appeared in such magazines as *Yankee*, *Mademoiselle*, and *Washington Review*. She served as a spokesperson for the Oregon Coast Aquarium and the Free Willy Keiko Foundation and currently lives with her husband, Nolan, and daughter, Kerry.